THE PARIS SPY

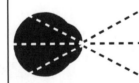

This Large Print Book carries the Seal of Approval of N.A.V.H.

A MAGGIE HOPE MYSTERY

THE PARIS SPY

SUSAN ELIA MACNEAL

KENNEBEC LARGE PRINT
A part of Gale, a Cengage Company

Farmington Hills, Mich • San Francisco • New York • Waterville, Maine
Meriden, Conn • Mason, Ohio • Chicago

Copyright © 2017 by Susan Elia.
Kennebec Large Print, a part of Gale, a Cengage Company.

Kennebec Large Print® Superior Collection.
The text of this Large Print edition is unabridged.
Other aspects of the book may vary from the original edition.
Set in 16 pt. Plantin.

LIBRARY OF CONGRESS CIP DATA ON FILE.
CATALOGUING IN PUBLICATION FOR THIS BOOK
IS AVAILABLE FROM THE LIBRARY OF CONGRESS

ISBN-13: 978-1-4328-4041-9 (softcover)
ISBN-10: 1-4328-4041-x (softcover)

Published in 2017 by arrangement with Bantam Books, an imprint of Random House, a division of Penguin Random House LLC

Printed in the United States of America
1 2 3 4 5 6 7 21 20 19 18 17

IN MEMORY OF NOOR-UN-NISA
INAYAT KHAN
*January 2, 1914–September 13, 1944,
a Special Operations Executive (SOE)
agent sent from Britain to Paris
during World War II and posthumously
awarded the George Cross for
her courageous service*

The German night has swallowed up the country . . . France is nothing but a silence; she is lost somewhere in the night with all lights out.

— ANTOINE DE SAINT-EXUPÉRY,
An Open Letter to Frenchmen Everywhere

No great country was ever saved by good men, because good men will not go the lengths that may be necessary.

— HORACE WALPOLE,
The Letters of Horace Walpole:
Earl of Orford, Volume 9

PROLOGUE

Only a single small sparrow, hiding in the high branches of the green chestnut trees, dared to pierce the Avenue Foch's eerie silence with her chirps and trills.

Even though it was afternoon, there was no traffic on Baron Haussmann's grand Neoclassical thoroughfare, which linked the Arc de Triomphe to the Bois de Boulogne. The vélo-taxis avoided the wide street itself, while pedestrians and bicyclists bypassed its *contreallée* — the inner road separated from the boulevard by a ribbon of lawn.

There were few cars in Paris, and even the large black Citroëns and Mercedes favored by the Gestapo seemed to glide silently, as if they, too, were unwilling to disrupt the quiet. Without traffic, the air on Avenue Foch was unexpectedly sweet and fresh.

The cream-colored limestone façades, with their wrought iron balconies, tall windows, and mansard roofs, were considered the height of Parisian elegance. But a more ominous factor lurked behind Haussmann's design: some of the architect's critics opined that the real purpose of his grand boulevards was to make it easier for the military and police to suppress armed uprisings. And so the elegant and distinctive city plan had made it simpler for the Nazis to invade Paris during the Battle of France in June 1940.

On the section of Avenue Foch closer to Porte Dauphine stood several anonymous buildings that gave the street its chilling reputation. Number 84 housed the Paris headquarters of France's section IV Counterespionage division of the Sicherheitsdienst, the German security service that interrogated arrested foreign agents. The Gestapo leaders had chosen Avenue Foch deliberately for their headquarters: it was named after the French general Marshal Foch, to whom the Germans had surrendered in November 1918.

The Sicherheitsdienst's chief, Obersturmbannführer Wolfgang von Waltz, lifted his head as he heard the low growl of a car pierce the silence of the street. He looked up from the papers on his massive walnut desk and out the window to see a gleaming

Benz pull to the curb. Two Gestapo officers in plain clothes emerged with a young brunette in handcuffs.

Von Waltz was in his early forties. He was of medium height, handsome, and immaculately groomed, with golden-blond hair and silvery sideburns, his midsection slimmed by an elastic waist cincher. Only one eye slightly larger than the other kept him from looking like the Nordic gods of the Nazis' propaganda posters.

Despite his high SS rank, he wore a double-breasted, gray-striped suit, Lanvin silk tie and pocket square, and handmade alligator shoes. He wore civilian clothes on purpose, to win over incoming prisoners. He left the actual torture, if necessary, to the SS henchmen in the elegant building's damp and chilly basement.

He stood, taking one last satisfied glance over his large office. It had high ceilings with elaborate meringue crown moldings and a glittering cage chandelier, light sparkling through its heavy spear crystals, grand enough to impress any prisoner. His eyes slid across the reproduction of Nicolas Poussin's *Rape of the Sabine Women* that hung on one wall, while on the other, over the marble fireplace, hung the gold-framed official portrait of Adolf Hitler. On the mantel stood an antique clock topped by a Jean Gille porcelain figure of a woman in repose — *The Sleeping Beauty* — one slipper teetering on a graceful foot.

But the centerpiece of the room was a plantation table topped with an enormous domed Victorian cage containing an African gray parrot — a gift from von Waltz's superior officer, Joachim von Ribbentrop, Nazi Germany's Foreign Minister, whose photograph was displayed in a silver frame on the desk. And even though von Waltz loathed the bird, he couldn't wring its neck as he might have liked. Ribbentrop had bought it at the Paris bird market, amused that a bird from Africa's Ivory Coast, with feathers scalloped like silver chain mail and long tail in Nazi red and black, could be taught to say *"Heil Hitler!"* on command.

The bird, whom von Waltz had named Ludwig, had intelligent orange eyes and a few bald patches from nervous overgrooming. Ludwig's ornate cage was lined with newspaper, which von Waltz's secretary had to change regularly. She also fed the bird his special diet of seeds, greens, chicken bones, and snails. *"Bonjour! Guten Tag! Grüß Gott!"* the parrot sang out, shifting his weight from one taloned foot to the other. *"Heil Hitler!"*

"Shut up," von Waltz snapped.

Ludwig replied, as Ribbentrop had taught him: *"Schupf di du Schneebrunzer!"* — *Get out of the way, you snowpisser.*

Von Waltz ignored the bird. He lifted the black Bakelite telephone receiver with one manicured hand and dialed his secretary with the other. "Fräulein Schmidt," he crooned, "our 'guest' has arrived from the Rouen office. Please serve us coffee and perhaps a few pastries? Yes, perfect."

Outside von Waltz's office, Hertha Schmidt rose from her desk and did as she was told. Coffee — real coffee, not the ersatz stuff made from chicory or roasted acorns — was as precious as gold or diamonds in occupied Paris. A broad-shouldered, thick-waisted German blonde in her twenties, Hertha relished the many luxuries, such as coffee and chocolates, that working for the SS in Paris afforded her. *"Terroristen,"* she muttered, measuring out the fragrant ground beans. *"Englische Terroristen."* It was bad enough to care for the horrible bird; treating prisoners of war to coffee and pastries was too much.

As von Waltz heard the heavy iron gate clang shut, he closed the file in front of him, then opened the top drawer of his desk and took out a pocket mirror to check his teeth and straighten his tie.

"You're stupid," intoned Ludwig from his swing. *"When you drink schnapps, you can't smoke — otherwise you'll explode."*

Von Waltz went to the cage and pulled a heavy velvet cover over it, silencing the bird. He heard footsteps on the staircase, then a rap at his door. He smiled, eyes glinting. "Come in!" he called in lilting, Austrian-inflected French.

The two SS officers who opened the door looked grotesquely large, towering over their captive — a petite young woman, trembling violently.

Von Waltz clicked his heels, then bowed. "Please sit down, mademoiselle," he invited, indicating a fragile gilt chair. "Would you like a drink? Coffee is on the way, but I can get you something stronger if you'd like. You look as if you could use it."

"Take those off," he ordered the two officers in German, indicating the heavy cuffs shackling the woman's delicate wrists. Once they did as they were told, he dismissed them.

"That's better now, isn't it?" Von Waltz took the seat across from the woman instead of returning to his desk chair. She knew her face was swollen beyond recognition, eyes slits in the battered flesh. Her hair was matted and dirty, the bruises on her neck purple, and she reeked of sweat and urine. She moved gingerly to test the use of her hands.

He clicked his tongue against his teeth. "I see you've shown the poor judgment to resist in Rouen. I do trust you will do better here. Ah, coffee!" he cried as Fräulein Schmidt entered bearing a silver tray with a silver sugar bowl, creamer, and plate piled high with pastries. "I do love the ones with the hazelnut crème filling," he confided as the secretary set the tray down. "Of course, German pastry is the best, but there is something special about Parisian pastry that makes it a very close second."

"Would you like me to pour, sir?" asked Fräulein Schmidt.

"I'm sure we can manage," he said, with a wink to the prisoner. As he reached for the coffeepot, he watched her take in his office. There were red Nazi flags on both sides of the hearth. On a rosewood table, a marble chessboard was set up with a game in progress.

"Would you prefer I call you by your code name?" he asked as he poured the fragrant coffee with graceful movements. "Or" — he said, abruptly changing from French to clipped English — "by your *real* name,

15

Erica Calvert? And do you take sugar or cream? Or both?"

Erica shook her head; von Waltz dropped two sugar cubes and a generous pour of cream into a cup for himself. "Well then, I shall call you Mademoiselle Calvert." He blew on his coffee before taking a sip. "You are Erica Grace Calvert, one of Winston Churchill's secret army of undercover agents, known as the SOE or Special Operations Executive, recruited to 'set Europe ablaze.' "

Erica avoided his direct gaze.

"You were captured in Rouen and held for questioning."

The agent remained silent.

"And you're so tiny!" he exclaimed, studying her as he set his cup and saucer down. "I had no idea when I read your file that you'd be such a petite thing — and so young, as well." From his jacket pocket, he took out a silver case. "Cigarette?"

Erica made a sound halfway between a snort and a mew.

"My colleagues, unfortunately, were not able to obtain any satisfactory answers from you. And so you have been sent to Paris, to me." He left the case open, placing it on the table between them. "I will ask the questions now, and, as you can see, we can make

16

this a civilized exchange. It is up to you, of course. What were you doing in Rouen, Mademoiselle Calvert?"

"I can't say," she managed through swollen lips.

"Oh, come now. Sabotage?" von Waltz suggested.

Erica shook her head.

"To whom were you reporting?"

"I can't say."

"With whom were you working?"

"I can't say."

There was a silence. "Where are the secret stashes of arms and explosives you and your colleagues are bringing over here?"

"I —"

"— can't say, yes." Von Waltz smiled as he leaned back in his chair and crossed one slim leg over the other. "And how did you enjoy your stay at Arisaig House? I hear the west coast of Scotland is quite beautiful, especially in autumn."

Erica's breathing stilled. There was no way he could know that location — the location of SOE's paramilitary preparation — or that she had trained there in September and October.

"You did quite well with your parachute school at Ringway. And how did you enjoy your time at Beaulieu?" The Obersturmbannführer pronounced it in the English way, *bew-lee*. Beaulieu was the SOE's so-called finishing school, where chosen agents were sent for their final round of training. "I hear even in winter, the weather in the south of England is surprisingly mild."

"How — how —" Erica stammered.

"We know a lot about you, my darling girl. For instance, how you've been leaving off your security checks from prison in Rouen, hoping your London office will notice and realize you've been captured." He smiled. "Meanwhile, the Baker Street agents *have* noted your lack of security checks — and sent messages back scolding you that in the future you must be more careful with your coding."

Erica hesitated for a moment. Then, "I don't believe you."

Von Waltz rose. He crossed to his desk, flipping through pages of her file, choosing one. Walking back, he handed it to her. " *'Your 5735 security check acknowledged,'* " he recited from memory, taking his seat. " *'You forgot your double security check. Next time be more careful.'* "

He studied her face, relishing the expression of abject shock on her bruised countenance. "Yes, we have a mole in SOE."

She flinched. But who was the mole? And

18

where? In France? Or in England?

Von Waltz continued, his voice still gentle. "We know how frightened you are, Mademoiselle Calvert. You've been confessing your fears in your letters home to your father."

"There's no way you can know that!"

Von Waltz ignored her outburst. "Fear in wartime, mademoiselle — well, it's nothing to be ashamed of. But I must speak frankly. Your superior, Colonel Harold Gaskell, has sent you — a woman — here, in direct violation of the Geneva Convention, as well as all the rules of gentlemanly warfare."

Despite her shock and fear, Erica let out a snort at the Nazi's hypocrisy.

"You have been sent here against all the rules of war," the Obersturmbannführer persisted. "A woman. In civilian clothes. As a secret agent. To commit acts of terrorism against us. You know what the penalty for that is, yes?"

Erica didn't reply. Of course she knew. *Execution.* By firing squad or noose.

"But I am a civilized man. I don't want you, a woman — a *lady* — to be sacrificed for the stupidity and rash decisions of your superiors. Your Colonel Gaskell dropped you into a trap — and then quite stupidly failed to recognize his organization's own security checks, put into place to keep his spies safe, were being left off deliberately to signal you'd been captured."

He stood again, then crossed the plush Persian carpet. "They think on Baker Street that we're bungling, ham-handed fools." At his desk, he picked up another file and pulled out another piece of paper. It was a chart of the SOE hierarchy in London, every name correct. When he walked over and handed it to Erica and she realized what it was and how much sensitive information it contained, she felt tears sting her eyes.

"I know you told your little cover story ad nauseam to the SS officers in Rouen, but let's dispense with it here, shall we, mademoiselle?" Von Waltz resumed his seat next to her. "I can't promise you everything, but I can tell you I can save your life. Instead of being executed, you'll stay here. You'll share all the information you know, then you will work with us. And when the war is over, you will find out who betrayed you — and get your revenge."

There was an ugly silence as the British spy struggled to process everything von Waltz was telling her. She'd been captured in Rouen, yes, but the Nazis still didn't know she'd come ashore on the west coast of France. They didn't know she'd studied geology and that she'd been sent to the beaches of Normandy to obtain sand and soil samples and to determine beach gradients.

If von Waltz learned the truth, the Nazis would realize that while Pas de Calais was the obvious choice for the inevitable invasion, Normandy was also being seriously considered. Sand samples, which would help the engineers know what sort of equipment and tanks to send when the Allies invaded, would serve as a red flag to the possibility of using Normandy. The enemy didn't know and they couldn't know — not because of her. The bag, with her notes and specimens, was with a fellow agent at a safe house in Paris. *As long as I can keep that from him . . .*

Von Waltz regarded her smugly. "A terrorist, sent against the Geneva Convention, out of uniform, behind enemy lines, seeking to sow seeds of fear and unrest." He shook his head. "A female terrorist at that. How badly things must be going in England for them to send their little girls! Sweet little doves, all of you. They should not have made you come."

"I wanted to come." She straightened. "I volunteered. It was my choice."

His voice was suddenly steel. "They

21

should not have allowed you." Then, in softer tones, "You know there is nothing you won't tell me when we're through, mademoiselle. Save me time — and your pretty face — and tell us everything now."

Erica stared at him in despair, then slumped over in submission. Like all other SOE agents, she'd been issued a cyanide capsule, in case of situations such as this. But hers was concealed in a fountain pen in her handbag, which had been confiscated.

"Yes, we know everything, Mademoiselle Calvert." Von Waltz moved to the edge of his seat. "Look — give us the names and locations of the remainder of the English spies, tell us where they're storing their arms and explosives, and we'll forget the rest. Those arrested as a result will be interned until the end of the war — they won't be killed. You won't have betrayed them." He smiled, revealing even white teeth. "This is an agreement we will make — you and I."

Erica sat with her head down, mute, seemingly broken.

"If this does not happen, the villages around where we believe the depots are will be burned. And all of the inhabitants, including your fellow agents, will be killed."

"No . . ."

"We are all afraid in this war, mademoi-selle. But now you can free yourself from fears. There's nothing dishonorable in it. *Help us!*" He leaned forward and grasped her hands, holding them gently in his.

Erica shuddered at the physical contact.

"Give us the location of your agents, weapons, explosives, safe houses. And no one will be hurt. I give you my word, as an officer of the Third Reich."

Erica peered up at him. "I think I'll have that drink now."

He dropped her hands and clapped his together with delight. "Good, good!" he exclaimed, rising and going to the bar cart. He splashed two fingers of scotch into a glass, then passed her the heavy tumbler.

She downed it in two gulps. "I will talk to you," she promised him. "I'll tell you every-thing I know. But I'm exhausted. I need to wash. Change my clothes. Eat."

Von Waltz's eyes lit up. "Of course, my dear."

"And I'd like my handbag — I have a compact in there. And some lipstick."

"I'm afraid that's not permitted until we've gone through everything. But we can show you to a place where you can freshen up. And I will have a hot meal prepared for you, for when you're ready, and some good

French wine. And after that, we'll chat."

"Yes," she said, struggling to her feet.

"You've made the right decision." He opened the double doors, gesturing to the guards outside. "Please take Mademoiselle Calvert to the lavatory on the fifth floor and allow her to freshen up. When she is finished, bring her back to me. And be certain to treat her as the esteemed guest she's proving herself to be."

The fifth-floor servants' quarters had a shared bath. The guards admitted her, then stationed themselves outside the closed door. Erica looked around. There was a dirty tub and a ragged towel on a hook. Over the chipped enamel sink was a mirrored medicine chest. She looked inside — nothing but rust on the shelves.

Grimly, she studied her reflection in the tarnished mirror. Her battered face stared back. She could break the glass and try to slit her carotid artery, but the guards would hear the crash, and they would surely stop her before she could achieve her goal. She'd already been through days of torture and deprivation. She couldn't take much more. Resolutely, she went to the window, opened the curtains, and looked out. From the fifth floor, it was a long drop to the pavement below. No one could survive such a fall.

While her courage from the scotch still held, she opened the window and crawled out, finding footing on a rain gutter. If she killed herself, the secret of the Normandy sands and soil would die with her. The planned invasion would have a chance. She had confronted death back in Rouen and made her peace with it. She knew what she had to do. Only one thing still tormented her: who was the mole in SOE? Who had betrayed her?

She stepped out into the air, hovering for a moment, like a bird, before she fell.

CHAPTER ONE

The time was wrong.

Maggie Hope startled when the ormolu clock on the fireplace's mantel struck the incorrect hour, metallic chimes ringing through the house's chilly, high-ceilinged library. Heart pounding, she snapped her head to look over at it. Gilt Gemini twins flanked its pearlized face, and the thin black hands that should have been set to 1:00 Paris time were instead moved to 3:00 — the hour in Berlin. The Nazis' first official act after the Occupation of France had been to impose the Reich's time on the captured country.

What, she wondered, would Albert Einstein think of the arbitrary positions of the hands? Hadn't he himself posited that time is only a relative construct? *Of course, he never counted on the Nazis and their hubris,* she thought.

As a mathematics major at Wellesley College before the war, planning to pursue her doctorate at the Massachusetts Institute of Technology, Maggie had often speculated about such things — time and space and numbers. Back then, her greatest ambition had been to become a professor of mathematics at one of the Seven Sisters colleges.

But she'd inherited her grandmother's house in London in 1937 and stayed on, even as war broke out, to work as a typist for the new Prime Minister, Winston Churchill. After she solved a mystery regarding an IRA bomb plot, Peter Frain, head of MI-5, asked her if she spoke fluent German and French, and if she'd be willing to do more for her adopted country.

She'd said yes, without realizing exactly what that would entail.

Now, almost two years later, in June 1942, Maggie Hope was a British officer with the rank of major. Officially, she belonged to the Auxiliary Territorial Service, the all-female service known as the ATS — as well as the one with the worst uniforms. But that was only a cover. In fact, she worked for a secret organization, the Special Operations Executive, responsible for deception and sabotage behind enemy lines. "Set Europe ablaze!" Prime Minister Churchill had thundered when he created the unit, and, across the Continent, his spies were doing their bit. At twenty-seven, Maggie was one of SOE's more senior agents, although back at headquarters at Baker Street, her opinions and ideas were mostly ignored.

Before coming to France as an undercover agent, she'd never understood Salvador Dalí's painting *The Persistence of Memory*. But now, after looking up endlessly at the gilt clock, she understood its warped imagery of time all too well.

She was in occupied territory, waiting for forged identity papers — and if she were found out, she would be tortured by the Gestapo, then hanged as a spy. Maggie had been in Paris for three months, and every minute of every day since she'd arrived she'd been tracking shadows from the corners of her eyes, flinching at strange noises, and swallowing her meager meals with the constant threat of discovery and capture lodged in her throat. Worry was her daily diet, ever since she'd left London for Paris on a two-pronged mission: to discover the truth about what had happened to her half sister, Elise Hess, a German Resistance fighter in hiding, as well as her fellow SOE agent Erica Calvert.

Staring at the clock chiming the hour was nothing new. In her ever-vigilant state, she'd discovered the building had its own music: squeaking parquet floorboards, the rattle of windowpanes in the wind, and the melody created by each person who entered. Maggie had developed a well-tuned ear for the songs of the structure — the pelt of raindrops against the glass, the creak of the foundation settling and resettling, the scuttle of rats in the walls. The strain of always listening was slowly driving her mad. To battle the tension, she kept the wireless on at a low volume, the music and conversation combating loneliness.

Maggie was staying, at least for the moment, in a three-story, nineteenth-century *hôtel particulier* in the first arrondissement, between the Louvre and Les Halles. It was the former residence of a princess, who'd left the city in the early thirties. A film actress had bought the townhouse — then fled before the invasion. In the spring of 1941, the dilapidated structure was purchased by Dr. Maurice Charcot and his twin sister, Agathe, to use as both a physician's office and private residence. In the year the Charcots had owned the building, they'd done little cleaning and repair, except for the doctor's office, which was ordered and tidy, and an adjoining small living space for the two of them.

The rest of the manse, a once-elegant house with six bedrooms, was crammed with what the former occupants had abandoned. Armoires stuffed with moth-eaten costumes, hats, and shoes. A staggering disarray of broken furniture, grimy taxidermy, and stacks of mildewed books — encyclopedias, dictionaries, Bibles, fairy tales — were piled on the floor. Stag heads, their glass eyes blinded by dust, watched over rooms overflowing with unstrung chandeliers, broken Chinese bamboo birdcages, and murky oil paintings. An unraveling Aubusson tapestry of a captured unicorn moldered on one wall, while chipped marble statues of St. Francis of Assisi with upraised palms holding doves leaned against another in awkward positions. It was as if the house, like time, like Paris — like France itself — was sleeping under some malevolent spell.

Maurice and Agathe Charcot were with the Resistance, helping SOE. They let the British organization's French Section use their empty rooms as a safe house, but made it perfectly clear that, if the agents were ever discovered by the Gestapo, both would claim ignorance of the entire operation.

When Maggie had first moved into the Charcots' house, she'd made the unused library her own. After a thorough cleaning, it was now a pleasant space, tidy and orderly despite the crumbling, chalky blue walls and water-stained ceiling. She'd carried in a desk, a small round table, feather-stuffed chairs with only a few holes, and a long, lumpy, deeply buttoned sofa she used for a bed. A gilt-framed reproduction of Rubens's *Leda with the Swan* hung above the fireplace's mantel, a trifold screen padded with shabby velvet stood in one corner, and large grimy windows covered with heavy brocade drapes looked out to the street.

Maggie spent most of her time either doing the exercises she'd learned at Arisaig — jack-knives, push-ups, sit-ups, and jujitsu — or reading or working out math problems. A stuffed owl, whom she christened Athena, now held a place of honor on the desk, with its neat stacks of blotters in every kind of fabric, a rusty pen resting beside an inkwell, and a sheaf of papers with sketches of the birds she could see from the windows.

Yet no matter how much she cleaned and arranged and then rearranged her space, she felt utterly alone. *What am I doing here? I should never have come. What on earth was I thinking?* Sometimes she fantasized about abandoning the mission and going back to London. But she knew she couldn't leave Paris — at least not until she found out what had happened to Erica Calvert and to her own sister. Nightmares of their possible fates haunted her; she couldn't return to her life in London until she'd done everything she could to find them.

Maggie picked her way across the chevron-patterned parquet floor, stepping over the squeaky spots, to the windows. She lifted the edge of a drape and peeked out at an angle — making sure to remain hidden.

She watched as a young woman in the window of a flat across the street peered out in an almost exact mirror image. *Who are you?* Maggie wondered, while the slim girl with her flowered dress chewed nervously on one finger. *And are you a resister or a collaborator? Or someone somewhere in between?*

It was impossible to tell by looking. Maggie knew there were many who felt the deepest pain, sorrow, and humiliation over France's loss. Open conflict was pointless — it could lead to arrest and execution. So there were those Parisians who reacted to the travesty of the Occupation by keeping to themselves and avoiding contact with the Germans as much as possible.

There were many who made significant sacrifices — workers who turned down well-paid positions with the occupiers, civil servants who refused to continue working under German command. There were also those, such as the Charcots, who sought ways to turn their anger into action. They waged their battles underground and in secret, publishing resistance tracts and hiding British agents.

Then there were those who were indifferent — and, really, wishing only for the nightmare to be over. Like mourners who go to a funeral with feelings of grief, but leave with an inner sense of relief that the worst has passed. And there were Nazi sympathizers. Without openly confessing any allegiance to the Germans, this group thought Nazi rule had its positive side, especially in its ideas about Jews. That it was one's patriotic duty to not only work with the Nazis but to show them the better side of France. At the very bottom were the lackeys, the thugs, the violent anti-Semites let off their leashes, who embraced Fascism with open arms.

As the sky grew darker, a greenish color, the girl across the street drew her curtain. Fat raindrops began to fall, and Maggie wrapped her thin wool cardigan around her. It was always cold in the library. She looked up and noticed a few shoots of buddleia sprouting from a gutter. Two plump pigeons with iridescent purple necks strutted and cooed in front of a row of chimney pots, undeterred by the wet weather.

She padded, catlike in stocking feet, back to her place at the round table, covered with the things she used to take her mind off the sense of impending doom she battled during the interminable days: a box of delicately painted bone mah-jongg tiles, a game of solitaire in progress, and the day's newspaper.

As she sat down on a spindle-legged chair, her body curving like a question mark, she opened the thin, ink-smudged pages of *Paris-Midi* to see if any new measures were being implemented. Radio France segued from Maurice Chevalier's "Toi, toi, toi" to Edith Piaf's "Un coin tout bleu." As the song ended, the staccato tapping of raindrops against the windowpanes picked up.

Maggie took a sip of cold catnip tea left over from breakfast as the announcer, Jean Hérold-Paquis, held forth in a blistering commentary, calling for the annihilation of the United Kingdom. A member of the French Popular Party — one of the two Fascist parties allowed under the Occupation — Hérold-Paquis was known for the catchphrase *England, like Carthage, shall be destroyed!*

She rolled her eyes in disgust and waited for the next song. *No one prepares you for the waiting.* In her training as a secret agent and all of her subsequent missions — in Berlin, in Scotland, even in London — she'd learned to wait, counting out all the decimal points of pi she'd memorized or running Fibonacci's sequence as far as she could go. *But nothing can prepare you for the reality.* The boredom and unease, mixed always with dread.

Although she hadn't been out of the flat in weeks, the broadcasts on the wireless, as well as the Fascist French newspapers her hosts subscribed to as part of their cover, painted a picture of how much Paris had changed, as if the city were a princess sleeping under a fairy-tale curse.

Nineteen forty-two was almost half over; the year so far had been a cruel one. In Asia, the Japanese, heartened by their success at Pearl Harbor, seemed unstoppable. In Africa, the Desert Fox, Field Marshal Erwin Rommel, kept up the offensive. Not only had the Wehrmacht survived the Russian winter, but as the snows melted, it was forging ahead, crushing everything and everyone in its path. In the Atlantic, German submarines and ships were sinking all in their wake. Nazi power seemed to be at its peak. Hitler's victory looked assured.

And in France there was, of course, the surrender. The armistice signed by Germany and France on June 22, 1940, was a one-sided agreement. In return for being allowed to administer part of a French territory without military occupation — a concession that allowed the German Army to redeploy forty divisions and encouraged Marshal Philippe Pétain, Chief of State of Vichy France, to say *"L'honneur est sauf . . ."* or *Honor has been saved* — France had to submit to all other demands. All German prisoners of war were freed immediately, while all French prisoners of war were to be held until the ultimate German victory. While 25 million people were living in the northern occupied zone, only 14 million were in the free zone, with its government, led by Pétain, in Vichy — the de facto capital of southern, "unoccupied" France.

As a young woman taking French classes, Maggie had gone to the college library to read *Le Figaro,* France's leading newspaper. Its motto, from Figaro's monologue in the final act of *Le Mariage de Figaro,* was *Sans la liberté de blâmer, il n'est point d'éloge flatteur: Without the freedom to criticize, there is no true praise.*

The august paper, whose writers had once

included Albert Wolff, Émile Zola, and Alphonse Karr, had relocated to Vichy. But eventually the editors suspended its publication, resisting the censorship enforced by the Pétain government. All of the Paris papers, including *Le Temps,* had been shut down, and new, Nazi-approved ones had sprung up in their place. Maggie hated them, yet felt compelled to read, both out of a sense of needing to know the worst and to practice her cover story.

As the wind picked up, sending the rain sweeping sideways, her eyes fell on a headline: LE FRANCE SE LIBERE DU JONG JUIF — FRANCE IS FREED FROM THE JEWISH YOKE.

She bit her lip as she read: *The arrest of 5,000 foreign Jews between the ages of 18 and 45, and then their removal to Pithiviers and Beaune-la-Rolande, has begun. All of the Jews were dangerous without exception — illegal traffickers on the black market who had become rich overnight. They are parasites who have finally received the proper though far too lenient punishment for their crimes against the long-suffering Aryan people. . . .*

She couldn't bring herself to finish.

Flipping through the pages, she spotted an advertisement for the Paris Opéra Ballet's *La Belle au Bois Dormant — Sleeping*

Beauty. She knew two of her fellow SOE agents and friends, Sarah Sanderson, code-named Sabine Severin, and Hugh Thompson, now Hubert Taillier, were working on the production at the Palais Garnier, in their new identities as dancer and cellist, until they could carry off their own mission. Maggie felt a frisson of fear but disciplined herself to ignore it. *Sarah and Hugh are smart and well trained. They'll be fine. More than fine — they'll succeed in their job and make it back home, safely.*

And when doubt nagged: *They will.*

The three agents had flown to Paris together on a small RAF plane, Maggie joining at literally the last moment. They had worked out all of their misunderstandings during the long flight. They were friends. They would all always be friends. And Maggie, despite her own past with Hugh, respected his and Sarah's burgeoning romance.

The rest of the newspaper was filled with countless photos of a detached-looking Marshal Pétain, as well as chirpy reports about the horse races at Longchamp, the new film *Mam'zelle Bonaparte,* and the upcoming Parisian premiere of Richard Strauss's *Capriccio.*

These were interspersed with articles on

the so-called Fatherland, patriotism, and warnings against the dangers of Bolshevism. *Travail, famille, patrie* — *Work, family, patriotism* — had replaced the Republican motto of *Liberté, égalité, fraternité.*

The tone of the newspapers published under the Occupation wasn't stoic or resigned but downright cheery; apparently, at least according to the articles, a new Europe was being built, helped by France's finest. While some political power had been "temporarily ceded," this transfer of power was lauded in the censored papers as a worthwhile maneuver.

But Maggie's head snapped up when she heard the wireless's disembodied voice intone: *Field Marshal Pétain, Head of State, will address you now from the Hôtel du Parc in Vichy.*

There was a knock at the double door, causing her heart to plunge in fear. "Come in," she called, finally finding her voice. Her hosts entered the library. Agathe carried a tray with Maggie's lunch, a bowl of steaming broth and a thin slice of what passed for bread. Maurice walked to the wireless to turn up the volume.

He was a dignified man, with a crisply trimmed white beard and mustache, wearing gray flannel trousers and a well-pressed shirt, a silk scarf tied around his neck. As he fiddled with the wireless's dial, he gnawed at the stem of an empty pipe that still gave off the smell of fruity tobacco. Agathe put down the tray on Maggie's makeshift desk.

"Merci," Maggie said to her with a smile.

The older woman gave an unmistakably Gallic shrug in reply. Agathe was a small, birdlike woman, with blotchy skin drawn over high cheekbones and iron-colored hair pulled tightly back in a bun. She wore a faded dress, lisle stockings, and scuffed leather shoes. A blue Bakelite swallow, wings extended, was pinned to her collar.

As Maggie spooned her lukewarm, watery soup, Agathe sat on the worn sofa, where she blinked nervously and crossed her thin arms across her chest for warmth. Her brother sat beside her, fidgeting at one of the loosening buttons on his cuff, as they waited to hear Pétain.

Maggie had the feeling that Maurice was the twin truly moved to offer up his house to the Resistance, while his sister was far less committed. *Fair enough,* Maggie thought. She was constantly aware that, by hiding her, the pair risked their lives.

Pétain began to speak in his high-pitched, nasal tones: *French people, don't make our situation worse by resorting to acts that give*

41

rise to tragic reprisals. It will be innocents who will suffer the consequences. Don't listen to those who try to exploit our distress. They will lead our country to disaster. France will save herself by observing the highest standards of discipline. Therefore, the orders of the government . . .

After Pétain's address, *La Marseillaise* came on. As the national anthem — a call for freedom and the fight against tyranny — played, Maggie watched Maurice's faded blue eyes cloud with disappointment. As a soldier during the Great War, he had no doubt seen Pétain as his savior. Now the general was his Judas.

Agathe cleared her throat, refusing to look at Maggie. Was the Frenchwoman thinking that, by harboring an agent, they were making things worse, as Pétain had said? Or was it that the woman just didn't like her? *Or, perhaps, my stay here is making me paranoid instead of grateful,* Maggie amended, remembering the warnings about how the mind could play tricks on missions.

The broadcast resumed: *The streets ring with the clatter of taxi-bikes in the championship race — a new Parisian sport and a product of the times. And one last surge takes the Dubois team to victory!*

Maggie broke off a piece of the bread. *An*

exhibition at the Berlitz takes a hard look at the Jewish problem. Since 1936, France has been paying for her kindness to the Jews. "Learn How to Tell a Jew from a Frenchman" is a chilling display of Semitic traits both physical and psychological and serves as a vivid warning against the Jewish peril. More Frenchmen must learn to identify the Jew and guard against his encroachments.

The wireless's introduction to a ditty by Charles Trenet didn't hide the thud of footsteps coming up the staircase. The trio froze. There was a loud *bang* as the door flew open.

There stood Jacques Lebeau, Air Movements Officer for SOE's F-Section, dripping with rain. "So sorry," he began in accentless French as he took off his wet hat and shook it. "I didn't mean to alarm you."

He was a tall, lean man in his early thirties, with sharp features, eyes that missed nothing, and a twitchy, sardonic smile. His straight brown hair was pushed back from his brow. His cheeks and chin, even though freshly shaved, were already shadowed with stubble. What was most striking about his face was his thick black eyelashes.

Jacques, you have sad, sad eyes, Maggie decided, her heart turning over. Even when he did smile, it was tinged with sadness, as

43

if he knew even momentary happiness was a deception. Then she shook the sentiment off. *For heaven's sake,* everyone *in Paris who's not a Nazi or a collaborator has sad eyes these days.*

Another man, short and lean with wet, sandy hair, stepped out from behind Jacques, causing one of the floorboards to squeak. He had a satchel slung over his right shoulder.

"This is Reiner Dupont —" Jacques began by way of introduction.

Agathe held up a frail hand. "Never mind that. We don't need to know names or details."

"You're the agent code-named Joan?" Reiner asked Maggie. She nodded. He patted the satchel. "I'm afraid I don't have any letters for you."

"I wasn't expecting any."

"Come with me," Agathe ordered the exhausted-looking Reiner. "I'll show you where you can wash up, then get you something to eat."

As they ascended the stairs, Maurice looked to Jacques and Maggie. "I'll give you two some privacy," he said as he left, closing the doors with a loud *click.* The two agents were alone.

Maggie had first met Jacques when the

plane carrying her, Sarah, and Hugh landed on a moonlit night in a field outside Paris. As he greeted them and led them to the safe house, Maggie noticed his hat, a gray fedora, was set at a jaunty angle. She'd found it both charming and irksome, that angle — as if he were acting the role of secret agent in a play or a film. And yet he was an important cog in the SOE machine, in charge of organizing secret RAF aircraft takeoffs and landings for agents. He was also responsible for the transport of the agents from the airfields to the various safe houses and back again when their missions were complete.

It had been Jacques who had hand-delivered the telegram that related her father was dead. And it was Jacques who had procured a bottle of brandy and drunk it with her as she absorbed the news in shock, then held her as she sobbed in an ugly way. When she finished, he'd given her his handkerchief and smoothed back her hair.

The voice from the wireless now disintegrated into static; Maggie rose to turn it off. "The weather's changing," she said, self-conscious now that they were alone. "The interference is getting worse."

Jacques stuck his hands in his pockets and

began to pace. "First it's sunny, then it's raining. Damn weather can't make up its mind. Er, sorry."

Maggie repressed a smile. She had heard — and said — much worse. "You missed Pétain's speech."

"Same old story." Jacques shrugged. "If the Germans don't want to die, they should have stayed at home. Still, everything is gray now, shades of gray — to us in the shadows at least." His voice turned hard, bitter. "And sometimes it's hard to tell one shade from another." There was a protracted silence, and Maggie wondered if perhaps he'd served too long, if he needed time off. Burnout was a real danger for agents.

"I hope the wait has given you time to grieve for your father," Jacques finally remarked, in softer tones. "I didn't know him, of course, but it must be hard — to deal with his death in a foreign land, to be unable to return for his funeral."

"The truth is, I didn't know him that well. I was — am — mourning the idea of never having had a real father." There was more to the story of her relationship with her father, of course, but this wasn't the time or place.

Jacques sat on the sofa and leaned back, stretching his long legs; the hems of his

46

trousers were mud-splattered. "SOE is quite cross with you, young lady. Everyone's still talking about it." He let out a whistle. "How you got yourself on that flight here by order of the Queen herself! Miss Lynd is still annoyed, in case you're wondering."

Maggie permitted herself a small smile. "Well, if the spy HQ is talking about it, they're not all that good at keeping secrets, are they? By the way, any news on Madeleine?" Madeleine was Erica Calvert's code name.

A shadow crossed the Frenchman's face. "No, nothing. As far as we know, though, she's still on the run. There haven't been any transmittals in the last few weeks. With or without security checks."

Maggie fought to stay expressionless. "She could be dead."

"Don't give up hope," he urged gently. Then, more briskly, "Speaking of which, I do have good news — a special delivery for you." He reached into his jacket's breast pocket and pulled out an envelope. "You're all set — passport, ration book, everything you'll need to pass in your new identity. And —" He rose and went to the double doors, opened them, and dragged in a large Louis Vuitton steamer trunk. "Voilà!" he said with a flourish. "There's a small suitcase, a toiletries case, and a few hatboxes down-stairs for you as well."

Maggie clapped her hands. "Thank you," she said, her face beaming with relief. Her time in limbo was over. "I can finally get to work!" She ran to the trunk, opened it, and rummaged through the tissue-lined haute couture clothing until she found what she was looking for. She took everything behind the trifold screen in a corner of the room.

"You know," Jacques opined as Maggie began to undress, "there are some French-men with our cause who wonder if what we're doing is having any real impact. But for me, and I'd say for most of us, the point is moot — there's a moral and psychologi-cal factor."

Maggie was naked for a moment. Between her old clothes and her new, suspended between identities. As she put on the clothes she personally would never wear, but those favored by the person she was to be, her heartbeat quickened.

Jacques went on. "It's a point of pride for us that we're not passively waiting for libera-tion. No 'someday my prince will come' for us."

Maggie emerged, pulling on pristine white silk gloves, buttoning their pearl closures. She was dressed in Chanel — an afternoon

48

dress in blue silk, her own pearl earrings, and wedge-heeled shoes. A surrealist brooch, an eye in platinum, diamonds, and enamel, with a ruby and diamond teardrop dangling from one corner, glittered on the ensemble. "A little something from the spring 'thirty-eight collection," she said, twirling. The skirt flared around her, revealing a lace slip and bare, slim legs that had already been painted beige with Creation Bien Aimée. "But still lovely." Changing her clothes had changed her posture, her carriage, and her bearing.

"Oooh la la." Taking in her transformation, Jacques grinned roguishly. "You clean up well, mademoiselle."

"It's all smoke and mirrors. Part of the job. *L'habit ne fait pas le moine.*"

"Well, it becomes you."

Reiner returned; he'd dried his hair and changed into fresh clothes, the official dark coveralls of a Paris sanitation worker, the satchel he'd arrived with in hand. "Some people have all the luck," he grumbled. "My assignment is quite glamorous, let me assure you. Garbage duty — in addition to getting the agents' mail in and out — but you never know what the Boche are going to throw away."

Maggie stopped midspin. "It's only a role.

49

Like an actor. If I needed to be a factory girl, I'd wear coveralls and put my hair up in a scarf."

"Sure you would." Reiner sounded anything but convinced.

"Let's go," she told Jacques. "There are things I need to put in place before I can start my mission." She walked to the door, heels tapping on the scratched parquet.

Jacques's eyes followed her.

"Well?" she said, turning in impatience, a hand on one hip.

A slow smile crept across his face, then he rose and made a formal bow. "I'm honored to carry your trunk, *ma belle dame.*"

Maggie lifted one eyebrow. " *'La belle dame sans merci.'* "

CHAPTER TWO

Against all advice from his cabinet ministers, his private detectives, and his beloved wife, Prime Minister Winston Churchill was presiding over a security meeting at Number 10 Downing Street.

Even though bombing from the Blitz had paused — at least for the moment — his staff would rather he worked at the Cabinet War Rooms, a secret underground bunker not far from Number 10.

But the P.M. loathed the dark and airless space and grumbled about turning into a "troglodyte." He much preferred working either in the Annexe, the Churchills' private wartime residence above the War Rooms, or back at Number 10, despite the fact that the two-hundred-year-old manse had sustained Luftwaffe bomb damage to its kitchen and state rooms in October 1940, while Churchill dined yards away in the Garden Room.

But who could say no to Winston Churchill? So the P.M.'s security meeting was being held in Number 10's rectangular Cabinet Room — though the windows were taped over, the portrait of Sir Robert Walpole was in storage, and the Victorian mahogany chairs had been replaced by metal folding ones. Weak light glimmered through narrow openings in the heavy damask drapes. It was just past one o'clock by the ticking timepiece on the mantel.

The men seated around the baize-covered table included General Sir Hastings Ismay, Churchill's personal Chief of Staff; General Sir Alan Brooke, Chief of the Imperial General Staff; Air Chief Desmond Morton of the Royal Air Force; Captain Henry Pim of the Royal Navy; General Sir Stewart Menzies, chief of MI-6; and Colonel Lord Robert Laycock, director of SOE. Churchill's head private secretary, David Greene, was there to take notes for the P.M.

The men sat at the boat-shaped table with the Prime Minister at its head, puffing one of his favored Romeo y Julieta cigars, enveloped in a cloud of smoke. There were times when Churchill could be amiable, with a quick smile and a twinkle in his clear blue eyes, but this afternoon he seemed sunk in gloom, his shoulders hunched as if braced for imminent attack. He had on his gold-framed glasses and was reading the latest memo from General Ismay.

"Our friend Stalin isn't pleased — wants us to create a European front immediately to divert troops from Russia." He looked up over the rims of his spectacles and glowered through the tobacco haze. "And I still don't know why you're so keen on Normandy as an ultimate invasion point, Pug!" The Prime Minister used his nickname for General Ismay, whose face and brows did have a distinct resemblance to those of a sad-looking dog.

The P.M. gnawed his cigar. "We need to see what happens with Jubilee before deciding anything — that should keep Stalin quiet. For the moment, at least." He was referring to the upcoming Dieppe raid, known as Operation Rutter during its planning stages but now by its final, official code name, Operation Jubilee. The attack was planned for the German-occupied port of Dieppe, on the northern coast of France, on August 19 — two months away. It was to be a relatively small raid, with about six thousand Canadian infantrymen, supported by the Royal Navy and the Royal Air Force.

The P.M. glared at each man around the table in turn. "After Jubilee, we'll see if it is indeed possible to capture a defended French deepwater port. Until then, we can't plan the main attack." He dropped the cigar into a cut-glass ashtray and picked up a glass of weak whiskey and soda.

"With all due respect, sir," ventured Menzies. "Jubilee is a military action to convince the Russians we're serious about a European invasion. It's like sacrificing a knight in chess — so that we can get back to North Africa and proceed the way we've planned."

"Winston —" General Ismay waved away the drifting cloud of smoke. "We're currently going over French beaches from Brittany to Dunkirk, and there are only two possible invasion sites — Pas de Calais and Normandy. There are advantages and disadvantages to each."

General Brooke cleared his throat. "I'm still concerned about the lack of intelligence we have on the coast. We have no actual geologists' reports — only scans from people's holiday photos we've amassed. *Holiday snapshots!*"

Churchill grunted.

"And, let me say, there are people on our fair isle who have no business wearing swimsuits in the first place, let alone being photographed in them. . . ."

A few of the men murmured, "Hear,

hear!" while Menzies lit a Player's cigarette and looked on impassively. The Chief of MI-6 never said much in these meetings, preferring to watch and listen, and to collect information he might use later.

"At any rate, the sand quality and beach gradients have been estimated using only beach holiday snaps," Brooke continued. "I will not even consider putting our tanks on French soil, let alone our boys, until we have hard scientific evidence to tell us about sand quality and depth of clay. This is no way to run a war, Winston!"

"Calm yourself, Brookie." The P.M. looked to Menzies. "And what do you think?"

"This is SOE territory," Menzies replied, not masking his distaste for the junior and "amateur" organization. "They're supposed to have provided us with the sand samples already." He pulled on his cigarette with thin lips. "If you'd given the job to my agents at MI-Six, sir, we would have had the information in hand months ago."

"Not at all," rejoined Laycock, bristling under the implied criticism. "SOE is on top of it. Colonel Gaskell of F-Section assures me that he has an agent with the Normandy sand samples, a young thing named Erica Calvert. Had to flit off to Paris apparently, on the run. But she'll surface soon."

Menzies stared down Laycock without blinking. "We hear your French agents are in a bit of trouble, old thing."

Laycock stilled. He was an average-size man, but with wide shoulders that hinted he'd once been an athlete and thick, chestnut brown hair only touched by white. "Not at all, I can assure you."

"Enough!" Churchill roared. "I won't have this infighting between MI-Six and SOE. All my children must get along. Now then — Captain, tell us about our options besides Normandy."

"Sir, we believe, regardless of sand, Calais would be too easily defended by the Germans — and the North Sea weather is far too unpredictable. Also, there are no beaches to sustain us in Pas de Calais." Pim adjusted the gold-striped cuffs of his immaculate uniform.

"You don't believe we can capture a deepwater port, Captain?"

"No, Prime Minister, I don't." Pim shook his head. "Unfortunately, I think Jubilee will only prove that."

"So." The P.M. drained his whiskey and soda. "It comes down to Pas de Calais and Normandy. We'll need to choose one. And soon."

"What about Roosevelt and the Americans?" asked Brooke. "I daresay they'll have an opinion."

"Let's establish our own playbook before bringing in the damn Yanks," Churchill rumbled. "I'll handle Franklin and his boys."

Brooke took a monogrammed silver case from his breast pocket and extracted a cigarette. "Hitler will expect us in Pas de Calais," he said, lighting it with his Dunhill. The tip glowed red in the shadowy light.

"No, the Hun is too smart for that," Churchill objected fiercely. "He'll assume Normandy. Normandy, I say!" He banged both fists on the table, rattling teacups and making papers jump. "He always expects the unexpected. The Bavarian lout has an uncanny talent for it."

"I'm all in favor of planning for a Normandy invasion, sir," Brooke observed, "but before we commit, I must insist on those geological samples. We need to know how to build our tanks, what our boys will require to navigate the terrain —"

"Laycock, get all your agents on this. Highest priority!" the Prime Minister ordered.

"Actually . . ." Laycock began. "Your agent, a Miss Margaret Hope, is in Paris now, looking for her sister — with your personal blessing?"

The P.M. looked to David. "Gimme scotch." David took Churchill's glass, then went to the bar cart at the end of the room and did as he was bidden.

"She's a bit . . . undisciplined . . . from what I hear, sir," Laycock remarked. "Colonel Gaskell has mentioned his doubts. Miss Hope's flight to Paris was certainly, shall we say, *impetuous.*" He arched an eyebrow. "If I may suggest —"

"Yet another female?" Menzies's phlegmatic face finally showed expression. "One of the most important pieces of information we need to plan the invasion, and you're sending a *woman* — ?"

"Miss Hope is one of the best agents we have!" the P.M. growled. "Used to work for me, you know! Damn fine girl. Patriot. Amazonian warrior!"

At this, David permitted himself a small smile. He'd been friends with Maggie Hope and was the one who had brought her on as the P.M.'s secretary, back in the summer of 1940. She'd saved his life during a kidnapping plot. He and Maggie had become even closer as she'd risen through the ranks of SOE, and as they both fought their own demons. If he hadn't been "like that" he probably would have married her, but, as things were, David thought of her as a sister.

"All right then, let's say we're theoretically going to make Normandy our invasion landing point" — at the Prime Minister's words, the assembled men stilled; history was being made — "but we first need those sand samples — we need to customize our tanks depending on the ratio of sand to clay. I'm making that a *priority.*" A twitch began beneath Churchill's left eye. "And I won't have MI-Six and SOE squabbling — we're all on the same side, damn it!"

David had seldom seen "the Boss" so frustrated. When battling Nazis, the P.M. was pugnacious. But today he looked as if SOE and MI-6's internal strife was taking a toll.

"Make a note, Mr. Greene — we need someone to coordinate the clandestine services — to supervise the invasion and all of the counter-information coming into and going out from SOE, MI-Six, and MI-Five. We need someone who can maintain absolute secrecy, has a certain fanatical enthusiasm, and complete reliability. 'Appointed Controlling Officer for Deception' — yes," the P.M. decided with a self-satisfied nod, as if picturing the title in his head. "That's what we'll call him."

Laycock looked to David. "Ring Colonel Henrik Martens, he's exactly the chap for it. Just back from clandestine SOE work in Norway. Injured in Operation Archery in the raid against German positions on the island of Vågsøy." He turned to Menzies. "All right with you?"

As the clock on the mantel chimed, Menzies nodded.

"Splendid!" The Prime Minister rose with effort; the other men scrambled to their feet. "Our highest purpose is to deceive the enemy about our intentions. We'll need to perpetrate the most important lie in history — where the Allied attack will *not* be."

Churchill looked to Menzies and Laycock. "SOE and MI-Six will work with our Controlling Officer for Deception to prepare ruses and shams, causing our enemy to waste military resources. You're not limited to strategic deception only but will need to mislead and mystify the enemy at every turn.

"In other words," the Prime Minister continued, making his way back to his private office in his inimitable rolling gait, "we need to use every dirty trick in the book to bugger those Hun bastards!"

Outside the Charcots', the slate pavement

was a glossy silver from the rain; Maggie's and Jacques's silhouettes reflected up from a puddle. Maggie's heart was in her throat, excitement and fear fizzing together. She held out a palm, looking up to the sky — half shimmering blue, half covered in dark clouds.

Jacques stood by Maggie's pile of luggage, panting. "Do you really need all of this?"

"Yes, I do," she assured him. "Some of us have guns and grenades — others, haute couture." Looking around, Maggie absorbed the beauty that was Paris after a rain shower. There was a warm, fragrant breeze, with only the slightest hint of a chill. She took a deep breath to compose herself, as church bells tolled the hour in the distance. *"Après l'ondée,"* she said over the deep-toned gongs, surprised to find herself so affected by the sound.

"What?"

Her lips twitched in a nervous smile. *"Après l'ondée.* It's a perfume — Guerlain — I used to wear. It smells like violets, cold rain, and warm sunshine. I never thought about the name before, not really, but Paris truly does smell wonderful after a shower."

"Paris smells good these days because there aren't any cars anymore. No petrol, so no more pollution. If you have a bicycle or decent shoes, it's not so bad — but forget getting anywhere in a hurry."

Maggie realized he was right — there were no automobiles in sight and there were no sounds of traffic, even in the distance. The only noises were the coos of pigeons and the swish of a broom as a man in denim coveralls swept water and bits of trash and yellow pollen from the gutters to the sewer grille.

No time to be afraid. "Wait," she said, eyeing her pile of luggage. "If there aren't any taxis, how am I going to move my things?"

Jacques gave her a sly grin, and, at that moment, what looked like a wheeled rickshaw turned the corner. He whistled and stuck out one hand to wave the driver down. "Vélo-taxi," he explained as the man, small but wiry, with yellowish white, greasy hair topped by a Basque beret, pulled up. He grimaced, revealing a steel tooth.

As the driver wrestled Maggie's trunk into the back, Jacques offered his hand to help her step up into the contraption. "Look, I know you've done this type of thing before, this work, but never in France. Never in Paris."

Jacques gave her a sudden, intense look, as if taking a mental picture to recall someday. Maggie adjusted her hat and smoothed her gloves, determined to look calm. "Any advice?"

He leaned in close. "It's the only rule you'll need while you're here," he whispered, mirth gone from his eyes. "Easy to remember: *Trust no one.* Nothing is clear here. Everything is shadows." He straightened and slapped one hand on the side of the vélo-taxi, letting the driver know she was in and ready. "Never forget that."

He brushed Maggie's cheek with his fingers. *"Merde alors,"* he said, the phrase agents used instead of *good luck.* Then, as the vélo-taxi pulled away from the curb, Maggie turned to watch as Jacques stuck his hands into his leather jacket pockets, tucked his head down, and stalked away with a long, loping stride. When he turned a corner and disappeared, she felt an unexpected jab of disappointment.

"Where to, mademoiselle?" the driver asked, as he strained at the pedals. With the extra heft of all the luggage, in addition to the weight of a passenger, he was already beginning to pant.

Maggie forced a smile she didn't feel. "Why, the Hôtel Ritz, of course!"

The man stood at a microphone, veins in his forehead bulging, perspiration glistening on his face, working himself into a fevered rage.

". . . the hidden forces which incited England already in 1914 were Jews! The force which paralyzed us at that time and finally forced us to surrender with the slogan that Germany was no longer able to bear homeward a victorious flag, came from the Jews! It was the Jews who fomented the revolution among our people and thus robbed us of every possibility at further resistance!"

He gestured to an imaginary crowd, fixing his intense silver eyes upon them. From his uniform's breast pocket, he pulled out a handkerchief embroidered with a border of black swastikas to swipe at his brow.

"Since 1939, the Jews have maneuvered the British Empire into the most perilous crisis it has ever known. The Jews were the carriers of that Bolshevist infection which once threatened to destroy Europe. It is no longer a question of the interests of individual nations; it is, rather, a question of conflict between nations which want to make the lives of their people secure on this earth, and nations which have become the helpless tools of an international world parasite!"

With that, he looked over to the producer of the radio address and made a slashing movement with his forefinger at his throat.

It was the end of the broadcast, and Adolf Hitler slumped down in his desk chair, breathing heavily.

As Hitler closed his eyes in exhaustion, rapturous applause erupted. The men were gathered around a small table in Hitler's private office in Wolf's Lair, his *Führerhauptquartiere* — Eastern Front military headquarters. The top-secret, high-security site was in the Masurian woods, five miles from the small East Prussian town of Rastenburg. It had been built in 1941 on damp swampland at the start of Operation Barbarossa, the invasion of Russia. According to Joseph Goebbels, the Reichsminister of Propaganda, Wolf's Lair looked like "a holiday resort" — although the guarded railway, armed walking patrols, machine gun towers, and antiaircraft artillery on the roofs belied his description.

The assembled inner circle consisted of Joachim von Ribbentrop, foreign minister of Nazi Germany; Heinrich Himmler, head of the SS; Adolf Eichmann, one of the architects of the roundup and extermination of the Jews; and Field Marshal Gerd von Rundstedt, Hitler's commander in chief of the West.

"A triumph!" Ribbentrop exalted, as the producer silently removed the microphone and other broadcasting equipment. The foreign minister's once-handsome face was aging; a softening jawline detracted from his cleft chin.

Eichmann nodded, one side of his mouth drawn up in its characteristic mocking half smile. "I would only add, my Führer, that in your speech for the Reichstag, you might include more about Roosevelt and his Jewish clique."

Hitler was still breathing hard, as if he had just run a race. He reached down to pet his Alsatian. "Good girl," he panted, stroking her head. The dog wagged her tail. "Good Blondi." He rummaged through his desk drawer and pulled out a treat for her, making her wait and beg until finally, almost with disappointment, he let her have it.

The Führer's office was surprisingly modest, with simple wood furniture, plain carpets, and cotton curtains. A tall-case clock ticked in the corner, its brass pendulum swinging. In a normal tone of voice, Hitler asked Eichmann, "What news from France?"

"We just received this telegram from Prime Minister Pierre Laval," Eichmann answered, rising to hand it to Hitler. "Laval suggests including the children in the July roundup."

"The children?" Hitler asked flatly, scanning the document.

"Yes, the Jewish children. Younger than sixteen. Laval says, and I quote, 'Children should remain with their parents.' "

Hitler pushed away the paper. "The fate of the French Jewish children does not interest me." He sounded bored.

Eichmann hesitated. Then, "If you have no objections to including the children, we must hurry. Before the international community — Eleanor Roosevelt and her Jew cohorts — can hear of it and start an outcry."

"There may be a hue and cry — for the moment. But who remembers the Armenian children now?" Hitler referred to the Ottoman Empire's Armenian massacres of the late nineteenth century. "In a few decades, no one will remember what we do."

A secretary knocked and then entered, carrying a tea tray with a plate piled high with *Lebkuchen* — spicy cookies. Young, with a full, childish face and pouty lips, the woman set it down in front of the men at the table, then poured a steaming cup for Hitler and brought it to him at his desk.

"Ah, caraway tea!" he exclaimed with a genuine smile. "Thank you, Fräulein Junge." The young woman ducked her head shyly, then left. "Caraway tea helps with the blood, you know," he proclaimed to the men. "Aids in digestion, too."

He blew on his tea, then raised the cup to his lips. "Now, we must turn our attention to other matters. The so-called Allies must be planning an invasion of Europe, even as we speak. I fully expect that sometime in the next weeks, months — or even years — Churchill and his band of thugs will land on the shores of the Continent."

His eyes closed. "It will be the final showdown. The destiny of the Reich and Occupied Europe hangs in the balance. It will be the decisive event of the war. If landings succeed" — he drew in a deep breath — "then the war is lost."

Von Rundstedt, a Prussian with hard features and an unflinching gaze, tugged at his sparse mustache. "Of course, we have the men and arms, sir — but the Allies have the element of surprise. We must not underestimate that."

"What we need to do is hand them a defeat, as we did with the Poles, the French, and now the Russians." Himmler pushed up the small silver spectacles sliding down his nose, then reached for a gingery *Lebkuchen*.

"Where will they land?" Hitler murmured,

as though to himself. "That's the gamble, the toss of the dice, the war game on which everything depends."

"Regardless, we have the forces to defeat them!" Ribbentrop insisted. "And when defeated, they will never have the strength, men, and materials to invade again — we'll see to that."

"What then, my Führer?" von Rundstedt asked.

"By then, not only will we have the V-One and V-Two rockets, but our atomic weapons will be operational as well. We'll conquer Britain. Then we'll turn to the United States and Canada."

"And what about Japan?" Ribbentrop asked.

Hitler waved a hand, as if discussing how to divide a loaf of bread. "We will give them the west coast of North America, Vancouver, San Francisco, Los Angeles. There will be a small unoccupied zone, split by the Mississippi River, no, the Rocky Mountains. We, of course, will take the East — Boston, New York, and Washington — and the Midwest."

He squinted at von Rundstedt. "Where do *you* predict they will land?"

"France, *my Führer,*" the field marshal replied without hesitation. "Definitely. We consider four sites most likely for the landings — Brittany, the Cotentin Peninsula, Normandy, and Pas de Calais. But Brittany and Cotentin are points — it would be too easy to cut off their advance. So I don't think those are serious options."

Von Rundstedt moved to the edge of his chair. "A landing in Normandy would permit simultaneous threats against the port of Cherbourg, coastal ports farther west in Brittany, and an overland attack toward Paris and eventually into Germany. However, the drawback of the Normandy coast — and it's a big drawback — is the lack of port facilities.

"And so I consider Pas de Calais the most likely initial landing zone. It's the closest point in continental Europe to Britain. Between England and Calais, there's barely twenty miles of open water. It's their best option," von Rundstedt continued. "They could deliver men and materials to a bridgehead in Pas de Calais four times faster than they could to Normandy, and six times faster than to Brittany."

"They can also use their airpower to best effect in Calais," Ribbentrop mused. "Their plan will most likely be to seize and open a major seaport — and Pas de Calais is the best option, with the most advantages."

Hitler gave them all a look that silenced

them instantly. "They will land in Normandy," he stated flatly. "If I were planning the invasion, I'd use Normandy."

The assembled men remained mute, no one wishing to disagree.

"They will not take the obvious approach. Surprise is their friend. However," Hitler stated, holding up one finger, "surprise expected is not surprise, is it?"

Ribbentrop cleared his throat. "Obersturmbannführer Wolfgang von Waltz, with Gestapo counterespionage in Paris, informs me he has a new lead on intelligence."

"What does Canaris think?" Admiral Wilhelm Canaris was chief of the German military intelligence service, Abwehr, and Ribbentrop's rival.

"Canaris isn't working with von Waltz," Ribbentrop clarified. "I am."

Himmler finished his cookie, then brushed crumbs from his uniform. "Von Waltz said he picked up an agent from Rouen."

"Yes, a female," Ribbentrop said. "British. Unfortunately, the woman killed herself before we could extract any information."

"Pity," Himmler murmured.

"A *woman*." Von Rundstedt sneered, steepling his fingers. "What depths they've sunk to!"

"It will be Normandy," Hitler repeated

quietly, as though alone in the room. "They will invade at the beaches of Normandy, then head to Cherbourg. Then spread across all of France.

"I say our enemies will choose Normandy, if they haven't done so already. And I am never wrong."

"Mein Führer," said Ribbentrop, "I will go to Paris, to meet with Obersturmbannführer von Waltz personally — and let him know how crucial his work with the English spies is. It is through this back door channel that we will confirm the invasion site."

Hitler nodded. "Go," he agreed, adding, "and bring me back a tin of those Flavigny anise drops I like so much."

CHAPTER THREE

The swastika was everywhere. The Nazis had branded the beautiful face of Paris with it, from the Eiffel Tower to the Arc de Triomphe and every public building and church in between. Some of the black-and-red banners shouted in bold, barbaric Fraktur script: DEUTSCHLAND SIEGT AN ALLEN FRONTEN — GERMANY EVERYWHERE VICTORIOUS.

Maggie felt fear, a primal reaction to the changed Paris she could see from the slow-moving vélo-taxi. She managed to control her breathing but could do nothing about the blood pounding in her ears.

Paris was gray now, Maggie realized. The limestone buildings with their rusticated bases and tall windows were grimy, the glass windows of the cafés reflected pewter, and the faces of the few people on the streets were ashen and drawn, their eyes haunted, their step nervous. Their sleepwalking quality reminded her of the people she'd seen on a mission to Berlin.

The massive double doors of the apartment buildings, which were usually open, allowing those passing by a glimpse of courtyard and children running and playing, were locked and chained. Windows were either shuttered or daubed with blue paint for the enforced blackout, the people inside unable to tell day from night. Even the Seine was a blackish gray, like tarnished silver.

Maggie was also taken aback by Paris's emptiness. Most of the blocks they passed were deserted. They rode in near silence, with only the infrequent long black cars adorned by Nazi banners, a few intrepid bicyclists, the occasional vélo-taxi, and a rare horse-drawn carriage for company.

The people she did see were lined up in queues in front of shops where Pétain's portrait hung in the windows. All waited, silent, their arms folded, their eyes unfocused. Crude wooden posts with signs bearing German names in Gothic lettering had sprung up everywhere, a forest of thorny branches, indicating the direction of this or that office.

As they wended their way closer to the Place Vendôme, more people appeared on the streets, mostly women of all ages. But the customary blue uniforms of French soldiers were absent. The *Feldgrau* of the German Army had replaced them — as had black-uniformed SS officers. Well-fed off-duty Germans strolled along the avenues with cameras in hand, gawking in shop windows, whistling at the pretty girls.

Paris was irrefutably under complete German control: signage and posters warned the locals in German and French to obey Occupation edicts, rationing laws, and the rigorous curfews — or face punishment. POPULATIONS ABANDONÉES, FAIT CONFIDANCE AU SOLDAT ALLEMAND! ABANDONED PEOPLE, HAVE FAITH IN THE GERMAN SOLDIER!

Maggie gave a grim smile as she saw someone had scribbled underneath in bold lettering, AND THEN WHAT? There were also posters warning of Jews and Communists with ET DERRIÈRE LE JUIF, EXPOSITION LE JUIF ET LA FRANCE, and COMMUNISME ENNEMI DE LA FRANCE. They passed a seemingly endless series of red posters on the walls — photographs of people who'd been executed on the order of General Schaumburg, the Commander of Paris, for treason.

As the vélo-taxi passed a cinema, she saw black lettering on the marquee: LEINEN AUS

IRLAND. Maggie had read a review about *Linen from Ireland,* a "comic" anti-Semitic propaganda film directed by Heinz Helbig. In it, Jewish textile company owners try to sabotage the German linen industry by buying linen from Ireland instead of having it produced in "the Fatherland." A long line of pallid-faced Parisians waited at a makeshift soup kitchen in front of the theater.

It's like witnessing a death, Maggie realized. *The death of Paris, the death of France . . .* Then, seeing two laughing children play hide-and-seek in their mother's skirts — *but perhaps the patient isn't quite dead, not just yet.* The Occupation was a trauma; Paris was numb, paralyzed, in a state of shock. Marianne, the national symbol of the French Republic, an icon of freedom and democracy, was sleeping under a Nazi spell.

As the vélo-taxi inched closer to the Place Vendôme, there was finally some traffic — long black Mercedes and Citroën saloon cars, their swastika pennants snapping in the breeze; camouflaged Wehrmacht squad cars; motorcycles with sidecars driven by soldiers in helmets and goggles. The Germans owned the chestnut tree–lined streets now.

Without warning, the vélo-taxi veered to

the curb and stopped. "Sir?" Maggie called to the driver. "What's wrong?"

But he was already out the door and wrestling her trunk and suitcases to the damp pavement. *"Excusez-moi!"* He ignored her. She grabbed her handbag and stepped out of the vélo-taxi. He was breathing heavily.

"Sir, I think we have a misunderstanding — I need to go to the Ritz —"

The man's face was flushed. He'd taken out a stained handkerchief to wipe beads of sweat from his brow. "Mademoiselle, you may go to the Ritz — with my blessing." As he grimaced, his steel tooth glinted. "But I'm not going to take you."

To be left, alone, in Nazi-occupied Paris? "But, sir, that's what we agreed on —"

He held up one grimy palm. "I don't know what you're carrying in that trunk — rocks and concrete maybe — but I'm an old man. I'm not going to risk a heart attack driving you and your wardrobe around." He got back into the vélo and tipped his beret.

"But I'll pay you!"

"I value my life more. *Au revoir, mademoiselle!*" he called as he pedaled off, the wheels making dirty spray of a puddle.

Sidestepping a stinking pile of horse manure, Maggie walked to stand near her luggage. As she watched him leave, her heart sank. *Now what?*

She looked around, considering her options, glancing up at the blue enamel street plaques. She spotted a *téléphone publique* and felt a wave of relief. Then she realized the telephone had no receiver.

The weather was changing again, the clouds blowing past to reveal a mackerel sky. *Mackerel sky, mackerel sky — Never long wet and never long dry,* she thought, remembering the old nursery rhyme. *Ciel moutonné, or fleecy sky, as the French say.*

She'd been left in a neighborhood with a Baroque church on one side, and a *coiffeur* and shops — a bakery, a butcher, a pharmacy — along the other. But there were hardly any goods on display in the shop windows. The only things of which there seemed an abundance were portraits of Pétain. In the window of an abandoned cheese shop, a dusty framed photograph of the field marshal's face stared back at her blankly. Below, in front of empty wine bottles covered in grime, a marmalade cat slept, reminding her of her own ginger tabby, Mr. K, back in London. Maggie was suddenly struck by a wave of homesickness, wanting nothing more than to bury her face in K's fur and hear his rumbling purr. *No time for that now.*

Next to the shop were the closed and chained double doors of an apartment building. Maggie squinted to read the swastika-covered placard: HERE LIVED FIVE JEWS, WHO KILLED THEMSELVES. COURSE OF ACTION HIGHLY RECOMMENDED TO OTHERS. She felt ill.

"Le Matin! Le Matin!" cried a news vendor in the distance, while across the street she could hear the grind of metal coming from Coutellerie Dubois & Fils, a knife-sharpening business. She could make out the approaching march of hobnailed boots, growing ever louder, along with the strains of a German folk song:

Es zittern die morschen Knochen,
Der Welt vor dem großen Krieg.
Wir haben den Schrecken gebrochen,
Für uns war's ein großer Sieg.

She realized what it was they were singing so merrily —

The rotten bones are trembling,
Of the World because of the great War.
We have smashed this terror,
For us it was a great victory.

Good God, she thought in horror, instinctively taking a step back, farther into the shadows. Here she was, alone in occupied Paris, with the German Army marching by. It was almost — almost — funny, and she bit her lip to hold back a peal of hysterical laughter.

The parade was followed by a second line of what could only be off-duty German soldiers — broad-shouldered, loud, and stumbling. A young man, well over six feet tall with corn-yellow hair and blotchy red skin, holding a map, asked in passable French, "Pardon, mademoiselle, but could you please tell us the way to the Eiffel Tower?" His breath reeked of beer.

One of his companions, shorter and darker, with a camera looped around his neck, grinned as he lurched toward her. "We're lost . . ."

The rest of the group guffawed in a good-natured way, one turning to stagger into the street, to photograph the church's bright blue clock.

The German with the map was too close. Maggie struggled to suppress the abject terror she felt. "Of course," she managed, trying to recall the layout of Paris. "First you —"

Before she could explain where they were

and how to get to the tower, there was a loud *crack*, a guttural cry, and then a *thump*. The staggering soldier had been struck by a thin, gray-haired man on a bicycle. As the cyclist realized what had happened and pedaled madly to escape, the German fell to the pavement, unconscious, his head bleeding.

Maggie ran to the fallen man; blood streamed down his forehead. She yanked off her gloves and balled them up to press on the wound. The white gloves were quickly stained red.

Like a wolf pack, the Germans ran after the man on the bicycle. Maggie looked up from the injured man's bloody face to watch in horror. The one with the map whipped a Luger from his inside jacket pocket and shot the terrified man in the back as he pedaled away. Both Frenchman and cycle dropped to the cobblestone street.

As the Germans returned to their fallen comrade, a Grosser Mercedes with swastika flags mounted on its front bumpers rounded the corner and stopped short. The driver, a sharp-featured man with a black eye patch, hopped out. He scurried around the car to open the passenger door.

A German officer emerged. He was not tall but was powerfully built, like a wrestler.

Maggie could tell from the gold bullion embroidered oak leaf on his peaked cap that he was a Generaloberst, one of the highest-ranking officers in the German Army. "What happened?" he barked without preamble, hands clasped behind his back, posture impeccable.

"That one" — the tall blond soldier pointed to the crumpled body of the Frenchman lying on the street — "hit our friend with his bicycle. We took care of it, sir."

The Generaloberst looked down at the hurt German photographer and grimaced, shaking his head. He then looked at Maggie, cradling the man's head in her lap. "How is he?"

Before she could answer, the injured man took a noisy breath and opened his eyes. "Why, hallo, beautiful Fräulein," he managed with an unfocused smile up at Maggie, who was still pressing her gloves to his wound.

The General snapped his fingers, pointed, and the soldiers dragged the Frenchman's body away into an alley. Another kept the bicycle. The hurt German struggled to sit up.

"He seems to be all right," she told the Generaloberst, doing her best not to look at the pool of the murdered Frenchman's blood staining the street not far away. "I'd recommend a doctor examine him, though — he could have a concussion."

The man wobbled to his feet.

"*You* — go see a doctor as the mademoiselle suggested. I'll speak with you about your conduct later," the Generaloberst rebuked.

The injured man hung his head.

Then the German officer extended his hand; Maggie grasped his fingers, rising. The Generaloberst took her in, from her chic Chanel hat to the balled-up, bloody gloves she held, then clicked his heels together and bowed. "May I see your papers, mademoiselle?"

"Of course." Maggie couldn't quite conceal the tremor in her voice.

She opened her purse, which she'd carefully prepared for such an occasion. Inside were Métro tickets, a silver compact, a deck of worn French playing cards, and a clipping from the Occupationist newspaper, *Je Suis Partout,* about Elsa Schiaparelli's new collection. There was also a large wad of francs in a wallet; if asked, she would say she was obliged to carry the sum for hotel bills.

"Here you go, sir," she said, handing over

her passport. It had been carefully and deliberately frayed, as though handled at dozens of security points, to correspond with her cover story.

He accepted it, eyebrows rising. "Irish," he said with some surprise, then handed it back to her. "Last weekend, I saw the film *Leinen aus Irland.* Excellent film. About the Germans and Irish working together."

"Yes," Maggie managed, voice stronger, dropping the passport back in her bag, along with the ruined gloves. "I read a review."

"Ireland is neutral in this war. We Germans like neutrals — 'The enemy of my enemy is my friend,' as they say."

Yes, I've heard that before.

The Generaloberst clicked his heels together. "You must allow me to replace your gloves. It was good of you to help a young German boy, so far away from home." He bowed again.

The German soldiers nodded in unison, staring at her with a mixture of admiration and longing. If they weren't so terrifying — and if a man hadn't just been murdered — it would have been almost comical.

"I would have helped anyone who was hurt," Maggie replied.

The Generaloberst gestured to the trunk

and cases. "Are these yours, mademoiselle?"

"Yes, my vélo-taxi driver became . . . winded."

"He was obviously not German, then," one of the soldiers said loudly. "A *German* would never have let a beautiful woman down!"

The Generaloberst made a dismissive gesture, and the soldiers hastily dispersed, two of them helping their injured comrade. "And where were you headed, mademoiselle — before all of this happened?"

"The Hôtel Ritz," she managed, folding her hands to stop their trembling. She noted there was blood on them, in half-moons under her fingernails. She battled a wave of nausea.

He inclined his head. "Permit me to escort you. To thank you for your service to the Reich." He snapped his fingers, and the waiting driver opened the car's trunk and began placing her luggage inside. "To the Hôtel Ritz."

"Yes, sir!"

Maggie realized the Generaloberst's *permit me* was merely a nicety. She had no choice in the matter. "Thank you," she said as he bowed again and then opened the door for her. She did her best to hide her trembling, blood-flecked palms. *A man is dead,* she thought. *And yet no one even notices. Or thinks it's important.* The driver started the engine, then pulled the Benz out into the street, splashing through puddles.

As they drove, Maggie distracted herself by studying the Generaloberst's face. He was somewhere in his late thirties, she guessed. Green eyes that sometimes looked blue. Brown hair. Tanned, with the beginnings of fine lines and a few sun spots on the bridge of his nose. Maggie guessed from his complexion that he'd served somewhere in the Middle East or Mediterranean before being transferred to Paris. He caught her gaze, and she looked away, out the window at the empty shops.

"Are you checking in to the Ritz?"

Maggie lifted her chin. "Yes."

"And how long will you be staying?"

"I — I'm not sure."

"Well, mademoiselle," he said, smiling for the first time. "Now I know where to find you."

Reiner left the Charcots' house not long after Maggie did. He knew only to go to Café Le Jardin, where someone would meet him to lead him to the head of his network.

At the café, Reiner took his ersatz coffee to one of the wobbly round tables near the window. He picked up an abandoned copy of *Le Petit Journal,* mouthpiece of Colonel de La Rocque's Parti Social Français, advocates of "Franco-German Peace and Balance," and opened it to a random page, pretending to read.

In his peripheral vision, he watched as a woman in heavy orthopedic shoes shuffled by. At the bar, she ordered what passed for Cinzano and carried her glass to a table near his. She was short and round, wearing a much-mended dress with what looked to be a new collar, her wispy silver hair pulled back with a lucite clip. Her face was the picture of annoyance.

Reiner put down the newspaper and strolled over. "Excuse me, madame. Did you call for assistance with your ceiling?"

She drained her drink. "You're the handyman?" She gave him a stare worthy of Medusa. "Monsieur Corbin Martin?"

It was the agreed-upon name. "Yes, madame."

She pursed her lips. "Very well, then," she said, rising. "Follow me."

Reiner offered his arm to the woman, but she refused it. "When you fix the ceiling," she said as they left the café, "I don't want you making a mess of things. Everything — sofas, tables, rugs — exactly the way it was.

If not, I'll take it out of your pay."

Even though he was terrified of being caught by the Gestapo, Reiner couldn't help but be amused by how she relished her role. Perhaps she'd once been an actress. "Yes, madame."

They walked together in silence until she led him down a narrow side street. "Number twelve," she whispered. He looked up to see where they were — already Number 10. "Third floor, right. *Merde,*" she wished him and kept walking.

Reiner opened the door, walked up the grubby stairwell, and knocked at the door. There was the sound of footsteps and then "Who is it?"

"Jules." It was another code name.

The man who opened the door was broad and squat. He, too, wore the dark denim boiler suit that was the uniform of the Parisian sanitation department. His skin was leathery, and his hair sprang from his shiny scalp in black bristles. "Well, what's wrong with you? Get inside!"

The flat was small, dimly lit, and reeked of fish. "Come, have some potatoes and herring," the man told Reiner. "You can call me Voltaire — it suits me, doesn't it?" His smile never reached his eyes.

"First I want to give you these." Reiner

put down his satchel and searched through it until he found what he was looking for: three radio crystals.

Voltaire took them, his stubby fingers surprisingly adroit. "Thank you," he said. "We've been waiting for these." He put them away carefully in a safe hidden behind a calendar, then went to the kitchen. Reiner followed. On the ancient stove, a cast-iron frying pan sizzled over the blue flames.

"Come, some food, some wine — and then we'll get you to work. Our shift starts tonight." Voltaire poked at what was in the pan with a wooden spoon. "Hope you're not squeamish. The garbage — not always exactly pleasant. But one man's trash is another man's treasure, no?"

Reiner sat at the scarred wooden table. "What's today's route?"

Voltaire set two plates down with a thump; the fish still had their heads. The Frenchman smiled, and this time it reached his eyes. "Avenue Foch."

The conference room was plain, with striped wallpaper and tufted leather furniture. A few of the Prime Minister's own paintings of the gardens of Chartwell, his family home in Kent, graced the walls. A whirring walnut moon-phase grandfather clock with a golden swinging pendulum, chained and weighted, tick-tocked loudly in the stillness.

The P.M., General Ismay, and David had assembled to welcome the newest member of their shadow organization. "He must report directly to you, Pug," Churchill was saying to Ismay as he made himself a weak scotch and soda at the bar cart. Outside the open windows, the bells of Big Ben and the Horse Guards Parade rang out, chiming the hour. The sky was cloudy, and a damp breeze fluttered the muslin curtains. "There are things happening in this war I don't need to know the specifics of, do you understand?"

Ismay, already seated at the mahogany table, nodded. "I do, sir."

As the Prime Minister brought his drink back to the table, David smoothly slipped a coaster under it seconds before the P.M. thumped it down on the glossy mahogany.

Churchill, in a chalk-stripe suit, settled his bulk into the carved chair, the only one with arms, then rubbed his palms together. "Now, who is this man we've chosen for the head of our clandestine forces?"

"As Colonel Laycock brought up at the last meeting, Colonel Henrik Rafaelsen Martens recently returned from undercover work in Norway," Ismay began. "Martens is

Welsh — born in Llandaff, Cardiff, to Norwegian parents. Educated at the Cathedral School, then Repton School in Derbyshire. Afterward, he went to Nova Scotia and hiked through Newfoundland with the Public Schools Exploring Society, then joined the Shell Petroleum Company, transferring to Dar es Salaam, Tanganyika. In 'thirty-nine, he joined the Royal Air Force."

"Ah, one of 'the few,' " the P.M. said approvingly.

Ismay nodded. "Yes, Martens defended our island nobly in the summer of 'forty. He then joined SOE, working with the Norwegian section under Captain Martin Linge, leading commando raids in Norway. Another injury sent him back to London a few months ago. I've spoken with him at length. He understands what's at stake."

"What else?"

"Of course we've thoroughly investigated his personal background. No ties to Communist or Fascist organizations, no issues with drinking or drug use, no known solicitation of prostitutes. Unmarried, with one broken engagement — but no known associations with homosexuals and the like."

Churchill flicked a glance at David, who reddened but didn't drop his gaze.

Ismay continued, unaware. "He's also a

lapsed Lutheran, with interests in nature photography and mountain climbing. And this injury . . ."

There was a knock at the door. "Well, come in then!" the P.M. bellowed.

"Excuse me, Mr. Churchill." A woman with hair pulled back in a steel-gray chignon opened the door. "Colonel Martens is here," she announced.

"Well, send him in then, Mrs. Tinsley! Don't keep the man waiting!" The P.M. pulled a cigar from the breast pocket of his suit and began to gnaw on it.

The man who entered was tall, with streaked blond hair, gray eyes, and a Viking's profile. "It's an honor to meet you, Prime Minister —"

"Yes, yes, yes — we don't have time for all that." The P.M. lit his cigar and puffed on it vigorously, setting the tip aglow. Smoke framed his round pink face. "Sit down, young man! Now, let me tell you what we're asking you to do."

"Yes, sir." Martens folded his long frame into one of the leather chairs facing the P.M.

"Master of Deception!" Churchill growled. "Wazir of Ruses! Wizard of Trickery! Marquis of Misinformation!" He removed his gold-framed glasses, glowering at Martens. "You are to be the point person in charge of all of the deception plans that will accompany the European invasion. For the truth is so precious she must be accompanied by a bodyguard of lies. You see that, don't you?

"You're not limited to strategic deception but will also mislead, misinform, and mystify the Nazis using every ungentlemanly trick in the book." Churchill pronounced the enemy's name in his idiosyncratic way, *Nazzi.* "As Sun Tzu said, 'Hence, when able to attack, we must seem unable. When using our forces, we must seem inactive. When we are near, we must make the enemy believe we are far away. When far away, we must make him believe we are near.' "

If Martens was surprised or shocked in any way, he hid it well. "Yes, sir."

"You will report only to General Ismay" — the two men nodded to each other — "and have an office in the War Rooms. Mr. Greene has prepared files for you, to get you up to speed." Martens looked to David, who inclined his head.

"You are to be the coordinator for all of the agencies — MI-Six, MI-Five, SOE, et cetera — that deal in deception. The only way our ultimate plan will work is if, and only if, we're all following the same playbook. And some of our agencies, well —

they don't play well with the others. MI-Six and SOE in particular don't get along."

David passed over a polished steel briefcase, complete with a set of handcuffs attached to the grip. "You will have safes in both your office and your flat," the private secretary told the Welshman. "Any information pertaining to the invasion or any secret work will be kept either in the safes or in the briefcase chained to your wrist."

"Do you have any questions?" Ismay asked.

"Only one," replied Martens, reaching for the briefcase. "When may I start?"

"Now!" the P.M. thundered, rising to shake Martens's hand. "Mr. Greene, please show our Norse god to his new office downstairs."

As the men took their leave, Churchill called rapturously after them, "Welcome to the Great Game, Colonel Martens!"

CHAPTER FOUR

Like France itself, the Hôtel Ritz Paris was divided.

It had always been made up of two edifices. The one that faced the Place Vendôme was originally the residence of the Duc de Lauzun, commander of the French troops at Yorktown during the American Revolutionary War. The other half was a building that happened to abut it on Rue Cambon. Lined with display cases, the long corridor that linked the two buildings was known as Temptation Walk.

But while César Ritz had founded the hotel in 1898 as a place where aristocrats and the wealthy could mingle, there was now segregation. The elegant front entrance, at 15 Place Vendôme, was for Germans and those from neutral countries only, while the less fashionable back entry, on the narrow, shady Rue Cambon, was for the French.

Because Maggie was posing as Irish, and

Ireland was a neutral country — even seen as friendly toward Nazi Germany — she was allowed to use the Place Vendôme entrance. And so the Generaloberst directed his driver accordingly.

Place Vendôme was less of a square than an octagon, with canted corners, severe Neoclassical pediments, and pitched mansard roofs — in the shape of Coco Chanel's iconic perfume bottle, Maggie realized. The Place was lined with shops such as Boucheron, Van Cleef & Arpels, Buccellati, and Chaumet, all seeming to be doing a brisk business with Nazi officers coming in and out as doormen bowed low.

At the center of the Place Vendôme rose a tall column, forged from melted cannons seized at the Battle of Austerlitz, topped with a bronze statue of Napoleon Bonaparte. As they circled, Maggie looked up at the emperor, imagining how pained he would be seeing this view, his square conquered, his people subjugated.

The Ritz itself was now the headquarters of the Luftwaffe. And as such, it looked less grand hotel than sandbagged fortress. Blood-red swastika banners flapped above the cream silk awnings and huge carriage-style lamps. Armed guards flanked the entrance in front of the curving topiaries.

Long, shiny black cars with flags, convoy trucks, and motorcycles with sidecars queued at the doors. As the Generaloberst's car pulled up, Maggie could hear officers shouting lusty *Heil Hitler*s to each other. She tried to assuage her fear by picturing Barbara Hutton Mdivani attempting to enter the Ritz in tennis shorts and being turned away, but couldn't quite manage it.

"Since I know where you're staying," the Generaloberst said as his driver opened the door, "may I call on you — when I arrive with your new gloves?"

Maggie accepted the driver's proffered hand. "I plan on going to the Café de la Paix often," she replied with a forced smile, as she stepped out of the car. She turned back to face the Generaloberst, hearing the approaching sound of marching jackboots in the square. She didn't want his gloves or anything else he could give her, and there was no way she ever wanted to see him again. But she couldn't say that.

"Perhaps we'll meet there." *Note — stay far, far away from the Café de la Paix.*

"I really do thank you — from the bottom of my heart," he said.

Do you have one? Maggie thought but didn't say, maintaining her glassy smile instead.

"So this is not *au revoir,* but *à bientôt,* mademoiselle."

A thousand times no. "Merci . . ." Maggie realized she didn't know his name.

"Generaloberst Ruesdorf. Christian Ruesdorf. At your service."

As a bellhop swooped to take her trunk, suitcase, and hatboxes, Maggie attempted to hold on to her smile. She gave a small wave before a barrel-chested doorman in a long coat with brass buttons doffed his hat and whisked her through the revolving door.

His low voice rumbled, "Welcome to the Hôtel Ritz, mademoiselle."

Inside was a different world — a hothouse of gilded mirrors, marble, and damask, the air perfumed by lush arrangements of orchids and roses, the ripples of a harp's arpeggios wafting through murmured conversations in both French and German. Maggie's first impression wasn't of a hotel but of a stately manor house, albeit one with its numerous Swiss clocks set precisely to Berlin time. Well-groomed men sat on Martin chairs reading freshly ironed newspapers.

But this was no fairy-tale palace — the lobby was also swarming with Nazis in gray-green uniforms. Maggie took a deep breath, raised her chin, and threw back her shoulders.

As she walked the long, carpeted hallway, past walls of silk moiré, Chinese pendant lanterns, and hopelessly banal artwork, she observed a slim, middle-aged man in a well-tailored suit. Topped by a dark widow's peak, his face was worn and haggard, but his jaw was noble. He stood listening respectfully to a high-ranking German, short and balding, his chest decorated with medals, the Iron Cross at his throat. "I wish to thank you for arranging last night's impromptu dinner party, Monsieur Auzello," the officer was saying. "It was superb, as always." He thrust out his right hand.

"You're very welcome, sir." Maggie watched as the Frenchman ignored the offered hand, then bowed gracefully, turned, and walked away — leaving the Nazi standing there with an outstretched palm and open mouth.

Resistance is alive, even at the Ritz, she thought, and instantly felt heartened.

Another French gentleman, this one with a lush mustache and fading hairline, passed Auzello and murmured, "Germans will come and go, my friend — but fly-fishing is forever," in Swiss-accented French. Maggie could only assume he was César Ritz, the legendary hotelier.

At the reception desk, a dapper, fussy, tortoiseshell-bespectacled gentleman looked up to greet her. "Ah, yes, mademoiselle!" he exclaimed, his eyes enormous behind thick glass, when Maggie said she had a reservation and showed her passport. "We've been expecting you."

He entered her information into the ledger with a fountain pen in script, adding, "As I mentioned on the telephone, our suites have been commandeered for high-ranking German officials. And so I'm afraid your room is on the top floor, under the mansard. It was originally intended to accommodate the traveling companions of the wealthy." As an aside, he whispered, "The German officers find the ceilings too low."

Maggie smiled as she signed her false name. "I'm sure it's charming."

"And, should you need it, our bomb shelter is renowned for its fur rugs and Hermès sleeping bags. France may have fallen, but not the Ritz! We —"

"The Rue Cambon entrance didn't have anything for me, André," a woman's voice interrupted. The newcomer was enveloped in a cloud of jasmine and cigarette smoke. "But I'm expecting an envelope with ballet tickets. Would you be a darling and check for me?"

She waggled bony shoulders in exasperation, glancing at Maggie. "Sometimes things for the Rue Cambon side are left here and vice versa — one really must be careful of that."

The woman was petite, slender, and somewhere in her fifties, Maggie guessed, although her gamine appearance defied age. Her skin was deeply tanned, her hair dyed black, and her cheeks rouged. She wore a simple black suit, but ropes of pearl and gold necklaces and bracelets rattled as she moved. She regarded Maggie with a basilisk gaze. "Nice dress," she said finally.

Maggie suddenly realized who the woman was. "Th-thank you, mademoiselle," she managed, glad she had chosen to wear the Chanel.

Gabrielle Bonheur Chanel, known by her nickname Coco, was one of the most famous couturieres and perfumers in the world. She was renowned for taking women out of heavy, frilly hats and fussy corsets, and dressing them instead in boyish toppers and creations of tailored, streamlined jersey. She'd also designed costumes for stage and film, alongside Jean Cocteau, Sergei Diaghilev, and Pablo Picasso, in addition to creating the world's most famous perfume, Chanel No. 5, named for her lucky number.

101

"They've put you up on the top floor, I suspect?" Chanel asked, her gold chain bracelets jangling as the receptionist looked through cubbyholes for any stray envelopes for her. Maggie nodded. "That's where I am now as well. I used to have a suite, overlooking the Place Vendôme. However, as you may have noticed," the couturiere continued, her voice hard, "times have changed."

"As always, you're correct, mademoiselle," André said, handing her an envelope with her name written in beautiful calligraphy.

Chanel took it and opened it, pulling out two tickets. "Excellent," she said. Then, as she unfolded the accompanying note, her crimson-painted lips pursed.

"Everything all right, mademoiselle?" asked André.

"Fine, fine." She waved a hand, brushing off his concern. "André here is the best in the business," she told Maggie. "Whatever you need he'll procure — an abortionist, a drug dealer, even an assassin. Anything goes at the Ritz." Maggie looked shocked, which seemed to please the designer. "And what brings you to Paris?" Chanel continued, tucking everything into her quilted lambskin handbag.

Maggie fixed a smile on her face. "I'm

pleased to say I'm in town for fashion, ma-demoiselle. My trousseau, to be specific. And a wedding dress."

"Aha! And whose ateliers will you be visiting?"

"Nina Ricci," Maggie answered, glad she had memorized the designers who still had shops open. "Jacques Fath, Germaine Lecomte, Jean Patou, Lanvin . . . and, of course, Schiaparelli —"

Chanel rolled her black eyes. *"L'Italienne."* Maggie could tell it wasn't a compliment. "Don't go to that one. Besides, she's left Paris for New York, the traitor."

"But I'm going to them only because *your* atelier is not open, Mademoiselle Chanel." Maggie had done her homework. Coco Chanel had closed hers in 1940, when the Occupation began, proclaiming it was "no time for fashion." However, she'd kept her boutique open and had made a wartime fortune selling No. 5 to eager Germans wanting a fragrant souvenir of their Paris sojourn to take home to their wives and sweethearts.

"You speak French well. But you're not French or else you would be using the Rue Cambon entrance." She grazed Maggie's cheek with an immaculately manicured, scarlet-painted fingertip. "And not German, either. Swiss?"

"Irish."

One tweezed eyebrow rose. *Irish?*

Maggie nodded. "Born there. But raised in America for most of my life, shuttling between the two countries. I'm living in Lisbon at present."

"Lisbon, yes — I'm thinking of opening a shop there. Madrid, too. Perfume only, of course — at least for now. Yes, Irish," she said, appraising Maggie, like a jeweler inspecting a diamond under a loupe. "I should have guessed with that red hair . . ."

"Your room is ready, mademoiselle," the receptionist said to Maggie, gesturing to a groom in buttoned uniform, white gloves, and cap, waiting with her key.

Maggie smiled. "Thank you."

"I'll walk with you," announced Chanel.

As the two women made their way through the lobby, a cluster of soldiers pushed a brass trolley loaded with large boxes. "So many Germans!" Maggie tried to make small talk. "They do seem busy."

Chanel glanced up with a gimlet eye. "They're colonizing."

"Colonizing?"

"What we did to Algeria, they're now doing to us. And plundering, too. Art, mostly. Perfume, too. And wine, clothes, foie gras, truffles . . . Anything and everything. Hitler's personal art broker, Karl Haberstock, has made the Ritz his home in Paris." She gestured, bracelets clinking. "That particular crew works for Goering."

"Reichsmarshal Hermann Goering?" Maggie repressed a shudder. She had met Goering in Berlin, in a different disguise.

"Of course — Herr Goering's the head of the Luftwaffe. He took over the Imperial Suite and is sending an endless parade of French art back to Carinhall." Chanel leaned in. "He takes our country — now he takes our paintings . . ." She tossed her head, shaking golden earrings with interlocking *C*'s. Maggie was suddenly aware of how much the linking *C*'s resembled the intersecting *S*'s of the swastika.

"And your suite as well," Maggie managed.

They approached the elevator, its doors frosted glass encased in a cylinder of limed oak, and stepped in. As the groom pushed the buttons, the lift groaned, then began to rise.

"Still, the hotel must be making a tidy profit from the" — Maggie wasn't sure how to phrase it — "new guests?"

Chanel tucked a stray lock of jet-black hair behind her ear. "They're lodgers 'on the

German plan.' " Maggie shook her head, not understanding. Chanel explained: "They're 'guests of the Führer.' And so they don't pay for their rooms. Or their Champagne."

"Ah." As they ascended, Maggie was aware Chanel was once again appraising both her body and the drape of her garment. Since the dress wasn't hers to begin with, the fit was slightly off — snug across the bust, loose in the hips. Only what a practiced eye would see. Maggie felt uncomfortable under the scrutiny, as though spiders were crawling over her. *It's from the 'thirty-eight collection,* she thought, trying to remain calm. *Anyone's body might change a bit in three years.*

When the elevator jolted to a stop on their floor, Chanel purred, "I do hope you enjoy your stay. Unlike some Parisians, I'm quite fond of neutrals." And then she was gone.

Maggie exhaled in relief, then followed the groom the opposite way down the carpeted hallway. He turned a ceramic knob, opening the door. "Welcome to the Ritz, mademoiselle," he intoned, bowing, then handing her the iron key. "Do you need help unpacking? I can send one of the maids up to assist."

"No." Maggie wanted nothing more than

to close the door and find solitude. But she forced herself to smile. "No, thank you." She reached into her purse and pulled out a few coins, which she pressed into his gloved palm.

He bowed low. "Thank you, mademoiselle. We hope you enjoy your stay."

She closed the door, locked it, took a breath of potpourri-scented air, then looked around.

As André had warned, the room was tiny, with a low, slanted ceiling, a small fireplace, and dormer windows. It was furnished simply, with a brass bed covered by a silk duvet and knife-edge pillows, a diminutive walnut desk and chair, and a cloisonné armoire. There was a vase of red roses on the bedside table and a few prints of exotic birds dotted the walls, as well as a gilt-framed reproduction of Gilbert's *La Belle au bois dormant.* Above the mantel, a Swiss carriage clock ticked, cutting through the luxurious silence.

Maggie dropped her handbag on the bed, slipped off her shoes, and unpinned and took off her hat. Outside, a sun shower was beginning. The drops thrummed against the windowpanes, though the sky above was blue.

She let out a long, shuddering sigh, finally

able to unclench — at least a bit — and to process what she had seen and experienced since leaving the Charcots' house.

The murder.

She went into the bathroom and ran both the sink's taps, scrubbing flecks of blood off her hands with a fresh cake of hyacinth-scented soap.

Then she went back to her handbag and took out the bloody gloves, and brought them back to the bathroom. She put in the sink stop, ran cold water, and dropped them in to soak, the water turning a rusty red. *The German's blood,* she thought. *But he, at least, will be fine — while the Frenchman on the bicycle is dead. Does his family know yet? What lies will they be told?*

She considered her reflection in the beveled mirror, seeing the remnants of the panic and horror she'd concealed at the time of the murder. She released her hair from its pins and clips. *What am I even doing here?* she thought, wiping at her ashen face with a damp washcloth, inspecting it for any traces of blood.

Her decision to come to Paris had been so fast — rash, even — and then, after flying in, she'd been so focused on her mission, on getting her identity papers, then finding Erica Calvert and Elise, that she'd never questioned anything. But now, finally, at her destination in her new persona, she was furious with herself. *Why did I ever think I could find not one but* two *missing women in an occupied city?* She refused to entertain the possibility that both Erica and Elise might be dead. *And why did I think I could make it out alive myself?*

Still, she was here for a mission, and that was what she would do. The first order of business was to settle in. She unpacked, starting with her toiletries case: Cadum tooth powder and toothbrush, Occupation-regulated shampoo, French-brand sanitary towels. An almost empty bottle of Joy perfume, memories wafting from it.

As she hung up her clothes, she heard a church bell strike the false Berlin time. She went to the window and opened it. The rain had stopped; the sun was shining unimpeded. Looking down at the Rue Cambon, she could see a line of men in suits and hats on the wet cobblestone pavement, still holding up black umbrellas. Hastily, she stepped back from the window frame and checked to see if she was visible from any sight lines, if anyone was looking.

When she realized what she was doing instinctively, she felt an almost overwhelming loneliness. She was an agent now. A *spy.* She hadn't talked to anyone for weeks besides Jacques, the Charcots, and then a few words with the agent who'd just arrived. The last time she'd seen her Aunt Edith was in Washington, D.C., and only for a scant day, fraught with frustrations and misunderstandings. Her father was dead, and her mother most likely was, too. It had been weeks since she'd been with her friends, the people who were her true family — David, Freddie, and Chuck. And even though her fellow agents Sarah and Hugh were also in Paris, it would be far too dangerous to make any contact with them.

As for her romantic life . . . John was courting divorcées in Los Angeles, Hugh was in love with Sarah, and she'd had only the occasional letter from the American soldier Tom O'Brian at Fort Bragg. And as for Detective Chief Inspector James Durgin . . . Well, they hadn't even had a proper date, only a brief connection while catching a Jack-the-Ripper-inspired killer. What kind of relationship did that portend? Not to mention he was older, divorced, a recovering alcoholic. . . .

Maggie was twenty-seven now, a veritable old maid. *So what's wrong with me?* She'd panicked when John had asked her to marry

110

him nearly two years before. She'd run to Hugh when she thought John had died — only to leave him. And then, when she and John had had another chance in Washington, she'd panicked again. Tom — well, that was easy — he was leaving. And then with Durgin . . . Well, nothing had really happened; there had been no time after the case closed and she'd left for France. Jacques was safe — off-limits — besides, she'd probably never even see him again.

Basically, I have no problem parachuting out of a plane or fighting Nazis, but I can't seem to fall — no, stay — in love.

Her Aunt Edith had raised her to be strong, self-sufficient, and independent. And she was. Except whenever she was with a man, part of her was always terrified. She couldn't be weak, couldn't be vulnerable, couldn't be out of control. She loved mathematics partly for its cold beauty, its lack of emotion. In math, either you were right, or you were wrong. Math couldn't hurt you, abandon you, leave you, damage you.

Freud would have a field day. Wasn't that what had led her to sabotage things with John in America? If she were honest with herself, she had to admit she didn't really think he was with a divorcée. Picking a fight with him had been easier than maybe moving to Los Angeles, getting engaged, starting a new life. Because what if she needed him? Would he run away and leave her, like her father did?

Her heart hurt, literally hurt, and she pressed her hands to her chest, as though to postpone its breaking. *I need to forgive my father for not being the man I needed him to be.* She put her arms around herself. *Maybe someday.*

No wonder finding her sister — her half sister — felt so important. She tried to picture Elise Hess, whom she'd met on her mission to Berlin over a year ago, and failed miserably, evoking only blond hair and the ghost of a sweet smile. *I don't even remember what she looks like. How am I going to find her?*

She ran the taps in the claw-foot tub and began to undress. *Pull it together, Hope.* All she wanted to do was get into a bath and wash away the horror of the day.

She threw in a generous handful of bath salts, then slipped under the surface of the hot water — courtesy of the Nazis, she realized; no one else in Paris had hot water. For a moment, she was able to lean back, relax the muscles in her neck and shoulders, and clear her mind.

But not for long. As she breathed in the fragrant air, she was startled by a knock.

"Who is it?" she called, heart racing. She stepped out of the tub and grabbed a peach-colored towel. Had she been found out? What could have given her away?

"It's Coco," came the hard-edged voice.

Maggie found a bathrobe and cracked open the door, flustered and dripping. Chanel didn't seem to notice. "Do you enjoy the ballet?" the couturiere asked without preamble.

"Er . . . yes?"

"I seem to have an extra ticket for tonight. The Paris Opéra Ballet," Chanel explained, as if Maggie were a slow child, "at the Palais Garnier. Would you like to join me?"

"Why . . . of course, thank you so much, mademoiselle."

Elise's father, Miles Hess, was a renowned conductor, who had undoubtedly played at the Palais Garnier. Maybe someone there, the evening's conductor, might know him, might know the address of the Hess family's flat in Paris. Going to the ballet could possibly bring her one step closer to finding her sister.

"The curtain's at eight, so I'll meet you downstairs at the Rue Cambon entrance at seven-thirty. My driver will take us."

"Of — of course," Maggie managed, fingers plucking at the neck of her robe. "But what about the curfew?" The Nazis had imposed a 9:00 P.M. curfew on Parisians.

"I have special papers that allow my companions and me to be out late."

Really, Maggie thought. *And how exactly did you get those?* But she said only "Thank you so much, Mademoiselle Chanel. This is so kind —"

"Call me Coco." The couturiere turned to leave, then swiveled back, as if on a runway. "By the way, you have the advantage — you know my name, but I don't know yours."

"Paige," Maggie answered with assurance. She'd practiced saying her new name over and over again, until it felt natural. "Paige Kelly."

Coco Chanel went back to her rooms down the hall, which always smelled faintly of No. 5, a modern mix of ylang-ylang, neroli, and rose, which the maids sprayed each day. She'd had to move most of her furnishings — her blackamoors, Jacques Lipchitz sculptures, and the silk divan she'd reclined on for Horst — to the rooms above her atelier when she'd moved from her grand Ritz suite to smaller rooms after the Occupation. But she would not part with her Coromandel screens, large burnished panels painted with flowers and exotic birds. They were precious reminders of her tragic love affair with "Boy" Capel.

Chanel stripped off her impeccable suit, revealing a girlish figure. She slipped into a rich paisley robe with satin lapels that flowed to her ankles, one of Boy's she refused to part with. She went to the second bedroom, which served as her closet, and examined dress after dress on padded silk hangers, looking for something to wear for the evening's performance. As she fingered the black sequins of a slim gown, she had a sudden thought and went back to her sitting room. There she perched on one of the gilt chairs and placed a phone call to her atelier.

"Yes, I need you to go to the files," she told the shopgirl on the other end of the line. "I want to know about a dress, the blue floral in the spring 'thirty-eight collection. Is there any mention of a Paige Kelly?"

During the pause that followed, Chanel examined her pointed, red-varnished nails, then opened the drawer of her dressing table, searching for something amid the stationery, envelopes, and fountain pens.

After a few minutes, the girl on the other

115

end of the line returned. "Yes, mademoiselle. You sold a number of pieces of that collection, including a blue floral dress, to a Paige Claire Kelly."

Chanel pressed her lips together as she removed a gold-tooled leather box. Inside was a syringe. "Did I make any notes?" she asked, taking out the syringe. She again went through the drawer until she found what she was looking for: an ampoule of clear liquid.

"We have Mademoiselle Kelly's height as five foot seven and recorded her measurements as thirty-three, twenty-four, thirty-six."

"All right, then," the couturiere said with a resigned sigh as she filled the syringe. "Close enough."

"Oh, mademoiselle, there is one more thing —"

Chanel, making sure there were no air bubbles in the needle, squirted a few drops of morphine-based Sedol into the air. "Yes?"

"You wrote in the margins that Mademoiselle Kelly was a blonde. A natural blonde . . . Mademoiselle?"

"That is all." Chanel hung up the receiver. *"Blonde,"* she muttered, eyes narrowing.

As the couturiere pricked the needle into her upper thigh, she murmured, "This little puzzle could make the evening much, much more fun than I anticipated."

CHAPTER FIVE

As were the other important buildings in Paris, the Palais Garnier — the grand opera house, home to the Paris Opéra Ballet — was shrouded in Nazi flags. Their presence negated the beauty of the arched windows, the double columns, the gilded adornments, and the graceful statuary, as did the sign on the front doors: INTERDIT AUX JUIF. A group of young German soldiers had clustered together on the front steps, singing:

Deutschland erwache aus deinem bösen
    Traum!
Gib fremden Juden in deinem Reich nicht
    Raum!
Wir wollen kämpfen für dein Auferstehn
Arisches Blut soll nicht untergehn!

"Mackerel sky, mackerel sky — Never long wet and never long dry," Sarah Sanderson muttered to herself as she walked quickly past the assembled Germans. She moved gracefully in her raincoat and jewel-toned Hermès scarf, despite the heavy dance bag she toted over one shoulder. But Sarah knew enough German to be able to understand the song's menacing lyrics:

Germany, awake from your nightmare!
Give foreign Jews no place in your Reich!
We will fight for your resurgence!
Aryan blood shall never perish!

She turned her head to avoid the sight of the assembled Germans. Two wizened women in black were walking arm in arm, followed by several giggling schoolchildren, and a mother pushing a pink and chubby-cheeked baby in a pram. She caught the baby's eyes and smiled; the infant rewarded her with a gurgle and a waved fist.

Sarah, a slim brunette from Liverpool, had performed with the Vic-Wells Ballet in London. But now, as an SOE agent, she was posing as a dancer with the Paris Opéra. She'd already taken daily class with the company that morning and had put in an afternoon's worth of rehearsals. Her long legs felt close to collapse, but there was still one more rehearsal onstage before the performance that evening. And then, after the ballet, was her actual SOE mission.

As she passed the singers, she saw a lanky French policeman in his gendarme uniform and cape walk by without saluting. A German sergeant, a dumpy man, with a florid, spongy face, wasn't about to let the perceived slight go unpunished. "You!" he roared.

The policeman stopped, spun around, and saluted smartly. "My apologies, sir — I didn't see you."

Sarah had spent her childhood summers in Paris with her grandmother, on Île St.-Louis. She knew firsthand Parisians had always enjoyed making jokes about buffoonish policemen. At the same time, there was a genuine affection for *Monsieur L'Agent.* Most French police officers had an easy and kindly manner. They seemed to represent the spirit of a free country. And they had never been required to salute French Army officers.

When the Germans arrived, all that had changed, and the French police had been turned into the Milice, the German-run military police.

"You will stand at attention!" the German sergeant bellowed.

The policeman did.

"You will salute me!"

The policeman did.

"And now you must run three times around the Palais."

Sarah turned away, her heart constricting with deepest shame at the humiliation of the Parisian police.

Passing through the back doors of the Palais Garnier, she stepped into an austere world the public never saw: a realm of classes and rehearsals and hard work and sweat — far, far away from the glamour and gilt of the front of the theater. It had survived on orders from Joseph Goebbels, who'd instructed that Paris's wheels of gaiety — music, dance, and theater — must keep turning at whatever cost.

She strode down a long corridor with plain stone floors, hearing the squeak of violins warming up and seeing a throng of wiry, long-limbed dancers, thick woolen leg warmers and sweaters over their practice clothes, congregate like Edgar Degas figures before a cork bulletin board. They smelled of fresh sweat, face powder, and sweet perfume. Pinned in the center was a sheet of thick paper embossed with a black swastika.

"What's this?" Sarah asked one of the coryphées in her deep, raspy voice, as she, too, rose on tiptoe to see.

"More decrees against the Jews," the younger dancer replied.

In the two years since the Occupation, the Nazis had passed anti-Semitic legislation in France, the Statut des Juifs. Jews were now excluded from public life, dismissed from positions in the civil service and the military, and barred from jobs in industry, commerce, medicine, law, and teaching. They were even forbidden to use public telephones. Thousands of Jewish businesses had been seized throughout France; Jewish-owned art and property had been "repossessed."

And in March, the Reich had also required all Jews in Occupied France, including more than eighty thousand Parisians, to register with the police. Sarah had heard rumors that the next order would have Jews identify themselves by wearing gold Stars of David emblazoned with the word *Juif* on their chests.

The dancer in front, a wiry étoile named Yvette Chauviré, large eyes accented by thick mascara, read the new regulation aloud: *"Decree of June 1942, concerning measures against the Jews —"*

"What do you make of it?" one of the other coryphées, Héloïse Guillemard, whispered to Sarah.

In her role as Sabine Severin, dancer from Monte Carlo recently come to the Paris Opéra Ballet, Sarah couldn't afford to raise any eyebrows. She shifted her weight to one side and lied, "It doesn't affect me."

"Well, I think there's another roundup coming." There had been two mass arrests of Jews already — men and foreigners. The prisoners had been taken to camps at Pithiviers and Beaune-la-Rolande in the Loiret. Rumors had swirled since early in the spring that they were being sent to Poland.

"Chez nous en France, tout cela serait impossible," Roland Petit, one of the company's premier danseurs, declared. *Here in France, that could never happen.* He asked Jean Babilee, "Still, if another roundup is coming, what will you do?"

Babilee, another premier danseur, was Jewish — his given name was Jean Gutmann. Sarah had heard he'd left Paris in 1940 when the Wehrmacht had invaded but returned not long after, still dancing beautifully. His dark eyes flashed. "If it comes to that, I'll run off to the mountains and join the Maquis!" Sarah knew of the Maquis. It was made up of bands of French Resistance fighters in the countryside, called Maquisards, both Jews and men who had escaped to avoid conscription into the Service du travail obligatoire — performing forced labor for Germany.

"Shhh!" warned a girl with a blond ponytail, frightened gaze darting up and down the corridor. "Someone will hear!"

"I don't care," retorted Babilee, his voice growing ever louder. "Let them hear. They can't deny my talent. Besides, my family may be Jewish, but we've been here since the Revolution. All of my ancestors fought for France — against the Prussians and in the Great War. I'm a Jew of French ancestry and proud to be French. I believe in the glory of France and always will. I came back to Paris out of loyalty to my country — and I will stand by her." He folded his arms across his muscular chest. "To the end."

"You *do* have a rather large nose," Roland Petit deadpanned.

"That's because I have a large" — Babilee paused theatrically — *"foot."* The assembled members of the company dissolved in laughter, dispersing and going their separate ways.

"It's an elegant nose," Héloïse said, as the two women made their way down the hall to the corps's dressing room. Sarah wondered if Héloïse had a bit of a crush on Babilee. "It looks Basque, don't you think?

124

Besides, it doesn't matter here." She gestured to the studios. "Here we are dancers, all of us. Artists. Art is the only thing that matters to people like us. *Are you any good?* is the only question worth asking."

Another dancer caught up to them — one of the quadrilles, one step down from the coryphées. Although her stage name was Daphné Gilbert, Sarah knew that her real name was Simone Dreyfus and that she, like Babilee, was Jewish. "France is the land of human rights," Simone insisted. "Nothing can happen to us here."

"I heard they're taking down the names and addresses of the Jewish children, too," Héloïse confided. "My cousin's boyfriend is a gendarme."

Sarah hadn't heard this rumor. "Children? Why?"

"Because they're planning on rounding them up as well next time."

"But they're *children!*" Daphné protested. "That's absurd! Thousands of Jews have taken refuge here. Do you know what they say in Poland? 'France is the Jews' salvation.' "

Héloïse moved her dance bag from one shoulder to the other. "I'm not so sure of that anymore. Maybe you should try America. I hear there's ballet in New York City.

That's where George Balanchine went, after all."

"America's turning away the Jews. Calling us 'undesirables.' " Daphné managed a coquettish smile. "Of course, I, myself, am *quite* desirable, don't you agree?" She ran her hands down the curves of her waist and hips. "Oh, here's a joke I heard — why don't the Germans like the Jews?"

Sarah and Héloïse waited.

Daphné chortled. "They only like barb-*Aryans*!"

The three dancers entered the spartan dressing room all the lower-ranking girls in the company shared. Sarah set down her dance bag and opened it, pulling out a slip of an evening gown, intended for the opening-night party after the performance, and hanging it up. She also took out her silver sandals, a chiffon wrap, and a beaded clutch — complete with a compact, lipstick with a sleeping pill concealed in the base, and a camera hidden in a cigarette case that, with any luck, she'd be using later that night.

As Pétain looked down impassively from his official portrait and a wall clock with long black hands kept the time, the female dancers all changed quickly from their street clothes into tights, leotards, and practice tutus, tying the ribbons on their worn pointe shoes. This last rehearsal, on the stage, was to perfect the blocking of the prologue before the curtain rose on the premiere.

As Sarah changed, Héloïse snuck a look at her figure. The tall brunette was usually slim, but, since she'd arrived in France, her body had become more rounded. "Ooh la la, your breasts, Sabine! They're huge!"

Sarah looked down. Her breasts had always been small, too small in her opinion, but they'd grown, she had to admit. And felt tender. "I'm going to get my period," she replied.

"Do you still get yours?" asked Daphné. "I didn't think any of us did anymore, not with the rationing."

As she had been instructed, Sarah left her black dance bag on the bench, and when another dancer, one she'd rarely seen, slipped hers beside it, Sarah picked that one up. The dance bags were identical. The other girl took Sarah's. The exchange was performed as gracefully as any pas de deux. Sarah lifted the new bag and slung it over her delicate shoulder, the straps biting into her pale skin. *Fait accompli,* she wished she could say aloud.

In the wings, it was dark. Dust motes

sparkled in the beams of blue and amber gelled lights. Dancers clustered about a freestanding barre, holding it lightly with one hand, bending forward then arching backward, doing demi-pliés and relevés to warm up. Others were stretched against pieces of the set or moved their weight from foot to foot, burning off excess nerves. A few girls sat on the wooden floor, sewing pink ribbons onto their slippers and darning the satin toe tips for extra traction. An African-looking man, a trombonist from New Orleans whom Sarah knew played jazz with Django Reinhardt at La Cigale, pushed a wide broom. He'd been allowed to keep his job as stage manager at the Opéra when Serge Lifar promised Goebbels and his men that no black man would ever be seen by the audience.

From the other side of the velvet curtain, they could hear the orchestra tuning up, various instruments doing scales, the violins performing a snippet of melody only to stop and repeat.

"I didn't know Babilee was a Jew," one coryphée whispered to another as they dipped their feet into the rosin box. "He seems so *nice.*" Around them, stagehands, burly men in black trousers and chunky black turtlenecks, adjusted lights and double-checked props.

Sarah stood at the barre, her feet in fifth position, the dance bag nearby. She did grand pliés deep and slow with her feet tightly tucked toe to heel — head up, shoulders down, neck long — all the while keeping an eye on the bag.

"All dancers to the stage, please," came the booming voice of the manager. *"All dancers to the stage. Positions for the prologue."*

With the other members of the corps who were ladies-in-waiting, Sarah made her way to the "throne room," standing still, waiting for the music to begin. This was the one time she had to take her eye off the bag, praying no one would take any notice, no one would look through for a pair of scissors or a skein of thread. Together, she and the other dancers stood in position as members of the royal court for the prologue, the "Entrance of the Fairies." They waited under the hot lights, staring out into the darkness, for the conductor to give the signal for the triangle to begin.

The Ukrainian Lifar had starred in Sergei Diaghilev's Ballets Russes in the twenties. In 1929 he took over the Paris Opéra Ballet as premier danseur and choreographer. The company had been on tour in Spain when the German Army had invaded Paris. When they returned, Lifar was confirmed as maître de ballet by French authorities to prevent German interference with ballet. Somewhere in the theater, Serge Lifar watched.

However, Lifar was rumored to get on well with the German overlords, including ballet aficionado Joseph Goebbels, and no one was quite sure if he was a collaborator or not. Regardless, the dancers, musicians, and everyone at the theater were relieved that the Paris Opéra Ballet was still under French control and they still had jobs. They practiced an ironclad ambiguity in order to survive.

Sarah gazed out across the stalls of the main floor, up to the four rows of balconies, a world of glitter and glamour. She knew Hugh was down below in the orchestra pit with his cello. She found that she danced better knowing he was playing. Hugh Thompson, with the French identity of cellist Hubert Taillier, was her "husband" as part of their disguise. During their SOE training in Scotland and England, they'd fallen in love.

Still, keenly aware of the dance bag left in the wings, Sarah could feel her shoulders inch up and her hands tighten. With the mission of the evening on her mind, she wasn't dancing her best. She took a deep breath, pushed her shoulders down, and unclenched her hands, trying to listen to the music, to dance, and to forget everything else for the moment.

Finally, Lifar clapped for them to stop. "Are you Arabians or Clydesdales?" he mocked. His jeer echoed through the empty theater.

Sarah thought they were in for a tirade, but he added only "All right, that was better. Rest now. Then get ready. It's a big night for us." The maître de ballet relaxed, shifting his weight to one side, a hand placed elegantly on one slim hip. "*Merde* to all," he said, the ballet world's age-old *shit* for good luck — just like spies — waving them offstage.

As they all trailed offstage, Sarah heard chatty Daphné Gilbert's unmistakable nasal voice. "You know Hitler blames the sinking of the *Titanic* on us?" she told Babilee, who'd been watching from the wings, warming up. He was playing Prince Désiré.

He had a towel around his neck, dabbing at the sweat rolling down his face. "Really?"

"Because it hit an ice*berg*!"

Sarah grabbed the bag, releasing a quick, grateful breath, then made her way to the orchestra pit.

Hugh was putting his cello back in its case, waiting. He smiled, green eyes bright, when he saw her. At the sight of him, her heart leapt for joy.

"Hello, my love," he said, kissing her full on the lips. "How was the tempo?"

"Fine." Sarah hadn't even noticed. "Fantastic." She looked around to make sure they were alone. "Here," she said, handing over the black bag.

"It's heavy."

"The less we know, the better." She took another glance at him. "You're wearing glasses," she said, finally noticing his silver frames.

"As it turns out," he said, slipping them into his jacket pocket with a disarming grin, "I'm a bit nearsighted. It helps, even though I know most of the music by heart now."

"Wherever did you find eyeglasses?"

"The conductor got them for me," he explained. "Where they came from — well, I try not to think about that."

Hugh looked down at the bag, then pulled on the zipper to reveal the contents. Inside, he rummaged through to see geological reports with readings, measurements, detailed field sketches of stratigraphic sections, and notes with drawings of various beaches and rock formations. Adding to the bag's weight were a compass and glass jars, neatly wrapped in layers of tissue paper. Moving aside the tissue, he could see each jar contained sand samples, neatly labeled: BARNEVILLE-PLAGE, CABOURG, GRANVILLE, ÎLES CHAUSEY, PORTBAIL, TROUVILLE. All beaches in Normandy.

Like Orpheus, he couldn't look away. His eyes widened, as he realized the implication. *"To see a world in a grain of sand and a heaven in a wild flower — hold infinity in the palm of your hand and eternity in an hour,"* he muttered.

"Put it away!" Sarah cautioned, refusing to look. "We don't need to know what it is — we just need to get it back to London."

She pulled away, then gestured for him to follow her. He acquiesced, and they walked backstage, where Sarah pulled him into a janitor's closet, tugging at a string to turn on the bare bulb.

"You make everything romantic," Hugh teased, closing the door. He lowered the bag and bent to kiss her. But Sarah was in no mood. Their mission after the evening's performance was simple — and yet not.

Since their arrival in Paris three months ago, Sarah and Hugh had been cultivating a relationship with Reichsminister Hans Fortner, a German ballet aficionado, although whether Fortner truly loved the dance or just liked watching girls in tutus, Sarah didn't know. Or care. What was more important was that he was the head of the Reich Ministry for Armaments and War Production in France. He would have the latest files on which French companies — such as Peugeot, Renault, Avions Voisin, and La Licorne — might be working with the Germans in violation of the terms of the armistice, aiding in the development of weapons. Once their collaboration was confirmed, the factories would be targets for RAF strikes or for SOE sabotage. Their mission — hers and Hugh's — was to photograph the precious papers so SOE would have the concrete evidence they so desperately needed to bomb the weapons factories.

They knew from a fellow Resistance worker, a woman who worked as a maid at Fortner's hotel, that the Reichsminister kept all of his files in a safe in his suite. Sarah had learned the safecracking skills needed to get the safe open and shut. Now she just had to get into his heavily guarded suite.

Through postperformance parties Lifar threw for the occupiers and collaborators who were ballet aficionados, Sarah and Hugh and Fortner had been introduced, then had become friendly, going out for drinks and for dinner, where Fortner flirted shamelessly with Sarah.

And tonight, after the party at Maxim's, they would make sure they were invited back to his hotel. There the plan was for them to get drunk, or at least seem to. Hugh would pretend to become ill and need to return to their flat, and then Sarah would seduce Fortner, drug his wine with the sleeping pill hidden in the base of her lipstick, and then, while the Reichsminister was unconscious, break into his safe and photograph the plans with the tiny camera hidden in her cigarette case.

Sarah pulled away, Hugh still clasping her waist. "I'm worried, Hugh. I might have to, you know —"

"You have the pill to knock him out."

"Yes, but how long will it take to work? This isn't an exact science, you know. I've never even used it before!"

"As long as we get the names of the factories" — he pushed back the tendrils of dark hair that had escaped her bun — "that's all we need. And then back to London —"

"Where we'll be married, for real, this time." They embraced, this time kissing passionately, until Sarah broke away, again. "I could tell him I'm having my period," she said against Hugh's chest, unable to look him in the eye. His arm cradled her head, and she could hear the faint tick of his watch.

"It won't come to that." He rubbed her back.

"How would you feel?" she asked softly. "If it *did* come to that? If I — had to?"

"It's a job, darling." He reached for her hands and looked her in the eye. "Think of it as acting."

But Sarah loved Hugh. And, even knowing how selfish she was being, she didn't want her actions to damage their burgeoning relationship. "But how would you feel about Fortner and me — in bed together?"

"I want us to complete this assignment and get safely back to London," he answered firmly, either unable or unwilling to entertain seriously the possibility she was asking him about. "Once we have the photographs of the papers, I can radio back to London that they can schedule a pickup for us. Eight days until the full moon — and then we'll be home!"

"So I should 'lie back and think of England'?"

"Sarah . . ."

"Oh, it's fine. Darling, people are being

asked to kill in this bloody war! Surely, in context, fucking an old German — if it even comes to that, which it most assuredly won't — isn't such a huge deal." Then, "If you were me, would *you* do it?"

"I would," Hugh reassured her without hesitation. "Soldiers in the field endure far worse. Espionage, well, there's a reason it's called 'the second oldest profession.' "

"All right then," she said resolutely, "if worse comes to worst, I'll do it. I'm a patriot, after all. I'll do what I need to," she concluded, feeling both angry and not a little betrayed by Hugh's reaction.

"Look," he reminded her gently, cupping her cheek with his palm, "these files could take out dozens of weapons factories. They could save hundreds of thousands, if not more, of British lives. Wars aren't won by respectable methods."

"Wars aren't won by respectable methods," Sarah repeated softly. "I understand. God gave me a mind and a body, and I shall use both. If Mata Hari could do it, so can I."

"I love you," he said, kissing her.

"I love you, too." She drew back and smiled. "I need to change into my costume and do my hair and makeup."

He picked up the bag. "And after the

performance, we drop this off, then have our own little performance."

"*Merde,*" she said.

"*Merde alors,*" he replied.

In addition to attending the ballet, Nazis in Paris patronized the brothels. With no wives or children in tow, and the imposed exchange rate at twenty francs to one mark, carnal pleasure on demand was practically free.

The officers went to the established bordellos: the infamous Le Sphinx near Montparnasse, 32 Rue Blondel in the Sentier, just off the infamous Rue Saint-Denis, or House of All Nations. But the pinnacle was 122 Rue de Provence, known as One-Two-Two. The brothel was housed in a mansion that had once belonged to a prince, and was run like a luxurious gentlemen's club, similar to the exclusive Travellers on the Champs-Élysées, but with certain *supplements.* Before the Occupation, one could have spotted members of the French Parliament, nobility, members of the Académie, and stars of the Comédie-Française enjoying themselves there. Now the French could go only during the afternoons, while Nazis took over the more desirable evening hours.

There were multitudes of women to

choose from, or else, for the shy or indecisive, proprietress Madame Georgette Jamet would make a suggestion and facilitate an introduction. The experience was further enhanced by differently themed rooms. Clients could select the hayloft, the Marquis de Sade dungeon, an igloo room — with a bed actually made of ice and covered in furs — a transatlantic liner cabin, or an Egyptian chamber complete with a sloe-eyed Cleopatra.

Von Waltz's favorite courtesan was an unblemished young blonde with peachy skin named Selena, and his preferred room was designed to look like an Orient Express cabin, including a recording of engine noise and a vibrating bed.

When his rendezvous with Selena was over, the Obersturmbannführer took a leisurely hot bath, then dressed once again in his perfectly pressed trousers, a burgundy smoking jacket, and monogrammed slippers to enjoy a cigar and cocktail with some of his fellow officers before the formal dinner. He was looking forward to it: the night's menu card read oysters, lamb, and strawberries with cream. But first, he wanted an aperitif.

Perfumed with Eau de Cologne du Coq, von Waltz entered, acknowledging various

German officers smoking cigars and drinking Champagne, and a group playing an especially intense game of skat with gold-edged cards in one corner of the room. The gentlemen's lounge was decorated to look like a Versailles salon, with boiserie panels, red brocade furniture, gilt sconces, cake-icing paneling, and an enormous glittering cage chandelier. A marble Louis XVI clock topped by a panther ticked faintly on the mantel, flanked by matching garniture.

"Bretz!" Von Waltz had spotted Hauptsturmführer Arlo Bretz. Von Waltz had trained with the younger Viennese man. Bretz was in charge of the Gestapo's radio intercept station, located on Boulevard Suchet. Von Waltz walked to him. "Who were you with this fine evening?"

Bretz picked up his glass of cloudy, diluted pastis and raised it to von Waltz. "Angelique, this time. 'The girl with the heart-shaped ass.' You?"

"Selena, of course," von Waltz replied, sitting opposite, a burr walnut games table between them. "I'm utterly faithful. If not to my wife, then at least I'm constant to my whore." The men laughed. "Cigar?" von Waltz offered, pulling two Gildemanns from the breast pocket of his smoking jacket.

"I don't think the girls like the smell of it."

"True, true. Now ask me" — von Waltz put one back, then cut and lit it with a lighter engraved with a swastika and eagle, puffing on it until it flared — "who the fuck cares what the girls like?"

"True, true." The two laughed again.

Von Waltz exhaled, blowing smoke rings one after the other. "Before I left the office today, I was talking to Ribbentrop about the little radio game our colleagues are playing with the SOE in Holland," the Obersturmbannführer said, namedropping shamelessly. "We must have the same success here, in Paris. We must fool the British — beat them at their own game. Alas, our last prisoner decided not to work with us, but we can still use her radio."

"Too bad," Bretz said, tapping the side of his glass, then drinking. "Any stand-in we use would have a different fist from the English agent." A radio operator's *fist,* the way he or she coded, was as distinctive as a signature. It was an assurance to those picking up the message that the agent was really who she said she was. "The different fist, as well as lack of security checks, might set off alarm bells back in London, you know."

"Oh, the SOE obviously doesn't notice or

doesn't care about such details. They don't even care that their security checks are compromised. We could include a few lines of *Mein Kampf* and the British still wouldn't believe their pretty operator's been captured. But you're right — we won't be able to get away with it forever. And so I have an idea. We tell them this particular spy has gone into hiding in Paris for a few weeks. This will explain her changed fist, lack of security checks, and missed times of communication."

"And then?" Bretz drained his glass.

"Then, after some time has gone by, we begin again, make London trust her. All the while either capturing more agents and commandeering their radios or letting them signal back as our prisoners, operating under our watch."

"And our endgame?"

"The Allies will be making plans for their eventual invasion attempt, of course," von Waltz answered, resting his cigar in an opaline ashtray. "To prepare, they will need covert agents in place, supplies, plans of destruction. By playing our *Radiospiel,* we'll learn the time and place of the invasion. Information invaluable to Himmler. And to our Führer. Ribbentrop is on his way to Paris as we speak."

" 'Radio game.' I like the sound of that!" Bretz swallowed the last of his pastis. "But the British might know. It's possible they are playing us at our own game. They could have given us this agent in order to have someone on the inside. She just didn't go along with the plan."

"I studied at Cambridge years ago and know a few things about the English," von Waltz replied. "They're smart, they fight hard when they have to, they always do their duty — but they have an idealistic sense of 'fair play' that never fails to trip them up. And they would never, *ever* deliberately sacrifice one of their own, even in the name of victory."

"But we can't have this agent 'in hiding' forever," Bretz objected. "And to truly use her radio, we're going to need more information about her network. *Specific* details, so they don't begin to suspect anything."

Von Waltz leaned closer. "I have a spy on the inside — a double agent. My relationship with him goes back to the Spanish Civil War."

"Ah. And what contacts does this agent have with the English?"

"Through the whimsies of war and his own quite considerable ambitions, he's risen to a position of critical importance inside

English intelligence. He's the SOE's round-house, through which most vital movements of their spy networks are scheduled. If we protect him and the British activities from any untimely discovery and arrest — keep the police and the Wehrmacht away from the safe houses and the Luftwaffe from their takeoffs and landings, at least as much as possible — he will continue to be extremely valuable to them." Von Waltz doused his cigar in a small pool of water in the ashtray. "They will grow to trust him more and more."

"Won't they get suspicious if their agents start disappearing?"

"We mustn't be greedy. We'll pick off only a few at a time, no mass arrests. After all, the more agents he gets home safely, the more confidence the English will have in him. And the more they trust him, the better an agent he'll be for me. We should follow these spies, see who they meet, find out the locations of the safe houses, and so on. By leaving their networks more or less intact," von Waltz continued, "we'll have access to unprecedented intelligence — up to and including the time and place of any Allied landings."

One of the girls, wearing only a satin robe, poked her head into the salon. "And pierce the heart of the British spy network." Bretz blew her a kiss. She giggled and left. "But why would your man be so keen to betray the British? After all, we invaded his country."

"He's no fan of the Reich, but he loathes Communism even more. He's appalled at the way the French Communists have joined the Resistance, collaborating with the British. He thinks the Commies are planning on taking over if the Allies win. And he'd rather see his country Fascist than Bolshevik. Besides, the money is very good. He likes the finer things in life." Von Waltz reached for his cigar. "As we all do."

"But the agents — they're not going to confide the details of their missions to this man. What information other than drop-offs and deliveries will he have access to?"

"This is where things become truly wonderful. In addition to smuggling agents in and out of France, he picks up their mail going back to London and various letter drops around Paris and hands it over to the pilots of outgoing flights. He brings it to me first, however, so that I can read and photograph anything of importance. In addition, to arrange a landing, the Allies will need to send their agents materials in advance. The information on maps, blueprints, and drawings can't be transmitted by radio. It'll have to be in papers handed off by courier. These pages will ultimately provide the secrets of the invasion."

"Tell me, who is this mystery man, this double agent?" Bretz was nearly giddy with pastis and curiosity.

"I can only tell you his code name: Gibbon. I chose it specifically — it's French for 'friend with a gift.' "

Bretz grinned. "Well then, let the Radio Games commence!"

"Come by Avenue Foch with me tonight. I'll give you a little demonstration."

"Now?" Bretz protested, grabbing his crotch. "I've barely begun!"

"No, after. *After*, of course!"

CHAPTER SIX

It was *l'heure bleu* — the blue hour, when one couldn't tell if it was afternoon or evening — when Maggie and Chanel arrived at the Palais Garnier. Signs outside the theater proclaimed the Paris Opéra Ballet's opening night performance of *La Belle au bois dormant* was sold out.

Once inside, Chanel gestured toward the monumental marble staircase. "Shall we?" Lights blazed, and golden reflections danced along the marble and gilt as if the theater were a palace in a Belle Époque fairy tale. Graceful female torchères, created by Albert-Ernest Carrier-Belleuse, held candelabra aloft. *Don't their arms get tired after all this time?* Maggie wondered, trying to distract herself. The ceiling above the sweeping staircase had been painted by Isidore Pils with a number of murals, including *Minerva Fighting Brutality Watched by the Gods of Olympus.*

Both women were exquisitely dressed: Coco, of course, in one of her own creations, a gossamer black tulle gown with a ruby Maltese cross brooch, Maggie in a clinging, pale blue silk, bias-cut gown by Vionnet with a black embroidered net overdress. She caught Chanel eyeing it with a look of both envy and approbation. Together, they made their way up the marble steps. The crowd, recognizing the iconic couturiere, parted before them.

It was clear to Maggie that Paris, like London, had turned to ballet to ameliorate the grim misery of war. From the German-inflected French she could hear, it seemed that the occupiers were great balletomanes — although whether it was because ballet had no language barrier or because it was a superb opportunity to see pretty girls in skimpy clothing, she couldn't say.

As they reached the top step, Chanel pulled Maggie aside to one of the balconies to watch the continuing procession on the wide staircase, her eyes wandering over the crowd. Maggie could smell cigarette smoke, perfume, and hair tonic; all around them rose birdlike chatter.

"This is *my* stage," the designer announced as they looked down over the people making their entrances. "The most important runway in all of France, perhaps in all the world. You know, Hitler adores the architecture of the Palais. It was the first thing he went to see when he came to visit."

On the grand stairway, Parisian socialites flirted with handsome Luftwaffe officers. Frenchmen in evening dress — powerful industrialists, designers, and politicians — held out their arms to be clasped by women clad in silk and satin gowns covered by ostrich-feather capes. In their gloved hands, they carried beaded evening bags, hanging by fragile gold chains.

Maggie looked up and around warily. The theater's interior was a bit ornate for her taste, but that was part of its charm. Looking down over the milling French and Germans, she realized that the Occupation was re-creating in real life the predemocratic era they'd craved. Like royalty of the good old days, these die-hard noblemen and noblewomen were enjoying outrageous privilege, while misery lay just outside the palace gates: the Jewish quarter was only minutes away.

Chanel leaned in, and Maggie realized that the designer was wearing Chanel No. 5. The same perfume Clara Hess — Maggie and Elise's mother — wore. *Stop it, Hope. No time for that.* "That one's mine" —

Chanel was saying, pointing to a gown — "and that one — and that one — and that —"

Finally satisfied, Chanel led the way to their seats, the first box near the stage, a grand red-velvet jewelry box completed by a formal antechamber with wide *fauteuil en Bergère* chairs, coat hooks, and a large girandole mirror for last-minute primping. *It's almost as if* we're *the performers,* Maggie thought as she took one last look to make sure she didn't have lipstick on her teeth before making her entrance.

As they took their seats in the box's front row, Maggie felt a bit like the girl with the pink roses in Renoir's *La Loge.* She looked around the theater, an otherworldly place of storybook glamour. The walls were gold and gleaming, and the seats upholstered in scarlet. Every inch of the high coffered ceiling was painted with cherubs and flowers or carved with scrolls and garlands of roses, illuminated by the infamous glowing crystal chandelier from Gaston Leroux's *Le Fantôme de l'opéra.* There was no question that Parisian cultural life was glittering under the Occupation — obviously, the Germans had money and wanted to be entertained. "It must be wonderful to see so many women wearing your fashions," Maggie murmured to Chanel.

"Darling, I don't *do* fashion — I *am* fashion."

To avoid rolling her eyes, Maggie opened her program. There was *Sabine Severin* in the long list of attendants, and *Hubert Taillier* in the orchestra listing. She looked down from the box at a perfect view of the orchestra members drifting in and taking out their music, adjusting their stands, rosining their bows. She saw Hugh taking his cello from its case and blinked. *When did he start wearing glasses?* Then she realized her hostess was once again speaking to her.

"Feminine Paris in the arms of masculine Berlin," Chanel noted, taking in the French women with German officers. "Do you know," she added, "that in the twenties and thirties, I was known as Mademoiselle Ballet?"

"Really?" Maggie responded. Hugh was now seated behind his cello, tightening the strings of his bow. *The new glasses suit him.*

"Oh yes." Chanel didn't seem to notice Maggie's distraction. "I worked with Picasso, Stravinsky, Dalí — designed costumes for Sergei Diaghilev's Ballets Russes — *Le Train bleu, Orphée, Oedipe roi* — I adore androgyny. 'Avant-garde perversity' is what one critic called it. We were all delighted by

151

that sort of review, of course."

Maggie realized that for the privileged few, like Chanel and her entourage, wartime Paris was really no different from peacetime; high society danced on much as before, just with a different partner. As Chanel pontificated, needing only the occasional nod or *mmm-hmm,* Maggie's eyes wandered around the spectacle.

It was the Palais Garnier, but in her mind's eye she saw occupied London reflected in a nightmarish image. Would the Sadler's Wells Ballet still be dancing under Nazi rule? Maggie had once met Ninette de Valois and thought no — at least not with Madame in charge.

But if the Nazis had invaded, Lord Halifax most likely would have been made Prime Minister and put in charge of some sort of shadow government. The Duke of Windsor would have been crowned King, Wallis Simpson made Queen . . . Maggie shuddered, suddenly seeing it clearly: Nazi banners flying from Buckingham Palace, the Luftwaffe put up at Claridge's, Hermann Goering taking his pick of art from the National Gallery. Germans in gray-green uniforms and jackboots marching past Nelson's column, as the clock of Big Ben chimed on Berlin time . . .

We shall fight on the beaches . . . she remembered typing for newly named Prime Minister Churchill in those fateful days of the summer of '40, but she knew it was true. If it had come to that, the Brits would have fought, with bottles and pickaxes if they had them, and stones and handfuls of sand if they didn't. Churchill's speeches, the indomitable will of the people, all those young RAF pilots defending Britain with their Spitfires like knights of yore. Maggie knew, in her very bones, that even if some of the anti-Semitic Fascist-leaning British aristocracy might have been wooed, the rest of London would not, like Paris, have gone so gently into the glittering night.

She heard a pause in Chanel's monologue and sensed an opportunity. "Do you know the conductor?" she asked, glancing down at her program. "Hugo Boulez?" Surely Coco Chanel, who seemed to know everyone, would know him — and he might know the famous German Maestro Miles Hess, and might even know where his Parisian flat was located. Which might lead her to Elise. *So many* might*s.*

"Why, yes. Yes, of course."

Maggie smiled. "I'd love to meet him, after the ballet — if you wouldn't mind introducing us."

"You're a music aficionado?" Chanel arched a penciled eyebrow. "Certainly you're not interested in taking him as a lover — Boulez is old as Methuselah."

Spycraft 101: Don't lie if you don't have to. "I'm not interested in him personally — but I do love music. And meeting conductors."

As the houselights dimmed and the low roar of conversations quieted, Maestro Boulez, a rotund, white-haired man in his seventies, entered to warm applause. He made his way to the podium, bowed to the audience, and then turned to the orchestra and lifted his baton. The overture began.

The gold-tasseled velvet curtains opened onto the interior of a Versailles-inspired palace, the courtiers wearing elaborately coiffed white powdered wigs. It was a ballet of pomp and ceremony, with decorous formations of royals and fairies. Even with the wigs, Maggie spotted Sarah immediately as a bejeweled noblewoman in blue silk. *She should be Aurora,* Maggie decided loyally. *Or the Lilac Fairy.* She loved her friend's dancing and thought she was better than Margot Fonteyn.

As the dancers spun and soared, Maggie watched, entranced. *Perhaps this is a different sort of resistance. A French, not a British, one.* Wasn't the very choice of performing

154

The Sleeping Beauty a battle cry in and of itself? The ballet was wholly French in spirit, with French technique, the story based on a French fairy tale, the architecture, décor, and costumes undeniably classically French. Wasn't this a reminder of France eternal, a vision and defense of nobility and court life, of chivalry and etiquette with high ideals and formal principles, symmetry and order?

Maggie started when the evil fairy, Carabosse, entered, costumed in black and red. *An allusion to SS uniforms?* Maggie looked over the faces of the audience below. No one seemed in the least perturbed. She smiled. *Resistance comes in all forms.* With that in mind, she enjoyed the performance much more than she'd expected. It was as beautiful and delicate as a butterfly, and a precious balm for her soul.

When the curtains finally closed, there was a standing ovation, and then endless bows and curtsies, with Maggie clapping especially hard for Sarah's group. As the velvet curtains at last closed, and the houselights came up, Chanel looked to Maggie. "We will meet everyone at Maxim's," she announced as the audience began to disperse, smiling and laughing.

"Will Maestro Boulez be there?"

"Of course, my dear — anyone who's *anyone* these days goes to Maxim's."

Chanel and Maggie were taken to the famed restaurant in the same long black Benz that had brought them to the ballet. Maggie didn't ask how Chanel managed a car and driver in the midst of such deprivation. *Most likely thanks to the same someone who got her papers to be out past curfew,* Maggie decided. *A high-ranking Nazi lover?*

"Your jewelry's beautiful," she told Chanel, when the silence felt strained.

"Can you tell if it's real or faux?" the couturiere challenged, fingering a necklace. Maggie shook her head. "It's best that way. A woman should mix fake and real, I feel. I adore fakes because I find such jewelry provocative, and I find it disgraceful to walk around with millions adorning your neck simply because you're rich. The point of jewelry isn't to make a woman look rich but to enhance her own beauty. It's *not* the same thing."

Maggie had no idea what the designer was talking about, but she smiled and nodded all the same. The streets between the Palais Garnier and Place de la Concorde, lit by moonlight, were nearly empty. A few people hurried by to make it to the Métro before curfew as the occasional vélo-taxi pedaled swiftly along. Maggie could see the anxiety and fear on the faces of those people they did pass. *The Germans are clever,* she realized. The curfew wasn't only a security measure; it was a form of psychological control.

As they were helped from the car by the fawning doorman at 3 Rue Royal, Maggie saw the distinctive golden font of Maxim's on the silk awning by the glow of the headlights, while tacked onto a streetlight was a government poster warning that cat meat was unsafe to use in stews. Across the street, in the shadows, a prostitute with a heavily made-up face and pushed-up décolletage posed against a wall.

Inside, the restaurant was a smoky scene from Franz Léhar's operetta *The Merry Widow.* The main dining room was a flamboyant Art Nouveau salon in gold and scarlet and jewel-like stained glass, where all lines curved, and lamps with red silk shades flattered every complexion.

Everywhere were huge and fragrant displays of burgundy roses, creamy carnations, and sheaves of gladioli in every color from mauve to canary. The waiters were dressed for French formal service in white coats, towels over their forearms. And in a dim corner, a balding pianist with half-moon glasses played *"C'est mon gigolo."*

"Coco!" came a man's cry over the chattering of the crowd. He was lean and taut, with striking dark looks and almost feline grace.

"Serge!" Chanel replied as she made her way over, offering both rouged cheeks to be kissed. "This is Mademoiselle Paige Kelly, here from Ireland by way of Lisbon. And this, my dear, is Serge Lifar." The designer's smile broadened. "*The* Serge Lifar."

"*Enchanté*, Mademoiselle Kelly," Lifar purred, bending low to kiss Maggie's gloved hand. She almost let out a hysterical giggle despite her omnipresent fear; the charismatic premier danseur and choreographer bowed to her so theatrically that she actually felt, for an instant, like a prima ballerina herself. At his table, Maggie recognized famous faces: the artist Jean Cocteau, the actress Arletty, and the playwright Sacha Guitry. *Like Boccaccio's Florentine youths and maidens, who fled to the hills and spent their days playing the lute and telling stories while plague ravaged their city,* Maggie thought.

Arletty, a dark-haired beauty and film star was saying, "My heart is French, but my ass is *international!*" The actress wore a low-cut

Chanel design with a black velvet bow and diamonds — real or fake, Maggie couldn't say — and a flirty birdcage veil.

"My dear!" interjected Guitry, whose good looks and elegant ease gave him the air of a boulevardier. "Naughty, naughty!"

Arletty smiled, her lips moist and scarlet against gleaming teeth. "Well, if you French-men hadn't let the Germans in . . ." She pushed a piece of baguette around her empty plate to soak up every last drop of buttery sauce. "I wouldn't be sleeping with them!" She popped the bite in her mouth with a satisfied look.

Her voice had carried. "Paris welcomed us with her legs open!" crowed a passing Nazi officer, drinking straight from a bottle of beer, despite the horrified looks of some of the French diners. He staggered. "It's not as if we burned the city, the way Napo-leon did to Moscow," he added by way of an apology.

One of the German officers at the table rose and went to Chanel. "I'm so glad you could come, darling," he said, kissing her on both cheeks.

"Ah, here he is, our gracious conqueror," she murmured in reply. Maggie watched their body language and guessed the officer and the designer were lovers. It occurred to her that, for some of the society ladies, the Occupation offered a certain kind of excitement that far exceeded any enjoyments or luxuries from before the war, as the "Nordic heroes" arrived.

Chanel turned to Maggie. "Let me introduce Baron Hans Günther von Dincklage — but feel free to call him Spatz. We all do."

"How do you do?" they each said in turn. Dincklage was in his mid- to late forties, with blond hair, steady eyes, and a suave manner.

"Mademoiselle Paige Kelly," the couturiere continued, introducing Maggie with a petulant look at odds with her age. Maggie noticed how Dincklage stroked the small of Chanel's back and whispered something in her ear that made the older woman smile.

"See, another Frenchwoman who's taken up with a German," called Arletty from the table, pointing at Chanel and confirming Maggie's suspicion.

As the designer peeled off her gloves, revealing nicotine-stained fingers, she quipped, "Really — a woman of my age who has the chance of a lover cannot be expected to review his passport."

Arletty raised her glass of wine. "War is no time to be alone."

"Sit, sit!" Lifar urged, as gilt chairs were

brought over and more places set. "Any friend of Coco's is a friend of ours." The table was already covered with food — caviar on ice with mother-of pearl spoons, pâté de foie gras, escargot swimming in butter and fresh parsley, rack of lamb, red lobsters, eel in aspic, roast chicken and crispy skinned duck, coupes of sparkling Champagne. After months of watery soup and hard bread, Maggie was nearly dizzy from hunger.

"Waiter!" Lifar snapped his fingers. "Menus for the ladies!"

The leather-bound menu looked as if it were the one from prewar days, offering oysters, different sorts of fish, bouillabaisse, rabbit, and chicken. Everyone, including the Germans, was speaking in French. A hedgehog-like Nazi officer with beady, dark eyes urged Maggie to try one of his oysters: "In times like these, my dear, to eat well and to eat often gives you a tremendous feeling of power."

Maggie demurred. Then he offered one to Chanel; she declined as well, but for other reasons: "I only eat oysters during months with the letter *r* in them."

"Well then, more for me!" he crowed, slurping one greedily, washing it down with gulps of Champagne. Maggie forced a smile.

161

"Mademoiselle?" A waiter appeared at Chanel's elbow, a starched white linen cloth draped over his forearm. "What may I bring you?"

"Soup," she stated. "Clear. A plate of white asparagus with no butter, if it's still in season. And a glass of Bordeaux — Château Lafite Rothschild, 'twenty-eight, if you have it."

"And you, mademoiselle?"

Maggie was in no mood to feast when the rest of Paris was getting by on stewed cat. "Nothing for me, thank you." The waiter bowed and took their menus.

"I eat lightly," Chanel said by way of explanation. Maggie didn't respond, as she'd caught a glimpse of Hugh and Sarah arrive arm in arm, with a large, fat German in uniform, his face like marzipan. They didn't notice her.

"You look as if you've seen a ghost, my dear."

Maggie took a sip of Champagne to cover her distress.

"I recently got a gorgeous fur coat — belonged to a Jew," Arletty was saying. "Long. Pure sable."

"I hear many of the Jews have gone into hiding," added Cocteau, as he lit a cigarette with long, tapering fingers.

"Ah, they may hide," said the hedgehog-like German, slurping at another oyster, "but we'll find them. You can count on it."

"Not many of them made it out of the country before the surrender, so there must be lots of them still around," Chanel observed.

The German lifted his glass. "There's another big roundup to come."

"Now we real French can control our businesses and economy," Chanel said. To Maggie, she explained, "The Wertheimers, my so-called business partners, tried to take over my perfume business. Swindled me out of every penny, the dirty Jewish swine. But I'll use my new status as an Aryan French citizen to get back what they stole." She looked to Dincklage with a smile. "Occupation has some advantages, after all."

Maggie blinked, stunned at the venom spewing from Chanel's red-painted lips and at the enthusiastic reception by the others at the table. "I really had no idea the Jews were as bad as all that, mademoiselle."

"You look shocked, my dear," said the dark-haired German. "But you, thank heavens, have few Jews in Ireland. You don't know them the way we do. And whether one hates the Jews for the Dreyfus affair and betraying France, or for killing Christ, or

163

for cheating you in a business deal" — he looked to Chanel, who nodded with approval — "all Frenchmen — and women — are anti-Semites in one way or another."

"France even now doesn't know what's hit her," Chanel agreed, her wineglass smeared with the crimson print of her lipstick, a half kiss on glittering crystal. "She's still in a daze, but has already come to sufficiently move her eyes and see what is going on around her. Soon she'll recover the use of her limbs, and then the trouble will start. I want to get my business back from those dirty Jews and under my control now, while I still can."

"Ah," Maggie said, rising, wanting with all her heart to leave the table and escape these monsters. "I see the conductor — and must go and congratulate him. Please excuse me."

Chanel looked up with a gimlet eye. "Enjoy, *ma chérie.*"

CHAPTER SEVEN

As Hugh and Sarah mingled with a crowd of musicians and dancers, people stopped to stare at the beautiful couple. Hugh carried the black bag with Calvert's papers and sand samples over one shoulder. "The drop-off's *here*?" Sarah said softly in his ear as they smiled and nodded to other members of the company.

"I was told I'm looking for a man in a blue suit with a pink carnation in his lapel," Hugh whispered back. "We're going to sit with him, have a short conversation. Then he'll take the bag when he leaves."

Sarah spotted the man with the pink carnation. "There," she said, pointing. He was small but wiry, with piercing eyes and an upturned nose. She pulled Hugh to the man's table.

"Bonsoir, monsieur," Hugh said to the man, in the prearranged signal. "Are you Raimond, the nephew of Lancelin Martin?"

When the man with the flower replied, "Lancelin Martin is my second cousin," Hugh knew he was the contact. He and Sarah sat at his banquette. Hugh slid the bag under the table.

The man gave an imperceptible nod, his eyes on the other diners. "Would you like some wine?" was all he said.

Maggie approached the conductor and his entourage, all talking loudly with animated hands. She caught his eye with what she hoped was a suitably ingratiating smile. "Maestro Boulez —" she began, and he glanced up at her. He was short, barely five feet tall, and plump, with white hair. On his face was a light but detectable layer of makeup.

"What a wonderful performance," she said, bending slightly. "I very much appreciated your tempi."

"Why, thank you, mademoiselle. You must be a music lover, to notice such things."

"I am," she assured him. "I play the viola — quite badly, I'm sorry to say. But I'm a fan of conductors — a huge admirer of Miles Hess."

"Ah, Hess!" Boulez exclaimed. "One of the greats. Back in Berlin now, I hear."

"I'm friends with his daughter Elise Hess,"

Maggie went on lightly, "and I heard she might be in Paris. Have you heard any mention of her being in town?"

"Afraid not, mademoiselle."

But Maggie would not be dissuaded. "Do you happen to know where the Hess family stays when they're here?"

"I don't." He looked to the other musicians around his table. "Anyone?"

"I do." The speaker was a handsome man with a beak-like nose, smoking a Galois. Maggie recognized him as the first violinist. "Clara, that is, Frau Hess, once invited me to a party —"

One of the other men gave him a light punch on the arm. "A 'party,' now, was it?"

"It was," the violinist protested, turning red. "I remember it perfectly. Had a great view."

"Do you — do you happen to remember the address?" Maggie pressed.

He shook his head. "I do remember Clara, er, Frau Hess, mentioning that they lived in Germaine Lubin's building."

Bingo! Maggie thought.

Without warning, the double doors of the entrance banged open. Half a dozen German soldiers carrying machine guns walked in briskly, led by an SS captain in uniform and black leather boots. The pianist stopped midmeasure. All conversation and the scrape of silverware and clink of glasses ceased.

Hands clasped behind his back, the captain strode through the restaurant. The Germans looked on impassively, as if bored. The French, with the exception of Chanel, kept their heads down, studying their plates. The designer lit a gold-tipped cigarette, sat back, and settled in to observe.

Maggie's heart caught in her throat when, on the other side of the restaurant, the captain walked up to Hugh and Sarah's table. But he spoke only to the man with the pink carnation. "Monsieur, you're to come with us immediately."

The man raised his hands. "But, sir, I've done nothing!"

The SS captain nodded. Two soldiers grabbed the man with the pink carnation by the shoulders. When he didn't get up, they dragged him. "Fucking Boche!" he screamed. One officer punched him savagely in the stomach.

As swiftly as they came, the SS officers were gone, taking the man with the pink carnation with them. The restaurant was left in silence. Leaning back with her cigarette between her teeth, Chanel clapped her hands, as if she had just witnessed a particularly delightful piece of theater.

"A round of Champagne for everyone!" Dincklage called. Slowly, people returned to their conversations and the piano started up again. Maggie, hands shaking, made her way back to Chanel's table.

"You look pale," the older woman observed, blowing smoke through her nostrils.

"I'm not used to this sort of thing."

"What about those IRA bombs?" Chanel parried.

"You know I met Mademoiselle Chanel through Diaghilev," Lifar interposed, before Maggie could reply. "I remember how he told Mademoiselle, 'I've been to see a princess and she gave me seventy-five thousand francs.' And then our Coco said, 'Well, she's royalty and I'm only a seamstress. Here's *two hundred* thousand.' "

Those around the table laughed, raising their glasses, eager to forget what they had just witnessed. Chanel nodded her head in acknowledgment, her eyes bright. "I prefer to give rather than lend money," she declared, picking up her own glass. "In the end, it costs the same."

On the other side of the room, Hugh looked to Sarah. "Are you all right?" Then, "It's here," he whispered in her ear as he reached for the bag. "We still have it."

She didn't respond. Her face was white.

"Something to drink, darling?" he asked, putting his arm around her. "Something to eat?"

"No." She shivered. "I'm fine, Hubert. Just need to splash some cold water on my face. Be back in a moment."

From across the room, a man cast his eyes on Maggie and approached. "Mademoiselle Kelly." The German officer placed one hand to his heart as if wounded. "You told me you frequented Café de la Paix — not Maxim's. You aren't trying to avoid me, are you?"

Maggie's heart sank. It was the officer who'd given her and her luggage a ride to the Ritz after the shooting, now out of uniform and in black tie.

"Heavens, no!" Maggie exclaimed while Chanel looked on, one painted eyebrow quirked with curiosity. "When Mademoiselle Coco Chanel invites you somewhere, you go, of course. Would you like to sit with us, er . . ." She couldn't remember his name.

"Generaloberst Ruesdorf. Christian Ruesdorf." He smiled. "But, please — call me Christian."

Chanel gave Maggie a side glance as he

pulled out a chair. "You didn't tell me you had friends in high places, Mademoiselle Kelly."

The Generaloberst laughed. "I was privileged to give our Irish friend a lift to the Ritz after her vélo-taxi driver had given up in defeat, done in by her heavy Vuitton trunk."

"The French are talented, especially with food and ballet, but lazy bastards in everything else," Spatz remarked. "A German would never have given up!"

"And I was most grateful for your kind assistance," Maggie lied, raising the corners of her lips in what she hoped looked like a smile.

"Mademoiselle and I spoke about German films with Irish themes — we have both seen *Linen from Ireland.*"

"I heard it was quite witty," interjected Chanel. "And I do love linen."

"Herr Goebbels has used Ireland as a setting for a number of his films. There's also *My Life for Ireland* and *The Fox of Glenarvon.* 'The enemy of my enemy is my friend, after all,' " Ruesdorf repeated, alluding to their previous conversation, smiling at Maggie. She felt ill.

"How do you know so much about film, Generaloberst?" Chanel took a delicate sip

171

of her wine.

"I've worked with Herr Goebbels," he replied, accepting a glass the waiter proffered. "He will be coming to Paris soon to inspect the cinemas, and I hope to arrange a special screening for him." He smiled. "Of course, you all must come, as my guests."

"Really?" Maggie's voice quavered. She had met Goebbels while undercover in Berlin, when she had also met Goering. If they met again, he would recognize her instantly.

The Generaloberst grinned, mistaking the tremor in her voice for excitement. "I must insist."

From the corner of her eye, Maggie saw Sarah rise and move toward the ladies' room. "Excuse me," she said to her companions.

Sarah was washing her hands in front of a carved trumeau mirror, her bloodless face lit by gaudy sconces dripping with crystal daggers and crowns. Maggie wished she could comfort her friend but instead disciplined herself to say, "Ah, it's Madame Severin, yes?" She added a reassuring smile.

Sarah nodded, giving Maggie a wary glance.

"You were wonderful in tonight's performance."

They were both keenly aware of the only other person in the room: the bathroom attendant, a stout woman with thinning gray hair and the faint shadow of a mustache. She stood in front of a table arrayed with a silver tray of combs and brushes, flagons of Mitsouko, Je Reviens, and Shalimar, and a bowl of violet breath mints.

"Thank you," Sarah replied to Maggie as the woman silently handed her a hand towel. "And — you are?"

Good, we're both playing the same game, Maggie thought. "Paige Kelly. Here in Paris from Lisbon, to shop for my trousseau." She, too, began to wash her hands.

"All best wishes for your upcoming nuptials, Mademoiselle Kelly," Sarah said in a measured voice, throwing the used towel in a basket. "Are you enjoying your time in Paris?"

"Well, this evening was quite . . . dramatic. And I'm speaking of the events just now, not those onstage."

Sarah nodded, fishing out a coin and putting it on the attendant's silver plate. "Yes." She turned to Maggie, adding, "I'm so grateful not to be alone. When you're married, you'll know what I mean."

"I *am* having a wonderful time at the Ritz,

though," Maggie said pointedly.

Sarah's gaze flickered in acknowledgment. "Ah yes, the Ritz bar is wonderful. I'd always hoped to see Marlene Dietrich and Ernest Hemingway there — perhaps after the war."

Maggie dried her hands on the proffered towel and she, too, placed a coin on the woman's plate. The ladies' lounge area was papered in a red Art Nouveau pattern and a trompe-l'oeil mural. A velvet recamier and a pair of Louis Quinze silk-covered fauteuil chairs ringed a low marble table. Sarah stumbled, then half-fell, half-sat on the sofa. Maggie's breath caught in her throat; she ran to her friend. But Sarah had righted herself. Sitting up, she raised both palms to her face.

"Are you all right, madame?" Maggie asked, sitting beside the dancer and placing a hand on her hard, muscular back.

"I'm fine," Sarah mumbled. Then, "No — no, I don't know what's wrong with me." The dancer once again tried to rise. Then she crumpled.

"Madame Severin?" Maggie managed to catch her friend as she fell. "Madame!" Sarah didn't respond. "Get a doctor!" Maggie called to the attendant. The woman scurried out the door.

For a moment, they were alone. "Sarah . . ." Maggie whispered urgently, laying her back on the cushion. "Sarah, can you hear me?"

The attendant returned, accompanied by a robust Frenchman whose fringe of sandy hair surrounded a shining bald spot, his face flushed from too much wine. "I'm Dr. Fournier," he announced crisply, kneeling beside Sarah. "What happened to the young lady?"

"She seemed to be feeling dizzy," Maggie told him. "Then she fainted."

The doctor placed his meaty fingers around Sarah's delicate wrist to feel her pulse. "Thready," he reported. "Is she a dancer?" he asked, taking in her physique. "Did she perform tonight?"

"She is and she did."

He snapped his fingers at the attendant. "Bring me a cool, damp cloth."

"Yes . . ." The woman wet one of the towels under the faucet, wrung it out, then brought it to him. He folded it and placed it across Sarah's temples.

Sarah's eyelids fluttered open.

"Mademoiselle?" he asked.

Maggie bent to wipe a smudge of mascara from her friend's lower eyelid. *Oh, Sarah, don't forget your cover now . . .*

175

But Sarah didn't break character. *"Madame,"* she corrected. "Madame Severin."

"Madame, you fainted, but you seem to be fine. You need to eat more." Maggie and the doctor both helped Sarah to sit up. "If I may ask, madame, have you been feeling fatigue lately?"

"Yes."

"And have you noticed any breast tenderness?"

". . . yes."

"And, if I may ask, when was your last menstrual cycle?"

"I — I don't remember. A few months ago, probably."

"Well, then, madame — may I offer you congratulations? I believe you and your husband are to be parents!"

Sarah sagged, her face instantly ashen. "I — I . . ."

"I would recommend seeing a doctor tomorrow for a full examination to confirm, but . . . madame — I'm sorry, but you didn't know?"

Sarah looked to Maggie with panicked eyes. "All best wishes, madame," Maggie intervened evenly, before the dancer could speak. "I'll take care of her, Doctor, don't worry. We'll just sit here for a moment, until Madame's a bit steadier on her feet."

When the doctor was gone, Sarah felt her breasts, then slid her hands down to her stomach. Maggie watched her face run through a storm of emotions — shock, joy, fear, then back to joy again. "It's . . . I think — I think he might be right. I mean, I haven't had my period since . . . But my body's changing . . . I guess with all the . . . excitement . . . I haven't been paying attention."

"Congratulations, Madame Severin," Maggie said a little too loudly, knowing the attendant was staring. "From the bottom of my heart — I mean it." But all she could think was *Pregnant? On a mission? We need to get you out of here — as soon as possible.* "And to your husband, too."

"It's not the . . . best time to have a baby, you know," Sarah said carefully. The attendant busied herself arranging the tray of combs and perfumes.

"No, not the ideal time." Maggie squeezed her hand. "But I'm sure you'll make a wonderful mother."

"A mother . . . I never even imagined . . ."

"This is good. A good thing, a *great* thing, in a world gone mad."

"I — I want this baby," the dancer said, making her choice plain. "But I can't . . . continue dancing."

"Well, then you should take . . . time off. Surely they can call in . . . an *understudy*? So you can go *home*?"

"No, I can make it through the run," Sarah insisted. "I don't want to let anyone down."

"Madame Severin, I'm sure you will make the right decision." They embraced. "Please find me at the Ritz, if you'd ever like to have tea and talk further. Remember, my name is Paige. Paige Claire Kelly."

Sarah's lips curved at the bittersweet irony of Maggie's cover name. "Oh, believe me," the dancer said, rising with the ghost of a smile. "I could never forget *that* name."

When Sarah returned to their table, she had a resolute look in her eyes.

"Are you all right, darling?" Hugh asked, frowning. "Is something wrong?"

"I'll tell you later, my love." Looking around, she caught a glimpse of Reichsminister Hans Fortner, who'd just arrived. He was over forty, sallow, and pot-bellied. His long thin arms and legs increased his unfortunate resemblance to a spider.

"Darling, I believe I see our friend Hans," Sarah said pointedly. They still had one more act in their performance tonight. "Shall we go to his table and say hello?"

Hugh studied her face, bewildered, then nodded, reaching for the dance bag. As the two approached the Reichsminister, he struggled to his feet and bent to kiss Sarah's hand. *"Mes artistes!"* he exclaimed. "You were dazzling tonight. Come, sit with me! Waiter — more Champagne!"

Maggie was on her way back to Chanel's table when she realized she was being observed. She scanned the room. Jacques was sitting in a corner banquette, engaged in conversation with another well-dressed Frenchman. Although he nodded to his companion, his eyes followed her.

When he saw her looking, he grinned. It was bad enough she and Sarah and Hugh were all in the same place, now Jacques, too? *And what's his excuse?* She felt a sense of deep disquiet, as if a black cat had crossed her path. And yet, she had to admit she was happy to see him.

As his companion rose and left, Jacques beckoned her over. Against her better judgment, she went. "Sit with me, mademoiselle," he urged. *"S'il vous plaît."*

"Who was that?" she asked.

"A shady businessman, whom I use as part of my disguise. You're not the only one with a cover. I'm a black-market racketeer

179

in my spare time."

Maggie sat with trepidation, realizing Chanel was watching. "You look so different," she remarked, noting his gold cuff links, embossed with Janus heads. "Aristocratic, even."

"I've found that the more you look like a collaborator, the less you're questioned. Speaking of which, if anyone asks why we're speaking, tell them I'm getting you a good price for Champagne for your wedding reception. Oyster?" He gestured to an icy heap topped by slices of lemon.

"I only eat oysters in months that end in *r.*"

"As one should." He opened a tarnished silver cigarette case, holding it out to her.

"I don't smoke."

"Then you must join me in some Champagne." The bottle read DOM PERIGNON GRAND CRU 1935. "A happier moment in time, between wars, bottled and preserved."

"No. Thank you."

He shifted toward her, his face suddenly earnest. "I called you over because I want to let you know . . ." He stopped speaking.

Maggie felt a rush of impatience. "Know what?"

He looked around to make sure they could not be overheard. "I've only just found out

— and I'm terribly sorry to tell you, but — Agent Calvert is dead."

"No." She was unable to absorb the news. "No, it can't be true."

"I'm afraid it is."

"How do you know? How do you know it was really her?"

"I have a friend . . . at the morgue. He gave me a heads-up and I went to look myself. It was definitely her."

"How . . . ?"

"A fall. The death certificate said accident."

"Where did she fall?"

"From the top floor of 84 Avenue Foch." Maggie and Jacques locked eyes, both thinking the same thing: *Gestapo.*

"She must have killed herself rather than . . ." Maggie shuddered, knowing all too well what young women on morgue slabs looked like.

"Yes," he agreed simply, sliding over the leather seat of the banquette and putting his mouth close to her ear. "Bar Lorraine is still the place to send and receive messages. The best way to contact me now is to go there."

"Understood. Now that our . . . *she* is . . . gone . . . there's only my sister left for me to find. How much time do we have? When's

181

the next scheduled plane out?"

"The next full moon's June twenty-eighth — a week from tomorrow. Wait for the signal on the BBC — it will be 'the night has a thousand eyes' — and be at the airfield where you were dropped. Just give word at the Bar Lorraine that you'll be there. We won't leave without you."

She stood. "Thank you. For letting me know."

He, too, rose, then seized her hand and bent to kiss it. "Try that again and I'll smack you," Maggie warned, pulling her hand away.

"We need a reason to meet. Our cover can be that we're lovers."

"Are you insane? I'm supposed to be engaged, here to shop for my trousseau."

"This is Paris, Mademoiselle Kelly. All sorts of things happen here." He winked.

"Do you have something in your eye, monsieur?"

The cocky grin was back. "I could be your 'Parisian dalliance.' "

Maggie leaned close and raised herself on tiptoes to whisper in his ear. "Do you know how many ways I know to kill a man? With or without my sister, I will see you on the twenty-eighth. Now, unless you have anything else relevant to say, good night."

"Is this man annoying you, Mademoiselle Kelly?" It was Ruesdorf; the sudden appearance of the German officer nearly made her gasp.

"No," she said, recovering quickly. "Not at all. But I'm ready to go back to my table now."

"Of course," he replied, offering his arm. As they walked, he remarked, "You look very beautiful tonight, if I may."

"Thank you, Generaloberst. But I must remind you — I'm engaged."

He nodded. "I am a gentleman. And your fiancé is a very lucky man, whom I respect. But please — call me Christian." He observed Maggie closely. "Are you ill? You're quite pale."

Maggie looked at the table of Chanel and her cohorts. All were speaking too loudly, acting like drunken fools. How much more of them could she endure? "I can take you back to the Ritz, if you'd like," Ruesdorf offered, as if he could read her mind.

Maggie was tempted. "I wouldn't want to curtail your good time . . ."

He pressed his lips together, taking in Germans swigging beer from bottles, the women who'd let their dresses fall off their shoulders. "As I said, I'm a gentleman. And this — well, this is not my sort of crowd, or

183

my idea of a 'good time.' "

"Then, if it's no trouble, I would appreciate a ride back to the Ritz. But first, let me thank Mademoiselle Chanel and take my leave."

As they were driven slowly through the darkened streets of Paris by the man with the eye patch, Christian ordered, "Turn on the wireless."

The song on the radio was *"Clair de lune,"* and they listened to Debussy's music, both silent as the bright waxing moon above them wove its way in and out of wisps of translucent clouds. The car pulled up in front of the Ritz. "Thank you," Maggie told the German officer.

"No, thank you. You gave me an excuse to get away. And to hear such lovely music."

Their eyes met. For a moment, Maggie thought the German might try to kiss her, and she felt a fierce panic rise in her chest.

"Good night, mademoiselle," was all he said, however. "Perhaps we'll meet again — at the Café de la Paix."

Maggie offered her gloved hand. He took it, clasped it, then lifted it to his lips, kissing it with a startling desperation, as if he were drowning and she could somehow save him.

The driver opened the door, breaking the

spell. As she emerged into the cool night air, Maggie let the hotel doorman help her through the revolving door, thankful the evening was over.

CHAPTER EIGHT

Later, after an evening of dinner and debauchery at One-Two-Two, von Waltz and Bretz returned to 84 Avenue Foch.

Although their appearance was impeccable, they spoke in too-loud voices as they navigated the grand marble staircase, holding tight to the iron filigree handrail so they wouldn't stumble. The office next to von Waltz's had been cleared out; the enormous room with gilt-painted moldings was now empty, save for a tiny, wizened man with a thick beard and mustache and a rumpled suit who sat at a long wooden table. He was bent over, his bald head shining, his veined hands hard at work adjusting the wires and tightening the screws on a radio transmitter. When von Waltz and Bretz entered, he looked up and nodded.

"The English call it a Mark A II," von Waltz said, leading Bretz in with a grand sweep of his hand. "It's a transmitter and receiver in one — extremely clever. As you can see, it's small enough to fit in an ordinary suitcase — only about thirty pounds."

"What's the range?" Bretz wanted to know.

"The frequency range is wide. But the signal is weak — twenty watts at best. It also needs about seventy feet of aerial. If you were to follow the wires out the window in daylight, you would see we have quite an elaborate antenna tangle in the back garden's trees."

Bretz rubbed at his stubbled chin. "How do you determine the frequency?"

"By changing the crystals — the English terrorists need at least two, one for night-time and one for daytime transmission."

"And what about the DF?" The German intelligence service used wireless direction-finding teams, known as the DF, to ferret out agents transmitting back to Britain. The DF worked from vans with hidden antennae, camouflaged as bakery or laundry trucks, and wore plain clothes as they wended their way around Paris. Bretz was still feeling the effects of all the alcohol he'd imbibed at One-Two-Two and chortled. "Wouldn't it be amusing if the DF showed up at Avenue Foch?"

"Hilarious," von Waltz responded. "No, you may be assured we have alerted them to our little operation here. By the way" — he gestured to the old man — "meet 'Erica Calvert,' English spy, part of Britain's SOE's F-Section."

"Fräulein Calvert, you really must do something about that facial hair," Bretz joked.

"I am Professor Franz Fischer," the bearded man replied with pointed patience. "British radio expert." Fischer looked with pale eyes to von Waltz, seemingly the more sober of the pair. "I have been practicing Calvert's 'fist,' as you instructed, sir."

"Good, good!" von Waltz enthused, clapping him on the back, a little too hard. Fischer gave a dry cough.

Von Waltz looked to Bretz. "The good professor here has been practicing by using recordings of Calvert's earlier coding from Rouen — they did have the agent send a few messages from Gestapo headquarters there before bringing her to Paris. From the replies SOE sent back, it seems they haven't noticed anything amiss about her lack of security checks." He elbowed Bretz. "A bit dim, these British, eh?"

Bretz whistled through his chipped teeth in admiration. "But are you sure this will work?"

"We haven't transmitted from here yet, but our professor is so good now, it's impossible London will be able to tell the difference. In fact" — von Waltz slapped the radio operator on the shoulder, face beaming — "let's send a message now!"

Fischer cleared his throat. "Yes, sir. What would you like me to type?"

Von Waltz considered. "Say, 'I am safely installed and will commence broadcasts as scheduled. Bar Lorraine is still secure.' "

Fingers to the keys, Fischer tapped out the message in Morse code:

CALL SIGN TRV
20 JUNE 1942

AM SAFELY INSTALLED IN PARIS STOP WILL COMMENCE BROADCASTS AS SCHEDULED STOP BAR LORRAINE STILL SECURE OVER

"How do you know about Bar Lorraine? Did your captured agent give it away before she —" Bretz grinned and made a slicing motion across his throat.

"I have my ways." Von Waltz smiled enigmatically. "We're going to take it over and have one of our own act as barman. This

189

way, any British agent counting on using the café will drop right into our lap."

Fischer's message was now flying through the airwaves to Britain; von Waltz nodded in satisfaction. "This is only the first radio in what I see as a small army of shadow agents. Our Radio Game. And, sooner or later, someone will radio back the secret location of the coming invasion. Another drink, my friend? I happen to have a bottle of Cognac."

He led the way to his own office. At his desk, he pulled a bottle from the bottom drawer.

Taking in the year on the label, Bretz raised his eyebrows. "Where on earth did you find *that*?"

"A certain Jew," von Waltz answered as he opened it. "He'll have no use for it where he's going."

"And what's this?" Bretz asked, flipping back the cover on the birdcage.

"My parrot. A gift from Ribbentrop."

The bird blinked its sleepy orange eyes, then shrieked, *"Drunken fool!"*

Von Waltz winced. "He has some bad habits." He took out two glasses and poured.

"Drunken fool! Bed wetter! Nut tree!" The parrot made the sound of a loud belch and then a long fart. *"He who chases two rabbits*

190

will catch none!"

"What's his name?"

"Well, every time I tell him to shut up, it falls on deaf ears. So I call him Ludwig — as in Beethoven." Von Waltz scowled as he handed Bretz a glass. "And if you'd like to drink in peace, my friend, I suggest you replace the cover."

After a long night of dinner and drinking and ingratiating themselves with Hans Fortner at Maxim's, Sarah and Hugh — Sabine and Hubert — were invited back to the Hôtel Le Meurice for more Cognac and cigars with the Reichsminister.

The Meurice wasn't far from Maxim's, on Rue de Rivoli, opposite the Tuileries Gardens between Place de la Concorde and the Musée du Louvre. And although Mata Hari had once been a guest at the hotel, the helmet-wearing guards carrying submachine guns at the entrance were intimidating enough that Sarah swayed slightly as she approached. When Hugh glanced at her in concern, she smiled. "It's nothing, darling. Too much Champagne."

"Never enough!" Fortner roared.

"Agreed!" called Hugh, and the trio laughed together merrily.

They bobbed and swayed through the

polished lobby to an intimate, wood-paneled bar. Inside, the light was dim, with Rococo sconces punctuating the gloom. In the shadows, a few off-duty officers in black tie and French girls in gowns lounged in oxblood leather club chairs as a pianist played the tango *"Schön ist die Nacht."*

They commandeered a corner table with a pâte de verre shaded lamp and a bouquet of velvety roses. As Fortner slumped into his chair, Hugh whispered to Sarah, "You have the pill, yes?"

The dancer tossed back her dark hair and gave him her most glamorous smile. Sarah was terrified — her palms damp and heart racing. But she had too much practice managing stage fright to show it. "Of course, darling."

"Let's have some bubbly, not Cognac, what do you think." It was not a question. Fortner raised one hand and snapped his finger at the bartender. "Champagne!" the Reichsminister called. "Make it that 'twenty-eight Krug I so enjoyed the other night!" He turned to Hugh and Sarah. "Wait until you try it — you'll understand why Dom Pérignon thought he was 'tasting stars.' "

As the waiter brought a bottle to the table and opened it, pouring for everyone, Sarah noticed that the label had a red stamp in German and in French. It read: RESERVED FOR GERMAN ARMY OFFICERS. NOT FOR RESALE OR PURCHASE.

"Again," Fortner announced, raising his glass, "to a brilliant performance! By both of you!" They clinked glasses and sipped. Looking at Sarah, the Reichsminister murmured, "You have such perfect posture — you look practically German!"

"Thank you, Hans," she cooed. "One of the many benefits of all those ballet classes."

"And you" — Fortner now looked directly at Hugh — "have a straight, solid frame, perfect for handling the cello." He turned back to Sarah. "And what great benefits does playing the cello impart?

"After all," Fortner continued, reaching over and seizing Hugh by the wrist to hold up his hand for examination, "this is its own instrument, to be played, to be honed, to be appreciated."

Sarah was bewildered. She glanced to Hugh, who gently but firmly pulled his hand away. "Um — thanks."

Sarah decided to take charge. "I'd like to thank you for all of the hospitality you've shown us," she ventured, placing a graceful hand on Fortner's arm, massaging the muscles.

193

"Ah." The Reichsminister smiled. "I would hate for this evening to end. But, you must be exhausted." He removed her hand. "After such a performance tonight, I think it's time we got you home, my dear."

Sarah and Hugh locked eyes, panicked. This wasn't what they had planned. Not at all. "But —" she began.

"No *but*s about it. A dancer must rest. Besides, Hubert won't be long." As he said this, he glanced to Hugh with an expression that suggested the opposite.

"What . . ." Sarah scrambled for words, her heart sinking. "What about the curfew? I can't go alone —"

Fortner snapped his fingers, and a guard approached. "See that Madame gets back to her apartment safely — on Avenue Frochot, in the ninth."

Sarah felt real fear. "H-how do you know the address of our flat?"

"I make it my business to know many things, madame." The German's tone was dismissive. Sarah's time with them was over and she was leaving, whether she wanted to or not.

As they all rose and Sarah put on her wrap, she turned away from Fortner and fumbled in her clutch to try to slip the lipstick case with the pill, as well as the camera hidden in the cigarette case, to Hugh — but her hands were trembling so badly, she dropped the purse.

Before Hugh could recover it, the Reichsminister bent, picked it up, and snapped it shut before he gave it back to Sarah. "Thank you," she said weakly.

Hugh picked up the black dance bag and handed it over. Of course, it would be safer with her. Fortner gave her a sharp look as she shouldered it. "What's that?"

"My dance bag, of course," Sarah replied.

The Reichsminister's forehead creased. "Looks heavy. What do you have in there?"

"Machine guns," she deadpanned. "Three."

"Ha!" Fortner rose and slapped his hand on Hugh's shoulder, letting it linger. "Come, Hubert! I have a handwritten Bach cello manuscript up in my suite. You simply must see it."

Hugh stepped toward Sarah. Gently, he kissed her lips. She loved his eyes, how green they were, how they sparkled, especially when he played the cello — and when they made love. But now, there was no light in them.

"Sleep well, darling," he said softly.

"This way, madame." As the guard gestured, Sarah hesitated. Finally, she acquiesced, looking back yet again at Hugh, who watched her go even as he was being led away by Fortner.

"Come, my dear Hubert!" The Reichsminister's face lit up. "The night is still young!"

Polly Bonner was Erica Calvert's godmother. Not in the literal sense; in SOE jargon, *godmother* was the name given to the radio operator assigned to monitor a particular agent's transmissions after the agent had been dropped in Occupied Europe.

Polly was a FANY, short for First Aid Nursing Yeomanry. She was one of nearly four hundred women who worked at a top-secret SOE listening post called Station 53a based at Grendon Hall, a manor house in Grendon Underwood, in the Aylesbury Vale district in Buckinghamshire. While the main house was appropriated by officers and administration, the radio operators and code breakers used the Nissen huts, surrounded by radio aerials in arcs, dotted about the grounds.

The code-breaking FANYs, only recently transferred from their original home at Bletchley Park, were constantly receiving and sending messages — from Africa,

Spain, Norway, Poland, Greece — and many, many messages to and from France. The agents' schedules were posted on boards in the transmission rooms, along with their code names and frequencies.

Inside the huts, which served as transmitting rooms, the women sat, earphones fixed to their heads, in metal folding chairs at long tables. In front of them were receiving sets, notebooks, and pencils. First, they had to find the frequency at which the spy abroad was broadcasting — not necessarily an easy task. Then they had to listen to the Morse code transmission. It was difficult work — if the agents were nervous, the dots and dashes would often run together.

The FANYs at Station 53a all realized how safe their jobs were, compared to the perils faced by the agents in the field. Some made sure to always acknowledge receipt of the message with "Good luck!" or even "God bless you." The agents and the operators never met — that would be against regulations — but they did "know" each other. Polly felt fiercely protective toward all of her agents.

Polly, like the other godmothers, became familiar with the fists of their agents if she picked up their transmissions long enough. Polly had noticed "Agent TRV" had been long absent from the radio waves; she was relieved to see the agent transmitting again.

"Thank goodness." Polly was a heavyset girl in her early twenties, her uniform straining at the buttons, with silky, fine hair that could never hold a curl, no matter how much she wanted to look like Rita Hayworth. She had a tic of blinking too much, which she did when she was particularly concerned about an agent. She'd been more than concerned about TRV — the agent's last messages had been so hasty and full of errors. Polly could only imagine what kind of duress the agent had been coding under.

When Polly had finished taking down Agent TRV's message, she was overcome by emotion. She sent back the receipt code and then added, *May God keep you, dear.* They might have been nameless and faceless to each other, but they did share a bond.

Wrapping a scarf around her throat, Polly made her way through the chilly night air to take the coded message to yet another hut on the manor's grounds. There more FANYs in their khaki drill skirts and bush jackets sat at long pine tables, translating the Morse code into English.

"Here you go," Polly told one of them, as she handed over the message from TRV. Elspeth Hallsmith was a slim, cool, elegant girl, who could somehow make even the FANY uniform look chic. It was rumored that she'd grown up in Windsor and knew the two young princesses. "It's TRV — thank heavens!"

"Excellent! Glad old TRV's on the air again," Elspeth said in a fluty voice. "It's been quite a while with that one."

Polly left Elspeth alone with the missive so she could get to work. Elspeth had decrypted TRV's missives before and had sent them on to SOE headquarters on Baker Street with a red stamp: SECURITY CHECK MISSING. She, too, was relieved to see the agent transmitting again — but her stomach clenched when she wondered if the checks would still be absent.

CALL SIGN TRV
20 JUNE 1942

AM SAFELY INSTALLED IN PARIS STOP WILL COMMENCE BROAD-CASTS AS SCHEDULED STOP BAR LORRAINE STILL SECURE OVER

Elspeth went over the transcribed message not once but three times. Again, Agent TRV had forgotten her security check. She bit her lip. Had TRV been compromised?

199

Everything else looked normal.

It wasn't up to her.

Once again, she stamped the decrypt with the red ink letters: SECURITY CHECK MISSING. Then, unwilling to let it sit in her outbox, she put on her coat and took it herself to the Hall. There, Harold Sheldon, the chief decoding officer — a grim man with dark, brilliantined hair and a glass eye — bundled it with a sheaf of decrypts bound for London by motorcycle courier first thing in the morning.

"Cigarette before we go back in, Miss Hallsmith?" Sheldon asked, taking a pack from his breast pocket and holding it out. All of the rules of SOE forbade them from discussing the decrypt.

"Thank you, Mr. Sheldon," Elspeth answered, plucking a cigarette from the pack with pink-painted fingernails. "I could really use one tonight."

Fortner and Hugh stood in the doorway of the Reichsminister's suite. "Please," the German invited, flipping on the light switch and waving Hugh in with a flick of his hand.

Hugh commanded his legs to move forward, entering the room reluctantly. His eyes darted, taking in the décor and the layout. But the beauty of the antique boiserie, as well as the gueridons and bergères, was lost on him.

Fortner closed and locked the doors with a series of sharp clicks that caused Hugh's heart to pound. Clenching his fists, he kept his back to Fortner, staring toward the window draped with blackout curtains.

The Reichsminister wasted no time. He strode up behind Hugh and spun him around. They were face-to-face, though Hugh was a good three inches taller. Fortner traced one stubby finger down Hugh's cheek. "I love the arts," the German cooed. "The beauty, the passion, the abandon. . . ."

Hugh stared at a corner of the room, a potted palm in a Chinese urn the only thing he could focus on.

"Relax, dear boy," Fortner crooned. "Relax."

Hugh did his best to gently extricate himself from Fortner's embrace. "But the Nazis are against homosexuality."

The Reichsminister turned and chuckled. "Rules are only for the little people. The *Volk* — they must make babies for the Reich. The SS officers, well . . . That's often a different story. We are like the Greeks, the Romans! Although we're always discreet, of course."

Fortner placed a hand behind Hugh's

neck and pulled him forward. At the last moment, Hugh twisted his face away to avoid the man's lips.

"Don't be coy," Fortner chided, taking Hugh's hand and leading him toward the bedroom. "I'm very attracted to you. Surely you must have known . . ."

"And I'm sure your mistress is quite attracted to you, too," Hugh said, for he'd met the pretty young Parisienne a few times.

"The girl's for show. As is my wife, back in Berlin. And my five children." He smiled. "That's one of the reasons I put in for a Paris assignment — you French are so much more sophisticated about these things. You love sex and don't worry too much about who's involved."

Hugh stood frozen. Was this really going to happen? Was he really going to go through with this?

Fortner whispered, "Take off your clothes."

Hugh let the Nazi kiss him. He did his best to switch his feelings off. It was a job. Sarah had been prepared to do it. Hadn't he even told her she had to, for the good of all? Once Fortner was asleep, he could get to the files . . .

"Ah, now you're getting in the spirit —"

"No! Stop it!" Hugh pushed at Fortner's

bulk. "Stop! Get off of me!" Without thinking, Hugh kneed the German in the groin. Fortner groaned, grabbed himself, and bent over.

And then came the jolt, the shock. Hugh closed his eyes in defeat.

When he'd caught his breath, Fortner straightened, eyes locked on Hugh. He reached over to the top drawer of the bed table near him and pulled out a Luger pistol.

Hugh hadn't just rejected Fortner, he'd done it in *English* — and blown his cover.

The instruction given at Beaulieu to SOE agents going abroad was that, if they were caught, they were to say nothing to the Gestapo for the first forty-eight hours. That way, everyone in the compromised agent's circuit would have time to move to new safe houses, to cover their tracks. When the two days were over, if the agent was still alive, she or he could say anything.

Hugh knew this going in, just as he knew his odds of survival were low. And so he was surprised when he was taken by two SS guards from the Hôtel Le Meurice to 84 Avenue Foch and then up the impressive marble stairs to von Waltz's office — not some sort of medieval-inspired torture chamber. The large room smelled of coffee

— the real sort. It smelled warm. Comforting. A mockery of safety.

"Come in!" von Waltz called pleasantly from behind his desk as the SS officers with Walther pistols dragged him in and threw him into a chair.

"Be gentle with our guest!" von Waltz chided them, clicking his tongue. "And take those cuffs off — we don't need them here."

As his handcuffs were removed, Hugh saw the portrait of Hitler over the marble fireplace mantel, the silver-framed photograph of Ribbentrop on the desk, and his hands began to shake. He rubbed at his red wrists, not only to ease the pain from the shackles but to disguise the trembling.

Von Waltz noticed with amusement. "Oh, come now, Monsieur Taillier — despite what you may have heard, we're not monsters. We're both gentlemen, you and I — and I can be quite reasonable, I assure you."

He slipped into the chair next to Hugh. "Should I use your code name, Hubert Taillier? Or should I call you Hugh Thompson?"

Hugh pressed himself back in the chair, the blood leaving his face.

"Yes, Mr. Thompson," von Waltz continued, a smile of amusement curling his lips, "we know your real identity. We know you were sent here, along with your fellow SOE agent Sarah Sanderson. We know your mission was to make contact with Reichsminister Hans Fortner, who has the records of all the major French auto manufacturers collaborating with the Nazis."

Hugh swallowed, his mouth dry, realizing he'd been betrayed. "Do you have a spy in London?" he asked. "Or here, in Paris?"

Von Waltz ignored his questions. "Would you like some water?" he asked solicitously, then nodded to one of the SS. "Go get our friend a glass." He turned back to Hugh. "My colleague at the Meurice says you were with Reichsminister Fortner in his suite. Let me guess — Sarah Sanderson was supposed to be the 'honey trap.' But what your friends at SOE didn't tell you is that Fortner is a noted sodomizer." Von Waltz cocked an eyebrow. "You'd kill for your country, but not have sex?" The German shook his head in mock disapproval. "And yet you'd expect Miss Sanderson to make the sacrifice?"

He chuckled as the guard brought in a glass and set it on the table beside Hugh. "And they say women are the weaker sex. Not very gallant, Mr. Thompson, asking a woman to do what you would not. And yet, that is how your SOE is set up, yes? You have women doing men's jobs — that's not exactly chivalrous, now, is it?" Von Waltz winked. "At any rate, it's understandable you wouldn't go through with it — Fortner's not exactly the Adonis type. No wonder you blew your cover. I don't believe a woman would have, though. . . . They're made of sterner stuff than we are. Do you think Miss Sanderson would have kept going? And going? Finished the job, so to speak?" The mocking words were having their intended effect on Hugh.

"Ah, but where are my manners? Please allow me to introduce myself properly." The German stood. "I am Obersturmbannführer Wolfgang von Waltz, but we can dispense with all that formality here. It's quite a mouthful to say, after all, even for a German." He chuckled at his own joke and clasped his hands behind his back. "Mr. Thompson, you're at 84 Avenue Foch, headquarters of the Sicherheitsdienst, the counterintelligence branch of the SS. At this moment, our agents are capturing Sarah Sanderson, who will join us here soon. Along with anything incriminating we may find."

Hugh raised his eyes. "Sarah!"

"We know how difficult this is for you, Mr. Thompson. We've read the letters you've sent home to your beloved mother, professing your fears — of capture, of torture. Of death." His voice was caressing.

"You've — read my letters?" Letters from SOE agents in Paris to family members, as well as messages too long and too dangerous to be transmitted over the radio, were smuggled out of France by Lysander when new agents were flown in. Hugh shook his head in disbelief.

Von Waltz picked up a folder from his desk and walked to Hugh. There, sure enough, were photographs of Hugh's letters home, in his own handwriting. "Work with us," the German coaxed, in his most persuasive tones, as Hugh slumped in shame and despair. "You are an officer, like me. There's a bond between us." Hugh didn't reply.

"SOE has sent you here in violation of all the rules of warfare: you're a traitor in civilian clothes. You're a spy. *A spy!*" Von Waltz paused. "Why give up your life for some stupid, inbred, Eton-educated snob working on Baker Street? Yes, we know all about Colonel Gaskell and his F-Section operation." At the mention of Gaskell's name, Hugh started. "And Diana Lynd, as well as the other 'Baker Street Irregulars.' " He leaned over to the desk and picked up another file, which he handed to Hugh.

In horror, Hugh scanned the paper. It was an organizational flowchart of all of SOE, rendered with stunning accuracy. "Who? Who betrayed us?"

"Work with us," von Waltz urged, ignoring his question. "I'm not going to make you any false promises. Life here won't be exactly luxurious, but you *will* survive if you cooperate. Now, we're going to make use of you. You will agree to code messages for us. You will pretend to your contacts back in London that you're still an agent at large. And we will use the information they send to you."

"Who betrayed us?" Hugh repeated, eyes dull with shock. *Who else was in danger of being exposed?*

"Work with us."

"No!"

"No?" Von Waltz was incredulous.

Hugh took a ragged breath. Softer now, he repeated, "No."

"I'm sorry to hear that. But perhaps you'll become more amenable after a little . . . encouragement." Von Waltz really did look regretful. "It didn't have to be this way, you know. You're bringing it on yourself."

Hugh raised his chin. "Can't be as bad as British boarding school."

Von Waltz gave him a pitying glance, then

looked to the two guards and snapped his fingers. "Take our friend down to the basement."

CHAPTER NINE

All prospective SOE agents were warned about vivid dreams. In fact, all trainees slept two or more to a room, to discover if anyone talked in her sleep — especially in English, a dead giveaway on a mission.

Maybe it was sleeping in a real bed after so many nights on the Charcots' hard sofa, but Maggie's dreams that night were surreal and strange, a vision in which she saw Paige Kelly, the friend whose identity she'd borrowed for this mission.

But the Paige in her dream was her old self, although imprisoned in a long mirror, like Alice in the looking glass. She smiled. And Maggie smiled back, their eyes meeting in the glass. Mirror Paige held up one palm, as if in benediction. Maggie opened her mouth to speak, but nothing would come out. Paige smiled sadly; she understood, but couldn't help.

Just as Maggie lifted her own hand to

reach into the mirror, she woke.

She deliberately kept her eyes closed as she lay in the tangled sheets. She didn't want to move, desperate to keep the connection she'd felt. But the thumps of doors closing, the faint sound of the elevator bell, then a room service trolley being pushed down the hall were enough to make the dream disappear. She opened her eyes reluctantly, seeing the day dawning red from the windows. She turned over and looked up. In the ceiling's corner, she could see a small brown spider spinning a web and comforted herself by thinking of math — after all, the French mathematician Descartes's inspiration for positions of points, coordinates, and the Cartesian plane had been a fly on the ceiling of his bedroom.

Maggie threw off the cover. Shivering in her cotton nightgown, she rose and walked to the windows, pushing aside the lined blackout curtains and then opening them as wide as she could to take a deep breath of fresh air.

It had rained again during the night. Looking down on Rue Cambon, she watched a line of nuns in black pass, their images reflected up from the wet pavement. A man with shoes resoled in wood clattered down the cobblestones, while in the distance a siren wailed.

Memories of the night before flashed before Maggie. While she was heartened by having learned the location of the Hess apartment, seeing a Frenchman murdered in the street, spending that much time around Nazis and collaborators, and hearing of Erica's death had left a noxious taste in her mouth.

And, if she was honest with herself, she had to admit that, although she was happy for Sarah and Hugh, the news of their baby was still . . . unsettling. Now she knew that things between her and Hugh were really and truly over. She felt wistful — and also slightly relieved.

After a bath and breakfast of decent coffee and a croissant brought up on a tray, Maggie was ready, dressed in Nina Ricci — a lilac silk suit and matching hat, with a pointy Robin Hood brim and bright blue feather.

But before heading to the Hess flat, she still had a cover story to keep up. She'd booked an appointment for the showing of the new collections at the House of Ricci, one of the few couturieres still doing business in Paris.

She left from the Place Vendôme doors of the Ritz for 20 Rue des Capucines, sidestepping puddles on the street. It was only a short walk, and she was early, but there was already a crowd waiting outside the atelier: elegant women wearing Ricci designs of past seasons in tribute; photographers with heavy black cameras; the French film stars Suzy Delair, Danielle Darrieux, and Micheline Presle; and the inevitable gawkers.

The entrance was cordoned off by a velvet rope, where a stylish man with formidable black eyebrows was checking names off a list. Behind him, plastered to the wall, were posters of delicate paintings by Christian Bérard for a promised new Ricci perfume, Coeur-Joie, interspersed with posters featuring a Nazi flag crossed with the Tricolor and the words *L'Europe contre Bolshivisme.*

"Paige Kelly," Maggie told the man with the clipboard when it was her turn.

He looked down the list, and back up at her. Then, to her relief, his frosty expression melted. "Welcome, Mademoiselle Kelly." He nodded. "Please come in."

She took a deep breath and entered the salon. A high-ceilinged space with a gray marble floor, the room was already hot and loud, filled with clients, department store buyers, salesgirls, and members of the press. The mirrored walls only added to the fun-house chaos and confusion as a pendulum

213

clock kept time.

Around her, she saw women in smart suits and witty hats, holding crocodile purses. They burst into peals of laughter on seeing one another, embracing and giving double air kisses, careful not to smear their waxy lipstick. With fabric shortages in effect, hats were more important than ever. Maggie admired one in particular: a narrow-brimmed boater with a tiny emerald bird perched on a branch of flowers pinned to netting, seemingly just escaped from a silver birdcage. She inhaled their perfumes: jasmine, rose, civet, and ambergris, along with the scents of smoke, face powder, and, on one woman's breath, the distinct aroma of brandy.

And she caught snippets of conversations: "You look ravishing, darling!" "How lovely to see you again!" "We'll talk after the show . . ." "I hear she went to New York." "Well, *I* heard —"

There were men in attendance, too. Those in suits were buyers for department stores in Italy, Japan, Germany, Switzerland, and South America, Maggie guessed, or possibly journalists, but there were also uniformed Wehrmacht officers. *Nazis looking for gowns for their wives back home or their Parisian mistresses? Perhaps both?* Although Maggie had known in theory what the situation was in occupied Paris, seeing the reality continued to be shocking — the French mixing with Germans at a public event without shame, even with a certain friendliness. She straightened her spine, knowing the Brits would never be caught doing any such thing. *Or would they?*

The atelier boasted a sweeping marble staircase, its iron balustrade and railing made of twisting vines, with leaves and even the occasional thorn. The stairs' plush steel-gray carpeting extended into a runway, lined by delicate silvery chairs arranged in rows. Maggie found her way to her seat, which had her name written in calligraphy on a tag tied with ribbon to the spindle-leg chair's back.

"Welcome, mademoiselle." A pretty salesgirl, dressed in a fitted black skirt and white blouse, handed her a small notebook and pencil. "Use this to check off the items you're interested in."

She accepted it in her gloved hand. "Thank you." For the purposes of her mission, Maggie — who'd been aware of fashion but never as attuned to its specifics as Paige — had studied it during her downtime in Paris, exactly as she had once studied mathematics. It was far more fascinating than she'd anticipated, with relationships to news, history, and the arts she'd never realized before. The war had affected fashion, too — because of the fabric scarcities, hemlines were now shorter in both evening and day wear. In fact, no more than thirteen feet of cloth was permitted to be used for a coat and only a little over a yard for a blouse; no belt could be more than one and a half inches wide.

Is fashion in France an act of collaboration or an act of defiance? Maggie wondered. As with the ballet, the last thing the French wanted was for fashion to be moved to Berlin, to be run under German rules and regulations. And French women had vowed to remain chic and elegant, considering it a matter of national pride to maintain their looks, to show the Nazis that they couldn't take away their beauty, confidence, and self-possession.

Maggie overheard the woman next to her, a patrician blonde, whisper to her neighbor, "I saw Reichsmarshal Goering on the Rue de la Paix this morning. He was coming out of his car with his baton. I hear it's made of ivory and all the insignia are real diamonds and rubies!"

Hearing Goering's name again, Maggie caught her breath.

The neighbor, the mirror image of the first, but brunette, replied, "*I* heard he bought his wife an eight-million-franc necklace."

"Well, I was told he wants his wife to wear French couture, rather than German styles, in spite of all the propaganda about 'degenerate Paris.' My friend at Poiret told me he picks out the most lavish silk pajamas and lace gowns there."

"I have a friend at Laroche who says the same — but swears they had them made in such a large size that it's possible Goering's keeping them for himself!"

As the women put their hats together and giggled, the clock ticked, and the crowd grew increasingly restless, even as flutes of Champagne were passed from silver trays. Finally, a woman with a glossy platinum-blond chignon and a triple strand of pearls as the only ornament to her severe black frock walked down the stairs, pausing on the next to last step. Instantly, the room hushed.

The woman smiled to her audience, then spoke in Italian-inflected French. "Welcome, ladies and gentlemen, to the House of Ricci."

All applauded as the woman beamed, her arms opening. "I am Madame Ricci and

217

today we're presenting designs that we hope you will love as much as we do. They'll show that, despite the times, French beauty and Parisian haute couture still thrive."

Madame Ricci raised one plump arm toward the top of the staircase, and someone put a needle to a phonograph record. A Lucienne Boyer song began to play, and the first model descended. An elegant, long-legged young woman with an unseeing gaze, she glided down, her pelvis thrust forward and her chin high. She was wearing a flame-colored wool suit trimmed in black fur and a tiny black top hat, and held a large white card with the number 1. The audience watched intently as she promenaded down the aisle, then twirled, and posed. There were clicks and explosions of light as flash-bulbs popped.

One by one, more young women holding numbered cards made their way down the staircase in dresses and suits of rich browns, blacks, and crimsons, all trimmed in furs — Persian lamb, mink, sable. The upcoming fall season's silhouette was elongated and narrow, and, as a nod to utility, topped by last year's hats. As more models walked down the stairs, there were *ooh*s and *aah*s of appreciation, as well as furious scribbling in the little notebooks.

One model appeared in an evening gown of midnight velvet and bugle beads, with a froth of red, white, and blue chiffon peeping out from beneath the skirt. It was a poem of elegance — of specifically French elegance. *Resistance!* Maggie thought, with a jolt of delight.

Around her, the audience responded, crying out, *"La, la!"* and *"Voyez c'est formidable!"* One fat gentleman thumped his cane against the floor, while the German officers in attendance looked on impassively.

"Ah, this one should be on the cover of *Vogue*," the woman next to Maggie whispered of the dress, her pencil scratching against the paper.

"Alas, French *Vogue*'s folded," replied her neighbor.

"No!"

"It's true — the editors refused to collaborate, and then the Nazis shut them down."

The last outfit of the collection was a wedding dress, a white confection of lace and organza. As the model passed, a German officer in the front row reached out to touch the fabric, as if the young woman were a mere walking mannequin, not a living being.

Maggie studied it, impressed by the beauty

219

of the image and by the technique and hours of stitching it must have taken to construct. But did she want it? Could she see herself, someday, wearing a bridal gown, walking down an aisle — or going to a courthouse in a simple suit? Marriage was, after all, most young women's life goal. And yet, the image left Maggie cold. *That's because you need to be in love first, dummy.*

When the parade was over, Maggie wrote a few scribbles in her notebook, for appearances' sake, then, out of habit, stuck the pencil through her bun.

The shopgirl reappeared. "May we help you with anything, mademoiselle? Did you see anything you like?"

"The wedding dress was lovely," Maggie replied, voice wistful. *Don't be a fool, Hope.* "But, alas, not for me," she added as she made her way out. *Maybe someday . . .* She tried to picture who might be waiting for her at the end of the aisle. Durgin? John? Someone she had yet to meet?

First, though, I need to find Elise. And she shook her head, as if to clear it of such unprofessional longings.

And the best place to start is the Hess family's apartment.

Sarah had left the Hotel Crillon the night

before with a feeling of dread and dismay. The evening had been a disaster.

As soon as the driver dropped her off at the flat she shared with Hugh near the Palais Garnier, she decided she was too easy a target there. She made her way instead to the Opéra House. In the pale moonlight and blue-painted streetlights of the blackout, she let herself in by the stage door. She had the heavy black bag slung over one shoulder.

In the women's locker room, she had changed quickly out of her evening clothes and back into her dress of the day before, along with raincoat and scarf, rubbing at the red welts the bag had left on her shoulder. She gave the middle finger to the portrait of Pétain, then lay down on one of the low benches. But she couldn't sleep. Horrific images of Hugh with Fortner haunted her.

In the morning, before any of the staff or dancers arrived, she'd made her way swiftly to the Hôtel Ritz. She avoided the main, German-guarded Place Vendôme entrance, arriving instead via the French-only Rue Cambon doors.

"I'd like to speak to Mademoiselle Paige Claire Kelly," she told the tiny elderly man at the desk. He was nearly hidden behind an urn of orchids. "My name is Madame

221

Sabine Severin."

"Of course, madame." The little man picked up the telephone receiver and dialed the room; after the seventh ring, he hung up and shook his head. "I'm afraid Mademoiselle Kelly is not here now."

"Merci." Sarah gritted her teeth. "Do you happen to know when Mademoiselle will return?"

The clerk shook his head, looking truly regretful. "No, I'm sorry, madame."

"May I leave this for her?" The dancer slipped the weighty bag from her shoulder, placing it on the marble countertop while keeping one hand on it possessively.

"Of course, madame." He wrote out a label — *Pour Mademoiselle P. Kelly* — then affixed it with a ribbon. "Would you like to leave a note to go with it?"

"No," Sarah replied. "No, thank you — she'll know what it is."

"Should I add your name to the label, madame? So she'll know who it's from?"

Sarah didn't want to leave anything incriminating with the bag. It was far too dangerous. "No, thank you. She'll know." She swayed, feeling a wave of nausea pass over her.

"Is something wrong, madame? You look distressed."

"I'm fine." Sarah straightened her spine, pressed her shoulders down, and lifted her chin, as if onstage. "Please make sure she receives it."

"Yes, madame — I'll keep an eye out for Mademoiselle Kelly." The man lifted the bag. "It's heavy," he remarked, smiling. "What do you have in there? Diamond tiaras? Ruby necklaces? Gold bars, perhaps?"

"Something like that."

High on an exposed hilltop stood the ancient stone convent of the Filles de la Charité, an order of nuns devoted to caring for the mentally retarded, epileptic, and incurably ill. Besides the sixteen sisters, there were forty female patients in an adjoining infirmary.

The convent was outside Paris; in fact, the nearest farm was a half-hour walk, the village and the train station another hour's walk on top of that. It seemed a world away from the Occupation.

The convent was the place Elise Hess had immediately thought of as a place of sanctuary when she'd been brought from Berlin to Paris against her will by SOE. They'd intended to take her back to England. But she'd both outwitted and outrun the British agents, and had ended up, miraculously, on this hilltop with the sisters.

It had been three months since she'd arrived at the convent, and Elise was fitting in as the novice Mademoiselle Eleanor — a young woman contemplating taking the vows of a nun. She dressed simply, not in a habit, as the sisters and the Mother Superior did, but in a plain dark blue dress with an apron. She wore the same thick-soled black shoes and baggy cotton stockings as the nuns, and a white linen veil covered her head, disguising her short hair, which had been shaved at Ravensbrück Concentration Camp.

Before the war, Elise had aspired to become a nun. She'd never taken the actual vows, though: she'd liked men too much. She'd been a pediatric nurse at Charité Hospital in Mitte, Berlin, working with St. Hedwig's Father Licht in the fight against the Reich's murder of the sick, and the physically and mentally disabled.

But that seemed centuries ago, although the women she and the sisters cared for so lovingly had the same diseases and issues that would have them exterminated in Nazi Germany. Here, the women were treated with love and respect. At least for now; with the Occupation, Elise had a feeling that it

224

was only a matter of time before the "undesirables" here were rounded up and taken away to be gassed, just as they had been in Berlin.

Before she went into the convent's dining hall for lunch, Elise perched on the low stone wall of the courtyard, swinging her feet and enjoying a few minutes of privacy and silence after a long shift at the infirmary. As the warm sun peeked from behind a heavy cloud and a goldfinch's song pierced the sweet-smelling air, she prayed, thanking God for allowing her to be useful in such a peaceful place.

One by one, the sisters arrived, walking past the walls of the courtyard. They were women from eighteen to eighty-nine, all dressed in bluish gray habits with white wimples. "Mademoiselle Eleanor!" she heard Sister St. Felix call. "We missed you at Mass this morning!"

"I know, I know!" Elise hopped down from the wall and brushed off her skirt, falling into step with her friend. Sister St. Felix was only a few years older than Elise, twenty-five and plump, with daffodil-yellow hair that occasionally sprang free in tendrils from underneath her veil.

"Wish *I* could skip early morning Mass some days," grumbled Sister Marthe, behind them. Just past forty, Marthe was lanky and gaunt, with large eyes, large nose, and a pronounced jaw that some might call handsome.

"Hush," Sister St. Felix warned. "Mother Superior said, 'Let her rest as much as possible, after everything she's been through.' "

Marthe had seniority at the convent and wasn't pleased to be told what to do. "And what exactly *has* she been through?" She narrowed her eyes at Elise. "No one will say!" When Sister St. Felix glared, she grumpily amended, "Ah, never mind, I know — don't ask."

Sister St. Felix pulled open the heavy, creaky door. Inside was a large room with a cool stone floor and whitewashed walls hung with paintings of saints and wooden crucifixes.

In the dining room, the women all sat at a long, low wooden table, as the Mother Superior, Mère St. Antoine, pressed her palms together and recited the prayer, her rosy eighty-something countenance and deep brown eyes framed by her veil. When she finished and they had bowed their heads and crossed themselves, Sister de l'Annonciation and Sister Marie-Bernard began to serve lunch.

Fresh food was far more plentiful in the

countryside than in Paris, so lunch consisted of slices of thick brown bread with sweet butter and fresh cheese, and steaming bowls of ersatz coffee made from chicory. After weeks on such fare, Elise was looking much healthier, and feeling stronger. Her angles were smoothing out, her collarbones not as sharp, and her face more pink than pale.

When Elise had first arrived at the convent, Mère St. Antoine had welcomed her and listened to her story with tears in her eyes. Then she showed the younger woman to what would be her new home: a white-washed room with a crucifix and a palm frond tucked behind it, and a narrow bed covered with lavender-scented linens. For the first time in what seemed like forever, Elise began to feel like a human, not a hunted animal. While she was still not out of danger, here she had miraculously found a reprieve.

The next day, Mère St. Antoine had presented, without comment, false papers, giving her a French identity — Eleanor Blanc, twenty-four, from Paris. Elise received them, also without comment, knowing whoever had provided them did so at terrible personal risk. "In my past life, I really did want to become a nun," she'd told the Mother Superior.

"This is a great blessing, my child," the older woman had replied. "To see what life as a sister is really like. And now, especially since you have medical training, I would like you to meet our *enfants.*"

The infirmary was adjacent to the convent. In actuality, the afflicted weren't necessarily children but rather females from five to ninety-three, brought to the convent by Assistance Publique, and all called *enfants* by the nuns with affection. And Elise went to work, thankful for the opportunity to be useful.

One of her favorite patients grew to be Thérèse, a woman in her seventies with high cheekbones and a brusque manner, who'd once been a telephone operator. Her days were spent in animated conversation on an imaginary telephone, with imaginary friends. When Elise came into her room with her pills and a glass of water, she would say into the pretend receiver, "Excuse me, I must ring off now."

Today, Thérèse eyed Elise warily. "Yes, but Mademoiselle Eleanor is here now," she whispered into her hand. "And what we're talking about does not concern her. I shall ring you back when I can."

As Thérèse swallowed her pills obediently, Mère St. Antoine found Elise. "When you're finished, I'd like to speak with you, child. I'll wait in the hall."

"Yes, Mère."

When Elise was finished and Thérèse had resumed her "telephone call," Elise went to find the older woman, who stood waiting with a serious face in the stone passage. "Walk with me, child," the Mother Superior said, leading the way out to the herb garden.

They trod the well-worn dirt paths between the sage and rosemary, passing a lichen-covered statue of Mary, her graceful palms extended in supplication. The sun had climbed higher and shone hotter, although the clouds were still heavy and the air thickly humid.

"You have been with us a few months now."

"Yes, Mère."

"We have kept your confidences and provided you with a new life."

"Yes, Mère." Elise felt fear at her throat. Was she in danger of being discovered? Would the nuns give her up to the authorities? Would she need to be on the run again?

But the Mother Superior continued, "You have proven yourself. We know your secrets. Now it's time you knew some of ours."

Elise was confused. "Mère St. Antoine?"

"We need your help."

The clock in the church tower rang the hour. Not only had it not been reset to German time but its time didn't actually correspond to standard measure. Instead, the white-faced clock moved its hands in ancient and mysterious ways — sometimes slower, sometimes faster — obeying its own abiding rhythm rather than the regulations of Berlin and Paris.

"Of course, anything I can do."

They reached the small chapel at the edge of the convent's land; next to it stood the morgue.

At the door, the Mother Superior knocked in a complicated pattern, then took a heavy iron ring from her pocket, chose a large key, and pushed it into the lock. She turned it, and the rusty hinges groaned. "Follow me."

They went down a cool and damp stone corridor to another room with a lock. This time, the nun used a different key, a smaller one, and opened the door.

Inside was a narrow bed and, on it, a sleeping man. It had been so long since Elise had seen a man other than Father Allard, who gave them communion every Sunday, she gasped.

The man was young, in his twenties, with badly cut hair. A coarse, dark beard covered his face. He woke and scrambled to sit up.

Terror flared in his eyes as they darted from the older woman to the younger.

"Shhh," the Mother Superior soothed. "It is only I — and this young woman is Mademoiselle Eleanor. She can be trusted. She's a trained nurse and I wish her to look at your wound.

"This is Royal Air Force Captain Augustine Preston," Mère St. Antoine told Elise. "The captain was shot down not far from here by the Luftwaffe. A few townspeople, at great risk, brought him to us, and we've done our best to treat the injuries he sustained from the crash. But he's not responding as we would like. It's impossible for us to call a doctor — we don't trust the one who attends the *enfants,* and so we implore you to do your best."

The captain's breathing calmed and he managed in English-accented French, "Thank you, Mère St. Antoine. How do you do, Mam'zelle Eleanor?"

Elise nodded, approaching the bed. "What is your affliction, Captain Preston?"

"Gus, please. Captain Preston is my father." The Englishman pulled off the sheet, then rolled up his pajama trouser leg.

Gently, Elise removed the bandages around his calf and examined the wound underneath. She didn't like what she saw.

"It's infected." She put her hand to his forehead. He was hot with fever.

"We need medicine," she told the Mother Superior. "Morphine for the pain."

"Medication is in short supply these days, my child — morphine is impossible to find."

"I — I can perhaps use some herbs from the garden. But, compared to real medicine . . ."

"I will leave him in your care."

Elise looked to the Englishman and gave her most reassuring smile. "I'll do my best." This wasn't the first time she had cared for a downed RAF pilot in hiding behind enemy lines; she had hidden and nursed one back to health in Berlin.

She walked out with the Mother Superior. When they were through the two doors and back on the path, the older woman looked to Elise. "Will he die?" she asked bluntly.

Elise chose her words carefully. She knew Mère St. Antoine had done her best. "Infection has set in his wound, and it isn't easy to treat at this stage. He needs a specialist."

"And that is impossible."

"All I can tell you is what I told him — I will do my best."

"Thank you." Mère St. Antoine placed one wrinkled hand to her heart. "And I will pray."

■ ■ ■ ■

When people asked Diana Lynd what she was doing for the war effort, she invariably answered, "A boring little job on Baker Street." Lynd was a statuesque woman with a quintessentially English sense of style. She was always dressed in impeccably tailored suits in shades of caramel, toffee, and cream, with a different brooch each day; today's was a golden bird in a pearl-and-ruby cage. She wore soft suede court shoes, and her honey-colored hair was rolled up at the nape of her neck. She gave off the distinctive fragrance of Jicky perfume and cigarette smoke, and her accent was clipped, with cut-glass consonants.

But her job was more important than she ever let on. When she was hired in 1940, she'd been recruited as a secretary to Colonel Harold Gaskell in SOE's F-Section, charged with running operations in France. She had the ideal qualifications for the support staff position: she spoke fluent English, French, and German, and had a keen knowledge of geography. In her late thirties, unmarried, with no dependents, she'd stated on the official paperwork that she had no political views. She had private means.

And she was exacting and tireless in her work.

By 1941, she'd become Colonel Gaskell's "Girl Friday" and an integral part of F-Section. When the opportunity arose for her to play a larger role in SOE, she grabbed it. In France, as the war went on and more Frenchmen were sent to work for the Reich, it was increasingly perilous for young male agents to travel around the country; they were often arrested and searched, making capture more likely. SOE's controversial solution, approved by Winston Churchill himself, was to send *female* agents abroad, despite the fact that women were technically barred from combat by the Geneva Convention.

Lynd was a pragmatist; she believed sending women abroad as agents made sense. Women were as capable as any man, as she well knew. And so she put herself forward to be overseer of F-Section's female spies, and Colonel Gaskell eventually agreed.

She recruited women to be possible agents, oversaw their training, and pored over their evaluations. If she assessed them as up to the job, she would officially enlist them, only then revealing the clandestine and dangerous nature of what they were being asked to do.

If they agreed to take the job, she gave them their undercover identities. She always accompanied them to the airfield in the south of England when they departed and personally made the final inspections of their disguises — no English cigarettes, all clothing labels French, no incriminating cinema tickets or chocolate wrappers in their pockets.

The women, often much younger, saw her as their leader. And she thought of the agents she oversaw as her "girls."

Lynd had finished lunch at Fortnum & Mason, where she dined every day unless she was meeting friends at Claridge's. She returned to 64 Baker Street, an anonymous gray limestone building not far from Sherlock Holmes's fictional address and Regent's Park, only one of the many unremarkable SOE offices scattered around London's Marylebone neighborhood. Because of lack of space in Whitehall, Baker Street and its surrounding area had become home for SOE, and several buildings had been fitted with discreet plaques reading INTER-SERVICES RESEARCH BUREAU. While that was considered off-putting enough for the general public, the staff and those in the know called it the Firm, the Org, or the Racket, and its employees were known as the Baker Street Irregulars, in honor of Sherlock Holmes's young informants.

The Baker Street offices were shabby and dimly lit, with SOE agents passing through, often swearing poetically in French and smoking stubby Gauloises. The reception room was small, with only one window and a low ceiling. When Lynd arrived, the receptionist, a plain young woman dressed in an ATS uniform, sporting a fat pimple on her chin, said, "This just arrived for you, Miss Lynd. By motorcycle courier from Station 53a."

Lynd nodded and accepted the large envelope. She made her way down the narrow hall to her tiny office, heels tapping. Inside, she unpinned her hat, then patted her hair into shape in a Venetian mirror she'd brought from home that hung behind the door. The window, with slatted blinds, looked out on a brick wall. The room was shabby but immaculate, with a banged-up metal desk, on which Lynd had a row of flip-flop card indexes, placed next to a silver-framed picture of the King.

Lynd settled herself at her wooden desk chair, opening the envelope and scrutinizing the missives inside. They were decrypts from Station 53a in Grendon Underwood.

Her cool exterior belied the stab of fear

she felt. Lynd had the ominous feeling that F-Section's agent Erica Calvert, known as TRV, was compromised.

When Maggie Hope, who'd worked as a receptionist in the office for a time in January, had alerted her and Colonel Gaskell to the missing security checks, he wasn't concerned. "Tell Agent Calvert to be more careful next time!" he'd bellowed, putting the spy's mistake down to stress and exhaustion.

Lynd had done just that. However, as time had gone on and more messages had come to her with the worrying red stamp, she became increasingly concerned about one of her "girls." Now the latest decrypt read:

CALL SIGN TRV
20 JUNE 1942

AM SAFELY INSTALLED IN PARIS STOP WILL COMMENCE BROAD-CASTS AS SCHEDULED STOP BAR LORRAINE STILL SECURE OVER

While the message was unexceptional, at the bottom, stamped in red ink, were the words SECURITY CHECK MISSING. Lynd stared.

Again, there was every indication that

Agent Calvert had been captured. And now, the message mentioned a specific place, Bar Lorraine. If the Gestapo knew about the café, any and all SOE agents who went there would inevitably be compromised.

She carried the communiqué to Colonel Gaskell's office.

"What the devil is it now?" he rumbled from behind his paper-stacked desk when she knocked on his closed door. A short, round man with thinning pale hair, Colonel Harold Gaskell had a fleshy, shining face, red with rosacea. Although he'd served in the British Army's Intelligence Corps as a doctor at the war's outbreak, he'd been evacuated from Dunkirk in early June 1940 and posted to London. Despite the fact that he was in charge of F-Section, he had no firsthand knowledge of, or training in, guerrilla warfare.

"Ah, Miss Lynd," Gaskell amended in a milder tone on seeing her. "What do you have there?"

"Another decrypt from Agent Calvert, Colonel. She's missed the security check yet again, and one of our girls at 53a caught it. The message says she's in Paris now and that Bar Lorraine is still operational."

"Good, good." Gaskell ran his hands through what was left of his hair.

"Sir, she left off her security check."

"She's probably hurrying to use the radio and sign off."

Lynd spoke carefully as she handed him the decrypt. "But, sir, we've already admonished her a number of times —"

Gaskell looked it over, gnawing on his left index finger. "Miss Lynd, do I need to explain yet again the realities of being an agent? It's nothing like the classroom. Who thinks about a security check when the Nazis are in hot pursuit?"

Lynd bit her tongue. She knew Colonel Gaskell had gotten his job through the old boy network, because he was an Eton alumnus. She felt he was woefully underprepared for the responsibility.

"Don't think too much, Miss Lynd!" She heard the unspoken words: *I still haven't signed off on those papers you need.*

"Yes, sir."

"What about Calvert's package?"

"She didn't mention it, sir."

"I received word from the top brass that package is more urgent than ever. We must recall her — *now.* Have Raoul give her word and get her back on the next Lysander. Let's see, the next full moon, that's — ?"

"In a week, sir."

"So, let's get on with it then. Get her and

her package back to Blighty posthaste."

"Sir, if her radio is indeed compromised and if we send them a message about the package, that may alert them to something she might have hidden —"

"Zounds, woman, stop your fussing!" Gaskell pounded a fist on his desk for emphasis. "Get Calvert on that plane! That's an order!"

Lynd wrote out a message to be sent to Raoul — code name for Jean-George Dubois, Air Movements Officer for SOE, known in France as Jacques Lebeau.

But she did so reluctantly, with a growing feeling of dread. What had happened to Agent Calvert? Not acknowledging even the possibility that an agent could have been compromised and captured was a horrible mistake, heading toward an even more tragic end.

Still, Lynd followed her orders. She had to. She didn't think Colonel Gaskell was stupid, not exactly. *Unburdened by brains* was how she thought of him and men of his ilk in the privacy of her own mind. And yet, Gaskell held total power over her.

She had lived a luxurious life in Bucharest. Raised by English nannies, she'd been brought up speaking French, English, and

German, in addition to Romanian. But by the 1930s, Fascism had risen to power, and the ultranationalist anti-Semitic movement, the Iron Guard, seized control of the government. In 1937, Miriam Rose Horowitz, age thirty-three, had fled to England — and then, on September 3, 1939, England declared war. By the end of that year, Romania had become an ally of Nazi Germany, and Miriam Horowitz, now known as Diana Lynd, was a citizen of Romania — what Britain now considered a "hostile territory." To avoid being sent to an internment camp, she hid the country of her birth.

One of the few people who knew Lynd's true identity was Harold Gaskell. She needed the colonel to keep her secret safe. She needed him for protection. And, as she was in the process of applying for British citizenship, she needed his support of her petition. And so her hands were tied. If Gaskell lost faith in her, she could easily lose the opportunity for British citizenship — and face imprisonment in an enemy internment camp.

And if the situation wasn't fraught enough, Lynd had even more incentive not to question Colonel Gaskell, for she had, illegally, contacted high-ranking German authorities at the beginning of the war.

While she and her mother had escaped to London in '37, their Jewish cousins, trapped in Romania, were in grave danger. Lynd had intervened on their behalf, making an extraordinary venture to Holland a year later, when she heard they'd been threatened with deportation to a concentration camp. She had traveled alone through Nazi-occupied Holland and into Belgium to bargain for their freedom. A large amount of money had changed hands, and they were saved from the camp.

While she had had absolutely no contact with the Germans afterward, that one incident, if exposed, would have landed her in grave trouble. And Colonel Gaskell knew about her dealings with the Nazis, too. He knew everything. And so she said nothing to challenge his authority. Even against her better judgment.

Looking down at her delicate gold watch for the time, she noticed it had stopped. She took it off and began to wind it, relieved when she could hear its gentle ticking again.

Leaving the Rue Cambon side of the Ritz, Sarah pulled a scarf over her hair and tied it under her chin. She put on sunglasses, then took the Métro — doubling back three times — to the Marché aux Fleurs, a flower market by the Quai de la Corse on the Île de la Cité in the shadow of the twin towers of Notre Dame Cathedral. It was the best place she could think of to lose a tail. The market consisted of rows of cast-iron Art Nouveau pavilions, near to bursting with cascades of cut blooms, flowering tree branches, fresh greenery, surrounded by tree-lined walkways. The air was filled with the fresh fragrance.

Despite the scattered raindrops, men in worn shirts with rolled sleeves, flannel trousers, and suspenders sold a seemingly infinite variety of plants. Beautiful, fragile, ephemeral flowers were the one commodity so perishable that Germans couldn't ship them home. And so fuchsia azaleas in clay pots were for sale next to tin buckets of crimson and lemon roses. Sarah walked past rows of cut flowers, unseeing.

A man was following her. When she stopped to sniff a poppy, he stopped as well. In her peripheral vision, she noted he was trim and athletic, well dressed in a dark suit and snap-brim hat, with the posture and mannerisms of a German. She wandered the aisles, seemingly idly shopping for flowers, but watching him closely. Wherever she went, he followed.

Sarah knew it was over. She broke and

ran, weaving between shoppers, pushing over vases full of flowers to slow him down. Water splashed across the pavement; her sunglasses fell off. The man swore and gave chase, hurdling over the upended buckets.

As merchants yelled and shoppers looked on in horror, her pursuer shouted, "Stop! Gestapo!" and pulled a Luger from inside his suit jacket.

Sarah turned a hard corner and made eye contact with one of the vendors, a swarthy, square man with thick, hairy forearms. He nodded, and she slipped into his stall, crouching behind tiered buckets of flowers.

"Where did she go?" the German demanded of the man and the customers, gun in hand. *"Wo ist sie?"*

Everyone remained mute.

"Wo ist sie?" the German insisted.

The vendor met his glare with stony silence. The rest looked down and shuffled their feet.

Finally, in frustration, the German kicked over a stand holding cups of lavender in frustration, then ground the wet blooms under his black boots. Muttering profanities, he made one more loop through the *marché* before stomping off.

The vendor watched him go. When the coast was clear, he nodded to Sarah, crouching behind the bank of flowers.

"Thank you, monsieur," she said, picking a pink rose petal out of her hair as she rose and turned to go.

His dark face creased in a sad smile. "Give 'em hell, mademoiselle."

Bar Lorraine, on an anonymous side street, was deserted. The room was shadowy and narrow; the bottles behind the dark wood bar were empty. The cracked tile floor was crowded with small square tables. The owner, Marco Mayeux, was cleaning for the afternoon and evening ahead; the bentwood chairs were up on the marble bistro tables as he mopped the floor. Mayeux was somewhere in his seventies, with tiny, round eyeglasses, a coarse mustache, and a shirt buttoned to the top under a gray hand-knit sweater vest. Suddenly noticing the quiet, he stopped cleaning.

"Delphine?" he called to his wife, who often worked with him. Usually she was chattering away, or singing along to the wireless. But the café remained silent. "Delphine, where are you?" Shoving the mop back into the bucket with a splash of dirty water, he wiped his hands on his smudged apron.

He found her in the kitchen, bound to a

chair and gagged. Two SS officers holding Walther pistols towered over her. A long-legged and elegant German in civilian clothes perched on a stool nearby. "Gestapo," the man said by way of laconic explanation.

Mayeux, stunned, looked from his wife's terrified eyes to those of the seated man.

"Monsieur Marco Mayeux." The German lit a cigarette. "You and your lovely wife are peaceful, law-abiding citizens, are you not?"

"Of — of course, sir." The man's voice was tight with fear.

"You have no contact with the so-called Resistance?"

The blood left Mayeux's face. "No."

"You do not run a letter drop for British terrorists?"

"N-no."

"You lie." The German looked thoughtful. "I know for a fact you collaborate with the English terrorists, with one of their Paris networks." He looked to the men. "Oh, why prolong this? I need to return to the office." He waved the hand with the cigarette, creating an arc of smoke. "You may proceed."

One SS officer shot Delphine and then Mayeux in the head.

"You," the seated man said to the first gunman. "You're his cousin, from Aix. You'll be running the café now."

"Yes, Herr Obersturmbannführer." The gunman fingered the long, ragged scar on his cheek.

"You," the officer said to the second. "You'll stay in the back, with the guns."

"Yes, sir! But — won't the British agents expect to find *him*?" He pointed at Mayeux's corpse with the snub tip of his Walther.

Von Waltz stood, tossed his cigarette to the floor, then crushed it under his heel. "Not if they've never been to Bar Lorraine before. You're the cousins, called in to take care of everything while they're away. *Everything.*"

"When do we start?"

"Why, you already have," von Waltz answered, brushing ash from his long black leather coat. He gestured to a dirty apron hung from a wooden peg. "No time like the present!"

CHAPTER TEN

At Bar Lorraine, a pair of wizened men in denim coveralls played backgammon. A woman in a striped dress and shapeless gray cardigan sat in one corner, reading the paper, eating what looked to be dandelion salad, while a man with hunched shoulders played *la belle lucie* with worn cards. The burly barkeep was doing a crossword puzzle with a broken pencil, the newspaper spread over the zinc counter.

At the bar, a German with a camera around his neck ordered a glass of vermouth in French. "Sorry for my accent," he said, reaching in his pocket for coins.

"No, it is *très jolie,*" joked the barkeep.

The restaurant stilled to absolute silence.

"It is not," protested the German, his face creasing in a wide grin. The atmosphere eased instantly, and the woman in the corner gave a nervous chortle of laughter.

Sarah arrived, out of breath, and waited

for the man behind the bar to finish at the brass cash register. "May I see Jeanne-Marie, the daughter of Ora?" she asked, as she'd been instructed.

When the barkeep replied, "Jeanne-Marie's not here," Sarah very nearly turned and ran.

The right response, the one she'd been schooled to expect, was "Don't you mean Babs?"

The man noted her panicked expression. He added, in a lower voice, "My brother, who owns the café, is on holiday. I'm helping him out this week. In *all* ways."

Sarah — sleep-deprived, hungry, and heart still pounding from her run-in with the undercover SS officer — nearly collapsed with relief. She whispered, "Thank you."

The barkeep nodded, and one of the waiters went to her, leading her through the tables to the kitchen. The waiter rapped at a door three times, then opened it. Inside, it was dark.

When he flipped on the overhead lights, Sarah winced against the glare, then let out an anguished cry.

"Bonjour, madame," an SS man in a black leather coat said, his gun pointed at her. "We've been waiting for you."

■ ■ ■ ■

When Maggie left the House of Ricci, half the sky was a brilliant blue, the other dark with clouds. She held up one palm, testing for rain.

Feeling no drops, she melted into the crowd of pedestrians going to the green-and-white-tiled Madeleine Métro station and followed them down the stairs. As the train arrived, she got on, but then bolted from the car at the very last moment — watching to make sure she wasn't being followed. As she walked back up the stairs to the street, a sudden breeze from the departing train tugged at her skirt, making it flutter around her legs. Feeling exposed, she did her best to smooth it down while walking as fast as she could in her fashionable shoes.

She emerged aboveground and doubled back: pausing before shop windows, checking who was around her in the reflections, relying on her memory to spot someone, anyone, familiar. She started when she noticed the pencil in her bun. It was unusual, it stood out, and it could get her made if she wasn't careful. She plucked it out and tucked it into her purse, trying to look absentminded rather than terrified.

At a bookshop a few blocks away, she ignored the prominently displayed photograph of Pétain to peruse the titles on a table at the front — St. John Perse's *Exil,* Salvador Dalí's memoir, and a translation of Ernest Hemingway's *For Whom the Bell Tolls.*

"Do you have a first edition of *The Man in a Hurry* by Paul Morand?" Maggie asked the shopkeeper, a man with dark, bushy hair and a round baby face; he was missing one arm, the shirtsleeve pinned up.

"No, mademoiselle. But you might try Librairie Michel Descours. Do you know it?"

Maggie smiled. "I'm afraid not."

"I will give you the address," he said, writing it down in tiny letters on a scrap of paper. As if on the trail of a rare tome, Maggie went to three more booksellers asking for *The Man in a Hurry.*

Finally reassured, she walked to a gated apartment building on an elegant square overlooking a park. The building had been designed in a flamboyant Art Deco style, looking almost like an ocean liner or a Miami Beach hotel. The entrance was black wrought-iron double doors; 2B had a placard inscribed HESS. On the pavement in front, children tried to catch pigeons with butterfly nets.

As Maggie considered her options for getting past the building's front gate, dark green tanks flying red-and-black swastika flags, moving slowly as if in funeral procession, lurched down the street. She repressed a shudder.

The horizon had turned mackerel again, with odd patches of alternating dark and light. *A dappled sky, like a painted woman, soon changes its face* popped into her mind. While the tank cavalcade passed, a slight man in a tweed suit, carrying a battered leather portfolio, walked by.

As he opened the gate, Maggie went up to him and smiled. He nodded, then held the gate, as well as one of the building's double doors, for her. As a young woman dressed in haute couture, even if a few seasons old, she aroused no suspicion.

She made her way up the circular steps; at the door of 2B, she knocked. Once, twice, three times. Then, looking around to make sure she was alone, she pulled a hairpin from her low bun to jimmy the lock.

The flat had high ceilings, boiserie detailing, and honey-colored parquet floors. The foyer was dominated by a Botke painting, *White Peacocks in a Forest,* reminding Maggie of the proud birds at the Hess estate in

Wannsee, Berlin. Beyond the foyer, the Art Deco rooms were fashionable — Hollywood glamour, gilt mirrors and glass — but now dusty and unused, with the furniture shrouded in sheets. She took the grand marble staircase to the second floor.

In what looked to be Miles Hess's study, the walls were dominated by two original oil paintings: one of Maggie's mother, Clara Hess, in costume as Isolde from the Wagner opera, above the enormous marble fireplace; the other, on the opposite wall, of her half sister, Elise, as a child, standing in what Maggie knew was the garden of their villa. On Miles's desk stood a silver-framed photograph of the three of them — Miles, Clara, and Elise — on a ski lift with craggy mountain peaks behind them.

A family, Maggie thought, feeling a sudden stab of longing and despair. *And where do I fit in? Not here, that's for certain.*

She carefully examined everything in the library before going to the private rooms. In one of the bathrooms she found a short golden hair in the sink basin — *Elise's!* she thought triumphantly. *She's been here.* Maggie's arms prickled with goosebumps. It was evidence, confirmation that Elise had been to the apartment since she'd escaped from SOE in January.

Everything in what must have been Elise's room was covered in sheets and dust, but in a grouping on the bureau, Maggie found a small silver-framed picture of her half sister, dressed for a party or dance. She slipped it into her pocketbook.

But though Maggie combed meticulously through the rest of the apartment, that was all she could find — no further signs of Elise, no clue to where she might have gone.

Then, in the study, she realized the plush carpeting had recently been walked over by someone wearing muddy shoes. Someone had come in and gone to the bookcase on the right side of the fireplace.

A secret room? Excitement jolted through her. She pressed on various panels. Nothing.

She pushed and then pulled on each volume in the bookcase. Nothing.

In frustration, she thumped her fists on the wooden shelves themselves. Nothing happened, except her hands became sore.

Muttering a few choice curses, Maggie flung herself into one of the chairs.

A dead end, she realized, kicking her feet like a disappointed child. *Elise might have come back here to the flat, but now she could be anywhere — Switzerland, Spain, Portugal . . . Even back to Berlin — who knows?*

Maggie stilled, her face hot with shame, feeling every inch the fool. Her impulsive journey to France, her quest to find Elise, was stupid, pathetic — a pipe dream. Her sister obviously didn't want to be found, didn't want anything to do with Maggie.

In this empty flat in a hollowed-out city, Maggie had never felt so terribly alone in her life.

Come on, Hope, she scolded herself firmly, finally rising. *You've tied up enough SOE resources. It's over. Erica Calvert is dead and Elise doesn't want to be found. You're done. It's time to go home.*

The chimes of church bells striking the hour could be heard through the closed windows. *Bells!* Elise had once wanted to be a nun. Even in Paris, even on the run, Maggie felt certain that Elise would have gone to Mass, and most likely gone to the neighborhood church.

Maybe someone there, at the church, has seen her?

She opened the shutters, then peered out the window, catching a glimpse of the pointed spire of a Gothic church tower, guarded by medieval gargoyles.

Well, as long as I'm here, she decided, giving her nose a good blow and squaring her shoulders, *what can it hurt to try?*

■ ■ ■ ■

Not far away, at 84 Avenue Foch, Professor Franz Fischer sat in front of the English agent's receiving station, headphones on, head rolled back, snoring loudly. He wore civilian clothes and not a uniform, despite the fact that he carried a concealed gun.

Ever since sending the message as Erica Calvert, he'd been on twenty-four-hour listening duty, her former radio tuned to the correct frequency. If SOE took the bait they'd set, he would, at some point, receive a reply.

The professor jerked upright when he heard the beeps of the first letters of the transmission. Righting his headphones, he began transcribing the dots and dashes. Joy pervaded him as he worked. Von Waltz's trap was a success! London believed they were radioing their agent, on the run in Paris!

He decrypted the Morse into text. He checked it twice, then walked, as fast as his bowed legs and arthritic knees would allow him, to von Waltz's office.

He banged at von Waltz's doors, causing Hertha to call, "Professor, wait —"

But the bearded man burst in, his collar unbuttoned, his tie askew. "Obersturmbannführer! You must see this!"

Von Waltz was finishing a telephone call. He hung up the receiver, then looked up. "Next time you arrive unannounced, Professor, I'll have you shot." It was clear, despite his mild tone, that he wasn't joking.

"Have you shot!" echoed Ludwig the parrot. *"Snowpisser! Beer idiot! Bed wetter!"*

The older man, still struggling to catch his breath, set the decrypt in front of his superior.

"Shut! Up!" von Waltz barked to the bird.

Ludwig replied, *"Parrot stew! Parrot stew!"* then gleefully made a loud farting sound.

The professor waited as the Obersturmbannführer read the decrypt:

YOUR MESSAGE ACKNOWLEDGED STOP RENDEZVOUS WITH RAOUL STOP YOU WILL RETURN TO LONDON STOP BRING BAG STOP OF UTMOST IMPORTANCE STOP DO NOT FORGET SECURITY CHECK AGAIN OVER

As he read, an enormous smile spread across von Waltz's face. "They took the bait!" he crowed. "And swallowed it whole!" He rubbed at the nearly imperceptible stubble on his chin. "Now, what was Calvert carrying that is so important?"

Fischer coughed delicately. "They realize we don't have the security check, sir."

"And the stupid fools don't seem to particularly care. We don't need to radio back quite yet — but we do need to find out about this bag she's supposed to have had."

"How do we do that?" Ludwig began to sing the Austrian folk song "Lieserl Walzer," fluttering from perch to perch in his cage.

Von Waltz picked up the telephone's receiver and waved Fischer away. "Back to the radio for you."

"Back to the radio!" Ludwig called after the older man. *"Have you shot!"*

Inside Our Lady of Sorrows Church, a few blocks from the Hess apartment, the light seeped around the edges of the taped and boarded windows and the damp air smelled of incense and candle wax. Maggie passed the cistern where worshippers dipped fingers into holy water to make the sign of the cross before walking past banks of candles flickering their hopes and prayers. Up in the balcony, an anonymous organist practiced; a Franck fugue echoed through the shadows.

A graceful, white-haired woman with impeccable posture was arranging blossoms and swags of greenery in a brass urn in front of the altar, where an ormolu-framed oil painting presided: Christ crowned by thorns, his bloody palms nailed to the cross.

Off-duty Germans with cameras looped around their necks walked along the aisles, gasping up at the great vaulted ceiling and Gothic windows. Some of the sightseers knelt in pews, eyes closed in prayer, which surprised Maggie — or at least made her wonder what they were praying for, exactly.

Maggie sat in a pew but didn't pray. She was a mathematician and believed in science. She would find Elise — or not — but she was certain that kneeling and mumbling ancient words wasn't going to help. She did like the contemplative feel of churches, though. They were good places to think and reflect, oases of comfort in an often disappointing world. She smiled, remembering Mr. Churchill's take on religion and his place in the Church of England: "I am not a pillar of the church, but a flying buttress."

After summoning her resolve, she made her way down the checkerboard marble aisle to the woman with the flowers. "Good day, madame — do you know where I can find the priest?" Maggie asked, noting the red roses, white lilies, and blue delphinium. *The Tricolor — another act of resistance?*

"Father Janvier is hearing confession now," the woman answered, cutting thorns off of a long-stemmed crimson rose before placing it in the large urn.

"Ah," Maggie replied. She had only a dim understanding of the Sacrament of Penance and other traditions of the Catholic Church. "Thank you, madame."

She walked to the elaborately carved confessional and stood waiting, listening. There was only silence. Surreptitiously, she checked under the curtain: no feet. The confessional was empty. She pushed aside the purple velvet curtain to enter the small booth.

Across from her was a metallic grille; behind it, she could make out a man dressed in black with a white collar — the priest. *"Bonjour, Father Janvier."*

"This is not how we begin confession, my child," he scolded gently. "Please kneel."

She did. "I'm sorry, Father, but I'm not looking for forgiveness today." *Or, at least, not from the Church.*

"Actually, I'm searching for a woman — who may have recently visited your parish. Her name is Elise Hess — she's young, twenty-five, with short blond hair. Probably quite thin, as she came to Paris after an incarceration in Ravensbrück. She was held

260

as a political prisoner, for helping a priest named Father Licht from St. Hedwig's in Berlin." She slipped her hand into her purse and pulled out the framed photograph. "Have you seen her?"

The priest pushed aside the grille so he could see Maggie clearly, and then, after a moment, took the photograph. "This is most unusual, young woman!" he exclaimed. He was sharp-featured, as if he had fasted for too long.

"I know, Father. And I wouldn't have come barging in on you like this, except I'm extremely worried about her. Her family's apartment is nearby and she's a devout Catholic. I'm hoping she might have come to Mass here, and that perhaps you may have seen her?"

He took reading glasses from the pocket of his cassock and studied the photograph. "What is your concern with this woman?"

"She's my sister." *Half sister. Still . . .*

"Well," he said, thawing slightly, "I don't know of this young woman, this Elise Hess, but I've only recently come to this church from Marseilles. Perhaps you could return and speak with one of the other priests, someone who's been here longer? He might know."

Maggie swallowed her disappointment as

she took the picture back. "Thank you," she said. *Yet another dumb plan come to nothing, Hope . . .*

But she had to try once more. "Elise wanted to be a nun at one point in her life — may still want to be one. Are there any convents associated with this church?"

"There *is* an order affiliated with our parish — the Convent of Labarde."

"Is it nearby?" she asked, her heart lifting.

"Not too far. The sisters run a hospital for the insane in the countryside near Chantilly, about fifty kilometers away. You can get there by train."

"Father, thank you. Thank you so much. This means — Well, it means more than you know."

"Good luck, mademoiselle — your sister is lucky to have you looking out for her."

Maggie's lips twisted into a wry smile. "I just hope she feels the same way."

He inclined his head. "I will pray for you both."

CHAPTER ELEVEN

Outside the church, Jacques leaned against one of the columns, hat at a slant, a collaborationist newspaper under his arm. He was dressed well, as he had been at Maxim's — flannel trousers, white shirt and striped tie, houndstooth jacket. When he saw Maggie, he grinned like a matinee idol and raised his hat.

Their eyes met. He made a "follow me" gesture with his head. She felt a stab of irritation — she had another lead on Elise — but she followed anyway. Jacques was her contact; he must have something important to tell her if he had made a point of tracking her down.

He led her to a park, a small one — only a city block's worth of space — but beautiful, with yellow and red roses and pleached trees. It was surrounded by boxwood hedges, and a fountain in the center was topped by a statue of Joan of Arc. A few dun-colored sparrows perched on her out-stretched bronze arms while others splashed in the water.

They reached a wooden bench, greenish with lichen and age. Jacques sat on one end and opened his newspaper. Maggie sat on the other. Except for two men in tweed caps playing chess in a far corner of the park, they were alone, with only the faint sound of a car in the distance and the occasional birdcall.

"You know, when they invaded, I left Paris — on a motorcycle, if you can believe," he said softly. "People were leaving in cars, on bicycles, with horses and carts, walking and pushing their belongings in baby carriages or strapped to their backs."

He turned a page of the paper. "When cars stalled or ran out of gas, people would scream at each other, cursing, ready to kill to gain a few more feet in the endless queue out." He gave a bitter laugh. "Crisis may bring out the best in the British, but it produces the worst in us French. I have never seen so much ugliness and selfish-ness. And that was *before* the Nazis got here."

"It must have been terrible," Maggie said.

"Others had it worse. I survived. And I made it to England."

"How did that happen?"

Jacques folded the newspaper, slid a bit closer to Maggie, and put an arm along the back of the bench. "I was a pilot for Air France and was offered a job flying planes for the Vichy government, which I couldn't turn down — or else they'd send me to a work camp. So I flew for Service Civil des Liaisons Aériennes de la Métropole." He glanced upward, as if remembering his time in the sky. "I'd fly from Paris to Vichy and back. To the colonies in North Africa, to Italy. At one point, I had a layover in Marseilles and through another French pilot made contact with British intelligence. We were transported out of France via the Pat line to Gibraltar. It was more than I'd ever hoped for — I had a chance to go to England. To fight for France."

The church bell behind them rang the half hour. Maggie watched as the birds, ruffled and wet with their bath, hopped to the edge of the fountain to begin their preening, and tried to be patient. "How did you end up with the Firm?"

"I was recommended to F-Section, because I was a pilot who knew France well, and could convince farmers to let us use their fields for landing our Lysanders and Hudsons. Before I came along, they were landing in bogs. Or running into trees on unchecked fields. And so I came to be an Air Movements officer, in charge of getting all of the SOE agents working in and around Paris in and out. I also coordinate with the farmers who own those fields we use and the various Resistance workers who run the safe houses here in Paris."

Maggie had looked away from him again, scanning the park to see if anyone was watching them. "What's that like?"

"We French can't agree on anything." He laughed, without humor. "We're a country with over three hundred types of cheese. How easy do *you* think secretly organizing a bunch of Frogs is?"

Maggie snorted. Jacques turned to her, and their eyes met. "What did *you* do before the war?" he asked, suddenly serious.

"I was a student. And then a secretary. And then a tutor." *No need to say to whom.* "Why aren't you flying now?"

"The people in the Firm — they want me on the ground. Organizing." He gave her a sardonic grin. "My parents died before the war. Perhaps they were lucky." He shook his head. "But I will continue to fight, to my last breath. My country is still at war with Germany, even if it looks like we've surrendered. Pétain and the generals have given

266

up, but the people have not. The war is still being fought, in the shadows. The Boche may have won this skirmish, but they have not won the war — and they will never win this war."

Maggie was moved by the fervor in his voice. Across the park, she could see a boy, dressed in raggedy clothes, searching through garbage bins.

She felt a sudden flash of hot shame. How could she wear such frivolous clothes in an occupied country? She knew she and Jacques looked like comfortable and well-fed collaborators. There were two versions of Paris, she realized. Versions that existed simultaneously, like Notre Dame and its rippling reflection in the Seine, like yin and yang — collaborator and resister. She bit her lip and tucked one ankle tightly behind the other.

A flock of ducks swooped down and landed on the grass, quacking and strutting, the drakes with their vivid purple sashes and iridescent heads waddling after the more dowdy hens. The boy at the garbage bins turned and smiled, taking a small slingshot from his pocket. He whistled to the ducks as he crept up to them, as softly as he could in his wood-soled shoes. "Hello my lovely L'Orange," he called, taking aim. "Come here, dear Salmis, darling Confit!" He had the face of a child and the eyes of an old man.

"And you," Jacques asked. "How are you faring in Paris?"

"This Paris" — Maggie gestured with one hand to the park, to the boy hunting ducks — "this is not the real Paris, the Paris I love. The one I knew before the war. That part is hidden now. And the rest — well, it makes me sick."

"I know. Me, too."

"So why did you need to talk to me —" But before she could finish, a group of Germans in uniform began to file in with instrument cases — a lunchtime brass band. As an officer carrying a trombone case passed by, Jacques slid across the bench to Maggie and kissed her — hiding their faces.

She found she didn't mind. As they drew apart, his hand caressed her cheek, and for a moment she savored the human contact. When she opened her eyes, she saw he was smiling. They stayed that way, gazing into each other's eyes, until the band started tuning. A cacophony of notes broke the stillness.

"I hate these bands," Jacques said abruptly, pulling away. "Nothing like our beautiful French music." Nazi officers were streaming in, wearing their various uniforms — green, gray, the grim black of the SS. They looked almost like actors in a play. But their "costumes," unlike those of the theater or the colors of a sports team, were reminders of a deadly moral order.

Maggie wasn't fooled by their posturing and ludicrous collections of badges and medals. One might secretly laugh at Hitler and his disciples, with their goose stepping and their shouting, but, as German philosophers long before the Nazis might have argued, abstract evil did not choose the form in which it emerged in the particular.

An off-duty German, a Teuton with close-cropped blond hair and a peachy complexion, ridiculous-looking in a paint-stained smock and black beret, began setting up a canvas on an easel. "Did you actually need me for something? If not, I have to go," Maggie said, rising.

Jacques didn't answer her question, only offering, "I'll walk you to where you're headed."

When she looked askance at him, he added loudly, "Really, mademoiselle, I can get you a better price for your wedding Champagne than anything those other thieves have promised you!"

The band started to play, and the birds

scattered. "I can come with you," Jacques said. "Wherever you're going."

"No — this is my mission. I need to do it alone."

A shadowy cloud passed overhead and a sun shower began, the raindrops marking dark spots on Maggie's ensemble. She knew a bit more about this man now, but still so little. *Perhaps this is what happens in wartime,* she thought. *There are few rules, after all.* She blinked away a raindrop that had fallen in her eye, like a cold tear.

The gritty streets of Paris with their compressed dust gave off a sort of shimmer when the sun hit them at a certain angle. Finally, she and Jacques reached the shadowed edge of the Place Vendôme. A man in a cap played the accordion, a cat perched on a ragged blanket at his feet; a passing Nazi soldier said *"Bonjour"* as he dropped a coin in the man's basket. The musician looked up with a wide, acquiescing smile, which vanished as soon as the German strode on.

"I'll go the rest of the way alone," she told Jacques.

"As you wish." He stepped closer.

She had the feeling he might try to kiss her again. She wanted him to — and yet it was wrong. Definitely wrong.

"Lovely to see you, mademoiselle," was all he said, stepping back. "Please keep me in mind for that Champagne." He turned on his heel and strode away, buttoning up his jacket against the rain.

Maggie ran to the revolving door of the Ritz, only now realizing the risks she'd just taken. The meeting about nothing in the park, the kiss, revealing real information about herself — it was all foolish for a spy, for an English spy in occupied Paris. And yet part of her wanted to find out if she could manage to see him again.

The man known as Gibbon shivered as the rain eased and the swirling breeze picked up. With his hat pulled low and collar turned up, he set off through the streets of Paris, documents in a courier packet tucked inside his buttoned jacket.

Looking both ways and satisfied he wasn't being tailed, he turned in to a glass-covered Belle Époque arcade, looked both ways again, then ducked into a stairwell. Taking the worn marble stairs two at a time, he climbed to the third-floor landing. Looking around, he rapped at one of the black doors, using its brass knocker in the shape of a two-headed snake.

A man opened the door. He was plump,

with a doughy face and glossy platinum hair brushed back without a part and wore a dark suit and a burgundy silk bow tie. He nodded when he recognized Gibbon, then stepped aside to let him enter.

The flat was unfurnished and shadowy. Any light from the windows was blocked out with taped-up newspapers. The living area was empty, except for a table, a chair, and a large black camera clamped to a wooden desk. The photographer's mono-light had a silver metallic interior, to reflect the light and increase brightness.

The man with the bright hair sat at the table, then held out his hand. Gibbon unbuttoned his rain-speckled jacket and took out the courier packet.

The seated man nodded. "Our boss wants to speak to you," he said in German-inflected French, as he took the packet.

"When?"

"As soon as I'm done photographing the mail. There will be an unmarked car waiting outside. When the door opens, get in."

A look of fear crossed the agent's face. "Where will it take me?"

The German centered the first document in the bright beam of light. He picked up the camera and squinted through the eye-hole before he pressed the button. "Avenue

Foch, of course."

"But what if I'm spotted?"

"The car will go all the way up the drive — you'll use the servants' back entrance."

At the Ritz, Maggie changed into a plain cotton dress, raincoat, and sensible shoes before heading to the convent. It was her last chance to try to find Elise.

Still, she wanted to check in at the Place Vendôme front desk before she left. She had a distinct feeling Sarah might have tried to get in touch. She half-smiled, remembering Scotland Yard's Detective Chief Inspector Durgin and all his talk of listening to "the gut." Still, the DCI had been right, and she had the nagging worry that, somehow, Sarah needed her. *"Bonjour, monsieur,"* she said to the man with the thick, tortoiseshell framed glasses. "Do you have anything for me?"

The receptionist looked at the cubbies behind him and saw nothing in the K cubby, then checked underneath the desk for any packages. "I'm so sorry, Mademoiselle Kelly," he told her. "Were you expecting something?"

"No, no," Maggie replied. *Gut? I must be getting paranoid.*

There were florists arranging massive banks of flowers around the lobby, even

273

more than usual. "Is something special going on?" she asked.

"There's a ball tomorrow evening," he replied. "A masked ball. Given by Reichsmarshal Hermann Goering. Didn't you receive an invitation, mademoiselle? All the hotel's guests are expected."

A party with Goering? Who would remember me from Berlin? No — no thank you. "As you know, I only recently checked in," she replied, hoping the bespectacled man couldn't hear the quaver in her voice.

"Well, if you're a guest of the hotel, you simply *must* come," said a woman in a smart suit and ropes of pearls passing by, leading an overweight poodle with an equally bejeweled collar. "After all, it's the event of the season!"

The sanitation truck rumbled noisily down Avenue Foch, stopping regularly to pick up each elegant building's trash. As Voltaire parked, Reiner opened the huge metal back doors, bracing himself against whatever insulting new odors he might encounter. Nodding to the German guards on duty, who waved him through, Reiner made his way on a side walkway to the back of Number 84, where the building's metal trash cans were neatly lined up. He dragged

274

them back, struggling to empty the contents into the truck. When they were all empty, he hoisted the last two onto his shoulders and made his way back to return them.

Later, at the dump, they would dig through the garbage until they found the trash from the Sicherheitsdienst offices and sifted through it — everything from coffee grounds and half-eaten pastries to discarded documents. They would report any important findings to F-Section via courier.

As Reiner wrestled the empty bins back into their row, a man dressed in civilian clothes cut through the garden. The man looked both ways, then approached the servants' entrance. His eyes slipped over Reiner in his overalls and cap. The agent felt a jolt of recognition but made sure to keep his head down, spending extra time lining up the cans perfectly as the other man knocked at the door and waited to enter.

Pulling his cap low, Reiner positioned himself to take a good look at the man's face.

Yes, he was absolutely sure: it was Raoul, another SOE agent working in Paris.

Who was now being warmly welcomed to the heart of the counterespionage division of Sicherheitsdienst.

"Gibbon!" von Waltz called. "Come in!" He stood. "Take Monsieur Gibbon's coat and hat, Fräulein Schmidt! And put on the coffee! Pastries, too — those delicious chestnut ones if we have them." The German clapped the Frenchman on the back with genuine affection. "It's good to see you again, my friend. It's been far, far too long." He pointed the agent toward the chairs in front of the fireplace.

Gibbon looked around, took a seat, and gave a low whistle. "Nice office you have here. Who would have thought back in Spain that someday you'd be a bigwig in Paris?"

"Ah, those were the days, my friend! Remember Madrid? The drinking, the *señoritas* . . . The Spanish Civil War was only a precursor to our partnership now."

"You're doing quite well for yourself."

"I've never had you here?" von Waltz exclaimed, also sitting. "Well, thank goodness we're rectifying that now."

"It's dangerous for me here," Gibbon countered. "Although I miss our drunken nights in Spain, I have no wish to be seen with you." He smiled. "No offense, of course."

"None taken," replied von Waltz. "And rest assured we're taking every precaution to make sure you're not seen. You've done a superb job for us. We've gleaned more from those courier packets to England than you'll ever know."

"I'm glad. It's not you Nazis that scare me — it's the damn Communists. The Resistance is all Commies."

"British intelligence must have complete trust in you now."

"They seem pleased with my work," Gibbon replied carefully. "But, of course, you never know." He shrugged.

"We have a little change of plans, here at Avenue Foch. What I'm doing now is setting up what I'm calling a 'radio game.' " As Hertha Schmidt brought in a tray, he rubbed his hands together. "Ah, we *do* have those chestnut pastries! How wonderful!"

"I'm afraid they're hazelnut, sir." Hertha studiously avoided his eyes by picking up the silver pot and pouring cups of coffee, then handing them to the men.

"Ah, how we suffer here in Paris —"

"Sir?"

"Thank you, Fräulein Schmidt. That will be all. Please close the doors on your way out."

Gibbon blew on his hot coffee, then took a small sip. "You have SOE agents here?" he asked the German.

"Yes!" von Waltz exclaimed. "We're using their radios to communicate with the British. I have one radio with no operator — poor Miss Calvert, I told you about her. I have just captured another agent and picked up his radio. He's in the basement being 'persuaded' to cooperate. And his partner's on her way. And already I've radioed our friends in England for more agents — with yet more radios!" He looked up with reverence at the painting of Hitler. "They will undoubtedly be flying in with the next full moon."

"Well that's . . . new," Gibbon ventured. "But if the Gestapo shows up at the airfield, the English will get wise to what you're doing. They'll stop the missions."

"Oh, we will be much more circumspect than that. We'll watch them land, then trail them to their safe houses. We'll follow them as they go about their business in Paris. Like wolves, we'll pick off the weakest. It will look natural. Inevitable. Besides" — von Waltz leaned back, crossing his legs — "what do you care?"

"I don't want to be caught, is all. I only signed on for letting you photograph the mail," Gibbon answered. "I didn't agree to turning over British agents."

"What is that British expression? 'In for a penny, in for a pound'?" Von Waltz grinned. "Oh, don't worry — we need you too much to ever betray you." He took a bite of his pastry. "Oh, delicious!"

Gibbon nodded, keeping his expression blank. He lowered his coffee cup to the saucer with a clink.

"At some point, perhaps even already, a crucial decision will be made by the Allies about where and when the invasions will take place," von Waltz continued, taking another bite.

"The spies sent over don't know that — they're deliberately kept in the dark."

"For now. But at some point, they'll be asked to prepare," von Waltz replied, wiping whipped cream off his upper lip with a napkin. "There will be details — when and where. That is our endgame: to obtain that information. As they say here, *Petit a petit, l'oiseau fait son nid — Little by little, the bird makes its nest.*"

"Do you ever worry that they might figure out your trap? Then play you at your own game?"

"Oh, no, never. Our English gentlemen friends would *never* knowingly drop an agent into an enemy trap. Their sense of fair play prohibits it. Above all else, the British are honorable." Von Waltz smiled and held out the plate of pastries. "Come now, these are marvelous. You simply *must* have one."

Gibbon shook his head, then asked, "By the way, what's in the cage? Under the cover?"

Von Waltz grimaced, a fleck of powdered sugar on his chin. "Don't ask."

It was impossible to know the hour in the basement of 84 Avenue Foch. The interrogation room was dim and stank of mildew and the faint metallic tang of blood. The walls were stone, and there was a drain in the middle of the concrete floor. Two muscular men, their denim shirts soaked with sweat, stood in the shadows.

Hugh Thompson stood under one of the fluorescent lights. He was naked. His hands were cuffed above his head, bound by chains leading from hooks on the ceiling. He was bleeding, from a cut below his eye and several on his chest. The first bruises on his torso and arms and legs were beginning to bloom, while his back was striped with long red welts.

A third man, stocky and dark, with the body of a boxer, circled him. "We know who you are, Hubert Taillier — or should we say *Hugh Thompson*, code name Aristide?" He wore thick-soled shoes, and the soles squeaked on the damp floor. The only other sound in the room was Hugh's ragged breathing.

The man continued. "We know you're working for SOE in F-Section, for the Prosper network. We know you and your partner, Sarah Sanderson, targeted Reichsminister Hans Fortner to steal information on the French automobile industry's assistance in Nazi weapons production, so you could prepare SOE sabotage targets. And we know you compromised yourself before you were able to obtain any information from Reichsminister Fortner."

Hugh grimaced; the knowledge that he himself had betrayed his cause, betrayed Sarah, hurt far worse than any of the blows the men had inflicted.

The interrogator lifted the Englishman's chin gently, with one finger. "What we want is for you to work with us. Do that, and this will all go away. You will be given a bath, clean clothes. Decent meals. And when this wretched, futile war is over, we will give you the name of the person in your organization who betrayed you."

Hugh looked away. "Piss off."

The stocky man nodded, and one of the men from the shadows flung a bucket of cold water at the naked Englishman. As Hugh struggled in his bonds against the icy spray, the man said, "Work with us, Mr. Thompson."

Hugh spat and shook his head, breathing hard. The water dripped down his face, mixing with blood.

The man backhanded the Englishman with all his considerable might. Hugh staggered and swayed in his chains, groaning low in his throat. With a look of disgust, the man gestured to the others. "Continue!"

They picked up rubber truncheons.

CHAPTER TWELVE

As Gibbon was shown out through the back, into a waiting unmarked sedan, von Waltz watched Avenue Foch from his window. Children played hide-and-seek on the *contre-allée,* their nursemaids overseeing prams and picnic baskets. Finally, a long, glossy Mercedes pulled up to the sidewalk.

The Obersturmbannführer clapped his hands in delight. "Another guest!" he called out cheerily. "More coffee, Fräulein Schmidt!" She narrowed her eyes, but rose to do his bidding.

"More coffee!" Ludwig gabbled. *"More coffee!"*

"Shut. Up!" Von Waltz yanked the curtain down over the bird's cage.

Ludwig managed, *"Snowpisser! Beer idiot! Bed wetter!"* before he quieted again in the darkness.

Two uniformed SS agents climbed the staircase with Sarah in front of them, pushing her with the tips of their guns. Her head was covered by a sack, her hands bound behind her. When they reached the second floor, they shoved her into von Waltz's office. She stumbled and fell.

Von Waltz eyed the two officers. Both looked the worse for wear. One had ugly red gouges down his cheeks, while the other's hand was bound in a bloody handkerchief.

"Gentlemen," he inquired. "What happened?"

The first SS officer poked the barrel of his gun into Sarah's ribs. "She scratches, Obersturmbannführer."

The second grimaced. "And bites."

"Lift her up." As they did, von Waltz sighed. "Well, remove the hood and untie her hands. Let's see our little hellcat." They removed the covering, revealing Sarah — eyes wild, lips chapped, hair snarled. A bruise bloomed on one cheek.

"Ah." Von Waltz eyed her. "You must be Madame Sabine Severin." He smiled. "Or should I say — Sarah Sanderson? We've been waiting for you, Miss Sanderson. We're well aware the British are recruiting and using women as terrorists in Europe. Colonel Gaskell of Special Operations Executive has no shame."

She stared at him, but said nothing.

"We know how frightened you've been," von Waltz continued in honeyed tones, approaching her slowly, as one would a cornered wild animal. "You confessed as much in your letters home to your mother. She lives where? Ah, yes — Liverpool. You're a long way from home, Miss Sanderson."

Sarah's eyes darted around the office; she recoiled when she saw the painting of Hitler.

"We know about SOE. We know about Sir Frank Nelson and Lord Selborne and Sir Charles Hambro. We know about Colonel Gaskell and F-Section. We also know about your paramilitary training at Arisaig House, about parachute school at Fulshaw Hall, about 'finishing school' in Beaulieu."

Sarah schooled her face.

"We have a friend of yours here in custody as well — Hugh Thompson." The Obersturmbannführer gave a sugary smile and paused. "Mr. Thompson has been rather . . . uncooperative. First with Hans Fortner and now with us."

Sarah's chest rose with a sharp intake of breath, but she refused to give von Waltz the satisfaction of an outburst. "I have nothing to say to you," she said, haughty as a princess despite her bound hands and bruises. "You represent everything I de-

285

spise."

Von Waltz pressed his lips together and knit his eyebrows in a facsimile of sympathy. "Work with us, Miss Sanderson. Work with us and you will live. Not only that, but you will live fairly well. And your Mr. Thompson, too."

Sarah said nothing.

"You'll make me do things I dislike by not cooperating," he mused. "I'm *your* victim, really. Miss Sanderson, I will ask you one more time: work with us."

Her gaze held steady, and she said in her best Liverpudlian accent, "Fuck you."

Von Waltz raised his hand as if to slap her, then dropped it. "We have your radio." Impatience crept into his tone. "We found it in your apartment. In a perfect world, we would like you to send a few messages for us, back to England."

"And I'd like to dance Giselle, but that's not happening either, is it?"

Von Waltz's manicured hands clenched. "Take this woman to the basement!"

Elise Hess had been busy in the convent's herb gardens and kitchen, preparing medicines for the English captain: echinacea tincture to reduce swelling and calendula ointment to heal infection. She returned to

286

the pilot's room with fresh bandages and her concoctions, as well as a vase of roses. When she knocked and then unlocked his heavy wooden door, she was surprised to hear music.

" *'Là ci darem la mano'?*" she asked, putting down her tray on a low table.

"Yes, I love Mozart." He smiled up at her from the bed. "Mère St. Antoine let me have her own personal wireless. And so I can listen to music. It's been a blessed relief."

"And I adore *Don Giovanni.*" As a conductor's daughter, as well as a pianist herself, Elise was well versed in music. She hadn't heard any in a while — not counting the nuns' hymns at Mass. There was no wireless for the sisters, as Mère St. Antoine's policy was "We should pray and not concern ourselves with politics."

Elise handed him the ceramic mug of herbal tea, and he sipped. "Ugh," he said, making a face.

For a moment, he looked like a little boy, forced to eat his greens. "This isn't a tea party, Captain. It's for your health."

"Gus, please."

"Gus." She undid the bandage on his leg and examined his wound, then cleaned it and applied the calendula ointment. "Your infection is deep," she said, wrapping his calf with fresh bandages. "I wish I had morphine to give you."

"Do you think my leg will need . . . amputation?"

As a nurse, Elise had always practiced honesty. "I can't say," she replied, looking him in the eye. "I hope not."

"Will I live?"

"I'll do everything possible to help you."

He looked away to the small wooden crucifix on the wall; Elise knew he was struggling to control his emotions. "Why did you decide to become a nun?" he asked finally.

"I'm not a nun, actually," Elise answered, pouring him more tea. "I'm a novice — meaning I'm staying with the sisters, trying to learn if the life of the order is right for me."

"Who tells you if it's right? Mère St. Antoine?"

"No!" She laughed. "God, of course."

"Ah."

Realizing that talking kept his mind off his injuries, she continued, "I always wanted to be a nun, though, ever since I was a little girl. But" — she smiled — "I liked boys. So I never took the vows." She laughed at his expression. "Though I seem to have found myself here, at a convent, somewhat unexpectedly."

"As have I," he retorted drily.

The corners of her mouth curled up. The aria ended, and, after a few words from the announcer in French, *"Ah! perdona al primo"* began.

"Another Mozart favorite." Gus looked up at Elise with gratitude. "You must be good luck."

"God is better than luck. Rest now and I'll check on you later."

Elise returned to the Mother Superior's office. "He's stable. But the infection is very bad. And it's spreading. I treated it with herbs, but I need real medicine. A doctor. In an ideal world, a surgeon."

"My child . . ." Mère St. Antoine began.

"I know."

"Will he live?"

"Most likely he won't, unless his leg is amputated."

"Can you do that here?"

"With the infection and the lack of sterile surgical equipment, no."

"I will pray for him, and for you, too." The Mother Superior opened a cupboard and took out a dusty brown bottle. "Brandy," she said by way of explanation. "Perhaps it will help our guest with the pain."

The stocky man flung another bucket of water at Hugh's face. "Wake up, Sleeping Beauty!" he called. "Are you going to work with us?"

"No," Hugh managed. He was slipping in and out of consciousness.

"No?" the man repeated, mockingly. "Well, maybe *this* will change your mind. Or, rather, *she* will."

He gestured to the two SS men at the door. They opened it to reveal Sarah, then pushed her forward.

It took a while for Hugh's eyes to focus, and when they did, he wasn't certain what he was seeing was really there. ". . . Sarah?"

She sobbed, then nodded.

"You already know each other," the stocky man interposed, "so we can dispense with the introductions." He snapped his fingers; the guards untied her hands.

The man walked to Sarah and put his face close to hers. She stiffened.

He tore off her scarf, balled it up, and threw it into the corner. He undid the belt of her coat and yanked it from her shoulders. He ripped at her dress until it was in a puddle at her feet.

Sarah was left standing under a bare lightbulb in a white chemise, shivering from fear.

The Nazi interrogator held Hugh's chin up, so he had to look. "You may be able to withstand your own torture, but what about hers? You don't want to see that, my friend, believe me." His voice softened. "Work with us. And we will spare your lover —"

"No, Hugh!" Sarah screamed. "Don't do it!"

The stocky man nodded, and one of the thugs stepped forward. He punched her in the stomach. As she doubled over, gasping for breath, the other grabbed her hair to raise her face. They took out truncheons and circled her, as though trying to choose the most vulnerable place to attack.

As one raised his arm to strike, Hugh could take no more. "Stop!"

The two men stopped. The Englishman looked up at the man. "If you guarantee her safety, I'll — do anything!"

"Hugh! No!"

"Give me your word — she won't be harmed!"

The man didn't smile. "I give you my word that as long as you both cooperate, she will be unharmed. And you as well. Obersturmbannführer von Waltz has a job for you."

"I'll do whatever you want. Just don't hurt her."

Elise knocked, then entered. "I've got something for you — a surprise!"

"A proper Sunday roast?" Gus asked hopefully. "Beef and Yorkshire pudding? New peas? A good claret?"

"Alas, no. But I think you'll be pleased anyway." When she produced the brandy bottle, his eyes lit up. "Mother Superior thought it might help with the pain."

"I won't say no."

She poured a fair amount into his teacup and handed it to him. It smelled of dried figs.

"Thank you," he said, taking it. "But it doesn't seem right unless you have some, too."

"Well, then," Elise said, pouring a tiny bit for herself into a water glass. She couldn't remember the last time she'd had alcohol. "If you insist."

"I do."

They clinked glasses. "Cheers," Gus said, taking a large gulp. "Oh, that's good."

Elise sipped, feeling the brandy's restorative warmth run down her throat.

"I suppose you're wondering how I got here," he said, after taking another swig.

"You don't need to tell —"

"No, I want to. You told me a bit about yourself, after all. I was born in Catford — in Southeast London. After a rather less than stellar academic career, I left St. Dunstan's College. When the war broke out, I joined the Royal Air Force."

He took another huge gulp of brandy, and Elise poured him more. "After training, I was posted to Ninety-two Squadron, based at Croydon, as a flight commander flying Spitfires. I was coming back from a raid on Dortmund — the factories on the outskirts, not the city itself. It was what Fighter Command called the 'Rhubarb raids.' Supposed to force the Luftwaffe to maintain aircraft in the west, helping to relieve the pressure on Russia . . ." He shook his head as if to clear it. "It was on the way home, over France. My Spit was hit in the engine. I was flying too low to bail out, so I shoved my canopy back and began looking for a field to crash-land. As you can see" — with a wry smile, he indicated his bandaged leg — "it didn't go as well as I'd hoped."

"But how did you get here? To the convent?"

"The farmer who found me in his field didn't know what to do, so he told his priest. The two of them brought me here, where Mère St. Antoine was kind enough to take me in and hide me. Although convalescing so close to the convent's morgue has been . . . an interesting existentialist exercise. And how did *you* come to be here, mademoiselle?"

"I was —" Elise had never told all of her story aloud before. "I was a nurse in Berlin once upon a time." Now was not the time. "I'm sorry, Gus — but I'd rather not speak of it."

As Maggie waited on the train platform, her eyes went to a large poster with bold lettering:

10,000 FRANCS REWARD!

Following the decree establishing the death penalty for all those who hide English soldiers or aid them to escape, the German High Command announces it will pay 10,000 francs reward to any person providing names and addresses of those engaged in this criminal activity.

A German officer was staring at her. A captain, from his uniform. Using a technique she'd picked up in Beaulieu, she stared fixedly at his feet in their gleaming black boots, allowing a quizzical look to cross her face.

He stopped staring at her and followed her gaze. He shuffled his feet, looking at them from all angles, trying to determine what was wrong. Maggie kept staring; finally, he became so uncomfortable, he moved to another part of the platform.

Ha! she thought, pleased with her small victory.

The train pulled in with a whistle and a shriek of brakes. She was relieved to secure an empty car for herself, sitting next to the grimy window. The city faded, giving way to plowed fields. She could see old men in coveralls with hoes, cows, and the flashing green of crops. She pulled her coat around her, trying to ignore her wildly beating heart.

Finally, the train arrived in Chantilly. Maggie got off at the very last minute. The countryside felt a world away from the heart of Paris. From the posted map, she knew she still had a several-mile hike on a dirt road through a dense forest. *Glad I changed my shoes,* she thought as she followed the road, scrambling over stones and jumping across mud puddles, stopping once to catch her breath, leaning on an ancient oak.

When she finally reached the convent, it

turned out to be a stone structure surmounted by a towering cross, encircled by a cluster of smaller buildings. Breathing hard, she made her way over worn paths, then climbed the steep stairs, hollowed by centuries of footsteps, and rang the bell.

The door of the Convent of Labarde creaked open. The nun facing her was very young, with freckles sprinkling her delicate face. She gave Maggie a wary look. "Yes, mademoiselle?"

"How do you do?" Maggie began. Then she stopped and took a deep breath. The entryway smelled of beeswax floor polish. *What exactly do I say?* Now that the moment had come, she realized how terrified she was of failing again. "I'm, well, I'm looking for someone." She held out the photograph she'd taken from the Hess apartment. "Do you know this woman?"

The young nun took the picture. As she squinted at it, she blanched. "Come in, mademoiselle, and wait inside. I'll get the Mother Superior. You can ask her."

Waiting in the entranceway, Maggie examined the crucifix hanging on the wall, made of rosewood and brass, Christ's carved ivory palms pierced. Moments later, an elderly nun appeared. "I am Mother Superior here," she said, nodding to Maggie. "Mère

St. Antoine. Let me take you to the parlor. We can speak there in private."

Maggie followed the Mother Superior into a sparsely furnished room, flooded with sunlight. Both women sat on a hard horsehair sofa below a reproduction of Bouguereau's *The Charity* — virtue personified as a young mother caring for twin infants.

"Thank you for seeing me, Mère St. Antoine," Maggie began. "My name is . . . well, my name isn't important. I'm — I'm looking for . . . Elise Hess. This is her picture."

The Mother Superior looked long and hard at the image of the girl in the silver-framed photograph. Finally, she looked up. "We have no one here who goes by the name Elise Hess," she answered.

"She might be using a different name," Maggie pressed. "And she might look quite different. She might have much shorter hair and be much thinner."

The Mother Superior's voice was gentle. "And how do you know this person, this young woman you're looking for?"

"She's my sister. Half sister — we have the same mother. I know she was a prisoner at Ravensbrück because of her Resistance work with Father Licht and the German clergy in Berlin. To the best of my knowledge, the last time she was seen was in

Paris."

"And why would you think she's here?" the nun asked.

"I was able to find her family's Paris apartment. At the nearby church, Our Lady of Sorrows, Father Janvier said he hadn't seen her, but that there was an order of nuns associated with the church — your order, Mère St. Antoine. I know Elise always wanted to be a nun when she was a girl. And she was a nurse at Charité Hospital in Mitte, Berlin. A convent with an infirmary like yours would be a place she'd be drawn to."

There was a long silence as the two women took each other's measure. "You must be tired from your journey." Mère St. Antoine rose. "Let us bring you some refreshment. Please wait."

The Mother Superior went to the kitchen and asked one of the sisters to prepare food and drink, then sought Elise. She found her with the injured Englishman, both of them smelling of brandy. "May I have a word with you when you're done, Mademoiselle Eleanor?"

Elise jumped to her feet and adjusted her wimple. "Of course." She followed the Mother Superior into the hallway and

298

closed the door. The two women stood, facing each other in the stone corridor.

"Someone claiming to be your sister is here."

"Sister?"

"A young woman, around your age? About your height? Red hair? She's here to see you. She knows you were at Ravensbrück. She tracked you to Paris."

"How —"

"Through Father Janvier at Our Lady of Sorrows, she heard of our convent." Her eyes considered Elise warily. "*Is* she your sister?"

"She is, Mère." Elise folded her arms across her chest. "But I won't see her."

"She says she's come a very long way."

"She's — she's not like us." Elise struggled to explain. "We have nothing in common."

Mère St. Antoine shook her head. "At least see her, child. These are troubled times. She may have something important to say to you. And who knows, you may not see her again on earth. If you're at odds, best to make your peace now."

"Are you giving me an order, Mère?"

"Of course not, child." She reached out to grip the younger woman's shoulder. "It's up to you. It's your decision."

Elise was silent.

"But if you do wish to see her, she's having tea in my study."

CHAPTER THIRTEEN

Colonel Henrik Martens, Prime Minister Churchill's newly named Master of Deception, whistled "In the Hall of the Mountain King" as he pored over files of top-secret documents. The door to his tiny office in the underground Cabinet War Rooms was cracked open.

George Rance, a former Army sergeant and head of the War Rooms, popped his head in. He had receding hair and prominent cheekbones, and his polka-dotted tie was in a perfect Windsor knot. "You must *not* whistle, Colonel Martens! The P.M. loathes it — and has absolutely forbidden it!"

The colonel grinned. "If I'm to work as a troglodyte, I must have a proper song for it, Mr. Rance."

"*No* whistling. If you please. Sir!" The older man closed the door firmly.

Martens's office was cramped, the white

walls smoke-stained, the low ceiling bristling with red-painted pipes, and a military-issue clock on one wall. The tall Welshman had folded himself behind his military-issue desk, lit by a green banker's lamp. The metal briefcase with the attached handcuffs was at his feet. A fan recycled the stale air.

Martens had requested all the relevant files transferred to his new office, and the space was stuffed with boxes of them, piled high on shelves, a metal bookcase, even in stacks on the floor. He was starting by going over all the back traffic from the agents abroad.

His first shock had come when he read a situation report on the Free French, stamped in red ink: FOR MOST LIMITED DISTRIBUTION ONLY. As he read over file after file, it became clear to him that Charles de Gaulle and the Free French were at odds with SOE — the two organizations were too busy belittling each other's achievements to learn from each other's mistakes in the field, let alone share crucial information.

Then there were the memos from MI-6. Everyone in the intelligence agency — from Sir Stewart Menzies, signature invariably "C" in green ink, on down — distrusted SOE. They loathed the start-up organization, considered them bumbling amateurs, called them "gung-ho incompetents" and the "Boys of Baker Street." In fact, one memo from MI-6 read: *It is a fact universally known that if you want to disseminate information widely, there are three sure methods of communication: telephone, telegraph, and tell SOE.*

Martens read over SOE's F-Section correspondence, noticing messages from the Rouen area flagged for lack of security checks. He was especially puzzled by the radio traffic of an agent named Erica Calvert. After a certain date, Calvert's messages had been stamped in red ink: SECURITY CHECK MISSING.

Scowling, Martens combed through Calvert's decrypts. Something else was wrong. Very wrong. At some point after the new year, Erica Calvert's went from the normal mistakes one would expect from an agent in the field, coding under duress, to absolutely error-free. And yet she consistently omitted her security checks, even after being reminded on multiple occasions.

Martens pushed back his chair and stood, banging his head on one of the low-hanging pipes. "What the bloody hell's going on here?" he muttered. There were two people he needed to speak with: Colonel Harry Gaskell, head of SOE's F-Section, and

Colonel George Bishop, head of MI-6's French Intelligence Department. And Martens could tell from the interdepartmental memos — both what was said and unsaid — that the men loathed each other.

Maggie was nervous, worrying her gloves in her hands. One of the nuns entered silently and put a wooden tray down in front of her with not only tea but beetroot sugar and goat's milk, as well as a ceramic plate with a slab of bread spread with butter and topped with a thick slice of smoked ham. When the nun left, Maggie poured the steaming, fragrant tea into a cup, then took a huge bite of the bread and ham.

Maggie had planned it so many times, her reunion with Elise. She'd played out so many different scenarios — in Paris, in Lisbon, in London. However, never once had she foreseen meeting her sister while she was chomping on a thick slice of ham and a particularly crusty piece of baguette.

And so, when Elise appeared, Maggie was unable to speak — at least not until she could swallow. She raised one palm in greeting.

Elise nodded, unsmiling.

Maggie took a gulp of tea and nearly choked. Finally, she managed, *"Bonjour!"* It came out far too cheery — embarrassingly chirpy. She felt herself blush as she swiped at her lips with a linen napkin, then rose, juggling her teacup awkwardly. "Thank you for seeing me," she said finally.

Elise sat across from Maggie. "You've come a long way to find me."

"You don't know the half of it!" Her words felt flat.

"No, I don't. And I may not want to."

"Touché."

Elise folded her hands in her lap and gazed steadily at Maggie. "You don't know me. You may think you do, but you don't."

"No," Maggie agreed. "No, I don't know you. But I'd like the opportunity to get to know you. If you'll let me."

There was a thick silence.

"I always wanted a sister." Maggie's words tumbled over themselves in her hurry to get them out. "When I was little I had an imaginary friend, a sister. Called Sister. Yes, I know — a bit redundant." She grimaced, but persisted. "Like you, I grew up as an only child. A 'lone child' — alone — I used to say. So I always had a fantasy of having a sister, even after I outgrew my imaginary friend. I always thought we'd play checkers and chess together and fight and make up and hug each other during thunderstorms.

I'd be Jo and you'd be Beth —"

Elise looked confused.

"*Little Women*? Louisa May Alcott? Well, never mind, she's an American author. Of course I always wondered what it was like to have a mother, too."

Elise raised her eyebrows. "With ours, you didn't miss much. *Diva* would be an understatement. Narcissus was nothing compared to our mother. She died, you know. I mean, you must have heard."

Maggie gave Elise a sharp look. "Actually, I heard they faked her death in Germany. And that she's in some sort of internment camp in Britain now. But I truly don't know."

If Maggie's words about their mother surprised her in any way, Elise didn't betray it. "In Germany, they are saying she's dead. That she died a martyr to the cause. A Nazi hero. That's the reason I was temporarily released from the camp — to go to her memorial service in Berlin."

"Don't believe everything you read in the news. Look —" Maggie leaned forward. "You're right. I don't know you, and you don't know me. And what you saw of me in Berlin wasn't my best. Although I will still defend my actions. However, if it makes you feel any better, I think of that boy, and his family, every day."

Maggie looked down at the low table with its tray of food. "Look at the beetroot sugar — beautiful, right? I hate beets. But I love chocolate and anything with chocolate, especially a chocolate cake my Aunt Edith used to make — well, buy and then try to pass off as her own. But still, she tried. And it was my favorite.

"And I love math, love it — love it obsessively. But I'm terrible at art — can't even draw a stick figure. And I was awful, tragically awful at sports, until, well . . . until this war gave me some pretty good incentives to improve." Maggie snorted as she remembered her original failures. "The first time I went to training camp, I washed out."

"Really?" Elise said. In Berlin, almost a year ago, she'd seen Maggie take down a German soldier.

"Really. I was awful."

"What happened?"

"I worked hard to catch up and then tried all over again. Made it through the second time. I fell in love, once — with John, you remember him. And I ruined that, too. He broke my heart, and I, well, maybe I broke his a bit. And then I really liked someone, and botched that up, as well. And then —" She laughed with practiced self-deprecation.

"It's complicated."

"I'm sorry to hear about John. I really liked him. Thought you two would be married by now, actually. Maybe a niece or nephew on the way."

I rather thought so, too. "Wartime isn't exactly conducive to happily ever after."

"True. But maybe someday?"

Maggie changed the subject. "How about you? Are you a nun now?"

"A novice — an apprentice nun."

"Do you think you'll take the vows?"

"I love God — I just have problems with promising lifelong poverty, obedience, and chastity." The hint of a smile tugged at Elise's lips. "Especially chastity. And really, obedience, too — when you get down to it."

"Yes, I can see that." Maggie pictured Elise's escape from SOE and her desperate dash into hiding. "I'd have a lot of trouble with obedience myself."

"I can see that." Elise continued, "You love math? Well, for me it was science. I used to take a straight razor to my dolls and rip them open — no, not like that!" she said, seeing Maggie's expression. "I not only always saved their lives but stitched them up, and gave them milk and cookies after. I wanted to be a doctor —"

"Before wanting to be a nun?"

"I thought I could do both."

"Doctor Sister?" Maggie smiled.

"Sister Doctor!" Elise smiled, too. "But then the war broke out and nurses were needed . . . I like chocolate cake, too, and sweets and ice cream — really, there isn't anything I don't like to eat, as my — our — mother often lamented. She wanted me to wear couture, like her, but I had too many curves."

Elise laughed softly, looking down at her thin frame. "Well, that's not a problem now. And I play the piano — but you know that."

"I play the viola!"

"We could perform quite the duet."

"I'd like that."

"How did you get here? To France?"

"By plane. SOE. The same organization that got you out of Berlin. Or tried to."

Elise shook her head. "I didn't want to be taken out of Berlin, to be 'saved.' I know you meant well and I apologize for running —"

"Please don't."

"But how did you manage it? Another mission?"

"I called in a favor."

"He must be someone quite important."

Maggie remembered Queen Elizabeth,

waving her off at the airport. "*She,* actually. . . . At any rate, I'd like to bring you back to England with me, when I go back. I have a house. And I have a cat, a tabby named Mr. K, who really has me. And my friend Chuck — Charlotte — and her baby are living with me while her husband's serving in the Middle East. It's quite nice, really."

"And what if I don't want to go back to England?"

"Then I will respect your decision," Maggie promised sincerely. "It seems nice here, removed from the insanity of Paris. You're interested in being a nun — this way you can see that sort of life up close, and make an informed decision. And Mère St. Antoine says you're working in an infirmary?"

"Yes." Elise nodded. "With mentally ill women."

"So you can practice medicine as well. Doctor Sister."

"Or Sister Doctor." Elise bit her lip, as if deciding how much she could trust Maggie. "Would you like to see our grounds?"

"I'd love to."

Henrik Martens arrived seventeen minutes early for his meeting with Colonel Gaskell at SOE offices. He was surprised to see the colonel emerge from the building wearing a light coat. "Let's take a walk," Gaskell said by way of explanation. "Jolly good day to get some fresh air."

The two men made their way up Baker Street to Regent's Park, passing John Nash's elegant white terrace houses, crossing the Outer Circle, and heading over gravel paths through lush green grass toward Boating Lake. All of the metal gates and fences had been removed — to be melted down for munitions — but the park had sustained little bomb damage and retained its beauty. They reached the "lake," which was more of a pond, filled with paddling ducks, two black swans, and a long-legged gray heron, posing on a fallen tree trunk. The paths were full of men and women in uniform; children played tag in a grove of trees.

"Stop here?" Gaskell suggested as they approached a wooden bench.

"Of course."

Gaskell caught sight of movement overhead. "Ah, a cuckoo. Most unusual. I'm a bird-watcher, you know. Wish I had my notebook with me."

The men sat in silence, the wind ruffling the dark waters under an opalescent sky. Gaskell took a bag of breadcrumbs from his coat pocket. Within moments, they were encircled by sleek ducks, flapping and greedily squabbling for their share.

"You're probably wondering why I asked to see you, Colonel," Martens began. "The thing is —" He was unsure of how to begin. What he was about to say could be considered an enormous criticism of F-Section. "One of the first things I did when I got this job was read through all the SOE agents' back traffic."

Gaskell continued to throw crumbs to the noisy birds.

"On some of the decrypts, the security checks were consistently missing. They were stamped as such by Station 53a, but no one at Baker Street ever followed up."

"What's your point?" Gaskell asked.

"Well, I'm asking you why. Why has no one followed up on the lack of security checks? Beyond reminders to remember for the next transmission — which also, invariably, was missing a security check."

"I want you to know," Gaskell said, his eyes not leaving the birds, "not only do we know all about this situation with the security checks but we're on top of it. And there's absolutely nothing to worry about, old thing."

A man in a bowler hat limped by, his glossy ebony walking stick, patterned with golden feathers, striking the gravel at regular intervals.

After he was out of earshot, Martens began again. "I don't see how you can say that, sir. Enlighten me — please."

"These agents — they operate under unimaginable stress. They don't have time to dot all the *i*'s and cross all the *t*'s."

"I was an undercover agent myself, sir. In Norway. My colleagues and I all found the time to include our checks, even in the midst of the most dire operating conditions."

Gaskell was silent. He had run out of crumbs to throw to the ducks. Disappointed, they waddled off.

Martens pressed on. "There's something else, too. There's a certain agent, an Erica Calvert, in F-Section. I read all of her messages. Her coding was riddled with errors for a while, then, suddenly, became perfect — absolutely flawless. No agent in the history of SOE has ever sent such error-free messages. And yet, none of those messages have their security checks in place."

"Women —" Gaskell waved a gloved hand. "They don't always remember things the way we do. Their brains aren't equipped to —"

"Colonel," Martens interrupted impatiently. "I believe it's not a question of *if* a French Section agent is operating under duress, but *how many.*"

Gaskell crumpled up the paper bag and slipped it back in his pocket. "You're going to have to trust me. Everything is under control."

"I can't recommend any more agents being sent to France, parachuting to their unknown fate, if this situation isn't addressed." Martens's voice became sharp. "We need to investigate what exactly is going on with the messages coming from France lacking security checks."

"And as I have already told you, our agents are fine."

"I read a particularly strongly worded memo on the direness of the situation by an agent from your office named Margaret Hope. Who is she?"

Gaskell rolled his eyes. "I haven't the foggiest idea, old chum."

"Really?" Martens had done his homework. "She worked for the P.M.? Went undercover on a mission to Berlin? Trained agents in Arisaig? Worked for your office for a few months last winter?"

"Oh, her." Gaskell didn't bother to hide his disdain. "She was just a receptionist."

"I've read Hope's file. She's not 'just a

receptionist.' "

Gaskell stood, brushing crumbs from his coat. "You'd best leave well enough alone, Colonel Martens."

Martens stood, too, blocking the shorter man. "Do you mean 'leave sick enough alone'?" the Welshman asked. "SOE is sick — and no one's paying attention. If the infection is not checked, it could poison the entire organization."

Gaskell drew himself up to his full height, still many inches smaller than Martens. "Under no circumstances are you to discuss this matter with anyone else in SOE. If you have any further questions, Colonel, come directly to me. That's an order."

Martens barked a laugh of astonishment at Gaskell's nerve. "You can't give me orders, Colonel. I don't report to you. I work for the Prime Minister."

As Gaskell turned and walked away, Martens called after him, "And remember — so do you!"

Elise led Maggie to the convent's herb gardens, where they silently walked the paths under leaden skies.

"There's a man," Elise began in a low voice, after a time. "He's one of yours, a Royal Air Force pilot, like John. He had to

315

bail out of his plane flying back from a mission. Not only is he in danger here, but he desperately needs medicine. Actually, he needs a hospital and a surgeon. His wounds are beyond my skills."

Maggie nodded, thinking back to the reward poster in the train station. "It's a risky situation. Do you know the Nazis are now offering ten thousand francs to anyone who can inform them of hidden British airmen?"

"No. We're quite isolated here. But it doesn't surprise me." Elise's voice was grim.

Maggie stopped and reached out to touch the novice's arm. "The penalty for hiding an English soldier is death. What you're all doing is unspeakably dangerous."

"Well . . ." Elise responded with a wry smile. "Wouldn't be the first time for that, now, would it?"

She and Maggie stared at each other. And then they began to laugh. Not demure, ladylike laughs, but real chortles, building into loud guffaws. When they had recovered, with a few snorts and hiccups, they looked at each other, intensely serious again.

"Well, I guess we really are sisters," Elise said.

"I hope so," Maggie agreed lightly.

They continued to walk. Elise glanced at

316

Maggie from under her lashes. "Can you help get this pilot out? Get him to London? Where he'll receive proper medical care?"

"Yes, of course," Maggie answered without hesitation, even as she wondered how in heaven's name she could pull it off. "We'll do everything we can for him. Is he here? At the convent?"

Elise bit her lip. "I'd rather not say."

Maggie nodded. "I understand. We always use the light of the full moon, so the next pickup will be approximately . . ." She counted off the days in her head. "Six days from now."

She looked to Elise. This was the moment. Would her sister agree to return to London with her? "Should I ask for a pickup for just the pilot? Or would you — ?"

"May I think about it?"

"Of course." Inside, Maggie was overjoyed by even the chance of having her sister come with her. But she knew better than to reveal it. "How can we stay in touch? Is there a telephone here?"

"There's one phone," Elise replied. "It's for emergencies."

"I'd say this qualifies. When I call, I'll use the name Paige Kelly."

"That's not a very French name!"

"No, it's Irish . . . a long story — I'll tell

317

you all about it on the plane ride home."
Then Maggie remembered herself. "If your
pilot's as bad off as you say, I'd better get
going."

Elise scuffed one boot in the gravel of the
path. "Thank you."

"You're welcome."

The two women did not embrace. After a
long moment, Maggie turned to go.

CHAPTER FOURTEEN

Outside 54 Broadway, close to St. James's Park Tube station, a blind man in a rumpled suit sold boxes of wooden matches. Martens dropped a few coins in his tin cup, then loped on. He looked up, past the taped windows of the building, to admire the magnificent mansard roof, bristling with a thicket of radio antennae. A discreet brass plaque at the sandbagged entry identified the building as the Minimax Fire Extinguisher Company. But Martens ignored the main entrance. Instead, he strode to the rear, at 21 Queen Anne's Gate, where there was another, smaller door.

Inside the building sat a receptionist, haggard and stoop-shouldered, but with a noble jaw, one of the legions of retired soldiers and sailors working as doormen and messengers all over London. He looked over Martens's identity papers and then nodded the Master of Deception through.

The building was a dingy, shabby labyrinth of wooden partitions and frosted-glass windows. Martens took the ancient lift to the fourth floor. At the end of a gloomy corridor, he climbed a short staircase, turning to find the image of his face distorted in a great fish-eye mirror. He started.

"May I help you?" came the shrill tones of a secretary. She was large and muscular, with beady eyes and an officious air.

"I'm here to see Colonel George Bishop."

"And you are?"

"Colonel Henrik Martens. My secretary telephoned this morning. I have an appointment."

She frowned. "Go in, then." He did.

The head of MI-6's French Intelligence Section was standing at one of the long taped windows, staring down at the street below, hands clasped behind his back. As he turned, a tiny sparrow on the sill flitted off. "I've been expecting you," he said in a flat, nasal tone. "Follow me." He opened a narrow door that led to a flight of even narrower stairs. Martens climbed behind the colonel until they reached the roof, home to a pigeon loft.

"Homing pigeons," Bishop said by way of explanation. "Neither Menzies nor I trust radio transmissions."

The two men walked to the edge and looked down, over the emerald expanse of St. James's Park. Martens had done his research on Bishop. Code-named V, Bishop was in his sixties, born into an aristocratic family in London, one of nine children. Educated at Wellington College, he joined the British Army at the age of twenty, serving in South Africa during the Boer War, making his way up the military ranks and befriending a young Winston Churchill. After the war, Bishop worked as a full-time agent for MI-6 in Italy, spying on Mussolini's Fascists. In 1939, concerned about the growing shadow of Nazi Germany, Bishop returned to London and was asked by Menzies to head MI-6's French covert intelligence operations.

"Actually, I'm here to see you because of that."

"Pigeons?"

"Radio transmissions."

"Ah." He didn't sound surprised.

"As part of settling in to my new position, one of the first things I did was start to read through SOE agents' back traffic. I haven't even gotten that far, and there are some troubling aspects to the messages from both N-Section and F-Section."

Bishop continued to look out over London. He gave a slight, almost imperceptible nod.

"On some of the decrypts, the agents' security checks were missing. They were stamped as such by Station 53a — but no one at SOE followed up."

"Hmmm."

"I just spoke with Colonel Gaskell for SOE's French Section, whom you know."

Bishop made an even more ambiguous-sounding "Hmmm."

"And I asked him why no one has followed up on the agents' lack of security checks. That is, beyond chastising the agent and reminding her to remember for the next transmission. The thing is, he didn't seem at all surprised. And then he told me he knew about the situation and that SOE's completely on top of it. He assured me I had nothing to worry about."

Bishop was preternaturally still.

"I pressed him on a particular agent, a woman named Calvert. Her coding, after a certain point during her tenure in France, became flawless. Which is, frankly, impossible. And yet *none* of these perfect messages have security checks."

"Erica Calvert is the agent with the sand samples from the Normandy beaches," Bishop remarked, surveying the cityscape.

"Yes, sir." Martens realized he hadn't told the older officer the agent's first name.

"Whom we are in the process of extricating."

"Yes, sir."

Bishop turned. "Do you believe this woman has been compromised?"

Both men knew what this admission would mean. "Yes, sir," Martens replied. "I do."

"SOE is Winston's special pet project," Bishop explained. "A start-up. Raging amateurs. For those of us who have spent our professional lives operating in the shadows, those idiots are a liability."

"Sir?"

"SOE and MI-Six agents often end up working at cross-purposes." He took a monogrammed silver cigarette case from his jacket pocket, opened it, and offered a Player's to Martens, who demurred. "They're a mob of second-raters, disorganized and dangerous. And they jeopardize my own agents and their missions abroad."

He took a cigarette for himself and pulled out a lighter. "They lack professionalism. And the grave mistakes they've already made should have been enough to eradicate the entire operation." He lit the cigarette and inhaled, pausing to pick a stray flake of tobacco leaf from his tongue. "But SOE is Churchill's brainchild — he won't let it be disbanded." Bishop let a stream of smoke pass through his nostrils. "I have long suspected the SOE agents in the Netherlands have been compromised and are operating under German control. It doesn't surprise me in the least that the Gestapo in France may be taking a page from their book."

Martens cleared his throat. "To the best of your knowledge, sir, have any SOE agents been captured and their radios turned?"

"No," Bishop answered. "Not officially, at least."

"Would SOE ever admit if their agents were caught?"

"That, my boy, is why you'll need hard evidence." Bishop looked at his watch. "Keep me informed on what you find out. You were right to come to me." He trained his eyes on the skyline. "But for the sake of God and country — don't put any of this in writing."

At Avenue Foch, Hugh was seated in front of his radio. Professor Fischer and Obersturmbannführer von Waltz were facing him, gazing at the Englishman almost fondly, as though he were an extremely intelligent dog about to perform a wonderful trick. Hugh had been cleaned up, the cuts on his face bandaged. He was wearing fresh clothes. But his eyes were dull, unseeing.

"Now then," said the Obersturmbannführer. "Let's begin, Mr. Thompson."

Mechanically, Hugh raised his hands; his fingers hovered above the keyboard.

"Let's see, what should we have him say?" von Waltz asked the professor. "How about a request for more agents? Let's build our little 'orchestra,' shall we?" He chortled. "Well, what are you waiting for? Start your message!" He leaned down to Hugh. "And be damn sure to include your security checks!"

Hugh began.

The F-Section agent code-named Clothilde was one of the few clandestine radio operators in Paris; they didn't tend to last long. Six weeks was the usual length of time before undercover agents were discovered by the Germans. "We have the shelf life of yogurt," they'd joke. But the German detection vans, listening for transmitted radio messages, were always circling, trying to zero in on transmission locations, which was why time on the air had to be kept as short as possible.

Clothilde was petite and young-looking, with heavy bangs shading bright brown eyes. Her radio set was open in front of her in Voltaire's kitchen, power from the six-volt dry-cell battery on. "All right." She cracked her knuckles, the antenna pointed out the window, rubber-coated aerial wires held up by tree branches while Voltaire kept watch for German vehicles. "What's the message you want me to send?" Although her voice was steady, her hands shook slightly.

Reiner had prepared the dispatch, coded in five-letter blocks. He handed over the scrap of paper. She nodded and put on her headphones, twisting the dial, listening for her call sign — *GJW*. When she heard it, she began to transmit, tapping on the key for dots and dashes, inserting her security check as she'd been trained.

The message read:

RAOUL SEEN ENTERING 84 AVE FOCH. STOP. PLEASE ADVISE. OVER.

Her eyes widened at the message's contents, but she didn't stop or question the two men.

Typing finished, Clothilde waited as her "godmother" in England confirmed the message had been received. She switched off the radio.

As she removed the headphones, rolled up the wires, and closed the set, Voltaire poured them all small glasses of wine that smelled faintly of vinegar. *"Á votre santé,"* he said as they clinked glasses. *To your health.*

They looked at each other, aware how dangerous making the transmission was, how there could be a traitor in their midst. *"Á votre santé."*

L'heure entre chien et loup was the French phrase that drifted through Maggie's mind as she made her way back to the Ritz in the blue-painted streetlight of the blackout. It was the expression for that uncertain moment at twilight when one couldn't tell the difference between a dog and a wolf — or friend and foe. "The gloaming," they'd called it in Scotland.

In the blackout and the silence of the curfew, Paris felt like a ghost town. An alley cat's yowl, a car's backfire, a random shout — together seemed menacing. Maggie reached a brick wall daubed with reflective paint that glowed, even in the darkness: a caricature of a Fagin-like face with wispy beard, bearing the legend SAXON + JEW +

TARTAR = THE BEAST. She turned her face away.

Maggie entered the Ritz through the Place Vendôme entrance. Buoyed by her meeting with her half sister, she wasn't the least bit fatigued by her long day and travels. She smiled up at the man at the front desk, working the late shift. "Any messages for Paige Kelly, André?"

"Nothing this evening, mademoiselle."

Still, the feeling there was something for her, something she needed to receive, nagged at her. "Packages?"

He bent to peer under the shelf and arose with a package in hand, wrapped in brown paper. "For you, mademoiselle!"

"Thank you," she said, taking it. *I was right!*

She walked to a deserted section of the lobby to open the box. Inside the brown paper was a long, flat box. She opened it and pulled apart the filmy tissue paper. Within was a pair of gloves. White gloves with pearl buttons — gloves exactly like the ones she'd used to help stop the bleeding of the injured German soldier.

There was also a thick, embossed card with the name crossed out, bearing the handwritten message:

To Mlle. Kelly,

        With my sincere thanks,

             Christian

P.S. I hope to see you at the masked ball tonight.

She walked back to the desk. "May I take the wrapping for you, mademoiselle?" André asked.

"Oh, thank you," Maggie said distractedly. Her immediate impulse was to throw the gloves away, but one couldn't do that in public. Instead, she slipped the pair into her handbag. "You're sure there's nothing else?"

As she asked, Chanel walked into the lobby, wearing a chic black straw hat with a scarlet quill feather in the band that matched her lipstick exactly.

"No, I'm afraid not, mademoiselle."

Maggie moved her lips into a glassy smile. "Thank you, anyway," she told André, turning to go. *"À bientôt. J'espère!" I'll see you later.* And as a reflex: *I hope.*

She'd wanted to avoid Chanel, but the couturiere had spotted her. "Mademoiselle Kelly!" she called before Maggie could make it to the elevator.

The younger woman stopped and forced

a smile. "Hello, mademoiselle. I'm sorry, I didn't see you."

Chanel's face indicated skepticism. "And how is trousseau shopping?"

"I went to Nina Ricci today." The morning seemed an eternity ago.

"Oh, how was it? Did you see anything?"

"I liked the red especially, but someone with my coloring really can't wear that color."

Chanel mused, "Yes, I heard there was a lot of red — and sable. And the wedding dress?"

Maggie remembered it in all its glorious detail. "Beautiful. But it might be a bit much for me. Perhaps an ivory silk suit might be better for these times."

"Nonsense! We must embrace excess — *especially* these days! We're dancing on the edge of a volcano, after all . . ." The couturiere peeled off her gloves. "I expect to see you at the masked ball tomorrow evening." It wasn't a question.

"Oh," Maggie said, "I'm hardly prepared . . ."

"A young woman like you?"

Maggie remembered she was supposed to be a society girl. "I — I don't have a mask."

"Somehow, I doubt that." Chanel quirked an eyebrow. "Still . . . come to my room tomorrow morning and I'll find you something. I'm a woman of many masks myself — and don't mind sharing."

CHAPTER FIFTEEN

The next afternoon, Henrik Martens made his way to Boodle's, a prestigious private gentlemen's club, located at 28 St. James's Street. When he arrived, he was shown directly to a smoking room. The walls were covered with gold-framed oil paintings of men on horseback surrounded by hunting dogs.

Bishop was waiting for him at a table in a dimly lit corner, glass of amber liquid in hand. "Sit down," he instructed. The small room was acrid with the odor of stale cigar smoke.

Martens obeyed, noting a silver-haired waiter leaving. Bishop called, "Close the doors!" which the man did. They now had the room to themselves.

"If you're going to have any power as 'Controlling Officer of Deception,' you'll need to know a bit more than what's in the files," Bishop told Martens. "The important things aren't necessarily written down. I know you have experience in the field with SOE's Norway Section, but there are any number of overarching intelligence plans in the works, and SOE's in the dark."

"Sir?"

"What a tangled web we weave . . ." Bishop's eyes went to a wall of leather-bound books, titles tooled in gold: *The Greek Tragedy* by Aeschylus, Euripides, and Sophocles; *The Art of War* by Sun Tzu; Carl von Clausewitz's *On War.* "Want a drink? You might need one by the time I'm done."

"Perhaps I should, then." Martens rose and made his way to the bar cart, pouring himself two fingers of scotch.

"Because the Allied landings will take place in France," Bishop was saying, "British intelligence operating there will be called upon to perpetuate the greatest lie ever told — the false location of the Allied invasion. We're outmanned and outarmed. Deception is our only chance for survival."

Martens took the seat opposite Bishop. "I was brought up with the adage that gentlemen don't read each other's mail."

"I was afraid of that." Bishop lit a Player's cigarette. "The gentleman's way of waging war died with mustard gas and trenches," he said with a certain waspish glee, "and now the British secret service is the best there is. We're ruthless, vicious, and cruel — and believe that the ends always justify the means. If you're going to work with us, Colonel, you're going to have to toughen up." Bishop exhaled smoke, the blue tentacles weaving around his head.

"You're educating me," Martens observed, setting down his drink and reaching for a cigarette.

"Why, yes." Bishop pushed the silver case across the table to him. "If we're going to work together, you need to be brought up to speed."

Martens plucked a Player's; Bishop lit it for him. "I specialize in what we call 'misleading deception' — creating an attractive possibility for the enemy that's dead wrong. I'm like a novelist — in that I create a setting, a cast of characters, and plausible details, all of which tell the same story."

"Story?"

"I'm talking about what we're calling 'Operation Fortitude.' It's still in the planning stages and we're still waiting on those damn sand samples. But once we get the official go-ahead that Normandy is the invasion site, my job — and yours — will be convincing the enemy that it will take place anywhere but there. *Everything* must point to an attack on Pas de Calais. If we can convince Hitler to believe the lies of Fortitude, on the day of the invasion the German Army will be massed in Pas de Calais — leaving the beaches of Normandy relatively free." He tapped his ash into a bronze tray with an embossed dragon.

"Even with the Yanks and the Canadians," Martens mused as he exhaled smoke, "we'll only have thirty divisions. If we're preparing to invade Normandy, how can we possibly convince the Germans of a Pas de Calais attack? We simply don't have enough men."

"A web of lies," Bishop responded. "A *story,* if you will. For a setting, we'll use the Thames Estuary and East Anglia, Dover, and Ramsgate. That's the logical place to build up our army of ghosts."

"You've lost me."

"Think! What would we have to do in real life if we were planning to invade Pas de Calais? Remember that old children's saying: 'Softly, softly, catchee monkey'?"

"Amass troops in East Anglia?"

Bishop looked like a headmaster let down by a star pupil. "*Wrong!* First, we'd need to widen the roads *before* bringing in men and tanks. And so that's what we're actually doing, of course. At night, using the cover of darkness. But the regular German aerial reconnaissance that flies over our fair island nation will soon note changes in the roads. They'll take the information back to Hitler. He'll know exactly what it portends."

"But then what? We don't actually have any men — or tanks — to spare."

"Ah —" Bishop tapped ash into a cut-glass tray. "This is where the dark magic comes in. We don't need real tanks, we just need something to *look* like tanks for the Luftwaffe's Leicas taking photographs at twenty thousand feet. Have you ever seen the Macy's Thanksgiving Day Parade? In New York City?"

"Yes?" Martens was now thoroughly confused.

"The balloons! We've gone to B. F. Goodrich, who makes the balloons for the parade each year. We've commissioned balloon models of Sherman tanks, two-ton trucks, guns . . . They ship them over, and we inflate them with an air compressor. Every night, we'll move them around — takes a few men for each — so that any Kraut flying over will be convinced he's photographing maneuvers."

Martens's eyes widened. "But — but what about people? The soldiers? The officers? All the support staff? You're talking about thousands of men!"

"Actors get drafted for war work, too," Bishop replied with a grim smile. "We're going to create a phantom army, voiced by radio actors. They'll be a cast of characters — real men with real issues. Not just the war, but men who need haircuts and have cheating wives. Who use toilet paper and condoms."

"That's insane!"

"Not at all, dear boy. We know Hitler can pick up radio messages. So we'll create fake wireless communications about fictional activity in real time."

"And you believe Hitler will buy it?"

"That's where counterespionage comes in. You've read up on the Twenty Committee?"

"Not yet," Martens admitted.

"Well, you should. You'll find out that all of the agents Germany sent to Britain as part of the so-called Fifth Column have been captured by MI-Five. They're all radioing back to the Fatherland under our control. Through their transmissions, we will pass the most vital secrets about Fortitude and the buildup for the attack. We'll have the turned spies send messages back about activity they're supposedly seeing — tank maneuvers and so forth that will corroborate our story."

"Then what?"

Bishop took a sip of his drink. "Then we pray Hitler swallows our lies."

"If you're building up a ghost army near East Anglia," Martens said slowly, "you must realize that the civilians nearby are in danger of being bombed. The Luftwaffe could decide to attack the fake buildup and kill some very real Englishmen."

"Yes."

"*Yes?*" He crushed out his cigarette. "People could *die* thanks to that scenario you've dreamed up."

"Ends and means, old thing."

"The British people will never stand for this!"

"The British people will never find out."

"Do General Ismay and the P.M. know?"

"We have their blessing to do whatever we need to do to win."

Martens shook his head. "Is there *nothing* you wouldn't sacrifice?"

"For survival?" Bishop gave a bitter laugh. "No, I have no limits. None at all. Before I let those Huns win, I'll sell my soul to the Devil himself."

Maggie had spent the day at various fashion shows and then returned to the Ritz for afternoon tea. Now, dressed and coiffed, with her face concealed, Maggie made her way to the ballroom with the designer.

"Well, it's not one of Elsie de Wolfe's soirées, but I suppose it will do," Chanel said as she swept through the doors of the Ritz's grand salon. Maggie looked over the scene. There were actually three salons, all connected, and each had a soaring ceiling, glittering chandeliers, gold-painted moldings, and velvet draperies. All had been transformed: the floors had been polished to a sheen, great gilded brackets held dripping candelabras, and bouquets of red roses and orchids overflowed on the linen-swathed tables.

Maggie had to fight the urge to turn and run; Goering was rumored to be attending. But instead, she pressed her mask — a confection of semiprecious stones and dyed feathers — against her face for concealment and descended the steps. The other hand demurely lifted the skirt of her dress, the pale blue hidden by a black lace gown she had worn to the ballet.

In the main salon, there was no shortage of haute couture on display. The ladies wore gowns of shimmering silk, frothy lace, and floating tulle. Jewels sparkled on their throats and dangled from their ears, and long kid gloves covered their hands and arms. The men were elegantly clad in evening dress, their shirt studs and gold cuff links glinting in the candlelight.

As the orchestra played a lilting fox-trot, the candlelit room swirled with dancers. The ballroom was a feast for the senses: the dancers in gowns of scarlet, crimson, and ruby keeping time to the sweet music of the strings. The fragrance of the women's perfumes and men's hair tonic combined with the heady scent of the flowers. And drifting above it all was the rise and fall of flirtatious conversation, mostly in French, but occasionally in German.

Maggie felt dizzy, from both the heat of the candles and the warmth of the dancers as they spun and twirled. A waiter stepped up to her with a silver tray. "Champagne?"

Maggie accepted a glass as Chanel was greeted by a group she obviously knew and took the opportunity to walk away, mask held firmly in place. The music finished and the assembled politely applauded. But before she could make her escape, a man blocked her path. "I couldn't help but recognize you by your hair," he said in German-inflected French. Despite his mask, Maggie recognized him instantly.

"Christian."

"May I have this dance?"

Maggie nodded, and set down her drink. The General led her to the dance floor. As they began to move to the music, he asked, "Did you know that legend has it Elsa Maxwell rejected a diamond Cartier bracelet at a dinner at the Ritz given in her honor, saying she preferred having Fritz Kreisler play for her?"

"Must have been a while ago," Maggie retorted drily. Jewels and gold were worth far more than francs.

"And at that, George Bernard Shaw proclaimed, 'This woman is the eighth wonder of the world!' I wonder, Mademoiselle Kelly, which would you pick?"

"Before the war, the violin performance." She gave a short laugh. "But nowadays, the diamond bracelet."

Christian spun her about, guiding Maggie across the crowded dance floor, one gloved hand holding hers, the other resting lightly on her back. In the arms of a German officer, even masked, she couldn't possibly relax. And then she caught sight of Goering.

Reichsmarshal Hermann Goering, towering and rotund, was wearing a specially made dress uniform trimmed in golden braid that stretched tightly across his broad back, dark sweat stains under his arms. His beaded and feathered black mask depicted the horned hunting god, complete with antlers. Christian saw the direction of Maggie's glance and immediately steered her closer. "Come, I'll introduce you!"

But before she could protest, another man cut in. "May I?"

Christian released Maggie regretfully. "We must dance again, mademoiselle," he said, then bowed and left.

The masked newcomer whirled her around the floor, away from Goering. Maggie stiffened in surprise, almost losing her step. "Jacques!" The orchestra began to play "A String of Pearls."

"You look beautiful, mademoiselle." His voice was thick with emotion.

"What's wrong?"

"Something's happened. We need to get to somewhere private to talk."

He took her hand to lead her across the floor. They went through the salon to the glass-walled atrium and then to the garden. There was no one else outside; the threat of rain was enough to ensure privacy.

As they walked the darkened paths, Jacques kept hold of Maggie's hand. "Are you cold? Would you like my jacket?"

"I'm fine."

But he took his black dinner jacket off and draped it over her shoulders. It was warm from his body, and she pulled it closer around her. They faced each other, hands clasped, palm against palm, soft glove leather against leather, but the touch was surprisingly intimate.

"You need to leave Paris," he said urgently.

The spell was broken. "Why? What's happened?"

"Two agents have been captured."

"What? Who?"

"I don't know. I only know they're at Avenue Foch. Who knows what they've said?"

"I promised my sister she could get out. And there's an injured British pilot —"

"First we have to get you to the safe house on Rue Curial. Then we'll worry about getting you all out. The full moon is less than a week away." He leaned close. Once again, Maggie was aware of the warmth of his body. "It's urgent. You'll need to go tonight."

"Tonight? What about the curfew?"

He looked at the face of his watch in the leaking light from the gala. "It's best we get you there as soon as possible. Go upstairs, change, and pack a bag. Take the servants' stairs back down. I'll be waiting on the street."

Maggie moved quickly, going up to her little

room, changing into plain, dark clothes, packing a small suitcase of necessities, leaving behind the large Vuitton trunk and all the couture. *Thank you, Paige,* she thought as she left and closed the door behind her. *You always were generous about lending your things.*

She ran down the stairs with her case; Jacques was waiting for her as he'd promised. She walked to him. "We might never see each other again." *And wouldn't that fit my pattern of romantic entanglements perfectly?*

"You never know. Let's say *à bientôt,* rather than *au revoir.* I'll walk you to the safe house. Make sure you go there."

"It's better if I go alone. We shouldn't be seen together." And yet Maggie set down her suitcase. In the shadows, his arms wrapped around her.

They kissed. *You fool,* Maggie thought, *you idiot — always falling for the unavailable man.* They broke apart and stared at each other.

"I —" he began.

"No," Maggie replied, drawing away. "Don't say anything more."

"Maybe after the war?"

Maybe. She picked up her suitcase again. "Stranger things have happened."

■ ■ ■ ■

At Station 53a, Elspeth Hallsmith bent over an encoded message, just received from the agent known as IDJ.

She didn't know IDJ well; he — or she — had been sent to France only recently, and she'd decrypted only three previous messages. It had been a long shift, and now there was only an hour to go before the next crew took over. Even Elspeth's usually perfect curl was falling out, her lipstick long since faded, her elegant fingers drumming restlessly on the long table. "All right, IDJ, let's see what you're up to," she muttered as she began to translate the Morse code into English.

CALL SIGN IDJ
22 JUNE 1942

MISSION ACCOMPLISHED STOP TARGETS IDENTIFIED STOP RE-QUESTING MORE AGENTS FOR IMMEDIATE ACTION OVER

Elspeth went over the transcribed message not once but four times. For the first time, IDJ had forgotten his security check.

She bit her lip. Another F-section agent leaving off security checks. It was becoming a far too common occurrence.

And so, like the others, she stamped the top of the decrypt SECURITY CHECK MISSING in bright red ink and put it in her outbox.

When Maggie arrived at the safe house, every window was dark and shuttered. All the doors were locked. *Great,* she fumed, *just perfect.*

Worried about being out after curfew, she made her way across the arrondissement to Bar Lorraine, still carrying the suitcase. Jacques had specified the safehouse, but she had nowhere else to go and couldn't stay out past curfew.

The bar was dim and smelled of herbal cigarette smoke. A man with an accordion finished playing "Flambée Montalbanaise" and began passing around his worn hat. The patrons in Thonet chairs at the marble-topped tables resolutely ignored him.

Two gray-haired men, one with a nervous blink, the other chewing on the end of an unlit pipe, played a silent but intense game of bezique at a table in the back. In a mirrored corner, Maggie saw a pretty French girl laughing and flirting over a tumbler of wine with a doughy-faced Wehrmacht officer, who leaned in to kiss her hand before he stood, bowed, and left.

The instant the German was out the door, a Frenchman with faded eyes and teeth stained by a lifetime of coffee and wine came up to the girl's table and, to Maggie's astonishment, slapped her across the face, hard. The girl's eyes filled instantly with tears as the man hissed, "Flirting with the Boche? Someday we'll shave your head and march you naked through the streets of Paris in your shame."

The girl rose. Her pretty face was very pale. "Be careful I don't get you arrested, old man!" she shrilled. Then she spat in his face and flounced off after the officer.

One of the gray-haired men called over, "*Non, monsieur.* Revenge is not the right way." His companion nodded in agreement. "That's not what we're fighting for."

Maggie made her way to the bar. *"Puis-je voir Jeanne-Marie, la fille d'Ora?"* she asked the man behind the counter, using the agreed-upon question. He was lean and broad-shouldered, with clipped brown hair. A shiny white scar ran down one cheek.

"Vous voulez dire Babs?" he replied, exactly as he should.

Maggie's entire body sagged with relief.

"Oui."

"Come." He took off his stained rondeau apron, then led her to the back hallway. There was a door; he knocked three times. Then he opened it for her, gesturing her inside.

She entered. Three Gestapo officers in long black leather coats stood facing her.

The man with the scar covered her mouth with his hand. "Don't make a sound."

CHAPTER SIXTEEN

Waiting in Obersturmbannführer Wolfgang von Waltz's office at 84 Avenue Foch, Maggie found herself in the grip of a cold intensity, a sort of trance, her mind closed tight to thoughts of anything except meeting the immediate crisis.

She felt oddly composed, her senses heightened, seeing the room around her with increased clarity — colors brighter, light and shadows more defined. Her ears seemed to pick up all the sounds of the Sicherheitsdienst headquarters — the secretaries, the guards, even the nightingale warbling outside the window. A gray parrot hopped and fluttered around its cage. *"Pretty Lady! Bonjour! Heil Hitler!"* He swayed from one foot to the other. *"Have you shot!"*

When the German in the elegant suit entered, he eyed her closely, as though she were an objet d'art that he couldn't quite evaluate without careful examination. "Mademoiselle Kelly," he said in silky tones, pulling the cover over the birdcage. "Please sit down."

Maggie did, taking a seat on one of the chairs with cabriole legs ending in gilded beast claws. He sat next to her.

"Permit me to introduce myself. I am Obersturmbannführer Wolfgang von Waltz. And I don't believe there would be any point in making matters more difficult for yourself by denying anything. In fact, your best course of action at this point is to tell us everything."

Maggie's mind was working furiously. What did they know of her? How much information did the Obersturmbannführer have? To the best of her knowledge, they had picked her up only because the café tabac had been compromised and she had used the code words. What else did they know? *Maybe nothing.* Her fear steeled into resolve to play the mental game and win.

"Your clock is lovely, Obersturmbannführer," she said, looking up at the Sleeping Beauty. "Louis Quatorze? Or Quinze?"

"You have a wonderful eye, mademoiselle." The officer smiled indulgently. "I have looked over your passport and papers — all seem to be in order. And we do not want to be obliged to imprison a citizen of

Ireland." He crossed his legs. "Believe me, what we should like most of all is to be able to release you at once. If you're a sensible woman — and your knowledge of décor suggests taste and breeding — you will simply tell us candidly why you were at the café, why you asked for Jeanne-Marie, daughter of Ora, and I assure you we shall then be able to let you go."

Maggie maintained her icy calm. "Because I was looking for Jeanne-Marie, the daughter of Ora. I didn't know it was a crime." *Deny everything,* she reminded herself, remembering her training. *Deny everything, even if they produce the most incontrovertible evidence.*

"All right, Mademoiselle Kelly, tell me why you are in Paris."

Maggie repeated her cover story, even describing at great length, and with colorful enthusiasm, the fashions she had seen at the House of Ricci.

Von Waltz was not impressed. "But, mademoiselle — why would you ask for Jeanne-Marie, the daughter of Ora, at the café?"

He sits next to me, and not at the desk — the obvious power position, Maggie thought. *He's trying to build a rapport, to use kindness to break me.* She cast her eyes downward. "I'm ashamed," she murmured girlishly.

He took a sharp breath. "No, mademoiselle, no need for shame. Just tell the truth."

"The truth is —" Maggie's fingers played with the folds of her skirt. "I'd heard there was someone at Bar Lorraine, someone named Jeanne-Marie, a woman who has access to —" Von Waltz had to lean forward to hear Maggie's whisper. "— what some call . . . 'Paris snow.' "

"Cocaine?" he asked in genuine amazement. *"Cocaine?"* Obviously, this was anything but the answer he was expecting. "And who the devil told you that?"

Maggie remembered what Chanel had told her about concierges: they could procure anything, truly anything, for their guests. "Someone at the Ritz — I don't remember who," she evaded, fluttering her hands. "One of the staff. And that's all I was doing at the café this evening, I swear to you!"

"I don't believe you."

Maggie straightened. "I'm sorry, sir," she said firmly, "but I refuse to answer any more questions at all until I have the advice of a lawyer, one appointed by the Irish Consulate, of course."

"Alas, mademoiselle, your request for a lawyer cannot be granted. Even if the Irish Consulate should send a lawyer here, he

352

could not be admitted to this building. This is the headquarters of the German Secret Police. No lawyers are permitted to interfere with our investigations."

Von Waltz changed tactics, interrogating Maggie — Paige — on her private life. Never taking his eyes off her for an instant, he asked question after question on minute details of her existence. Maggie was thankful she'd known Paige for so long, and had lived in close quarters with her. She answered easily, even managing to sound bored. *Just the way the real Paige would deal with an inept waiter.*

Over two hours had passed by the time von Waltz rose from his chair. His friendly smile had vanished. He looked like a schoolmaster, but a bad-tempered one, furious his pupil had outsmarted him.

Despite her exhaustion, Maggie felt a small glow of pride. Still, she was quick to temper it. *Be careful. Don't let your guard down. He's not done yet.*

A rap sounded on the door. "Come in!" von Waltz snarled.

The Gestapo agent with the white scar who had brought Maggie in swung open the double doors and stood in the frame. "Obersturmbannführer, is our prisoner cooperating?" he asked in German. "Has she

353

talked?"

Von Waltz answered, also in German. "Yes, she talked. I'm quite satisfied with the results. The interesting part wasn't what she said, but what she attempted to conceal."

Maggie's emotions churned. *They're speaking in German because they think I don't understand it. What did I say? Did I inadvertently let some detail slip? Instead of my outsmarting him, has he outsmarted me?* Maggie went over every word she'd uttered.

Of course, they might be saying I attempted to conceal something to try to confuse me, as part of their *game.* Her head hurt. The shock of her capture was beginning to wear off, and she was starting to feel real fear.

There was a scuffling sound in the hallway. Sarah was being marched through by a pair of uniformed guards, her hair matted and face bruised.

Maggie kept her face still, as did Sarah, but there must have been some flicker of recognition. Von Waltz pounced on it. "You know each other!" he exalted. "You are working together!"

"I don't know what you're talking about," Maggie replied with hauteur. "I've never seen this woman in my life —"

"At Maxim's!" Sarah interrupted, her eyes on Maggie's. "We met at Maxim's! You were kind enough to help me, in the ladies' room, when I was feeling unwell. Remember?"

"Of course!" Maggie exclaimed, as if just remembering. "The ballet dancer — Madame . . . Severin, wasn't it? I'm sorry — you do look a bit . . . different." She looked to von Waltz. "A woman? Tortured?" She rose from the chair and clicked her tongue. "You should be ashamed of yourself!"

"You said if Hugh cooperated, you wouldn't hurt me, you wouldn't hurt either of us," Sarah said — letting Maggie know Hugh had been captured as well. "Lies, all lies!"

Von Waltz looked to Maggie. "Hugh Thompson — do you know him, too?"

"No." Maggie lied without hesitation. "Never heard of him."

Von Waltz examined his buffed nails. The cuticle of his index finger had torn, and he began to pick at it. "Have you ever noticed, Mademoiselle Kelly, that when a string of pearls breaks and one of them drops off, the rest invariably follow, one after the other? It seems we have broken a string."

He waved his hand. "Take them both up to the fifth floor!" he ordered the guards, then turned back to the women. "Sleep well, ladies. We'll speak further tomorrow."

355

Maggie and Sarah climbed the winding stairway; on every landing was an armed sentry. They were taken to the former servants' quarters, which had been converted into small prison cells. The hallway walls were covered with yellow, faded wallpaper of swallows and satin ribbons.

Each of the women was thrust unceremoniously into a narrow, low room, with no furniture except an iron cot with a dirty mattress and a blanket, lit by a bare bulb hanging from a mold-stained ceiling. As the door of her prison room slammed shut, Maggie ran to the Judas grille cut into the door. She couldn't see out. She twisted the lock, then pounded on the door until her fists were raw.

Defeated, she made her way to the low bed, where she sat, stomach churning and mind buzzing. As she struggled to calm her thoughts, she counted out the Fibonacci sequence of numbers: *1, 1, 2, 3, 5, 8, 13, 21* . . . Then she read the graffiti scrawled on the wall behind the bed. NEVER CONFESS read one. FRANKREICH ÜBER ALLES — *France above all* read another with biting irony. BELIEVING IN YOURSELF GIVES ONE

THE POWER TO RESIST DESPITE THE BATH-
TUB AND ALL THE REST, reassured another.
There was DON'T TALK. And, in tiny let-
ters: I AM AFRAID.

Maggie was forced to admit that she, too,
was afraid. Deeply afraid. But a childhood
of benevolent neglect had taught her self-
reliance, study of mathematics dispassion-
ate thinking, and work with SOE bravery —
and so she refused to give in to fear.

Think, Hope, she schooled herself. *This is
like chess — logic, not emotion, is what will
get you through.* She remembered von
Waltz's metaphor about the string of pearls.
So, who broke the string? Who had revealed
the café and the question and answer? Who
had betrayed them? She thought back to
the poster she'd seen on the train. *Who
among us would be willing to earn a reward
by betraying us?* She thought of the Charcots. Had hunger and fear led to betrayal?
And then she remembered Sarah's battered
face. Or had pain and torture caused someone in Paris's SOE networks to break?

The overhead light blinked and went out.
Left in darkness, Maggie became aware of
the building's rhythms: the clank of the
radiator, the whistle of the wind through
the branches outside the barred window.
And then she heard it — a tapping. A tap-

ping on the pipes.

Maggie listened intently. After a moment, the tapping resolved into Morse code.

Sarah! She was in the room next to Maggie's, tapping out code and trying to communicate.

Go to loo was Sarah's message. *Check cabinet.*

Maggie rose and rattled at her door. "Guard!" she called. Then, louder, "Guard!"

She heard footsteps and then, through the grille, a curt "What do you want?"

"I need to use the lavatory."

The door was unlocked and opened. The guard was burly and so white-blond and fair-skinned he looked almost albino. "Fine, fine," he grumbled. "But be quick about it."

Inside the mildewed bathroom down the hall, there were newly installed bars over the window. Quickly, Maggie searched and finally, in the cabinet under the sink, found the note. It was from Sarah, scrawled in a simple code on a scrap of torn-off wallpaper, looking as if it had been written in blood. The note read that Sarah was able to communicate secretly with Hugh, who was in the cell on her other side. And the three of them could communicate through notes under the basin. Also, had Maggie picked up the bag?

What bag? she wondered, bewildered. Then she remembered the odd premonition she'd had earlier. *So Sarah did leave something for me at the Ritz. But what is it? And where is it now?*

"Hey," the guard yelled, banging on the door. "How long are you going to be in there?"

"As long as necessary!" Maggie replied, tearing up the note and flushing it down the toilet. "I'm having some . . . feminine issues."

"Mein Gott," he muttered.

Ten minutes later, she was escorted back to her cell, feeling connected to the prisoners in the adjoining cells, and not quite so alone. She remembered reading *A Little Princess* as a young girl, about how Sarah Crewe and Becky had lived through the privations of their life in the cold and lonely attic by pretending they were prisoners in the Bastille and Miss Minchin their jailer.

She tapped on the pipes: *Found note. What bag?*

Top secret. From Calvert. Left at Ritz.

Maggie started. Agent Calvert? She'd killed herself, yes. But if, somehow, they could get whatever she had been trying to bring back to London, her death wouldn't have been in vain . . .

Nothing at Ritz, Maggie rapped out.

Left for you yesterday, Sarah responded. *Nothing.*

There was an ominous silence from Sarah's end. Suddenly Maggie remembered Chanel's ballet tickets — and how they'd been left at the Place Vendôme entrance and not the Rue Cambon, in error. Was it possible that whatever Erica Calvert had been carrying — something so crucial to the war effort she'd committed suicide rather than let her Nazi captors find it — was sitting on a shelf under the desk on the Rue Cambon side of the Paris Ritz?

I know where, Maggie tapped. *Safe for now.*

There was no more messaging. What else was there to say? And how long before someone looked through the bag and discovered its contents? Maggie went back to the bed; she lay down and managed to doze off briefly. In a half dream, Mademoiselle Charcot's birdlike face and talon-like hands floated before her eyes. Maggie jerked back to consciousness, trembling with fright, thoughts of betrayal racing feverishly through her brain.

She tried to reason with herself. *If I don't crack under interrogation, the Gestapo can't pursue its investigation. And then no other pearls will drop off the string.*

As Maggie lay on the bed, eyes open, she looked up through the gloom to the water-stained ceiling. Above her was the skylight, with three iron bars, fixed on a wooden frame. Hugh and Sarah most likely had bars on their windows, too. *If only . . .*

A surge of adrenaline ran through her. *All I have to do is escape before they break me.* The insanity of trying to break out of Gestapo headquarters wasn't lost on her, but still, she was determined to focus on her plan — to escape with Sarah and Hugh, collect Erica's precious package, pick up Elise and her RAF pilot, and somehow make it to the airfield by midnight on June 28.

She had five days.

CHAPTER SEVENTEEN

Diana Lynd laid the latest decrypts, just delivered from Station 53a, on Colonel Gaskell's desk.

"What's all this?" the colonel asked, searching for his reading glasses, although even the most nearsighted could read the red ink stamp across the top: SECURITY CHECK MISSING.

"It's another decrypt, this one from Agent IDJ — that's Hubert Taillier, code name Aristide."

Gaskell gave her a blank look.

"IDJ's real name is Hugh Thompson."

Shoving his glasses up his nose, Colonel Gaskell read the decrypt:

22 JUNE 1942

MISSION ACCOMPLISHED STOP TARGETS IDENTIFIED STOP RE-QUESTING MORE AGENTS FOR

"Why so glum, Miss Lynd? This is excellent news! Jolly good show, indeed! He'll be coming back with a list of targets from Fortner. In the meantime, they need more agents, for more work! Maybe even a new cell!"

Lynd did not share in his enthusiasm. "He's omitted his security checks, sir."

"We've been over that, my dear."

"If Thompson's been compromised and we send in more agents, we'll be sending them straight into a trap."

"Believe me, Miss Lynd, I'm on top of it."

"Please read the next decrypt. It was sent by GJW — Clothilde — from HJW. That's Leo Ackerman."

Gaskell gave her another uncomprehending look.

"You may know him as Reiner Dupont," she explained patiently. "He's our agent in Paris sanitation. And you'll note all of his security checks *are* in place."

"Ah, the garbageman," Gaskell mused. He read the message and then turned to stare out the window overlooking Baker Street. "Well, well. There could be any number of reasons why our man was coming from Avenue Foch."

Lynd folded her arms across her chest. "Am I to understand, sir, that you believe a message sent without security checks and doubt one sent with?"

"You don't understand, Miss Lynd!" spluttered Gaskell. "Carry on with your duties! Leave the questions for your superiors!"

Lynd turned smartly on her heel and left Gaskell's office before she said what was really on her mind.

Maggie was once again in von Waltz's office. This time, it was daylight, the sky out the window low and sooty, with only a lone patch of blue on the horizon.

"Perhaps you don't realize the position you're in," he began, this time sitting behind his carved desk, hands folded. He looked to be freshly shaven, smelling of lemon cologne. "Perhaps that's why you're so stubborn, mademoiselle, not because you're guilty, or completely guilty, yourself. I will give you one more chance. I will give you until six o'clock this evening. If you haven't become reasonable by then, I will have no option. I shall have to use stronger methods of persuasion."

Despite the tang of fear in her mouth, Maggie gave him her most supercilious smile. "I can assure you, Obersturmbann-führer, I do in fact realize the position I'm in. I was sent by the concierge of the Ritz on a fool's errand, to ask for a certain person, which overlapped with something else — something that has nothing whatsoever to do with me." She waved an imperious hand. "Obviously, Jeanne-Marie and Ora are common names. This is a simple misunderstanding."

"As you know, we have captured Sabine Severin and Hubert Taillier. But we prefer to call them by their real names — Sarah Sanderson and Hugh Thompson."

"So?" Maggie kept her expression placid. "Again, this has nothing to do with me. This is not *my* war."

"We know all about SOE's operations in France — F-Section, as you call it."

"I have no idea who's operating in France. I'm just an Irish bride-to-be here for my wedding trousseau."

"We know about Colonel Maurice Buck-master, Air Commodore Sir Charles Ham-bro, Colonel Gaskell, and Diana Lynd. We know about training in Scotland and parachute school, and your so-called finishing school at Beaulieu."

Maggie shook her head, although her knuckles whitened. "These names mean nothing to me. I've never even been to Scotland. You have arrested me in error. And, I will say again, Obersturmbannführer, I insist upon speaking with someone at the Irish Consulate."

"A fine idea," von Waltz agreed genially. "Surely we can call the Irish Consulate — find out about a certain Paige Kelly — if that's even your name, mademoiselle. Where were you born?"

"In Belfast, on the fifth of June, 1915. And I don't need until six o'clock tonight to make up some story to satisfy you, Obersturmbannführer. Perhaps it is stupid of me, not to try to secure my release by making up some information which might deceive you into believing I know something. But the fact of the matter is —" She paused, doing her best to look vulnerable. "I'm a pretty girl, not a clever one — and certainly not cut out for your games. I'm telling you the absolute truth, sir, and that's all I can do, regardless of your threats. It's cruel of you to frighten me like this."

He stared at her a moment, then reached over his desk and picked up the telephone receiver. "Ah yes, Fräulein Schmidt. Please place a call to the Irish Consulate here in Paris. Ask them if they can verify the existence of a young Irish woman named Paige

Kelly —"

"Paige *Claire* Kelly," Maggie interrupted, deciding to go for broke.

Von Waltz held up a hand in annoyance. "Born in Belfast, Ireland, on the fifth of June, 1915." He replaced the receiver. "And now we'll see if you are who you say you are, Mademoiselle Kelly." He leaned back in his chair. "And you'd better hope to God they confirm your story."

The heavy blond guard led Maggie back up the steep stairs. On the landing of the fifth floor a cleaning woman, spewing foul language, was bent over a dented metal carpet sweeper.

"Madame Bonhomme!" the guard admonished.

The petite woman merely shrugged bony shoulders. Maggie could see she'd once been handsome, but was now pinched from too much work and not enough food. "Yes, Sergeant Schneider," she said to the pale man. "The damn thing's broken — again." She gestured to the carpet sweeper.

"I can fix it," Maggie offered impulsively.

"You?" scoffed the guard.

"I can. When I was a little girl I liked to see how things worked, even carpet sweepers. I'll need some tools, though."

367

The guard returned with a metal box, watched suspiciously as she handled the tools. She fixed the sweeper and handed it back to Madame Bonhomme, who thanked her profusely. Even the guard looked at her with admiration. Maggie put the screwdriver back in the toolbox reluctantly, feeling her heart sink as Madame Bonhomme latched the box and took it away.

Her only hope had been to mend the carpet sweeper ineptly. But how soon would it break down again?

Martens had been copied on the same decrypts as Gaskell. As he finished reading the file in his underground office, he reached for the telephone receiver, to call the colonel.

But then, remembering the F-Section head's lack of distress — as well as MI-6's concerns with the professionalism of SOE — he pulled his hand back. What if SOE itself was compromised? What if the head of the snake were Gaskell himself? It was too horrible to contemplate, yet he had to. He had to consider every possibility. And he didn't want to tip his hand.

He was, after all, Winston Churchill's Master of Deception. Something was going on, something was very wrong, and something needed to be done — and fast. It was time to go on a spy mission of his own.

"Miss Pinkerton," he called to his secretary, an ancient gargoyle of a woman. "I'd like the letters and other paperwork sent back from France with the SOE agents. The real documents, not just copies."

"Yes, sir."

"And I'll be working out of the office today. Please call Colonel Mason, at Station 53a. Let him know I'll be dropping by in a few hours for a little visit."

"Yes, sir," she replied. "Very good, sir."

"No — wait. On second thought, don't telephone," he said, putting on his cap. "Let's make this visit a surprise."

The Racing Club de France was located in the heart of Bois de Boulogne, on the Route of the Lakes, not far from Longchamp racecourse. All sports could be played — fencing, badminton, rugby — but SS Ober-gruppenführer Ulrich Friedrich Wilhelm Joachim von Ribbentrop, just arrived by train from Berlin, was meeting von Waltz to play tennis.

The two officers, dressed in their whites, met in the lobby of the clubhouse. When the inevitable *Heil Hitler*s had been exchanged, Ribbentrop asked, "Would you like to play indoors or out?" The Racing Club had both indoor *terre battue* courts with skylights and outdoor courts surrounded by perfectly pruned shrubs and tall trees.

"The weather could go either way." Von Waltz glanced out the windows at the gathering clouds. "You choose, Obergruppenführer," he said deferentially.

Ribbentrop was trim and muscular, with retreating blond hair, a cleft chin, and thin lips. "Outdoors then," he decided. "We are Aryans, and must get out from behind our desks and into the fresh air as often as possible, regardless of weather."

They passed a red clay court where the great champion Bernard Destremau was volleying. Since tennis balls were scarce due to the German ban on rubber for anything but war production, Ribbentrop had brought a new Slazenger. When he pulled it out of his pocket, von Waltz grinned. "Excellent, Obergruppenführer."

They took their positions on opposite sides of the net; Ribbentrop served, and the men volleyed. Both were decent players, scrambling with speed and agility over the traditional *en tous cas* — the packed brick-dust surface — and well matched. But when the first drops of rain spattered, von Waltz lowered his game and let Ribbentrop win. "Back to the clubhouse for a drink?" he suggested as they shook hands over the net.

"Of course!"

In the clubhouse, they waited for their Champagne to be poured. Von Waltz nodded to René Lacoste as he passed. "If you could devote all your time to practice, you'd be ready for Roland Garros in no time at all!"

Ribbentrop nodded. "Perhaps after the war."

The two Germans clinked their heavy crystal flutes. After they'd drunk, von Waltz asked, "And how long will you be in Paris, Obergruppenführer?"

"Alas, only a few days, then down to Vichy, to meet with Pétain and Laval about the upcoming roundup. And arranging for French troops in North Africa to be placed formally under German command."

Von Waltz nodded his head.

"I was talking with the Führer before I left, at Wolfsschanze," Ribbentrop said, never inclined to let anyone forget his close connection to Hitler. "About the expected Allied invasion. The discovery of the precise date and location of the Allied landings has become the overriding objective of the German Secret Services working in the West. I brought up your name, of course."

"Ah," said von Waltz. "Thank you, Ober-gruppenführer."

"The Führer is convinced the invasion will be on the coast of Normandy. The rest of them — Himmler, Eichmann, and von Rundstedt — believe it will be Pas de Calais. We've received some aerial photographs of Dover, across the channel from Calais. They've begun to widen the roads there, bringing in building materials. It certainly looks as if they're creating a massive base from which to launch a future attack."

Von Waltz raised an eyebrow.

"Our reconnaissance aircraft will, of course, continue to sweep up and down the British coast, to monitor what preparations are being made and where." Ribbentrop looked to von Waltz. "What do you think?"

"I think, Obergruppenführer, that if we continue to play the radio games I've begun, we shall get a clear answer about Calais versus Normandy — with plenty of time to assure victory."

"How are these 'radio games' progressing?"

Von Waltz heard the tinge of doubt in the other man's question. "We have two agents' radios under our control. We will soon commandeer others. We're in contact with SOE in London — they suspect nothing."

"And your man in Paris, this Gibbon — he can be trusted?"

"As much as anyone. But, yes, I've known him for years. He hates the Communists enough he's willing to help us." Von Waltz couldn't resist adding one more tidbit. "There is also a package that one of the agents was supposed to deliver. One London is *most* keen on retrieving."

"Where is this package?"

"We're following up a few leads," von Waltz evaded.

Ribbentrop drained his glass. The waiter rushed to pour him another. "Would you like to have dinner with me tonight? I have a reservation at Prunier. That's near your Avenue Foch, isn't it?"

"It is, and one of my favorite restaurants," confided von Waltz. "They have a wonderful Breton lobster there, flambéed in Cognac — absolutely delicious."

"And you're still enjoying my gift? What did you name him — Ludwig?" Ribbentrop asked. "He must liven up the office considerably."

"Honestly, Obergruppenführer," von Waltz answered with a stiff smile, "I can't tell you how much I adore that bird."

■ ■ ■ ■

In the attic of 84 Avenue Foch, Maggie pondered her options. She didn't have the screwdriver yet, but if she did — *when* she did, she corrected herself — she'd need the bed underneath the skylight — it was too high for her to reach without assistance. If she moved the bed directly to the center of the room, the guard would be suspicious. And so she began by moving it to the other wall.

A guard heard the noise and rapped at the door. "What's going on?" he demanded through the grille.

"I'm moving the bed," she replied, in an isn't-it-obvious? tone.

"Why?"

She shrugged, in the way she'd seen French women do: part charm, part fatalism. "Because I want to change the view."

"Hmph," the guard replied. And although he wasn't pleased with the explanation, he slammed the grille shut and didn't pursue the matter further.

While von Waltz and Ribbentrop had been playing tennis, Hugh was being tortured. The Gestapo's brutal methods were authorized by German law, the fundamental principle of which had been laid down by Wilhelm Frick, who served as Reich Minister of the Interior in the Hitler Cabinet: "The law, as the state does, serves only the *Volk.*" And, in case there was any doubt, Heinrich Himmler had just officially authorized the "third degree," a euphemism for torture, to obtain information.

The stocky man had moved on from cutting to burning to what was called *la baignoire* — the bath — forcing water into Hugh's mouth and lungs until he was nearly drowned, then reviving him at the last moment.

Von Waltz strode into the dim basement chamber holding a decrypt he'd received from England, acknowledging Hugh's message but asking for his checks in the next transmission. "You fool!" the German raged. "How dare you lie to me? You left off your damn checks!"

Hugh's bloody and bruised head, still dripping from the *baignoire,* rolled back.

"I'm talking to you!" Von Waltz gave Hugh a kick in one shin with an alligator loafer. "But they don't even care, your stupid SOE handlers! They merely told you to 'remember your security checks' next time!"

Hugh groaned and opened his eyes.

"That's what they said? I should remember my checks?" He looked as though he'd been hurt more by SOE's overlooking his missing security check than the torture.

"You were at Maxim's the night we arrested a man with a pink carnation in his lapel," von Waltz insisted. "What did he give you?"

"Nothing!"

"So you do remember a man with a pink carnation."

Hugh was silent.

The German kicked him again. "What did he give you?" Von Waltz's eyes were wide and crazed. He kicked Hugh's shin a third time, like a child having a temper tantrum. "And where have you hidden it?"

"I don't know," Hugh sobbed, knowing he had to protect Sarah. "I don't. *I don't know!*"

Von Waltz nodded to the stocky man. "Continue."

Hugh couldn't endure much more without giving up all he knew. And the truth was, he knew too much. He'd peeked inside the dance bag, seeing the sand samples from the Normandy beaches. He'd opened Pandora's box, even though it was against every rule they'd learned at SOE. The one thing he didn't know was what Sarah had done with the bag after she'd left the Hôtel Le Meurice. But he knew she'd taken it — and he couldn't bear the thought of her being tortured.

I'm sorry, darling. I love you. As the guard forced his head under the dirty water in the sink, this time, instead of fighting, Hugh breathed in deeply. Liquid flooded his lungs.

When the guard realized what was happening, he yanked the prisoner's head out. But it was too late. Hugh was dead.

CHAPTER EIGHTEEN

Von Waltz ordered Sarah to the radio room and had her sit at the table in front of Hugh's set. Sarah was exhausted, every nerve frayed. Fischer stood by the window, observing. The professor gave a loud sniff, then wiped at his nose with a handkerchief.

"I won't try to sugarcoat it, Miss Sanderson. Your fellow terrorist Mr. Thompson died early this morning, rather than give over his security checks."

She sat absolutely still. "No," she said, quietly. "No — Hugh can't be dead."

"Yes." Von Waltz smiled at her. "And so, although we didn't wish to involve a woman if we didn't have to, we'd now like you to use his radio to send messages. Messages we will dictate. We of course expect you to include *your* security checks."

"No," Sarah moaned. Her stomach heaved, and she bent over.

"Miss Sanderson," von Waltz warned in

stern tones.

"I — I'm going to be sick."

"Oh, for Christ's sake —" He snapped at the professor, who fetched the wastepaper basket for her. She gave a few dry heaves, then quieted.

Von Waltz waited, then asked, "Do we have to take you down to the basement to make you cooperate?"

Sarah placed her hands on the table in front of her and pushed back. The chair's legs made a horrible grinding screech, and then she rose, slowly, with a dancer's poise. "Do what you want with me." Her voice was broken. "If Hugh's dead, I don't care anymore."

Von Waltz stared at the resolute woman in front of him, then saw the blood trickling down her legs, puddling on the floor.

"What — what's this?" he yelped, in real shock.

Sarah's ashen face was etched with profound sorrow, like the Madonna of a Pietà, her eyes black holes of grief. She held back her sobs through sheer force of will.

Fischer coughed. "It's blood, sir."

"I know it's blood, you idiot! Why is she bleeding? Why are you bleeding?" The Obersturmbannführer rounded on her. "My men did not touch you! I ordered it!"

"If it's not from rape, then perhaps she's losing a child," Fischer observed mildly, as though commenting on the weather.

"Women!" von Waltz thundered. "Women in war! This is why it's wrong! Guards! Get her cleaned up! Then take her to her room!" When she was gone, he clasped his hands behind his back, and began to pace.

"Sir, we've picked up communications between Gibbon and his handlers in London," the older man ventured.

"Yes?" von Waltz snapped. "Well, come now — don't keep me hanging!"

"They've asked for him to return to London. On the next flight out." The two men locked eyes.

"They might suspect something," Fischer said finally, taking out his handkerchief and blowing his nose.

"They might."

The sun was setting over St. James's Park, exploding in fiery reds and oranges on the horizon. "I'm afraid there's no doubt about it." Henrik Martens wrapped his striped university scarf tighter around his neck. "All the F-Section's mail from Paris to London has been photographed. SOE is compromised. And I believe agents leaving off their security checks have been captured. They

380

are either in Gestapo custody or dead."

"This is terrible," Colonel Bishop said, looking as if it were anything but. In a bowler hat and wrapped in a long black overcoat, the head of MI-6's French Intelligence Section nearly melted into the shadows. "But I don't see how you know for certain."

"These."

The colonel looked at the letters, turning them front and back, holding them up to the light from the window.

"You can't tell by looking at them. But believe me, they've been lit and shot. I used to be an amateur photographer — I took letters that had arrived in the last batch and used chemicals to determine if they'd been exposed to bright light. They have."

"But that doesn't mean anything," Bishop argued, unexpectedly looking like the cat who'd caught the canary.

"The only reason they'd be exposed to such a bright light is if they're being photographed."

"What does Colonel Gaskell say about all this?" Bishop asked carefully.

"When I spoke to him about agents leaving off security checks, he insisted he had it under control. He doesn't know about F-Section's mail being photographed yet.

I've come to you, sir, because I'm extremely concerned there is a mole at SOE. Maybe a few moles. In addition, we have a message from one of our agents in Paris that Raoul was spotted entering 84 Avenue Foch."

"If all this is true . . ." Bishop mused.

"Then we have a spy in our midst. We'll need to get Raoul out of France. And quickly. Before any more of our agents are compromised. Lock him up."

"But first we need to know what he's done exactly — and how much damage there is to the network. It's essential we find that out."

"I'll send a message telling him to be on the next flight back."

"Yes, good, but we must be delicate when he arrives. Otherwise he'll realize what we're doing and make a run for it."

Martens nodded. "I'll let Colonel Gaskell know."

"No! Say nothing to Gaskell! If he asks why you're bringing Raoul back, just say you're doing some reorganizing of the network and want the agent's advice, based on his experience and expertise. It's imperative we get to the bottom, and I mean *very bottom,* of all of this without tipping our hand to Gaskell."

"Agreed."

"And what's the story with that damn sand from Normandy?"

"Still missing in Paris."

"It's imperative we get it back to England. And find out if anyone else knows about it and what secrets it contains. Let me know when you expect Raoul. I want to be there when he arrives."

Maggie moved her bed to a new part of the room every few hours, until Sergeant Schneider lost interest in the noises coming from her room. Then she moved the bed to the room's center.

She wasn't tall enough to reach the window, so she called for the guard. "I'd like a chair," she said pleasantly through the grille, thankful that Sarah's room had a regular window.

"A chair? Why do you need a chair?"

"To put my things on, at night." She leaned forward, appealing to the most German part of his nature. "I do hate a mess, don't you?"

There was a round of questions, but in the end, Maggie got her chair. If she put it on top of the bed, she might be able to reach the bars.

But before she could test her theory, she heard the muffled but unmistakable sound of sobbing through the wall. She got down and went to the pipe. *You all right?* she tapped out. *Sarah?*

Her only answer was moans, animalistic and raw. Maggie pressed her whole body against the wall, as if somehow she could reach her friend and comfort her. But she couldn't; she was powerless. For the first time since Maggie arrived, she began to contemplate utter and complete defeat.

The professor's cold was growing worse; along with his headphones, he now wore a scarf wrapped tightly around his throat to protect from drafts as he listened for any communications from London. Fräulein Schmidt had brought him a mug of the old German cold remedy, boiled beer. Although the older man was dubious of the beverage possessing any antibacterial properties, he sipped it, thankful for the woman's thoughtfulness.

The Germans had been monitoring Gibbon's messages coming and going from London since he and von Waltz had started working together in '40. The latest was less than reassuring. As he finished decrypting it, Fischer forgot his runny nose and scratchy throat in his haste to reach von Waltz's office.

"Gibbon, our 'gift giver,' has been summoned back to London!" the professor managed.

Von Waltz looked up from his papers. "He was spotted by one of the British terrorists entering this building! They must know he's meeting with you!"

"Let me see." Von Waltz grabbed the decrypt and scanned it. He picked up his telephone receiver. "Fräulein Schmidt, arrange through the usual channels for Gibbon to meet with me. Immediately."

The sweeper had broken again and the housekeeper appealed to the guard to let Maggie fix it once more. "In my room, if you don't mind, madame," Maggie suggested. "There's not enough space for me to work in the hall."

In her cell, Maggie examined the sweeper as intently as a surgeon would a body. "I'll see what I can do, madame. I'll need the toolbox again, of course."

The cleaning woman's shoulders sagged with relief. "Of course!" As she went to fetch the toolbox, Maggie summoned all her courage. The woman brought the box, and, as Maggie worked on the sweeper, the maid and the guard flirted, retreating to the hallway. Maggie could hear Sergeant

Schneider asking her to dinner and Madame's "yes" and nervous, high-pitched laughter in reply.

Maggie fixed the sweeper, then, taking a deep breath, she tucked the screwdriver down the front of her dress. Schneider stuck his head in. "How long is this going to take?"

"Done!" She smiled broadly and closed the box. "Here you go!" she said, giving the sweeper back to the wiry woman. "Good as new." Hiding her elation and fear, she latched the toolbox and handed that back as well.

When both had gone, she tapped on the pipe to Sarah: *Have plan.*

Again, there was no response. Maggie's stomach churned with fear and worry. And grief. She didn't know what had happened to Sarah, but given her friend's sobs, it must have been something terrible. What if Sarah had been tortured? And what of Hugh? Had something happened to him? She lay on the bed and, through the barred window, looked up at the stars. She felt as if her heart had cracked.

As she did in times of strife, she took refuge in math, almost as a form of prayer or meditation. In her mind, she turned numbers over, upside down, and inside out, observing. *Why is it that when you pick a number, any number, then double it, add 6, halve it, and take away the number you started with, your answer is always 3?*

If God is both all-powerful and all-good, why does he allow such evil?

Why are there never any real answers?

Gibbon spotted von Waltz, his elegant legs crossed, on a verdigris metal slat bench in the Bois de Boulogne, not far from Porte Dauphine, and sat down next to him. The park was nearly empty in the slanting sun, only a few mothers pushing prams and older men in caps playing a game of petanque in the distance.

Von Waltz looked to the sky. "No hot-air balloons today."

"And no Proustian strolls." But Gibbon was not in the mood for small talk. "I assume you asked to see me because you overheard the message from London. They want me back. It could be a trap."

Von Waltz nodded. "I want you to know if you don't feel it's safe to go, we will keep you here, take care of you. You've served the Reich well. We'll honor that."

Gibbon shook his head. "I must go. If I don't, they will know I've betrayed them. And I'll be no further use to you. But if I go . . . First of all, they might, as they say, merely want help with the network's reorganization. Even if they don't, I can always talk my way out of it. No," he disagreed, meeting the German's eyes. "I'll take the risk."

"You're a brave man." Von Waltz inclined his head. "Come back to us safely."

Gibbon squinted at the sky. "Maybe I can find out something useful while I'm there," he offered as he rose to leave.

"We have a redhead in custody now, a woman — young, very pretty. Insists she's Irish. She's one of yours, I assume."

Gibbon stilled, then shook his head. "No, not that I'm aware."

"Well, of course you'd know! You know all of them coming in and out of France!"

"Well, I don't know *this* one — if she's as pretty as you say, I'd remember, I'm sure!" He gave a brusque laugh. "I'm afraid you're on your own."

He left, not noticing that Reiner, cap pulled low over his eyes, emptying trash cans, had observed the entire meeting.

In the dark, relieved only by the fast-rising waxing moon, Maggie set the chair on the bed, which was now in the middle of the floor, then climbed on top of it, using the skylight's bars to steady herself as she worked. She had the bedsheet draped around her shoulders. The screws that attached the bars to the wooden frame were tight and rusted, and she was working at an awkward angle; with a sinking heart, she realized it was going to take much longer than she had expected.

Maggie heard the scrape of the key in the lock and the bolt sliding back. She slipped the screwdriver up her sleeve as the door opened. "Get down, *Fräulein!* What the devil are you doing?" Sergeant Schneider exclaimed.

Maggie gestured with the sheet. "What do you think I'm doing?" she sobbed.

"You're trying to kill yourself?" The guard ripped the sheet from her hand. "*Nein!* You will not die — not on my watch!" He sounded surprisingly disturbed. "The other one — the one who jumped — she should not have died. I was on duty that night."

So he'd known Erica Calvert. Maggie placed the chair on the floor, then collapsed on the bed in elaborate sobs. "Fine, fine," she managed. "I will live. I will live for you, Sergeant Schneider . . ." she whispered through crocodile tears. ". . . for you."

As he left, the German called back, not unkindly, "I will pray for you, *Fräulein.*"

389

When she was sure he was gone, Maggie took a breath, smoothed her hair, put the chair once more up on the bed, and went back to work.

As the sun rose, Maggie left the screwdriver in the cabinet in the lavatory for Sarah, to pass it between them until they had managed to loosen the bars on their windows.

Although she didn't hear anything through the pipes from Sarah, she was relieved to see the screwdriver had disappeared from the cabinet the next time she used the lavatory.

The screwdriver reappeared the following morning.

Finally, Maggie was able to loosen the last bar. It was June 25. They had only three days before the scheduled pickup. She passed back the screwdriver. Sarah signaled that her bars were off as well. *Tonight is the night,* Maggie tapped back. *Take sheet. Wait for signal. Tell Hugh.*

After lights out, Maggie waited, heart pounding, watching the moon as it rose through the clouds, once again listening to the music of the building. When she was convinced Sergeant Schneider and Madame Bonhomme were deep in conversation, she tapped on the pipe. *Now.*

Gently, she removed the window bars and placed them on the floor. Then she climbed up on the chair. Opening the skylight, she grabbed on to the ledge and pulled herself up.

Sarah was already there, holding her sheet in her arms. The two women nodded, then edged across the length of the rooftop. It was a cool night, with the moon darting in and out of the clouds.

"Where's Hugh?" Maggie whispered.

"Dead."

Maggie stopped and gasped. She grabbed Sarah by the arm. "No." But the pain in her friend's eyes confirmed what she'd said. "Oh, Sarah!" Maggie bit back a sob.

"We can grieve later," Sarah said, with a coldness that chilled Maggie. But she was right: they had to go.

Once they reached the house on the other side, each tore her sheet and knotted the strips together to make a rope. Story by story they climbed down, silently as cats. Maggie stepped over a bird's nest on a rain gutter and slipped, one leg dangling over the black abyss of the garden. She bit back a cry as, slowly, she righted herself.

Together, they shimmied to the ground. Once they'd reached the grass, they put on their shoes. But just as they slipped through the back garden and out the gate onto the street, the air-raid siren sounded, a low, insistent wail.

"The RAF?" Maggie groaned, incredulous. *"Now?"* Already, anti-aircraft fire was exploding upward as searchlights swept the skies. It wouldn't be long until the guards checked their cells and discovered they'd escaped. "Once they figure out we're gone, they'll cordon off the area," Maggie whispered to Sarah. "We need to get as far as we can, as fast as we can, even with the bombing."

Keeping to the shadows, the two women crept down Boulevard de l'Amiral-Bruix to the park. They could see armed soldiers in helmets patrolling the gated entrance. "We're going to have to make a dash for it," Maggie whispered. Sarah nodded.

As they reached the entrance of the Bois de Boulogne, there was a terrifying whine overhead and, immediately, a volley of answering fire from antiaircraft guns on the ground. When the clouds parted and the moonlight spilled down, a Spitfire dropped its cargo. The wind from the dropped bomb whistling in her ears, Maggie grabbed Sarah and rolled into the park's underbrush. The shell exploded on impact yards away, bursting into hot orange flames. The guards dove for cover as fire threatened to engulf them.

Around them, roused birds took off, calling and squawking. Tiny animals ran through the grass. Maggie's ears were ringing. "You all right?" she asked.

"That was . . . close," Sarah managed.

Praying the officers were distracted by the bomb and the fire, they made their way quickly through the shadowed park, keeping to the trees, listening for German hobnailed boots on pavement or the French Milice officers on their bicycles.

They found shelter under some overgrown shrubs, deciding to stay there until daylight. As the moon set and the sun rose, bright red in the east, Maggie whispered to Sarah, "I'm sorry. I'm so, so sorry. Hugh should be with us."

Sarah flinched but did not reply.

"How are you — how's the, I mean —"

"I lost it," Sarah answered bleakly. Maggie bit her lip and squeezed Sarah's hand tightly.

Maggie wanted nothing more than to console her friend, but first they needed to escape. "We'll take the train to Chantilly — my sister is near there. She's got an injured pilot we also need to rescue. Then, once we get the all-go signal, we'll head to the airfield."

"No." Sarah shook her head. "We need to go to the Ritz."

Maggie was ready to cut their losses and run. "We don't have time to go, Sarah. Whatever it is, we need to leave it behind. The SS is no doubt already looking for us."

"Hugh died for what's in that damn bag. We're going back to get it."

"Delaying leaving Paris is suicide."

"I'm not leaving without it."

Maggie knew Sarah's tone; there was no arguing with the dancer. And she wasn't about to leave her friend behind. "All right then — we'll go." She heard a ghost of a chuckle from her friend.

"You can't go to the Ritz looking like that, darling. Your dress is a disaster and you've got twigs in your hair."

CHAPTER NINETEEN

Sarah steered Maggie to the Rue Cambon entrance. "Ah, so this is why I didn't find it before I was captured," Maggie murmured. "As an 'Irish national,' I used the other entrance."

"Well, how the bloody hell was I supposed to know?"

"No, no — it's good — if I'd picked it up before, the Germans would have it now. We can only hope it's still there. What does it look like?"

"Medium-size bag. Black. Anonymous. Heavy. They tied on a label with your name on it."

Maggie entered the smaller lobby and approached the desk. The concierge was a man she'd never seen before, with sparse white hair combed over a sun-spotted pate. "*Bonjour, monsieur.* I am Mademoiselle Paige Kelly." She smiled. "I'm a guest, and while I usually use the Place Vendôme entrance, I believe someone mistakenly left a package for me here."

"Of course, mademoiselle, but first I need to see your identification . . ."

"I don't have it," Maggie said, her heart beating faster. "I mean, I don't have it with me. I, er —" She leaned in. "In truth, I spent the evening with a . . . friend," she confided. Continuing the ruse, she looked down at herself, then back up at the concierge. "Which perhaps explains my *dishabille*. In my hurry to get back, I seem to have left my handbag behind." She attempted a Gallic shrug. *"L'amour,"* she added by way of explanation.

The man was still hesitating when Maggie caught a whiff of jasmine and rose; Coco Chanel entered the lobby in a cloud of No. 5, en route to her Rue Cambon shop; her black silk scarf covered in white camellia flowers and green leaves. She took in Maggie and her wrinkled dress. "What are you doing, Mademoiselle Kelly, using this entrance and not the Place Vendôme side?" she demanded. "Slumming with the locals?"

"I — I'm picking up a package. And I seem to have left my passport with a . . . 'friend' last night."

"Hmmm . . ." said the couturiere, raising a penciled eyebrow. She turned to the concierge. "I vouch for this woman. She's an Irish citizen named Paige Kelly. She has —" Chanel paused. "High-ranking Nazi friends."

The concierge ducked his head. "Of course, Mademoiselle Chanel, Mademoiselle Kelly." He bent under the counter. "I'm so sorry. I don't see anything for you, mademoiselle."

"It was left several days ago," Maggie insisted. "It's a bag, black. It should have a tag with my name on it." She gave him her most persuasive smile. "Perhaps you could check again?" She tilted her head and widened her eyes. *"S'il vous plaît?"*

The man sighed but deigned to look again. "Oh, this old thing?" he said. Maggie's heart lifted. Then, reading the label, "I guess this *is* for you, mademoiselle. A thousand apologies." He passed it over. Chanel watched the exchange without a word, an intrigued expression on her face.

Maggie took the dance bag and slung it over her shoulder. "Thank you," she told the concierge, then nodded in gratitude to Chanel. Maggie began walking out to the narrow Rue Cambon; the couturiere joined her. Across the street and to the left, Maggie could see Chanel's boutique, with its white awnings and distinctive bold black lettering.

"I'm going this way," Chanel said, indicating her shop.

"And I, the other."

As they parted, Chanel leaned in to kiss both of Maggie's cheeks. "I don't know what game you're playing, Mademoiselle Kelly — or whatever your name really is —" she murmured, taking the jasmine-scented scarf from around her neck and wrapping it around Maggie's. "But it's been droll to watch." She gave a world-weary smile. "And war is so rarely amusing." She pulled away and turned to go. She called over her shoulder, *"Bonne chance!"*

Sarah was waiting at the café across the street. "Here —" Maggie handed her the bag. "You do the honors."

"Happy to." Sarah's smile was grim.

Maggie took in Sarah's bruised face. "Wait —" She draped the scarf Chanel had given her over her friend's head and tied it under her chin, in an effort to camouflage the damage. Then, "After all this fuss, do you know what it is?"

"No. And I have no desire to. Did you look?"

"No. If we get recaptured, the less we know the better."

"Hugh looked," Sarah whispered. "That's why I think he let them kill him — rather than tell —" Her eyes filled with tears.

Maggie put her arm around her friend's thin shoulders. "Then we must get it back safely. For Hugh." She squeezed. "Let's go — the nearest Métro is —"

"Why, Mademoiselle Kelly!"

Maggie braced herself, then turned. It was Christian Ruesdorf, eyeing them both curiously. She forced the corners of her mouth up into a smile. "Why, Generaloberst, how lovely to see you."

He crossed the café toward them, smiling broadly. Then, to Maggie's astonishment, he bent and whispered in her ear, still smiling, "They're searching everywhere for you. And for your friend, too." Maggie stared up at him, wondering if he was part of a trap, desperately trying to think of a lie to tell.

"The German man you helped that day — the drunken fool sightseeing — was my younger brother," Ruesdorf continued. "I didn't mention it at the time, because I didn't want to seem as if I were giving him preferential treatment," he said, his blue-green eyes sincere, his smile serene, as if they were discussing favorite teas. "I would like to repay you in kind. What do you need?"

Maggie had no choice but to trust him. "Your car," she replied urgently. "We need your car."

"I have a little sports coupe today. Pale gray. It's parked just down the block." He reached into his pocket and drew out the keys, pressing them into her hand. "Be careful taking turns at high speeds. I just want you to know" — Ruesdorf leaned closer — "I like to read. I have a garden. I used to have Jewish friends. I never wanted to be a Nazi."

"Thank you," Maggie stammered, stunned by this sudden turn of events.

"Enjoy your drive, mademoiselle." He rose, clicked his heels together, and bowed. *"Au revoir."*

Before he could turn away, Maggie rose impulsively. Standing on tiptoe, she kissed him on the cheek. *"Au revoir — et merci, Christian."*

Maggie drove while Sarah navigated, lying down on the backseat in case any of the other cars were looking for a vehicle with two women. She was using a map they'd found in the glove compartment. As the gray of the city segued into bright green countryside, Maggie kept checking the rearview mirror, making sure they weren't being followed. Sarah finally spoke. "Maggie — when they were questioning you, did they . . . know things?"

Maggie thought back to von Waltz and shuddered. In the tension of the escape, she hadn't had time to think about all she and the Obersturmbannführer had exchanged during her interrogation. "He knew about Beaulieu. And about Arisaig." She rubbed at one eye; a piece of grit had gotten in.

"He knew my real name. And Hugh's, too. And" — Sarah faltered, remembering — "he'd read my letters home. He referred to specific things I'd written to my mum. Very specific." Sarah looked to Maggie. "Did he read any of your letters?"

Alas, my branch has fallen from the family tree. Once again, Maggie checked the mirror. "I didn't send any. And he didn't know my real name — at least as far as I know."

"But how could he have read my letters?" Sarah mused aloud. "The Germans must have someone in London . . ."

Without taking her eyes off the road, Maggie blinked hard until the mote finally came out. "— or someone in Paris." *Oh, God.* She felt dizzy. "Jacques's associate — Reiner — picks up the letters from all the agents that are left at Bar Lorraine. When there's a departure, Reiner puts them on the returning plane. He could stop off at any time — have them transcribed or photographed . . . Taken the copies straight to von Waltz."

"If Reiner's working for the Nazis, every agent coming into France is compromised." Her eyes widened. "But why aren't we all getting picked up at drop sites? Or shot down? Why are they letting agents *leave*?"

"Because — because they're letting us go *on purpose.* Because they're playing the long game." Her thoughts roiled. "The Luftwaffe must be working with von Waltz, Sarah — they're *letting* us get through. If he allows the SOE networks to grow under his watch, they'll know a lot more about what our side has planned, including —"

"Oh, Maggie!" Now Sarah, too, knew what was at stake.

"— the location of the invasion." Maggie glanced once again at the mirror. "When we get back to London, we'll report Reiner. But first we need to get Elise."

When Maggie and Sarah arrived at the convent, Elise made sure they ate, then waited for them to bathe and change into clean clothes — novices' dresses and veils, the same as Elise wore. When the two agents met up in the Mother Superior's parlor, they startled at the sight of each other, then laughed.

"Of all the costumes I've had to wear . . ." muttered Sarah. "And I've had to wear quite a few over the years."

The Mother Superior knocked, then opened the door. "Welcome, ladies," she said. Elise stood beside her.

"Thank you, Mère St. Antoine, for your kindness," Maggie told her. "We know the great risk you and the sisters are taking —"

"You are quite welcome," the nun replied. "And thank you for helping our . . . guest. Elise tells me you'll all be leaving soon. Of course you're welcome to stay as long as you need."

"Thank you, Mère," Maggie repeated. "If it's possible, I need access to a wireless today. The BBC makes coded broadcasts about the flights' departures. I must be certain our flight is still scheduled before we make the trip to the airfield."

The Mother Superior gestured to Elise. "Please show them to the radio our guest is using."

"Also," Sarah said, "how will we all get to the airfield? Won't we all be conspicuous?"

Elise smiled, a glint of mischief in her eyes. "You'll go in coffins!" she exclaimed.

"Sorry?"

"Coffins," Elise repeated. "You see, we

403

have an infirmary. The *enfants* are here for life. And so we have a morgue and, well . . . coffins."

"If they are without family, we bury them here, of course," Mère St. Antoine added. "But sometimes their families wish them to be in ancestral plots or mausoleums. And so one of our sisters will drive the body, in its coffin, to the *enfant*'s church. They handle the arrangements from there."

"And how do you transport the . . . coffins?" Sarah asked, face pale. Maggie knew she was thinking about Hugh, so recently dead.

"We have a funeral coach, of course."

Maggie and Sarah looked to each other. "Of course."

"No, I'm *not* going in a coffin," insisted Gus. Maggie, Sarah, and Elise were all in the pilot's room in the chapel near the morgue, listening to Gilbert and Sullivan on the wireless:

Things are seldom what they seem,
Skim milk masquerades as cream;
Highlows pass as patent leathers;
Jackdaws strut in peacock's feathers . . .

Elise was sitting on the edge of his bed,

404

cleaning his wound, while Sarah paced, standing guard near the door. "Gus," Elise admonished, "you're a pilot, a captain — you've been shot down in battle over enemy territory — and survived. Surely you can get into a coffin for a bit." In the church tower, the bells rang out. It was getting late.

"No," he insisted, real panic in his voice. "I'm not doing it! Small, windowless spaces terrify me! What's that called again?"

Sarah rolled her eyes. "Inconvenient?"

Maggie was perched on a wooden stool in front of the wireless radio, moving the dial by increments through static and atmospheric crackles to keep Radio Londres coming in.

Black sheep dwell in every fold;
All that glitters is not gold;
Storks turn out to be but logs;
Bulls are but inflated frogs . . .

"Claustrophobia," Elise corrected.

"Hush," Maggie admonished. "Try counting backward from a hundred," she told Gus.

"What happens when I get to zero?"

"Start again."

They listened as the BBC announcer came on with the evening's deliberately obscure *messages personnels.* "Before our next song, please listen to some personal messages. 'Mathilde has blond hair,' 'There is a fire at the bank,' 'All good men will come to a party.' 'The dice are on the table.' " And then, " 'The night has a thousand eyes . . .' "

"That's it!" Maggie twisted the radio's dial off. "The night has a thousand eyes" was their cue the rendezvous was on. "It's tomorrow night!"

"Where are we going?" Gus asked, his face white.

"There's a field near Amboise, where we flew in. The plane will be there."

"Amboise," Elise repeated thoughtfully. "That's nearly thirty kilometers away. We'll need to leave as soon as possible."

That night, under the light of the full moon, Elise drove the convent's hearse through the shadows, the headlights covered with slatted blackout covers. Maggie navigated. She read from a worn Michelin map by the moonlight pouring through the car's windshield, the heavy black bag at her feet. Sarah and Gus were hidden in wooden coffins in the back. "We're not being followed," Maggie said. But she looked back, just to be sure.

"A mercy. But I'm more concerned with

roadblocks and checkpoints."

There was an uncomfortable silence, then both women began to speak at the same time. "You first," Maggie said.

"No, you."

"Please."

Elise took a breath. "I was just going to say that even though I got the parents and you didn't, we both made our own families, didn't we? I with the nuns here, and you in England, with your friends. Even in the brief time we've been together, I can see the bond you have with Sarah."

Maggie thought of Sarah and of her friends back home — David and Freddie, Chuck and Griffin, even K. And, yes, John across the ocean in Los Angeles. Elise was right; *they* were her family now. "Do you ever think of what you'd be doing if there weren't a war?" she asked her sister.

"We spoke of it lightheartedly before, but I'd like to think maybe I can still be a doctor," Elise replied seriously. "Go back to university when all this is over. Because I do believe this war will end someday. Somehow."

"I saw how you were with Gus. You're obviously a wonderful nurse. You'd make an excellent doctor, if that's what you want."

"What do you think you'd be doing?"

"I'd probably still be in graduate school, studying mathematics. Not Princeton, as I'd always wanted — they don't admit women — but at MIT. Still, when I think of myself there, I see myself as bookish and closed off. Living in a black-and-white world of numbers and theory, not truly alive." She adjusted her wimple. "Passive."

"So, in some ways the war has been good for you?"

"War is never good," Maggie retorted with bitterness. "*Never.* There's never a 'good' war — but I do think we're fighting a *just* war. That said, we don't get to choose the times we live in, do we?"

Elise rubbed at her nose, then confessed. "That's why I was so angry with you — so afraid of you. When I saw you kill, I thought you had lost your humanity."

"I hated it," said Maggie. "I hated doing it and I still hate that I did it. I'll remember that young man as long as I live." Her hand crept to her own bullet scar. "But Elise, I — I had to do what I did. I had to. I've made my peace with killing him. And I won't apologize —" There was a loud explosion. Elise slammed on the brakes and the hearse skidded to a stop.

A muffled voice called from the back. "Did they shoot us?" It was Sarah.

Elise grimaced, reaching for the door handle. "Just a tire."

"A tire," Maggie repeated, getting out to take a look in the moonlight. *The fun never ends.*

Together, Maggie and Elise took the spare off the back of the car, then slid the jack under the axle. "Can you believe," Elise managed as she worked, "that some men don't think women can change a tire?"

Maggie stopped and looked up. "For goodness' sake, keep quiet!" she whispered. "There's a checkpoint ahead!" A uniformed German soldier was approaching. "Keep working," she muttered.

"I'll throw the jack at him if he gets any closer —"

"Keep your voice down, Sister." Maggie realized after the words were spoken that Elise might think she was trying to force their relationship rather than stay in character as a novice nun. Well, there was nothing to do about it now.

The officer stopped a few feet away from the women. "My goodness! Nuns! What on earth are you doing here this time of night?"

"Flat tire," Maggie explained easily. "We're from the convent of the Filles de la Charité, which houses an infirmary for the mentally ill."

The soldier crossed himself. "I can help you if you'd like."

"Thank you, sir." Maggie knew refusal of his offer would only mean more suspicion.

"It's my pleasure, Sisters," the German assured them as he rolled the damaged tire off the road and bent to attach the new one. "You know, most of you French women snub us. Won't let us help with anything."

"Well, *we're* certainly grateful," Maggie gushed, desperate to mask the fear in her voice. *If he finds Sarah and Gus . . .*

"It's shortsighted of the French not to be kinder to us — not speak to us, not invite us to visit their families. I should very much like to get to know Paris from the inside. Yet these cold Frenchmen hold us at arm's length — and women, well, they're even worse!" he complained, tightening the lug nuts on the wheel. "It's so sad to see Paris under these circumstances. The so-called City of Light is famous for its good living and beautiful women. Wine, women, and song, right? Not for me. At least *you* have been polite to me, Sisters." He spun down the jack, and the car settled on its tires.

"Of course," Elise responded with forced cheer.

"Thank you," he said, handing the tools back to her. "Oh!" he said, peering in. "Are those . . . coffins?"

"They are, sir," Maggie said, heart in her throat. Would he want to search them?

"Alas," Elise explained, "two of our charges have died, and we're transporting them back to their home parish."

He shuddered. "God bless you both." He came around to the front of the hearse. "I'm a bit lonely here," he admitted, before saluting smartly.

"Sometimes loneliness can be a good thing," Maggie said as they climbed back into the hearse.

Jacques was waiting for them. In the moonlight and the glow from the hearse's slatted headlights, Maggie saw his silhouette as he stood in front of a corrugated-metal shed at the end of a makeshift airfield. An RAF Lockheed Hudson was parked in the rough grass.

The air was damp and cool. Maggie's shoes sank into the spongy earth as she stepped out of the vehicle. Somewhere, an owl called mournfully.

Jacques ran to embrace Maggie. "You made it!"

"It was close," she admitted. "A little side trip to Avenue Foch."

He kissed her forehead. "But you made

411

it." Then he turned to scowl at the hearse. "What's in there?"

Maggie walked back and swung open the doors. "More passengers."

The coffins were heavy. Gus was wild-eyed and breathing heavily when he was finally released.

"It's all right," Elise comforted him as he flailed and tried to stand.

"You did it!" Maggie said as she handed Sarah the precious bag.

"I thought we were done for at the check-point," Sarah said softly.

Elise nodded. "So did I."

"Jacques," said Maggie, "this is my half sister —"

"Sister," Elise corrected.

"Sister," Maggie agreed, smiling broadly.

"Ah." He was wearing a fleece-lined leather jacket and scarf. A messenger tote was slung over his shoulder; Maggie noted it was the same one Reiner had carried when he'd arrived at the Charcots' house, six days ago. "One more passenger than expected — shouldn't affect the fuel we'll need."

"You're the pilot?" Maggie asked, surprised. She remembered he'd told her that he could fly. Still, she wasn't expecting to see him personally taking the plane to England.

"I am." He winked. "I'm needed back in London, so — two birds, one stone, et cetera."

As Gus took a step forward to offer his hand, he buckled and collapsed; Jacques caught the Englishman in his arms as he fell.

"What's the matter with him?" Jacques asked Maggie.

"Injury and infection."

Elise was bent over his leg. "So much blood. . . . His wound must have reopened during the drive — all those bumps in the road." In the moonlight, the bandages looked black and wet.

"Is he strong enough to travel?" Jacques asked.

"He *must* get back to London. He has blood poisoning. He needs to be in a hospital." Elise looked to Maggie, then rose. "I want to thank you," she said slowly, "for coming to France for me."

And all at once, Maggie knew what was coming. The tone in Elise's voice was a regretful prelude to goodbye.

"No . . ." Every fiber of Maggie's being had led her to this moment, to getting Elise on this flight to London, to safety. *We're so, so close* . . . "Elise, you have to come with us," she insisted. "Please."

"The *enfants* need me," Elise explained gently. "And maybe I'm meant to be a nun. But I'll never know if I don't stay. Go," she urged. They embraced fiercely.

Finally, the younger woman drew back, smiling, although tears glimmered in her eyes. "I'll pray for all of you. Especially for you, Maggie, my dear, dear sister. Now that I've gotten to know you better, I think you may need my prayers most of all. But I feel better, knowing you're fighting this war with us."

Maggie felt tears sting her eyes. *To have come so far . . .* "Elise —" she pleaded.

"Shhh," Jacques warned. "Voices carry."

"Promise me, Maggie," Elise whispered, "you'll never kill again."

"I can't promise you that," Maggie answered. "But I *do* promise I'll do everything in my power not to."

"Yes — I understand. And the next time we see each other, there will be a Tricolor over the Tomb of the Unknown Soldier."

"Well, you never know — I may be back to France sooner than you expect . . ."

"You need to leave." Elise kissed Maggie and embraced her once more, holding her close. "It isn't safe to linger."

Elise was right: for a moment, Maggie had

414

forgotten they were in enemy territory. She looked to Jacques and Sarah. "Let's get Gus on the plane. It's time to go."

The interior of the twin-engine Hudson was constructed of gray metal, dented and drab, with benches along each side of a narrow aisle. A row of small windows lined each wall. Tiny flickering green lights cast a sickly glow.

Jacques dumped his leather satchel on a bench, checked his watch, then made his way through the open door to the cockpit. Maggie lifted a heavy box of tools and set it on the floor as Sarah helped Gus to the bench and strapped him in, propping him up between them. The pilot closed his eyes, head lolling. The engine roared as it came to life.

Maggie put a hand to Gus's forehead. "He's burning up," she called above the noise, feeling safe enough to switch from French into English.

"He'll make it," Sarah replied grimly. "He's got to. *Someone* should."

For the first time, it occurred to Maggie that this part of the mission was just as dangerous as what had come before. Perhaps even more so. They could be attacked by the Luftwaffe, they could crash, they could . . . *Stop it!* She forced herself to take a shaky breath. *You escaped the Gestapo — you can make it across the English Channel.*

Maggie reached over and grasped her friend's hand. "Look, whatever you need when we get home, Sarah — if you need a place to live, my house is yours. If you want to be left alone, I'll make you meals on trays. If you want to go out and get drunk every night, I'm your girl. If you want to go back to the ballet, I'll sew ribbons on your toe shoes and darn your tights. I'm here for you — whatever you need."

Sarah looked her friend in the eye. "Honestly, Maggie, I don't know how I'm going to get through the next two minutes, let alone the next two days. It hurts. I never thought anything could hurt so much."

"I'm here for you," Maggie repeated. "And I'll always be here for you." The aircraft lurched forward, then began to move, rattling and shaking as it rolled faster and faster over the grass.

And then they were airborne.

CHAPTER TWENTY

Inside the cabin of the plane, it was cold and noisy. Maggie and Sarah both slipped into shearling-lined flight jackets and helped Gus into his. The Englishman was falling in and out of consciousness. Over his head, Maggie met Sarah's gaze; the dancer had the black bag next to her, with its own safety belt. They nodded, acknowledging what they'd been through. *Hugh should be here with us,* Maggie thought, blinking back hot tears. *Hugh should be going home, too.* From the closed-off expression on Sarah's face, she knew her friend was thinking the same.

The plane climbed steadily. Maggie stared out the window; with the full, bright moon, there were few visible stars. Far below, shadows shrouded the farms.

And Elise — Maggie felt a pang of bitter disappointment. Her sister wasn't returning with her to London. But they'd made a connection, and that was something. Her loneliness had been eased. She had a sister. A sister who might be in Occupied France, but still — a sister. Family.

And, really, she admired her sister's commitment to the *enfants* and to finding her path in life. *This is where you belong, Elise. And, maybe — if we're lucky — we'll see each other again . . .*

The aircraft leveled off. They flew smoothly for minutes, until, without warning, the plane lurched sideways, causing them all to rock violently. "The wind," Maggie said, if only to reassure herself. One of the gray-painted panels began rattling.

Sarah pulled something from Gus's breast pocket. "I saw your sister put this in," she told Maggie, holding up a small flask. "Don't think he'd mind if I had a sip, do you?"

"Go ahead."

Sarah took a long pull, then put her feet up on the toolbox. "Your sister has good taste in Cognac." She offered the flask to Maggie, who shook her head.

"Maybe later."

"I wish I had a cigarette," the dancer said, taking another swig.

"You might want to pace yourself."

"Sod that." Sarah tipped back the flask, then wiped her mouth with the back of her hand.

"Sarah — you remember how we were talking about Reiner and the letters? Reiner's not the only one who has access to the letters."

"Bollocks." Sarah unbuckled her safety belt and made her way to the satchel Jacques had left. "Let's see what we have here."

"Sarah —"

She opened the bag; it was full of papers and letters. The dancer rifled through the envelopes and pulled one out. "This is my last letter home — I wrote it the day before Hugh and I were captured. Left it at the assigned drop-off." She examined it in the sickly light of the cabin, then slid next to Maggie. "It's been opened."

Maggie didn't see any rips or tears. "How do you know?"

"Look here — it's wrinkled, like it's been held over steam. And there's too much glue on the envelope flap. Someone opened it, then resealed it."

Maggie suddenly remembered Jacques's warning: *Trust no one.*

"My God." Her heartbeat was so loud in her ears it almost blotted out the engine's roar.

Jacques appeared from the cockpit. "We're good," he told them. "The weather's holding and no Messerschmitts in sight."

"So who's flying the plane?" Maggie asked, keeping her voice level.

"She's on gyroscopic autopilot — we should reach Tangmere in no time." He looked to Sarah. "My condolences about Hugh."

She said through clenched teeth, "Thank you." The rage radiating from her was palpable.

"His mother will be proud," Jacques said gently.

Maggie stiffened. "His mother?"

As Hugh's friend, Maggie knew the Englishman's mother was alive and his father was dead. With their intimacy, Sarah must, too. *But why would Jacques?*

"I — I assumed," he stammered.

"But why would you 'assume' his mother — and not his father? Why not say 'his parents'?" Maggie pressed. "Unless you've read Hugh's letters home . . ."

"I spoke with him when you landed," Jacques replied easily, recovering. "He must have mentioned her."

"No," Sarah responded. "He didn't. I never left Hugh's side when we landed. He never discussed his family with you. And that was the only time you had together."

Maggie looked into Jacques's eyes; they

420

were blue and brown. They were also sad and shrewd.

"You . . ." She felt the sting of betrayal. "It's you! Oh my God — it was you all this time . . ."

His expression shuttered, and he pivoted swiftly to step back to the cockpit.

"Wait!" She jumped up and followed. "What are you doing?"

"Turning this plane around. Taking us all back to France."

"And giving us up to the Gestapo?" Maggie challenged.

"You've burned me. I'm already under suspicion for working with the Germans — that's why they've ordered me back. If I return to England, and they know I've been going through the letters, I'll be shot as a traitor."

"And if we go back to France, we'll be taken by the Gestapo again. To be tortured by your friend von Waltz."

"I'll do what I can for you. Put in a good word."

"How dare you!" Sarah was the picture of cold fury.

"I'm not your enemy —"

"You are. You're worse than the Nazis."

He shrugged. "I'll save you the Nazi-versus-Commie lecture for when we return

421

to Paris."

"I hate you," Maggie said, a vein throbbing beneath one eye. She put her face up to his. "And I hate that damn French shrug! You *are* a traitor. People have died because of you! So we will get you back to London — and they'll deal with you there. *Va te faire enculer, fils de pute!*"

Jacques gave her a twisted smile. "I see we've gone from *Qui vivra verra* to profanity. Be very careful," he warned. "You can't do anything to me. Who'll get us home?" Maggie and Jacques were so engrossed in their argument, they didn't notice Sarah rise and move to the toolbox.

"Gus," Maggie said resolutely. "Gus will get us home."

"*Gus* can't even keep his eyes open. And if I'm not mistaken, he's wet himself. He'll get you home all right — in a ball of fire."

"You never had a friend at a morgue," Maggie said, thinking it through. "You *knew* von Waltz killed Calvert. It was the Germans who were using her radio. That's why her messages never had their proper security checks . . ."

"Erica Calvert committed suicide," he said. "I had nothing to do with having her killed. She died rather than collaborate with the Gestapo."

422

"So, the letters home — did you have them transcribed for your Nazi friends? Or photographed?"

"Photographed," he said. "In a little flat not far from Avenue Foch. Didn't take long."

"And Bar Lorraine," Maggie pressed. "Has it always been compromised?" She looked to Sarah. "Is that where they captured you?"

Sarah moved closer to the two, hiding the wrench behind her back. She nodded.

"I told you *not* to go to Bar Lorraine, to go to the safe house instead!" Jacques cried. "I tried to *save* you!"

The wrench in Sarah's hand slammed into Jacques's skull with a wet crunch. Maggie gasped as he collapsed like a puppet with its strings cut.

Sarah dropped the bloody wrench and took a step back. "He betrayed Hugh and got him killed. I'd rather take my chances in the sky than go back to France," Sarah rasped. "You?"

Maggie didn't reply. She knelt beside the injured man to take his pulse. "He's alive."

"Too bad."

Maggie examined the gash on his head. "It's superficial. He won't be out for long. We've got to tie him up."

423

Sarah dropped the wrench and went to the toolbox to get a length of rope. "We might die up here," she said matter-of-factly, stooping to bind his wrists.

"Better in a plane than the basement of 84 Avenue Foch. We need to wake Gus up."

"How?"

"We have those pills we got in case we needed to keep going — Benzedrine. If we give him a few, it might shock him awake." Maggie sat down on the bench and took off her right shoe, twisting the heel. It moved, and the cellophane packet with two round pills dropped into her waiting palm.

"You're sure that's not the cyanide?"

She gave a sad smile. "No, those pills are in my lipstick case."

Maggie lifted Gus's head. She placed the tablets in his mouth, then poured liquid from the flask down his throat. He spluttered noisily, then swallowed. "Good boy," Maggie said, patting his back as he gagged and his eyelids quivered. "That should work in a few minutes."

"Maggie?" Sarah asked.

"Yes?"

"Autopilot or no — someone should probably be flying this plane."

Moonlight was streaming through the cockpit windows, illuminating the instrument panel. Maggie was as terrified as she'd ever been. Still, she forced herself to slip into the pilot's leather seat. She rested her hands lightly on the yoke, staring out at the cloud formations in front of her. Her heart was hammering.

She was petrified to take her eyes off the sky, but she knew she had to look down at the instrument panel. She checked the altitude. Miraculously, the plane seemed to be holding steady. She checked the fuel — the tank was just shy of full. *We're in the equivalent of a tin can hurtling through space and time,* she realized, simultaneously wanting to cry and giggle.

She looked up as Gus staggered in, supported by Sarah. In the shadows, the pilot's eyes were rimmed with red and his skin looked clammy. "Here you go," the dancer said, helping the injured pilot into the navigator's chair.

"Oh, you should be the one in the pilot's seat —" Maggie said, starting to rise. She wanted nothing more than to relinquish the terrible responsibility.

"I can't operate the rudders with my injury," he slurred. "If we're . . . going to do this, you need to be my legs."

"Are — are you sure? I barely passed my

425

driving test back home in the States. Never did learn to parallel-park, if we're being completely honest."

"No need for parallel parking up here." Gus attempted a grin and failed. "I'm afraid if I try to move, I'll pass out from the pain."

"I've had far too much Cognac to fly anything." Sarah clapped him on the shoulder, and he winced. "All right then — you two do what you need to do. I'm going to keep an eye on our Judas in the back."

"So," Maggie said when she and Gus were alone in the cockpit, her heart a cold fist. "This is flying."

"You can do it, miss."

"Sure." Maggie sounded less than convinced. "Just like driving my Aunt Edith's 'thirty-two Ford back home. And it's Maggie, please — not miss."

"All right, then. That's the altimeter, that's the vertical speed indicator, that's the artificial horizon, and that's the compass." Gus pointed to each in turn.

A sudden patch of turbulence made the aircraft sway. Maggie squeezed her eyes shut, reciting the decimal places of pi. *Three point one four one five nine two . . .*

"*Don't* close your eyes — whatever you do!" Gus insisted. "We're going to Tangmere, yes?"

426

She somehow managed to nod.

"Good — I've taken off and landed there before." He eyed the compass. "Three hundred fifteen degrees magnetic — we're on course. Keep her steady."

They flew in silence for a while. "How do you feel?" she asked, desperate to break the tension.

"Not up for the Lindy Hop, I'm sorry to say. But the pills helped."

Without taking her eyes from the sky, Maggie put her hand to his forehead. He was on fire. "You've got a fever."

He grimaced. "We'll deal with that on the ground. In the meantime, I'd like to get above this cloud. We're at three thousand feet. I need you to take us to five thousand."

Maggie pulled back on the yoke and the plane jerked up, slamming them backward. Back in the cabin, Sarah yelped.

"No! Not so fast!" Gus cried.

Maggie adjusted the altitude.

"All right, better, better. . . . Now, just make sure you keep climbing — maintain the climb rate using the vertical speed indicator at five hundred feet per minute. Don't raise the nose too fast or too far up, or you'll stall."

"And if we stall?"

"Don't ask."

427

In moments they entered what looked like cotton, and she realized they were actually in the clouds. "I can't see!" Maggie said, a crackle of panic in her voice. "I can't see a thing!" A fine mist swirled at the cockpit's windowpanes. "Where are the windshield wipers?"

"Afraid there aren't any. The instruments are our eyes — watch your artificial horizon to keep your wings level. And have faith."

"We could hit a mountain!"

"We're nowhere near the Alps." She could hear suppressed laughter in his strained voice. "There are no mountains in this part of France."

The cloud thinned. "All right now — gently — level her off," he instructed.

Maggie carefully adjusted the yoke, eyes flicking between the windshield and the instruments, as the plane's engines droned on. She glanced at Gus, at his increasing pallor, the bruise-like smudges under his eyes. "Do you need water?" she asked.

"No, I'd really prefer not to have to take a piss on the floor in front of you. Er — sorry about the language."

"Gus, we're five thousand feet in the air in a glorified sardine can. Do you really think I care about your damn language?"

"I do try to be a gentleman."

"And I'm sure your mother's very proud."

They flew in silence. "All right," Maggie said, "let's have a quick lesson. I know how to change altitude. But how do we control the speed?"

"The engine controls are here on the center console. These two levers are the left and right engine throttles. Push forward to give it more power."

"All right — good to know. What else?"

"You won't need to worry about the flaps and landing gear until later." Gus was squinting at the horizon. "Shit! Er, sorry."

"What?"

He pointed. "Messerschmitt — ten o'clock, climbing." He pointed.

"Oh, bloody hell!" The German plane was still in the distance, but as it climbed closer, Maggie could see the distinctive black crosses on its wings. She felt nauseous. "Because we didn't have problems already —"

"It's a Messer 109." Gus explained it as if they were out on a nature walk and had spotted some harmless animal in the underbrush. "She's fast and light, with two machine guns mounted in the cowling. They fire over the top of the engine and through the propeller arc. He'll definitely try to shoot us down. We're going to have to brace for impact. Are you strapped in?"

"No . . ." He glared at her, and she bristled. "We didn't exactly have time for all the niceties, what with capturing the double agent and taking control of the plane!"

"Grab that strap and put it around you," he said, doing the same for himself. Maggie managed with trembling fingers.

"Your friend should, too."

"Sarah!" Maggie shouted.

Sarah poked her head back in. "What?"

"We've got company — buckle up." Sarah left. "All right then, Gus, what do we have? Where's the artillery?"

He looked around, then grimaced. "I'm afraid we have nothing."

"Nothing?"

"They took out the gun turrets to make the plane lighter," he explained.

"So we're completely defenseless?"

"Yes. We need to hide — fly into another cloud — find cover. There —" Gus pointed. "Go there."

She adjusted the yoke with shaking hands, muttering obscenities. As the enemy plane edged closer, Maggie could see bright flashes. She heard the chilling *rat-a-tat-tat* of gunfire.

They had not been shot.

Yet.

The Messerschmitt flashed past them, then arced, swooping in for another pass. As it approached, it opened fire again. The sparks flared red and orange in the night sky.

The left wing was hit, the bullets punching through the aluminum skin. The sound was terrifying. "It's all right," Gus reassured her. "Just as long as he doesn't hit the fuel tank."

"Oh, you bloody, bloody, buggering *bugger*!" Maggie's anger felt good, and swearing even better. Better to be furious than frightened out of her mind.

"All right — it's all right," Gus said by way of comfort. "We're still in the air, after all. And we're almost there. Just keep going toward the cloud."

As the German plane banked and prepared for a third pass, they reached the safety of the cloud. "Now change direction," Gus instructed.

Maggie did so, smoother this time. They'd lost the German plane and now flew in silence. Maggie didn't know what Gus was thinking, but her thoughts were of Jacques. His betrayal.

"May I ask what happened to the original pilot?" Gus ventured.

"We knocked him out."

"Ah. And we did this — why?"

"Because our pilot turned out to be a slimy, two-faced, traitorous, Nazi-loving Frog. Who was planning to take us back to Paris and the Gestapo when we found out what the bastard was up to."

"Righty-o, then," Gus ventured. "Probably a good decision to take over the plane after all."

"We thought so."

As they finally left the cloud, Maggie spotted a gray-blue stripe below, shimmering in the moonlight. "Is that the Channel?"

"It is."

"Oh!" Her heart leapt for joy; they were crossing back to England. "Hello there, Blighty!" *Home. Normality. Laughing with David. Having tea and toast with Chuck. The sweet fragrance of baby Griffin's downy head. K's purr. These are the things that matter,* she thought. *Love is what matters.*

Gus wiped at his eyes with a fist. "I'm not crying."

"No, of course not. I have something in my eye, too." Then, "How long until we get to Tangmere?"

"A bit. The base is on the south coast, near West Sussex."

"I've been there," Maggie told him. "But only as a passenger." RAF Tangmere, about

432

four miles east of Chichester, was often used as a base during the moon periods because the airfields were so much nearer to their target areas in France than those at Tempsford.

"Well, I hate to tell you . . . but it's not flying that's hard, it's landing. And from what I've heard the boys say, these Hudsons can go up in flames if they're not brought down gently."

"Gus," Maggie said tightly, "if you're trying to reassure me, it's not working."

"Swear all you want if it helps."

She let out a dazzlingly creative string of profanities, making the Englishman blush. "You're right, that does help!"

He looked both horrified and impressed. "Do you, er, know what all of those words actually mean?"

"Most of them." Maggie peered through the cockpit window at England in the silvery light right before dawn. Below her was a patchwork quilt of farmers' fields, copses of trees, rivers, lakes, and ponds. Despite her fear of the task ahead, she had an unmistakable urge to sing "Rule, Britannia."

Finally, Gus pointed. "That's Tangmere, there — do you see? Look for the lines of runways and the control tower."

"I see it. Should we let them know we're

coming? Use the radio?"

Gus tapped the instrument panel. "No radio."

There's no radio? "Let me guess — to make the plane lighter?"

He didn't reply.

Maggie took a shaky breath. "Right then. Let's land this thing."

"There." He pointed to a runway slicing through the center of the airbase. "Go for that one. Runway heading is two hundred and sixty-three degrees. Drop your flaps and landing gear when you get below a hundred twenty-five knots."

Maggie pulled the lever back, and, as the engines' roar eased, the plane began to descend. Her heart was trip-hammering.

"Don't overdo it — nice gentle descent," Gus instructed.

"Easy for you to say," Maggie muttered.

"Now drop the gear and flaps. Aim for the runway." It seemed they were almost touching the ground. The airfield fence line flashed past, and they were skimming the airstrip.

"You've got to bring her down now," Gus said. "Or we're going to hit the tower."

"Bloody hell."

"Cut the engines back the rest of the way to idle." There was a long moment that seemed to stretch forever — then a bump as the wheels finally made contact with the earth. The plane bounced up again instantly, then crashed back to the runway. But at least they were on the ground and rolling.

"Brakes!"

Maggie screamed, "Where?"

"Pull on the Johnson bar in the center console!"

"This?"

"No!"

"This?"

"Yes!"

The rolling aircraft slowed with a shudder and a louder roar than any they'd heard in the sky. As it finally came to a stop, Maggie couldn't help herself. She burst into tears.

"You did it!" Gus exclaimed.

"*We* did it!" But before she could undo her safety belt, he'd passed out.

CHAPTER TWENTY-ONE

Dawn was breaking at RAF Tangmere, the sun turning the high, silvery clouds pink. From the cockpit window, Maggie could see two men in dark suits and two Coldstream Guards. She stepped past Gus with a "sorry" and ran for the door. Together, she and Sarah managed to open it.

"Here!" Maggie yelled. "We have an injured man in the cockpit!" As soon as the gangplank was extended, the guards boarded the plane. She watched them place Gus on the stretcher and carry him out. As Sarah stood over Jacques with the wrench, Maggie called out the Hudson's door to the other two men in dark suits. "And we have a prisoner."

She led Jacques out, his hands still tied behind his back. Sarah followed, holding the dance bag in both arms.

England, Maggie thought as she made her way down the plane's narrow stairs, greedily breathing in the sweet morning air. *Home.* She felt dizzy with a heady mix of joy, sorrow, anger, and relief.

She watched anxiously as the guards lifted Gus's stretcher into a waiting Range Rover. She owed it to him, and to Elise, and to Mère St. Antoine, to make sure everything was done for the injured pilot. "We'll take good care of him, miss," one of the men assured her. It was wonderful to hear people speaking English.

The two men in suits, Bishop and Martens, stared at Jacques, his face angry and defiant. "Raoul, I presume. I'm Colonel Bishop, head of MI-6's French Intelligence Department. This is Colonel Henrik Martens. And you must be Jacques Lebeau, real name Jean-George Dubois. Tell me, what did the Nazis call you?"

Jacques stuck out his chin. "Gibbon." His hair was matted with blood.

"Care to explain why an SOE agent would be consorting with the Sicherheitsdienst?" Martens asked the Frenchman.

"Sir, it's a misunderstanding —"

"No, it's not. He's a double agent," Maggie clarified. "He's been working with von Waltz and the Sicherheitsdienst — photographing agents' mail, compromising our communications. He betrayed Hugh and

437

Sarah and me to the Nazis by letting us think Bar Lorraine was safe." Then, to Jacques, "You're the lowest of the low — a double agent. A traitor. God help you." She had to look away — the sight of him was too much to bear.

"Take him in the Range Rover. We'll question him later." Bishop gave a signal to the soldiers, who herded Jacques into the vehicle and drove off.

Colonel Martens scratched his head. "If Raoul was tied up, who landed the plane?"

"Maggie did," Sarah answered.

"Gus and I did it together."

Martens raised an eyebrow, then extended a hand. "You're Miss Hope? I've been eager to meet you." As they shook hands, Maggie realized how cold hers were. She felt chilled to the very bone.

Martens seemed to read her mind. "Here," he said, taking off his coat and wrapping her in it. Bishop did the same for Sarah.

"Oh, dear," Maggie said, remembering her abrupt departure to France. "You haven't been talking to Miss Lynd, have you? Whatever she's told you, don't believe her." She looked around. "She usually attends both the departures and the arrivals — where is she?"

Bishop ignored her question. "Where is

Mr. Thompson?"

"Dead," Sarah whispered.

Martens removed his trilby. His lips tightened into a thin line, but he said nothing.

"Were you able to complete your mission?" Bishop asked. Sarah shook her head mutely, and he scowled before turning to Maggie.

"Agent Calvert?"

"Also dead," Maggie admitted quietly. "But we did get her bag." She motioned to Sarah, who was cradling it in her arms like an infant.

"Sir, we —"

"Not here." Bishop held up a peremptory hand. "Colonel Martens and I will be handling your debrief at the house. Tell us everything then."

Maggie turned away, looking up at the rising sun and gold-tinged clouds, momentarily overwhelmed. *Another mackerel sky,* she thought.

"You're between worlds," Martens told her gently, once again uncannily seeming to read her thoughts. "It's hard to get used to, I know. Only a few people understand."

"And you're one of them." Maggie realized this was his way of telling her that he, too, had been on missions abroad. "What is

439

it that you do again, Colonel Martens?"

"The Prime Minister recently appointed me 'Minister of Disinformation.' "

Maggie made a sound halfway between a snort and a laugh. "That sounds like Mr. Churchill."

"You worked for the P.M., didn't you? As a secretary?"

"Yes, a long time ago." Maggie looked to Sarah, standing alone, lips pressed together so hard they looked white, and realized this was only the beginning of grief for her friend.

Bishop put a hand on her shoulder. "Miss Sanderson. I believe you have something for us."

For a moment, it looked as if Sarah was going to refuse to hand the bag over, then, without speaking, she thrust it toward him.

Bishop accepted it, bowing his head in acknowledgment of its cost. "Thank you, Miss Sanderson. And please let me thank you on behalf of a grateful nation, although one who will never know all the sacrifices you — and Mr. Thompson — made."

Martens cut through the heavy silence. "Right then — let's get you two ladies back to the house. You can freshen up and have some breakfast. And then, when you're ready, we'd like to have a little chat."

■ ■ ■ ■

They drove on a narrow hedgerow lane across gently sloping, green hills. The car's windows were open to the warm air. On the edge of the grounds was a roadblock where an RAF sergeant asked them for identification. Bishop showed it, and the guard waved them all through.

They passed through a tall gate and then made their way down an overgrown drive. Hidden in the trees and bushes was a brick, slate-roofed Victorian manor house, guarded by more uniformed men. People in intelligence regularly joked that the initials "SOE" stood not for Special Operations Executive but for Stately 'Omes of England, as so many had been requisitioned for war work.

Another guard opened the car door for Maggie and Sarah, and they were guided through the front door and hall, down a smoke-filled corridor. It was loud inside, filled with pilots in uniform and men in khaki trousers and navy turtlenecks — Maggie assumed they were either just returning from missions or about to take off.

"You back from bombing Paris?" one called to the two women.

441

"Not exactly," Maggie called back.

"Officers of the One Sixty-one Special Duties Squadron," Martens explained. "Most of them flying SOE agents in and out of occupied territories, armed with only a compass, a Michelin map, and a full moon."

Despite the early hour, another shouted, "You ladies want a drink?"

Oh, you have no idea. "No — but thank you." Maggie smiled and the officer grinned back at her.

They were led up the massive staircase to bedrooms. Maggie's room was shabby but pleasant, sunlight streaming through the windows into a golden pool on the chintz-covered bed.

After a long, steamy bath, ignoring the five-inch waterline, Maggie dressed in the clean uniform that had been left for her. She didn't miss couture in the slightest. Despite the fact she had never been over-joyed to wear the frumpy, belted ATS uniform and dreaded lisle stockings, today was different. She put everything on and, for the first time in months, felt like herself again.

She went to the window and looked out. Life continued, despite Hugh's death, despite Jacques's betrayal. She opened the glass pane, letting in grass-scented air, admiring the banks of pink roses. The early morning's clouds had burned off, revealing a brilliantly blue sky. She thought of Elise and realized her sister would probably see a time like this as a chance to pray to the God she so firmly believed in. Maybe — just maybe — there was a God. Not the old angry man of the Bible, but a force of order, growth, beauty, and harmony. And in the long-running battle between light and darkness, Maggie vowed to play her part.

A robin perched on the sill, peering at her with bright, inquisitive eyes. "Well, you're a cheeky little fellow, aren't you?" Maggie observed. As the robin flew off, just as swiftly as he had come, she realized she was absolutely starving.

The former dining room was now the officers' mess; even without a fire, the décor was cheerful. A number of small drawings, mostly pen and ink with a few watercolors, were tacked up on the paneled wood walls. The table and chairs were military issue. From a side table, Maggie helped herself to scrambled eggs, tiny fried mushrooms, toast, and tea.

She sat down at the long table and began to eat. Food — plain English food — had never tasted so good. Sarah, also in her ATS uniform, sat down beside her. "You must have something," Maggie urged her.

"I don't want anything."

"At least have some tea then." Maggie rose and poured a cup, pressing it into her friend's hand. Sarah didn't drink from it, nor did she set it down. Instead, she clasped it firmly, as if for warmth.

A young woman with a long nose and slightly bulging eyes appeared at the door. "Miss Hope?"

"Yes?"

"Colonel Bishop and Colonel Martens would like to speak with you now."

In what had been the house's library, foxed glass reflected the sunlight, and a banjo clock ticked away the minutes. From above the fireplace, a mounted boar's head with curved yellow tusks stared down at them. "Thank you for joining us, Miss Hope," Martens said, standing. "Please take a seat."

Maggie perched on a metal folding chair. Despite the room's grandeur, the furniture was all government issue. Martens settled his lanky frame behind a metal desk, while Bishop stood at an open window, hands clasped behind his back. There was a framed needlepoint sampler on the wall: *Any fool can tell the truth, but it requires a man of some sense to know how to lie well. — Samuel Butler*

Bishop turned. "We'd like to commend you for the remarkable courage and ingenuity you showed, in escaping the Gestapo, but also in retrieving Agent Calvert's bag. And taking down Jacques Lebeau."

Martens added, "Not to mention flying the plane. And landing it."

"I had a lot of help. The bag was Sarah's — Miss Sanderson's — doing. And there are people over there taking far greater risks than I. The truth is, I wasn't able to save Agent Calvert." Tears stung her eyes. "Two of our own made the ultimate sacrifice."

Bishop's frown deepened. "You're referring to Agents Calvert and Thompson."

"Yes."

Martens looked over his papers. "You knew Hugh Thompson?"

"We worked together on a case for MI-Five a few years ago. We were . . . friends."

"Miss Sanderson seems most distraught," he observed. "They were close?"

Maggie wasn't going to reveal her friend's personal business, but she wasn't going to lie, either. "Yes," she said simply.

"I see."

"The bag," Bishop interjected. "Did you

445

look inside?"

"No, sir. 'The less we know the better' is what we were taught at Beaulieu."

He exhaled. "Very good, young lady, very good." Maggie felt as if she had sidestepped a land mine.

Martens continued, "We learned that while you worked for SOE at Baker Street earlier this year, you noticed the lack of security checks on Agent Calvert's decrypts. We just want you to know that you were right. She'd been compromised — and was trying to signal SOE."

"It's bitter consolation." Then, "Who finally realized there was a problem?"

"That's under internal investigation," Bishop evaded smoothly.

"I want our agents to be safe," Maggie insisted.

"Of course — as do we all, Miss Hope." Martens glanced down once again at his notes. "You had a special dispensation to look for your sister. Did you manage to find her? What happened?"

"I did find her. But she decided to stay in France." Maggie swallowed. "She's doing important work there."

Martens studied her face a moment, then rose. "Thank you, Miss Hope. We'll ask you for a longer, written report later. After we've spoken to Miss Sanderson, someone will drive you both back to London."

"Thank you," Maggie replied. "May I use a telephone to call the hospital? I'd like to see if there's any news on Gus — the injured pilot."

"Of course." Martens nodded. "There's a telephone in the front office you can use."

Bishop turned back to the window. "Before you make the call, would you please let Miss Sanderson know we'd like to speak with her?"

Maggie stopped at the door. "I want you both to know — I'd like to go back."

Martens raised one eyebrow. "To France? Despite your experiences with the Gestapo?"

"Yes. I'd like to be useful. Do my duty, as they say. *Qui n'avance pas, recule.*"

From his position at the window, back to the room, Bishop translated, " 'Who does not move forward, recedes.' "

"Exactly," Maggie said. "Sir."

"Understood, Agent Hope." Martens nodded. "We'll be in touch."

"Please sit down, Miss Sanderson."

"I'd rather not."

"Would you like a cigarette?"

She nodded. Martens pulled out a case

from his jacket pocket and opened it, letting her pick one out. He lit it for her.

"You're a patriot, Miss Sanderson. We can't thank you enough for your actions in France. And, of course, for those of your partner."

"We never got the names of the French automobile companies," she said dully.

"Your original mission is nothing compared to bringing back Agent Calvert's bag safely," Martens told her.

"Did you look inside?" Bishop asked.

"No," Sarah replied.

The two men exchanged glances. "Did Jacques Lebeau look inside at any point?"

"No. He never even touched it. But, whatever's in there" — she took a long drag on her cigarette, her hand trembling — "I hope it's bloody well worth it."

"Yes," Bishop assured her. "It is."

"What's going to happen to Jacques now?" Sarah asked. "Will he be executed? I'd like to kill him myself."

"He will be dealt with," Martens assured her. "Miss Sanderson, we need to know — would you ever be willing to go back?"

"Never." She flicked ash to the floor, unconcerned. "I'd work in a factory making bombs or drive a tractor before I'd do anything like this again. Are we finished?"

"Close the door," said Bishop after she'd left. Martens did.

"Neither of them knows what's in that bag — which is good," Martens began, walking back to the desk. "Where is it now?"

"I've sent the sand samples off to our lab for analysis." Bishop paced the length of the room. "They'll be able to find out quite a bit about the beaches of Normandy, information that will help us immensely as we go forward with Fortitude."

Martens sat, then straightened his papers. "Still, that information cost two agents' lives." He looked up to Bishop, now staring thoughtfully at his reflection in the tarnished mirror. "I must speak with Colonel Gaskell — inform him of everything that's happened and alert him that he needs to disregard anything and everything coming from Agent Thompson's radio. And then we have to transport Lebeau to the Tower. I predict he'll be shot for treason before the new year."

"No." Bishop turned away from the mirror. "Not so fast."

"Sir? I don't understand."

"But I think you do."

The silence between the two men stretched.

"There's something you should see." Bishop took a manila folder out of his briefcase and handed it to the younger man. "Read it. Then ask yourself about sacrifice."

Martens pressed his lips together as he read the folder's contents. Finally, he raised his head and closed the file. "I see," he said slowly.

"I'm glad you do. We'll work together on this, then?"

"Yes." Then, "I'm going to return to London. I'll take Miss Hope and Miss Sanderson with me."

"We need to win this war, Martens. Chivalry died with the poison gas and trenches — when we attacked cities and civilians. There is no nobility now — only victory. Or defeat."

Martens nodded as he stood. "What about Gaskell? We can't keep him in the dark forever. Eventually he'll figure it out."

At that, Bishop nearly smiled. "Let's see if Miss Hope is willing to take over his job."

Chapter Twenty-Two

Martens pulled the Vauxhall to the curb in front of Maggie's house on Portland Place. Sarah, who'd been sitting in the backseat, left the car without a word. She'd been fighting back tears the entire way and looked relieved finally to be let free from the confined space.

"Thank you for the ride," Maggie said, reaching for the door handle and stepping out of the car.

"Of course," Martens replied.

Maggie closed the door and began to walk up the pavement to the entrance.

Martens reached over and rolled down the window. "Miss Hope!"

She turned. "Yes?"

"I — er, nothing. Sorry." As Maggie stood and watched, bewildered, he drove off.

Inside, things were unchanged — David's hand-painted mural of the Union Jack and the Stars and Stripes in brilliant colors brightened one wall. A curved staircase dominated the foyer, with a grand dining room to the left, parlor to the right. "Maggie!" she heard.

"Chuck!" They hugged tightly. "And where is Master Griffin?" Chuck — really Charlotte — as well as her young son, Griffin, had been living with Maggie since their own flat was destroyed in a gas main explosion. Chuck's husband, Nigel, was serving with the RAF in the Middle East.

"Taking a nap right now, thank heavens. Oh, you'll see — and hear — him soon enough. His Nibs learned to sleep through the night — and then promptly forgot. Be warned." Chuck leaned close to Maggie. "Sarah ran through here without even saying hello. Is she all right? She looked godawful." Chuck was never one to mince words.

"She's — she's had a big shock."

"Understood." Chuck nodded. "When — if — she's ready, she'll tell me. In the meantime, lots of tea, a good meal, and as much alcohol as we can beg, borrow, and steal."

Maggie felt the softness of fur around her ankles, then heard the unmistakable, odd *"Meh,"* of her cat, K. She scooped him up. "You!" she exclaimed, kissing the top of his head. "I've missed you so! Have you missed me?"

"Meh!"

Maggie looked to Chuck. "Has he been good for you?"

"Define *good.*"

"Ah."

"Why don't you go up and change? I'll put the kettle on and we'll have tea."

Tea, Maggie thought. *Home.*

"And I'll bring some up to Sarah, too. It might not help, but it can't hurt. By the way," Chuck added, a twinkle in her eyes, "that charming Detective Durgin called while you were gone. I told him you'd call him back when you arrived home. Left the number on the notepad in the kitchen."

"I'll call him back later," Maggie said. "Right now, all I want is to change and have that cup of tea."

That evening, after dinner, there was a knock at the door.

It was Henrik Martens, hat in hand, blond hair glimmering in the moonlight. "I know this is quite unusual," he began, looking sheepish, "but I didn't have your number, and I wanted to speak with you again."

"Oh," Maggie said, surprised.

"I'd like to take you and Miss Sanderson

out, to say thank you. And welcome home."

"I'm a bit knackered, actually . . ."

"It's, well, it's important. Official."

"Well, please come in, then. I'll check on Sarah."

She ran up the stairs and knocked at her friend's door. "Sarah? It's Maggie — may I come in?"

There was only silence.

Maggie called through the door. "Colonel Martens is here, Sarah. He's invited us both out for a drink."

More silence.

"Don't you think it would do you good to get out?"

Maggie heard the rustle of bedclothes and then a sniffle. "Leave me the hell alone!" There was the sound of something hitting the door and then smashing.

Guess that's a no, then. "All right, darling, I'll check in on you later." There was no response.

Maggie hesitated, then went back downstairs. "I'm afraid Sarah's not up to coming."

"Of course," said Martens. "I'm sorry to hear that, but it's completely understandable, all things considered. Would you like to go to the bar at the Ritz?"

"No," Maggie replied, her voice firm.

"Not the Ritz. *Anywhere* but the Ritz."

"Actually, it's just as well Miss Sanderson isn't joining us," Martens said as they drove slowly through the blackout.

"Oh?"

"There's something I want to ask you."

Maggie raised an eyebrow. "At your flat?" She was well acquainted with the tactics of lonesome soldiers. "No, thank you."

"No! Nothing like that! At the Cabinet War Rooms," he amended.

"Drive on then, Colonel Martens. You've certainly piqued my curiosity."

He was silent for the remainder of the trip. It gave Maggie time to soak up the sight of London in the moonlight. How keenly she'd missed this city, bombed and battered as she was.

Martens pulled the car up to the curb and they both got out. He showed his ID to the guards at the door, then led her down the stairs and through concrete corridors to his office. Once there, he closed the door behind them.

"You used to work down here in the War Rooms, didn't you? Underground?"

"A long time ago." Maggie looked around his office. *Yes, the same low-hanging red pipes, the same black fans, the same stale air* . . . "Although unless bombs were actually dropping, Mr. Churchill preferred to work at Number Ten or the Annexe."

"Still does." He offered a chair.

Maggie sat, crossing her ankles and folding her hands in her lap. "I must say, sir, you definitely have my attention."

He cleared his throat and went to his desk. "Miss Hope —"

"Maggie, please," she said as he took a seat as well.

"And I'm Henrik. Maggie, I know you've signed the Official Secrets Act and have a high-level security clearance —"

"Yes, of course."

"And I've read through your file — it's quite the page-turner. You've performed multiple missions at a top-secret level. You're used to a life of discretion."

Maggie shrugged. "Part of the job."

"Yes." Martens opened a metal briefcase with handcuffs attached.

"Oh, that does look rather cloak and dagger, doesn't it?"

He pulled out some files. "Before we proceed, Maggie, I need to ask — do you plan to continue working for SOE?"

"Well, yes — as long as they'll still have me. I'm hoping to be sent back to France. With the experience I've gained in Paris, I

456

think I can be of use to the networks over there."

"I want you to know that I read over your notes about Agent Calvert's decrypts. And you were correct. She wasn't using her security checks."

"But at least F-Section knows now."

He blinked. "The truth is, there was nothing sinister about their not acting on the absence of security checks, just amateurish incompetence."

Maggie remembered Gaskell's ordering her to fetch his tea while dismissing her safety concerns. She leaned forward, frowning. "But they know *now,* yes? The Sicherheitsdienst has control of Hugh Thompson's radio. If they don't know, they'll just send agents into a certain death trap."

"They don't know. And we're not going to enlighten them. At this juncture of the war, it's what we want — no, need — to do."

Maggie wasn't sure she'd heard correctly. "Colonel Martens — Henrik — I don't understand."

"I think you do, Maggie."

Maggie gnawed at her lip. "No — we need to tell Colonel Gaskell — inform him of everything that's happened and alert him that he needs to disregard anything and everything coming from Hugh's — Agent Thompson's — radio. Immediately!"

"Not so fast. We have an incredible intelligence opportunity here."

"What?"

Martens went to the desk, picking up a framed official photograph of a glowering Winston Churchill. "We're playing a deadly game here, Maggie, and the odds are badly stacked against us. The endgame is the location and day of the Allied invasion. Already, we're going about a slow and painstaking process to create disinformation. We need to use every tool we find, even if it's one we stumble upon." He put down the photograph and reached into the breast pocket of his suit jacket for his pack of Player's cigarettes. "Especially then."

"I still don't understand."

Martens pulled out a cigarette and stuck it between his teeth. "But I think you do."

"No."

He reached in another pocket for his lighter. "We don't imprison Lebeau — or execute him. We send him back to Paris." With a flick of his thumb, a bright flame appeared.

"No —"

Martens stuck the end of the cigarette into the flame, pulling on it until the tip glowed red. He waited a moment, then said thoughtfully, "It's perfect. A double agent will become a triple. We're going to turn Lebeau to our side. Then we'll send him back to Paris, to continue just what he's been doing." He exhaled, returning the lighter to his pocket. "But this time we'll know everything. He'll be working for us."

"But he's not only photographing letters and documents. He'll be turning over agents and their radios to the Sicherheitsdienst."

"Exactly."

Maggie was still at a loss.

"You know what I'm saying." Martens gave Maggie a moment to absorb the idea. "Think about it — it will work. Lebeau will feed von Waltz and his cronies false information about the place and day of the invasion. In the meantime, any messages von Waltz starts sending via the captured agents will be quite revealing — his questions will become more expansive once we start to satisfy his greed for information. A patient process of listing, collating, and cross-referencing his messages will gradually reveal what our enemy already knows, as well as his preoccupations and priorities. We'll be able to get a clearer picture of Sicherheitsdienst operations in France."

"But that means —" Maggie protested.

"Colonel Gaskell will never agree! You're talking about" — she lowered her voice — "deliberately sacrificing agents."

Martens didn't blink. "We don't tell Gaskell."

"SOE in the dark? Gaskell as a stooge?" Maggie swallowed. "My God," she exclaimed, realizing.

"You can see the endgame now, can't you?"

Maggie constructed the formula aloud: "You'll get information about what the Germans know from the messages they send back. And you'll be able to plant false information about what we're doing. About battle plans. About —" *What's the biggest secret of the war, Hope? Think!* "About the Allied invasion."

At the realization of the extent of the deception, she was breathless. "You're going to let the Gestapo torture our agents and turn them, aren't you? You and Bishop — sending agents over, like lambs to slaughter." She thought for a moment. "They will know, though? You'll tell the agents what will be expected of them before they go, yes? It will be their choice?"

"Think."

She did and the realization made her ill. "No. . . . They must be convinced the information they're carrying is good. So, if they break under torture they won't give away the game. That *when* they break under torture, they'll reveal what you want them to — and *not* the truth about the invasion." She sucked in a breath. "Good God — it's like Kipling's tethered goats. A blood sacrifice."

"I have no qualms about exploiting a man and an agency that's proven over and over again to be utterly incompetent — do you? Before this, SOE was a liability. Now we can use that ineptitude to our advantage."

The silence between the two agents stretched. Finally, Maggie shook her head. "You're condemning SOE's F-Section agents to torture and death."

Martens blew smoke out through his nostrils. "War is sacrifice," he said, his voice harsh. "I sacrificed in Norway. We sacrificed at Dunkirk. We sacrificed at Coventry. We're going to make sacrifices at Dieppe. It's like sacrificing the queen in chess —"

"We're talking about the lives of real people, not chess pieces!"

"A few lives to save millions and millions," Martens said harshly. "We're at war with a savage empire, people who are determined to debase and enslave and eradicate races, who slaughter and plunder with impunity.

If they win, it's the end of the world as we know it. Our survival overrides *any* moral consideration. They are waging total war, and so we must have total commitment to winning. As they say, 'No country was ever saved by good men, because good men will not go to the length that may be necessary.' "

He continued: "You see the logic — follow it to the very end. And then you'll realize I'm right. We'll run this as a church-mouse operation. Nothing on paper. No one will ever know."

Maggie wasn't ready to give up. "People will be killed!"

"People will be killed regardless. And in far greater numbers. If you can't live with what we must do — all of it — consider the alternative. What will happen to us, to England, to the entire world, if the invasion fails?"

Maggie stared at him, speechless with horror.

"Before you decide to hate me, there's something else you should know." Martens took a manila folder out of his briefcase, the one Bishop had given him, and handed it over to her.

Maggie looked down at the first page:

Republic of Poland CAP
Ministry of Foreign Affairs
The Mass Extermination of Jews in Occupied Poland CAP
Addressed to the Governments of United Nations

"Read that," Martens ordered. "Then ask yourself whether you still have issues with sacrificing a few individuals."

Maggie began to read. As she turned the pages, certain words and phrases jumped out at her: *extermination camps* and *cattle cars. Showers* and *Zyklon B gas.* There was a photograph of a crematorium.

When she'd finished, her hands were shaking. "Genocide?" she said, putting it together. "The Germans want to . . . exterminate the Jews? It — it can't be!"

Martens got up to retrieve the folder and return it to his briefcase. "I'm afraid so. In addition to everything else, this — an official extermination of the world's Jewry, as well as the physically and mentally infirm, political prisoners, homosexuals, and gypsies — has begun in earnest in Eastern Europe."

"Of course we knew things were bad, but . . ."

"The Allied governments will be making a

statement and releasing this information soon. Then the whole world will know."

"This is what we're fighting." Maggie said it softly. "For the success of the invasion and also because of . . . this."

"Yes."

"This is why you're willing to sacrifice SOE agents."

He sighed deeply. "Yes."

"I feel sick." She forced herself to take steady breaths, then looked up. "It's going to *work*! That's the worst part, isn't it?"

He nodded somberly.

Fury flooded through her. "I hate this! I hate all of it. I hate the way the world is. I hate knowing these things. I hate what we're becoming. I hate who *I'm* becoming."

"If we loved it, we'd have to worry. We'd be no better than the Nazis."

There had to be a way to stop this. "I'll — I'll tell Fleet Street!"

"I'm afraid you'd simply be arrested and discredited."

"I'll tell Mr. Churchill!"

"You know the P.M. needs plausible deniability. And don't fool yourself that the same man who let Coventry be destroyed in a Luftwaffe attack to protect the secrets of Bletchley Park will be sympathetic to your moral qualms. Really — do you think he'd hesitate to use *any* weapon at his disposal? I read in your file you know about the chemical weapons, the anthrax, already."

We shall fight on the beaches . . . Maggie recalled typing for him, when she was his secretary back in the summer of '40. And she remembered their conversation here at Number 10 in Churchill's office the previous fall, when she heard the terrible truth about what he was willing to sacrifice, when she bargained for Elise's rescue.

No, no I don't believe the P.M. would hesitate, she thought. *If only math could help. But the value of human life is immeasurable, and so neither option is morally acceptable. How do you measure and compare the quantity of* x *versus the quantity of* y + z *if you don't know the values of any of them? How many angels can die on the head of a pin?*

"How can you keep on" — Maggie began, her voice raw with emotion — "knowing what you know? It's so . . . cynical."

"A cynic is what an idealist calls a realist."

"It's wrong. It's evil."

"We need to win this war, Maggie. As someone said to me, chivalry died with the poison gas and trenches, when we attacked cities and civilians. There is no nobility now, no good and evil — only victory. Or defeat."

"History will judge us."

465

"That's why we put nothing down on paper. You must understand one thing — never, ever admit anything. No matter what happens, never reveal what you know, what you've done. You must resolve to go to your grave resolutely denying anything ever happened. Remember that."

"No! No, I won't be part of it."

"You need to grow up," he replied harshly. "And learn the meaning of *duty*. In fact, we need you to continue to do your duty — and work for us. Colonel Bishop and I would like you to take over Gaskell's position — to run F-Section."

"Me?" It was what she'd wanted — to have a position of authority where she could use her brain — but not like this. "No — my God — no." Maggie shook her head. "I can't. I'm not like you. The men and women of SOE give their hearts and souls! They sacrifice everything! They trust you! *We* trust you!"

"Our agents will still be able to give their hearts and souls — and achieve the same ends."

"Which justify the means? No, just — no. You're as corrupt as the Nazis."

"I'm afraid that, in this war, things aren't as black and white as the propaganda reels would make them seem. I'm merely willing to be a part of something that's hateful and dangerous for the sake of victory. Believe me — I didn't like it at first, either. But then I saw the logic."

"When your moral sense begins to rot, it's worse than if you had none to begin with." Maggie stood. "I'm sorry, Colonel, but I can't work for SOE in that role — knowingly sending agents to their deaths. I won't be a part of it. *No.* An unequivocal no."

"I was afraid of that." He rubbed his hands together. "And now you know too much." He rummaged around in one of his desk drawers. "I'm sorry."

"I'm leaving." She rose.

"I don't think so." Martens stood as well, both hands clasped behind his back. "I want to assure you that I respect your decision not to work for SOE. We don't consider you a traitor, you haven't betrayed anything — but now, alas, you know too much. It's in your own interest that you be kept safely."

"Kept? What — ?"

As Martens stepped around the desk, his right arm rose, swiftly sweeping toward Maggie's head. Instinctively, she raised her hands. This threw Martens off balance, allowing her to use both hands to swing his arm up as she rotated under. He gasped at the pain as Maggie forced him over. He hit the desk sideways. His right hand opened.

"A pen?" As Maggie voiced her disbelief, Martens's left hand came up behind her, covering her mouth with a cloth wet with chloral hydrate. She struggled, then went limp.

After she'd lost consciousness, he laid her gently on the floor, then walked back to his desk. He picked up the red telephone receiver. "It's Colonel Martens," he said. "Let them know that Miss Hope will need to be detained indefinitely."

ACKNOWLEDGMENTS

Thanks to my husband, Noel MacNeal, and son, Matthew MacNeal, for their love and patience.

Thank you to the incredible team at Penguin Random House: Kate Miciak, Julia Maguire, and Alex Coumbis, as well as Victoria Allen, Dana Blanchette, Kim Hovey, Vincent La Scala, Allyson Lord, and Maggie Oberrender. You are brilliant and dedicated professionals; I am blessed to work with you, as well as the intrepid Penguin Random House sales force. Hats off.

Cheers to the wonderful (and wonderfully patient) Victoria Skurnick and the fabulous team at Levine Greenberg Rosten Literary Agency.

Hugs to Idria Barone Knecht, as always, for everything.

Thank you to Phyllis Brooks Schafer — friend, translator, retired Berkeley professor, London Blitz survivor — who is kind enough to read over my manuscripts for historical accuracy. Thanks to Ronald J. Granieri, director of research and lecturer in history at the Lauder Institute at Wharton at the University of Pennsylvania, for also checking the manuscript.

Gratitude to Blake Leyers and Rebecca Danos for her knowledge of French mathematicians.

Bravi to Caitlin Sims, and daughters Calista and Lily Sims, who looked over the dance sections. And wild applause for former New York City Ballet soloist and now choreographer Tom Gold, for background on the Paris Opéra Ballet.

Gratitude, as always, to Meredith Norris, M.D., for sharing her medical expertise, despite her insanely busy schedule.

Merci to novelist and Francophile Cara Black, author of the *New York Times* bestselling Aimée Leduc mystery series, for advice on traveling to Paris and then her invaluable notes on the manuscript.

And a special salute to the pilots — Dave Bermingham, author Twist Phelan, and her friend Shawn Kelly, for kind assistance with the flight scene.

HISTORICAL NOTES

Was there actually a triple agent working for SOE, the Gestapo, and under the ultimate control of MI-6? Were SOE agents deliberately sacrificed to protect Fortitude, the secret of the Allied invasion?

There are no definitive answers to these questions — and the issue is still fraught with controversy.

Of course *The Paris Spy* is fiction and only fiction — what could be imagined to have happened. However, even distinguished historians continue to dispute what *exactly* happened to SOE agents in Paris during World War II.

Jacques Lebeau is based on the very real Henri Déricourt, a French agent for SOE. He definitely worked as a double agent for the Sicherheitsdienst in Paris — but whether he was working only for the Germans, or really as a triple agent for MI-6, remains unclear.

Colonel Henry Gaskell is loosely inspired by Colonel Maurice James Buckmaster, the leader of SOE's F-Section. Despite receiving multiple messages lacking agreed-upon security checks, Buckmaster refused to believe that F-Section's networks — especially the Prosper network — had been compromised — thus sending many SOE agents to their arrests and deaths.

Diana Lynd is modeled on Vera Atkins, a British intelligence officer working with SOE's F-Section under Colonel Buckmaster. She also failed to pull agents out (or convince Buckmaster to pull them out) from France when they repeatedly omitted the security double-checks on their transmissions.

Lieutenant Colonel Sir Claude Edward Marjoribanks Dansey of MI-6 and the London Controlling Section, who served under Major General Sir Stewart Menzies, is the inspiration for Colonel George Bishop. By all accounts, Dansey disdained SOE, considering them "bumbling amateurs." M. R. D. Foot, the official historian of SOE in France, alleges that Dansey was responsible for the betrayal of the Prosper network. Foot writes: "It was widely believed in France that [Francis] Suttill's circuit was deliberately betrayed by the British to the Germans even directly by wireless to the Avenue Foch [German military headquarters in Paris]."

Here's what makes coming to any definite conclusion about what *really* happened in France tricky: the relevant files either were destroyed or are still not allowed to be opened. In 1945, the SOE's files, including F-Section's, were supposed to be given over to the Foreign Office. They were marked: "Important Historical Records. Never to be destroyed." Those records burned in a fire before they could be moved.

Other files on SOE's and MI-6's wartime activities — ones that may shed light on F-Section and the roles of Henri Déricourt, Colonel Buckmaster, Vera Atkins, and Colonel Dansey in the deaths of SOE agents in France — remain sealed until 2037.

Until then, we wait and wonder.

I must express special appreciation for the excellent book *Asylum: A Survivor's Flight from Nazi-Occupied Vienna Through Wartime France,* by Moriz Scheyer and P. N. Singer for its vivid descriptions of Scheyer's time in hiding at a French convent.

The escape from Avenue Foch was inspired by the one made by SOE agent Noor-un-Nisa Inayat Khan (January 2, 1914–September 13, 1944), to whom this novel is dedicated. Also known as "Nora Baker," "Madeleine," and "Jeanne-Marie Rennier," Khan was sent from Britain to Paris, to work with the French Resistance. Khan was betrayed, either by Henri Déricourt or Renée Garry, and sent to Avenue Foch. She attempted to escape from the SD Headquarters, along with fellow SOE agents John Renshaw Starr and Leon Faye. However, they all were recaptured on the roof of Avenue Foch during an air raid alert (detailed in *Spy Princess: The Life of Noor Inayat Khan,* by Shrabani Basu). Khan was ultimately moved to Dachau Concentration Camp. On September 13, 1944, she and three fellow female SOE agents (Yolande Beekman, Eliane Plewman, and Madeleine Damerment) were executed by shots to the back of their heads. Khan's last word was recorded as "Liberté."

BOOKS CONSULTED

SOE's F-Section

SOE: An Outline History of the Special Operations Executive 1940–46, by M. R. D. Foot
Fighters in the Shadows: A New History of the French Resistance, by Robert Gildea
Shadows in the Fog, by Francis J. Suttill

Bodyguard of Lies, by Anthony Cave Brown

Spy Princess: The Life of Noor Inayat Khan, by Shrabani Basu

A Cool and Lonely Courage: The Untold Story of Sister Spies in Occupied France, by Susan Ottaway

A Life in Secrets: Vera Atkins and the Missing Agents of WWII, by Sarah Helm

The Women Who Lived for Danger: Behind Enemy Lines During WWII, by Marcus Binney

All the King's Men: The Truth Behind SOE's Greatest Wartime Disaster, by Robert Marshall

Double Webs: Light on the Secret Agents' War in France, by Jean Overton Fuller

The German Penetration of SOE: France, 1941–44, by Jean Overton Fuller

Déricourt: The Chequered Spy, by Jean Overton Fuller

Paris and the French Resistance

Fighters in the Shadows: A New History of the French Resistance, by Robert Gildea

Paris Was Yesterday, by Janet Flanner

Swastika over Paris: The Fate of the Jews in France, by Jeremy Josephs

Queen of the Ritz, by Samuel Marx

The Hotel on Place Vendôme: Life, Death,

and Betrayal at the Hôtel Ritz in Paris, by Tilar J. Mazzeo

Elsie de Wolfe's Paris: Frivolity Before the Storm, by Charlie Scheips

Asylum: A Survivor's Flight from Nazi-Occupied Vienna Through Wartime France, by Moriz Scheyer and P. N. Singer

Les Parisiennes: How the Women of Paris Lived, Loved, and Died Under Nazi Occupation, by Anne Sebba

Paris Underground, by Etta Shiber

The Unfree French: Life Under the Occupation, by Richard Vinen

Books on Ballet in Paris During the War

The Paris Opéra Ballet, by Ivor Guest

When Ballet Became French: Modern Ballet and the Cultural Politics of France, 1909–1939, by Ilyana Karthas

Ma Vie — From Kiev to Kiev: An Autobiography, by Serge Lifar

And the Show Went On: Cultural Life in Nazi-Occupied Paris, by Alan Riding

Books on Coco Chanel

Coco Chanel: An Intimate Life, by Lisa Chaney

Mademoiselle: Coco Chanel and the Pulse of

History, by Rhonda K. Garelick

Coco Chanel: The Legend and the Life, by Justine Picardie

Sleeping with the Enemy: Coco Chanel, Nazi Agent, by Hal Vaughan

Documentaries

Robert H. Gardner's *Enemy of the Reich: The Noor Inayat Khan Story*

The BBC/Imperial War Museum's televised *The Secret War* series, specifically the episodes "The Dutch Disaster," "The Spymistress and the French Fiasco," and "The French Triple Agent"

Museums and Exhibits

Musée de la Mode et du Textile, Louvre Museum, Paris

Imperial War Museums, London

Mémorial de la Shoah, Paris

Musée Carnavalet, Paris

Musée de l'Armée, Paris

Paris Opéra House tour, Paris

ABOUT THE AUTHOR

Susan Elia MacNeal is the *New York Times* and *USA Today* bestselling author of the Maggie Hope mystery series. She won the Barry Award and was nominated for the Edgar, Macavity, Agatha, Left Coast Crime, Dilys, and ITW Thriller awards. She lives in Brooklyn, New York, with her husband and son.

susaneliamacneal.com

Facebook.com/maggiehopefans

Twitter: @susanmacneal